W9-BBP-637

LIGHTS OUT

LIGHTS OUT

PETER ABRAHAMS

THE MYSTERIOUS PRESS

Published by Warner Books

A Time Warner Company

Grateful acknowledgment is given for permission to excerpt from *Samuel T. Coleridge's The Rime of the Ancient Mariner* by John W. Elliott. Copyright © 1965 by John W. Elliott. Reprinted by permission of the publisher, Monarch Press, a Division of Simon & Schuster, New York.

Grateful acknowledgment is made for permission to quote from *Surveiller et Punir* by Michel Foucault, © Editions Gallimard 1975, and Georges Borchardt, Inc.

 Mysterious Press books are published by Warner Books, Inc.,
1271 Avenue of the Americas, New York, NY 10020.

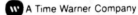 A Time Warner Company

The Mysterious Press name and logo are registered trademarks of Warner Books, Inc.

Printed in the United States of America

First printing: March 1994

10 9 8 7 6 5 4 3 2 1

Library of Congress Cataloging-in-Publication Data

Abrahams, Peter.
    Lights out / Peter Abrahams.
       p.   cm.
    ISBN 0-89296-482-0
    1. False imprisonment—United States—Fiction.   2. Caribbean Area—
Fiction.   3. Ex-convicts—Fiction.   I. Title.
PS3551.B64L5   1994
813'.54—dc20   93-28634
                                                                    CIP

To Peggy and Anthony

The author is grateful to Mary Owen at the Barnstable County House of Correction and to Tom Connolly at MCI-Cedar Junction for their patient assistance.

Justice pursues the body beyond all possible pain.

—Michel Foucault,
Surveiller et Punir
(Discipline and Punish)

Inside

Chapter One

Man is the word. You can't stop hearing it when you're inside. "You crazy, man?" "You fuckin' with me, man?" "Fuck you, man." "Shi', man." "Sheet, man." "Shit, man." It doesn't mean a thing. It's just an itch that no one can stop scratching, a sore tooth no one can stop probing.

Fifteen years is a long time for scratching and probing, longer when there's nothing to do but mop floors and sew mailbags, all for fifty-five cents an hour. You've got to find ways of making time go faster. Nails—during his third year they started calling him Nails, but his real name was Eddie Nye—Nails took up weight lifting. That made time go faster, but not fast enough. What he needed was a way to make time disappear. That's what led him to reading. Nails probably hadn't read a book in his life, except for high-school assignments, and, much earlier, *Muskets and Doubloons*, but in the room they called the library, with its blue-white strip lighting, steel chairs and tables bolted to the floor, yawning corrections officers, he ploughed through everything on the shelves. He started with Max Brand. After a while he learned that the better the book, the closer time shrank to the vanishing point. Seven years later he was reading Tolstoy, still searching for the story so perfect it would kill time dead. Old books were better. Nothing written in the twentieth century worked at all.

Poems were best, especially long ones with rhymes and a beat. One day Eddie came upon "The Rime of the Ancient Mariner."

He returned to it over and over, not unlike a child who can't stop looking at a bloody crucifixion on the wall at Grandma's house.

Eddie read the papers too. Funny thing about the papers. Although he read every word, including the weather in places he'd never heard of and subjects he had no interest in, like the stock market, recipes, dance reviews, he somehow didn't get it. Everything just floated by—megabytes, Japanese cars, yuppies, the end of the Cold War, all that. Eddie knew things were happening, but they were far away and meaningless. Like looking through binoculars from the wrong end. Of course, you could say it was Eddie who was far away. He had to be, to get away from time.

Not that he didn't want out. That happens to some of the longtimers, but didn't happen to Eddie. It wasn't that he had plans: he couldn't form any. But he wanted out, all right, so bad that with two or three months to go he started getting wired. Couldn't eat, couldn't sleep, couldn't sit still. In consequence, his memory of events in those months wasn't too clear. It lacked, for example, some of the details, the nuances, of El Rojo's first contact.

At the time, Eddie had a cell on the first tier of the north wing of F-Block. Cell F–31 measured four paces from the bars to the seatless steel toilet, a pace and a half from the steel bunks to the steel side wall. Eddie had the top bunk, Prof slept on the bottom. Prof wasn't in for long. Forgery. Three and a half to eight, but probably much less with parole. Eddie had had lots of cellmates— Gerald, who had split his wife's skull with his son's Little League bat; Moonie, who'd shot some bystanders in a drive-by; Grodowicz, who'd botched a kidnapping by detouring to sodomize the hostages; Rafael DeJesus, a smuggler and occasional killer of illegal aliens who'd taught Eddie Spanish; a kid whose name Eddie no longer remembered, who hadn't been able to stop stealing cars and had finally run over twins in a twin stroller at the end of a high-speed chase; Jonathan C. McBright, a professional bank robber and by far the easiest to live with; another guy who'd killed his wife, but unlike Gerald denied it and cried in the night; and others, who'd done more of the same.

They came, they put up their decorations, they served their time or got paroled, got transferred, got killed, or killed themselves. Eddie kept his distance from his cellmates, from everybody. That was the secret of being a successful con. When they were gone, Eddie took down their decorations, tossed them in the corridor at mopping-up time, nodded hello to the next arrival. He never put up decorations of his own.

Prof was almost as austere. He'd taped just two pictures to the wall above his bunk. One was a studio portrait of his wife, Tiffany, and their two kids, all wearing matching reindeer sweaters and smiling like the kind of family used for selling something wholesome. The other, much bigger, was a photo of a powerfully built woman with a two-pronged dildo inserted into her body and an impatient expression on her face, as though she was already late to her next appointment. The juxtaposition of the pictures didn't seem to bother Prof; maybe he didn't even notice. Eddie noticed, but it didn't bother him. In fifteen years he'd seen everything, everything that could be taped to a wall.

Something clicked in the steel walls of F-Block. Eddie heard Prof sit up on the bottom bunk. "Hey, big guy, whaddya know?" he said. The barred door slid open. "We're free." Prof had a sense of humor. Not as good as Rafael DeJesus's though. DeJesus had been really funny. He'd even performed at Catch A Rising Star once, after jumping bail.

Prof went into the corridor. Eddie heard it fill quickly with restless, noisy men. They'd been in lockdown for five days, all because Willie Boggs had lost another appeal. That had led to a demonstration of Willie's supporters outside, a demonstration covered by local news and therefore seen inside. The footage had fed delusions of hope on death row, causing a commotion that spread to Max and then to F-Block. Lockdown reminded everyone what the situation really was and that all Willie's pastors, ACLU lawyers, and anti–death penalty crusaders—including the head of Amnesty International, the justice ministers of two Scandinavian countries, and Mother Teresa—couldn't put Humpty together again. The only appeal left was to the governor's clemency, of which in his ten years of office he had shown none.

Eddie climbed down off the bunk. He took his Remington cordless from his lockless locker and shaved his face by touch. Mirrors had been confiscated years ago, following a shard slashing on the third tier. Fat drops of blood had plopped down onto the floor outside F–31, as though from a roof after the passing of a red storm. Eddie ran his fingers over the top of his head, felt stubble. He shaved that too, feeling the razor buzz against his naked skull. Not unpleasant.

He went out, into the line of men moving toward the checkpoint that led to the mess hall. He smelled their smells, saw the details on their unsunned skins, the details he always saw, couldn't not see, although they no longer made an impression: the scars, the bruises, the dried semen stains, the open sores, the tattoos. Eddie had a tattoo on the inside of his left biceps, self-administered with a sharpened pocket comb and a bottle of red food coloring during his only stay in the hole, at the end of year two. In block letters about half an inch high it said "Yeah?" It was a joke he no longer got.

Eddie passed through the scanner but turned into the east wing before he got to the mess hall, and walked to the library. "Not eatin', Nails?" said the C.O. outside the door, patting him down. Eddie went inside, making no reply. "Got to keep your strength up," the guard called after him. "For when you're in the real world."

Eddie sat in his favorite chair, the only one in the library not bolted to the floor. Left over from an earlier era, it was a sagging armchair, spavined and sprung, too heavy to be used as a weapon. He was almost finished with the morning paper, in the middle of a book review on the last page that was panning a novel because it contained "elements of melodrama," when Willie Boggs shuffled in, a C.O. on either side, loosely grasping his mahogany-colored arms above the elbow. Willie had a proud face and erect bearing; he only shuffled because of the shackles around his ankles. He saw Eddie and nodded. Eddie nodded back. Willie looked the way he always did, except that the skin bordering his lips might have been a little chalky. He took a few books off the law shelf and sat at a table. The C.O.s unlocked his handcuffs and sat beside him, eyes glazing almost at once. Willie opened a book, found the page he wanted, took out a note pad, started writing. He was the best writ-writer in the system. That's why he was still alive.

Eddie folded up the paper and took down the collected Coleridge. Coleridge opened to "The Ancient Mariner" by itself; in fact to page 248, where the central problem was. Eddie stared at the stanza:

"God save thee, ancient Mariner!
From the fiends, that plague thee thus!—
Why look'st thou so?"—With my cross-bow
I shot the ALBATROSS.

No explanation, unless you count the small-print text in the left-hand margin—"The ancient Mariner inhospitably killeth the pious bird of good omen"—and Eddie didn't consider it much of an explanation, didn't even know if the small print was part of the poem or added later by someone else. No explanation. In one verse everything's cool with the bird, in the next the guy plugs it. Why? Eddie had been through it a thousand times, without getting any closer to the answer. That didn't mean much. Eddie knew there must be plenty he didn't understand about "The Ancient Mariner." For example, it had only recently struck him that there might be a reason the mariner stopped only one of the three wedding guests, instead of telling the story to all of them. Maybe the wedding guest wasn't saying, *"Wherefore stopp'st thou me?"* but, "Wherefore stopp'st thou *me?"* So Eddie wasn't sure he even understood the first verse.

Just shot the albatross. Why? Because he was jealous it could fly? Because he wanted to suffer? Because he was afraid of sailing fast? Or just because it was possible to do? None of those answers felt right. It occurred to him that the shooting was melodramatic. Maybe the whole goddamn thing was melodramatic. The reviewer would have panned Coleridge too, if he'd been alive at the time.

Eddie looked up. Willie Boggs and his guards were gone. Another man sat at the long table, alone. He was reading *Business Week*. This, Eddie realized, was his first close look at the state's most famous inmate. El Rojo, they called him. His face had been on the cover of *Time* magazine the week they'd caught him. The face reminded Eddie of a picture he'd seen in one of the books, a picture of a Spanish king, Charles the Something. He had red hair, translucent skin, a long nose, a long chin, long delicate fingers with long manicured nails. The only difference was that, as one of the founders of the Medellín cartel, he had probably been richer than all the kings of Spain put together. Maybe he still was. El Rojo shook his head at something he read and turned the page.

Eddie closed his eyes. True, he hadn't been sleeping lately, but he'd been sleeping for almost fifteen solid years before that. He couldn't be tired. But he kept his eyes shut anyway. Everyone said he had to make plans. He tried to picture himself in the future, outside. All he saw was the red lining of his eyelids. "Her lips were red, her looks were free, her locks were yellow as gold." The specter LIFE-IN-DEATH. Was it important that she was a woman? Woman, in fact, with a capital *W*. Why?

"Arsewipe. Hey. I'm talkin' to you. Arsewipe."

Eddie opened his eyes. Standing over him was an inmate Eddie had never seen before. He was big. Prof called Eddie "big guy," but Eddie wasn't really big. When he'd come in, at nineteen, he'd been six one and weighed about one seventy. In fifteen years he'd added twenty pounds, mostly muscle, but he wasn't big, not compared to the man calling him arsewipe. This man must have weighed three hundred pounds; not svelte, but not fat either. He had a slack, heavy face, long greasy hair, a long greasy beard, a few teeth, and a half-healed hole in his upper lip where a ring must have fit—jewelry was forbidden. It was like waking to a nightmare. Eddie closed his eyes. It wasn't the first time.

"Hey. Arsewipe." Eddie felt a kick on the sole of his right foot. A hard kick. He opened his eyes.

"I'm talkin' to you. You're in my chair."

"Guess again," Eddie said, conscious as he spoke of El Rojo's gaze.

"Huh?" the big man said. He thought for a moment, mouth open. Eddie noticed that the big man was wearing a ring after all—a gold one stuck in the fleshy tip of his tongue. He gave Eddie another kick.

"You're new," Eddie said.

The big man's forehead creased. "I'm new *here*. I'm not new to the scene, you fuckin' fuckhead. I did four fuckin' years in fuckin' Q, man. And I always had a favorite fuckin' chair in the fuckin' library at fuckin' Q. See? So get up. Unless you want me to tear your fuckin' head off." And he kicked again, this time with a windup. Eddie winced; he couldn't help himself.

"You're not giving me much choice," he said.

"Move, faggot."

Eddie rose. The big man, a head taller, took him by the shoulder and gave him a push to help him on his way. Eddie let himself be pushed, but at the same time he pivoted and stuck his hand into the middle of that slack face, stuck it right into the fleshy wet maw, sliding his index finger through that stupid tongue ring. The big man's hands went up then, but he was much too slow. Eddie had curled his finger around the tongue ring; now he yanked.

First there was a ripping sound and the ring came free in Eddie's hand. Then the big man spouted blood. The pain hadn't quite hit him when Eddie caught one of his massive wrists in both hands, spun behind the broad back and jerked the wrist up as high as it would go. Something snapped in the big lump of shoulder; muffled by all the muscle, it sounded no louder than a breaking wishbone on Thanksgiving. The big man bellowed and fell forward on the table, not far from El Rojo. Did El Rojo move away at all, or simply sit there? That was the kind of detail Eddie couldn't remember later.

The big man was moaning and writhing when C.O.s came bursting in. Eddie was sitting in his chair.

"What the fuck?" said one of the C.O.s.

"Melodrama happens in real life," Eddie explained.

"What the fuck are you talking about?"

El Rojo spoke. "The señor bit his tongue," he said. "You know how that . . . what is the English word? Smarts? That doesn't sound right."

The C.O. opened his mouth, as though to say something. Then he closed it. They took the big man away. He left a pool of blood on the table. El Rojo noticed that it had spread to one corner of *Business Week* and seeped through the pages. He pushed the magazine away with distaste.

"Thanks," Eddie said.

"Don't mention it." El Rojo examined something in his hand: the tongue ring. Eddie couldn't remember how he'd gotten it. El Rojo slipped it into his shirt pocket and looked at Eddie. He had liquid amber eyes, like pools of maple syrup. "Melodrama happens in real life?" he said.

Eddie shrugged.

El Rojo smiled at him. He had the whitest smile Eddie had seen in fifteen years, marred by a missing canine. "Smoke?" he said, as though they were sitting in a quiet club somewhere.

"I'm trying to quit." Quitting wasn't easy inside, where cigarettes were money and the American Lung Association had no influence.

"For when you are released?" asked El Rojo. His voice too reminded Eddie of maple syrup; smooth like some old black-and-white screen star's, one with a trace of accent.

Eddie made that connection, but he said: "How'd you know I was getting out?"

El Rojo answered with a question. "You're the one they call Nails?"

"Yeah."

"Everybody knows you. Or almost everybody," he added, glancing at the pool of blood. Then he laughed. There was nothing cultured about his laughter. It sounded more like the utterance of a crow than of some black-and-white smoothie.

El Rojo shook two cigarettes out of a pack. "How can one more hurt you?" he asked. One of Eddie's rules for life inside was to take nothing from anyone, and he was in El Rojo's debt already, but he took the cigarette. What the hell. He was getting out. El Rojo lit a match, offered the flame to Eddie, then sucked at it himself. They exhaled two smoke clouds that became one in the air. "My name is Angel," said El Rojo, giving it the Spanish pronunciation.

"It is?"

El Rojo showed his beautiful teeth. "Angel Cruz," he said. "Cruz Rojo, you see. Kind of a joke."

"Because you supply the medicine."

El Rojo laughed his cawing laugh. "That's part of it," he said. "You've got brains. I like that." He held out his hand. Eddie took it, felt the long, slightly damp fingers wrap around the back of his palm. Those fingers reminded him of something in "The Mariner," but he couldn't think what. He drew deeply on the cigarette. Cigarettes helped you think.

"See?" said El Rojo. "What's one more?"

"Yeah," Eddie said, blowing another cloud of smoke. "I'm getting out."

Chapter Two

He was nineteen, still in many ways a boy; an athletic boy with a swimmer's body, light hair, unmarred skin. Three lifers got him in the showers. One was called Louie. Louie was the best bridge player in the joint; he'd been working on his game for twenty years. Before that he'd raped and killed a sorority sister in Pennsylvania, was still cutting her up when the police arrived. The other two were overgrown and mildly retarded brothers from the Ozarks who did what Louie said. Louie could have used one more helper. It took too long to get the boy down. They had to break his jaw and a few of his ribs. Even then, the boy kept thrashing until hit on the head with a cast-iron shower faucet ripped out of the wall. After that, they did what they wanted.

Day 5,478: his last. Eddie Nye awoke before six, remembered, disbelieved. Maybe it was only day 300 and he had dreamed the rest. "Christ," he thought, but must have spoken aloud, because from the bottom bunk he heard Prof say, "What you got to be pissed about?" and he knew it was true.

Before breakfast, Eddie went through his locker. The clothes, all state issue, he tossed on the bunk. The books, magazines, and Remington cordless he left for Prof.

"Not takin' the razor, man?" said Prof, watching from his bunk.

Eddie shook his head. He unstrapped his watch and handed it to Prof as well. "Hey," said Prof.

"Just take it," Eddie told him. He could feel Prof thinking:

But I already got a watch; and What's he pullin'? But Prof was too smart to say anything; at least, he wanted to leave the impression he was smart. Forgers were supposed to be smart, and maybe some still were. But Prof was a modern forger—he dealt in official documents, bribing government clerks for the real thing. And Eddie was past caring what was going on in Prof's mind. All he wanted was to walk out of there clean, completely clean.

Eddie rummaged in the locker. At the bottom lay his mail. Four letters. The first, almost fifteen years old to the day, was a consolation note from his lawyer. Eddie had forgotten his name. He checked the letterhead: Glenn Weems, of Smith and Weems. Eddie tried to picture him and couldn't.

The second, from Wm. P. Brice, Investigation and Security, was dated a few months later.

Dear Mr. Ed Nye:
As I informed your brother, all our best efforts to locate the individual known as JFK have to this point in time been unsuccessful. Lacking further funds to continue, we are obliged to terminate the investigation.
Sincerely,
Bill Brice

The third letter had come two years after that.

Dear Mr. Nye:
We at the Red Legal Commune obtained your name from a list of state prisoners and have since learned something of your case. Although there is nothing we can do to assist you in a legal way, we are committed to demonstrating solidarity with our incarcerated brothers and sisters. Many of our supporters are interested in corresponding with inmates. If you are interested, please let us know at the above address.
In peace and in justice,
Molly Schumer (assistant coordinator)

Eddie had written back, asking Molly Schumer to send a picture of herself. She had sent back letter number four: an envelope containing a photograph of the entire Red Legal Commune, posed on a lawn outside a brick row house with a raised fist painted on the door. Molly Schumer had circled her face in the photo. A round face, maybe a little plump, but laughing, and framed by golden curls that glinted in sunshine. She wore a tie-dyed shirt, tight around full breasts. A man in granny glasses had his arm around her shoulder, but everyone had their arms around everyone. Eddie had written back, asking for a picture of Molly all by herself, at the beach maybe. There had been no reply.

Eddie held his collected correspondence over the toilet, lit a match. The old paper ignited and flamed immediately, like a torch. Eddie was aware of Prof watching in fascination, not because he was burning letters or because fires were against the rules, but simply at the sight of fire itself. Eddie dropped the flaming wad into the steel bowl, wondering whether the Red Legal Commune still existed. "Do they still have communes, shit like that?" he asked Prof.

"Whaddya mean, exactly?"

Someone rapped on the bars. Eddie, stepping in front of the toilet, turned and saw a guard he didn't know. He smelled smoke, heard Prof unwisely sniffing the air; but the C.O. didn't appear to notice anything.

"Man wants to see you," he said to Eddie. He had a pink pass in his hand.

"What man?"

"I don't do interviews," the guard said. "Move."

Eddie moved, out of the cell, past the scanner, out of F, across the yard, into C, past the scanner, up to the third tier, along to C–93, the last cell. It was a single, the same size as all the other cells but containing only one bunk. El Rojo was sitting on it, staring at a photograph on his wall, or perhaps at nothing, listening to his cassette player. Eddie recognized the tune: "Malagueña." El Rojo felt their presence and turned.

"My friend," he said. *"Ven aca."*

Eddie went in.

"Five minutes," the C.O. said, and went away.

"Sit down," El Rojo said.

Eddie sat on the bed. He looked at the picture on the wall. It showed a dark-haired boy of about nine or ten, riding a white horse. He wore an all-black cowboy outfit that looked like real leather and was aiming a pistol right at the camera. The pistol looked real too.

"My son," El Rojo said. Eddie felt the other man's gaze on his profile. "We call him Gaucho, although his real name is Simon. After the Liberator."

Eddie wasn't sure what liberator El Rojo was talking about, but he nodded anyway. Simon the Liberator was smiling; he had beautiful white teeth, a lot like his father's.

"A fine boy," El Rojo said. "And a dead shot."

"Isn't he a little young for that?"

"Too young to learn the importance of self-defense? I find that amusing, coming from a man of your reputation." El Rojo smiled, revealing the missing tooth that differentiated the father's smile from the son's. "You must be something of a marksman yourself, amigo."

"I've never fired a gun in my life."

Pause. "You shock me." El Rojo's maple-syrup eyes held Eddie in their gaze. "But you don't do badly with a nail and an elastico, do you?" He laughed his crow laugh, kept laughing it for a long time, until a tear ran down his cheek. Then he laid his long hand on Eddie's shoulder and gave a little squeeze. "To business," said El Rojo. "Tell me your plans."

"A steam bath," Eddie said. "After that I'd only be guessing."

He expected more laughter, but there was none. El Rojo nodded, as though a hunch had been confirmed. "I could use someone like you."

How, Eddie wondered, flexing his shoulder slightly. El Rojo got the message and his hand fell away. I'll be out and you'll be here.

Did El Rojo read his mind? "Who can predict the future?" he said.

The judge who sentenced me, Eddie thought, deciding that El Rojo still didn't know how bad it was. Why should Eddie be the one to tell him?

"Think about it," El Rojo said.

"About what?"

"Employment. Good salaries and generous bonuses. No benefits, I'm afraid."

"What kind of employment?"

"Steady employment, amigo. Do you mind if I offer some advice?"

Eddie didn't mind.

"You've never been locked up before, have you?"

"I've been here for fifteen years."

"I know that. But this is your first sentence."

Eddie nodded.

"Then you've never been released before. Unlike me. As a young man, I spent two years in La Picota. My own fault. I failed to understand the system then, even the primitive system of ours. Two years. An important period in my development, I see now. But even more important was the lesson I learned when I got out." He started to put his hand on Eddie's shoulder again, changed his mind. "Time changes everything, amigo," he went on. "So you cannot simply resume life where you left off. And I suspect that is what you want to do."

"I wasn't busted in a steam bath," Eddie said.

El Rojo showed his teeth. "I admire spirit," he replied. "Regrettably, it counts for nothing in this world."

The guard was at the door. El Rojo rose. Again they shook hands, again those long damp fingers stirred some memory. "Be seeing you," El Rojo said.

Was it a joke? El Rojo had one of those three-digit sentences that get a judge's name out in front of the public. Walking down the corridor with the C.O. behind him, Eddie laughed.

"What's so funny?"

"You," said Eddie. "Running errands for a con."

The back of Eddie's neck prickled, in anticipation of a blow. But the guard didn't hit him; he just said, "Fuck you, asshole," and without much force.

Before breakfast, Prof handed Eddie a cardboard tube. "Mind mailing this when you're out?"

"Sure," Eddie said, checking the address: 367 Parchman Ave. #3, Brooklyn, NY.

"A present for Tiffany. Here's a pack of Camels to pay for the stamps."

"Forget it."

Breakfast was fried Spam, tapioca pudding, coffee. Eddie just had coffee. He didn't want to take anything with him when he went, not even inside his body. With that in mind, he returned to F−31 and sat on the toilet. He was wiping himself when a C.O. came, one he knew. "Move it, Nails. You can jerk off all you like on the outside."

"How's that different from here?" Eddie said, getting up.

They went down to the showers. It was an open room off the gym with a cement floor and faucets spaced around the walls. The C.O. stood outside the door while Eddie stripped off his inmate denims and scrubbed under a stream of water that was never hot enough. He thought to himself: Yes. I can go to a steam bath somewhere. I can do it today.

The Ozark brothers had been easy. They liked to work out together with heavy weights, one lifting, the other acting as safety. The boy had walked up one morning when they were all alone at the bench press, Brother A on his back, grunting under a bar bent with weights, Brother B leaning over him to help lower the bar in the bracket at the end of the set. They had the music cranked up and didn't hear a thing. The boy didn't think. He just picked up a ten-pound barbell and brought it down on the back of Brother B's head. Brother B fell forward onto the heavy bar Brother A was just raising on his last rep. The bar came down on Brother A's Adam's apple—the boy caught the look of comprehension dawning in his eyes as it slipped from his grasp—then crashed to the floor. They found A and B lying face to face, belly to belly, on the bench.

Eddie toweled off. The C.O. handed him a brown-paper package. Inside Eddie found a suit of clothes. Not a suit, exactly—a bright green short-sleeved shirt, beige trousers with belt loops, a brown leather belt, white socks, BVDs, a khaki windbreaker—but civilian clothes. Eddie found that his hands were trembling as he got dressed. He realized he was nervous. It was a sensation he hadn't felt in a long time. What did he have to be nervous about? He was getting out.

"No shoes," the C.O. said. "The taxpayer won't spring for shoes. But they still throw in the belt."

It was the belt that counted, of course. Eddie hadn't worn a belt in fifteen years. He buckled it and said: "Now I can string myself up whenever I want."

"Be my guest."

Eddie laced on his old and smelly basketball high-tops and picked up Prof's cardboard tube. Then they went up the stairs, through the scanner, and out of F-Block. The yard was full of men in denim. Eddie felt a little funny in his green shirt. They went past a touch football game. There was a brief pause as Eddie went by. He felt eyes on him. Then someone said, "Snap the ball, shithead," leather smacked flesh, and Eddie walked through another scanner and into Admin.

The C.O. knocked on a door that said "Director of Treatment." The door opened, but before Eddie could go in, an inmate came out. El Rojo. He stopped, smiled his white but gap-toothed smile.

"Amigo," he said. "Today's the day, no?"

As if they hadn't been talking an hour ago. "Yup," Eddie said.

"Excellent." El Rojo leaned against the wall, in no hurry, took out cigarettes, offered one to Eddie.

"No, thanks," Eddie said.

El Rojo laid his long-fingered hand on Eddie's shoulder. Gentle, but Eddie felt the strength in those fingers, and the dampness. And he remembered the image that had eluded him:

> The very deep did rot: O Christ!
> That ever this should be!
> Yea, slimy things did crawl with legs
> Upon the slimy sea.

"Smoke it later, my friend, outside," El Rojo was saying. He lowered his voice. "After."

"After what?"

El Rojo kept his voice low. "After you get laid for me." A burst of crow laughter followed, was quickly throttled.

"Get laid for you?" asked Eddie, looking into the maple syrup eyes, aware of complexity in their depths, beyond his understanding.

"It will make me happy just to think about it," El Rojo replied.

Eddie shrugged, took the cigarette, and put it in the pocket of his green shirt. El Rojo removed his hand from Eddie's shoulder, extended it for shaking.

"Adios."

"So long." That was the truth, given El Rojo's sentence and the fact that Eddie wasn't coming back.

Eddie went in. He smelled a piney smell and thought of Christmas. The director of treatment, sitting at his desk behind a sign saying "Floyd K. Messer, M.D., Ph.D.," had the right body type for the Santa role. He had fat cheeks, reddened by the sun— photographs of him posing beside hooked game fish hung on the walls. He had curly graying hair and a trim gray beard that, grown out, might have looked just right. All he needed was to learn how to make his eyes twinkle.

Dr. Messer was gazing at a computer screen, his fat white fingers poised over the keyboard. "Take a pew, son," he said, without looking up.

Eddie sat down on the other side of the desk. The piney smell was stronger. "What kind of treatment program you putting him on?" Eddie said.

Dr. Messer looked up. "Who would you be talking about, son?"

"El Rojo, or whatever the hell his name is."

Dr. Messer gave him a long stare. "Is that any business of yours?" Dr. Messer waited for an answer. When none came, his fat fingers descended on the keys. "Nye," he murmured, tapping slowly. "Edward Nicholas." There was a pause. Then he put on a pair of glasses and bent closer to the machine. From where he sat, Eddie couldn't see the screen; he watched the tiny green letters reflected in the doctor's glasses.

"You've done a long stretch," Dr. Messer said, still murmuring but a little more loudly now, so that Eddie wasn't sure if he was still talking to himself. "Comparatively," the doctor added. He looked puzzled. For a wild moment, Eddie thought that something had happened, that they weren't going to let him go. The pores in his armpits opened; a drop of sweat rolled down his ribs, under the new green shirt. Dr. Messer tapped at the keys. "You should have been out in less than . . ." Tiny words scrolled down his lenses. Dr. Messer searched for their meaning in silence. Eddie realized that everything was all right. It was just that Dr. Messer didn't know who he was, didn't remember.

How many years had passed since he had last been in this office? Eddie wasn't sure, but he recalled the occasion clearly. It was during the period of Dr. Messer's enthusiasm for soliciting inmate volunteers for drug-company tests. Eddie had agreed to take one little red pill a day for six weeks. At the beginning, someone from the drug company had given him a local anesthetic and taken one gram of muscle from inside his forearm. At the end, another gram was required, for comparison. By that time, Dr. Messer had been trained in the procedure. He took the gram himself, but something went wrong with the anesthetic, although Dr. Messer hadn't believed Eddie about that, and then, with the big square-ended instrument dug deep in his flesh, it was too late for Eddie to do anything without making things worse. The arm had been useless for months. The drug company paid Eddie ninety dollars—forty for each procedure and ten for taking the pills. He'd spent it at the canteen, mostly on Pepsi, ripple potato chips, and cigarettes.

Dr. Messer said: "Ah." He nodded to himself, removed his glasses and turned to Eddie. Christmas-tree smell wafted across the desk. "Well, son. Got any plans? Thirty-four's not old, not in this day and age."

Eddie said: "What were the results of the experiment?"

Dr. Messer blinked. "Experiment?" His forehead creased in a way Santa's never would. "I asked you about your plans."

"Plans?" said Eddie.

"Like what you're going to do tomorrow, next week, next year," Dr. Messer explained impatiently.

"Steam bath," Eddie said.

The forehead creases deepened. "You want to work in a steam bath?"

Eddie was silent.

Dr. Messer took a deep breath and said: "What did you do before?"

"Before?"

"Before here." The impatient tone was back, beyond the control of deep-breathing techniques.

Eddie considered his answer. What had he done? There'd been

swimming, of course. And Jack, Galleon Beach, Mandy, the Packers, the whole fuckup. "Not much," Eddie said. The names, their syllables strange and familiar as returning to the house you were born in, stayed in his mind. "But as a friend of mine says," he added, "you can't expect to take up where you left off."

"Your friend sounds wise."

"For an ax murderer," Eddie said, stretching the truth a little.

Dr. Messer, long accustomed to conversation with those less bright than himself, took another deep breath. "The point is it's expensive outside these walls. In here we give you your three squares per and a place to sleep. Out there you got to earn it. You're gonna need a job. Unless you're in line for a fat inheritance or something." Dr. Messer turned up the corners of his mouth to show he was being funny. Eddie said nothing. Dr. Messer's lips turned down. He tapped the screen with his glasses. "Says here you're an 'inadequate personality.' Know what that means?"

"Sounds like bullshit to me."

Dr. Messer's fat fingers tightened slightly around the frames of his glasses. "That just proves the point, son." He tapped the screen again, harder now. Maybe it was a symbolic way of knocking sense into Eddie. Or just knocking him. "Five to fifteen, but everybody knows you're out in three and a half, four. Any half-assed adequate personality would've been. Any half-assed adequate personality wouldn't have fucked up his parole. But you did the whole nickel and dime, like the dumbest con in the joint."

All at once, Eddie thought: Why do I have to listen to this anymore? I'm gone. He looked into the untwinkling eyes and said: "In your opinion."

"In my opinion?" Dr. Messer's voice rose, but not much, a few decibels. The door opened and the C.O. stuck his head in.

"Everything okay, Dr. Messer?" He wasn't gone yet.

"Couldn't be better."

The door closed. "Tell you something," Dr. Messer said, starting to smile. "I've been in corrections for twenty-three years. It's the shittiest work in the world. The pay is shitty, the benefits are shitty, the hours are shitty. But the shittiest part is, you got to deal with the likes of you. One look and I know your whole story, past, present, and future. And you know something, son? Summing up, so to speak? I'll be seeing you again. Soon." He was smiling broadly now, but resembling Santa less and less. He tossed a brown envelope at Eddie. Eddie caught it and started to rise.

"Count it," Dr. Messer said. "Just so's there's no misunder-standings."

Eddie opened the envelope and counted his gate money. Three hundred and thirty-eight dollars and twenty-five cents. It wasn't a gift. That's what he'd earned, minus what he'd spent in the canteen.

"Sign here."

Eddie wrote "Edward N. Nye" on a form Messer slid across the desk. Then he stuck the money in the pocket of his new pants and went out. There were no good-byes.

The C.O. led him along a corridor and down a damp stairway. They entered a dark space. The only light came from a dusty ceiling bulb. It shone on a white station wagon with government plates. "Get in," said the C.O.

Eddie stepped forward, fumbled for a moment with the door—it had a recessed handle he was unfamiliar with—and climbed in the backseat. From the front came a voice: "Hokay?"

"Okay what?" said Eddie.

The driver turned to him and shrugged. He was a dark-skinned man with a thin mustache and a Tampa Bay baseball cap. Did Tampa Bay have a team? *"No hablo ingles,"* said the driver.

He switched on the engine. A big door opened in front of them, exposing a rectangle of dazzling light. They drove out into it.

Out, along a couple hundred feet of pavement that led to the perimeter fence, where guards checked under the hood, under the seats, under the chassis, and waved them through. The guards, their shotguns, the fence, the gate, all blurred in Eddie's vision. The light was so bright it hurt his eyes, made them water uncon-trollably. Was one of the guards staring at him? Don't think I'm crying, motherfucker, Eddie thought. It's nothing like that—just this light.

Out, past a woman in black holding a sign that read "Free Willie Boggs," and onto a highway with other cars, a highway lined with other signs, signs Eddie tried to read through the dazzlement: Motel 6, Mufflers 4U, Lanny's Used Tires, Bud Lite, Pink Lady Lounge, All the Shrimp You Cn Eat $6.95, XXX Video, Happy Hour. The driver turned on the radio. ". . . skies overcast, temperature in the mid sixties," it said; then the driver switched to a Spanish station where an announcer was saying the same thing. Overcast? Eddie looked out. He saw no clouds, but the sky wasn't blue. It was gold—thick, dense, rich; all the way down to the ground.

And then his gaze fell on the side mirror. He saw a medieval vision in it: a fortress of stone, shimmering in the glare. Eddie had never seen his prison before, not from the outside. They had brought him in at night. Now he watched in the mirror as the gray walls shrank, their lines lost distinction, wavering in the golden light. It might have been a mirage.

Louie. Louie hadn't been so easy. Louie knew what had happened to the Ozark brothers, even if no one else did. Had the boy made plans or simply seized an opportunity? Louie didn't know, and what difference did it make? He could never be alone, that was all.

It took two years. The boy—although there wasn't much boy left by that time—found a half-inch-wide elastic band one day, wrapped around a discarded envelope in the yard. If he'd had a coat hanger or a cleft stick the rest would have been easy, but coat hangers were forbidden and there were no trees in the yard. He tried to stretch the band between his thumb and index finger, but it was too thick. The only way was to take one end of the band in his teeth and pull with his left hand. That left the right hand free.

He stole a four-inch nail from the shop, carried it through the strip search glued to his palate, hanging down his throat. Back in his cell he took it out, along with part of the lining of the roof of his mouth. Late at night he would practice, holding the band taut between his teeth and his left hand, setting the head of the nail in the band, pulling it back, firing into his pillow for silence. A technique that took a long time to perfect, but that was the one thing he had.

Louie liked to play bridge at a table in a corner of the rec room. The boy took to playing Ping-Pong. The first time he came in, Louie didn't take his eyes off him. The boy didn't even glance at Louie. He just played Ping-Pong. He was good at it. He came every afternoon. Louie got used to his presence. He got used to the fact that sometimes the ball got away and a player had to come over to the bridge table and pick it up. He got used to the boy coming to pick it up.

Money was bet at those bridge games, although it changed hands later. And Louie took most of it—he knew how to bid, how to count cards, how to cheat if he had to. It was a lot to think about. One afternoon, Louie was wondering whether to go to six spades when the Ping-Pong ball came bouncing across the floor. Louie heard it but didn't look up, not until he felt a stillness in the room. Then he saw the boy kneeling on the floor, at the far side of the table, in a funny sideways position, yanking at a rubber band held between his teeth and squinting right at the middle of Louie's forehead. It was so weird, he never saw the nail at all.

"Hokay," said the driver, pulling into a Dunkin' Donuts parking lot.

Eddie got out. The white station wagon backed, wheeled around, was gone. Eddie stood in the middle of the lot. From the sky came a tremendous chirping din. Eddie looked around, not aware at first of its source. He located it, finally, in the branches of a sick-looking scrub pine at the edge of the lot—a single brown bird he couldn't identify. A bird. Its song stunned him. He remembered:

> Sometimes a-dropping from the sky
> I heard the sky-lark sing;
> Sometimes all little birds that are,
> How they seemed to fill the sea and air
> With their sweet jargoning!

Eddie never had figured out "jargoning," but now he understood the exclamation mark and, wiping his eyes, thought of getting down and kissing the pavement of the Dunkin' Donuts lot. A funny idea; it made him laugh out loud. He heard his own laughter, didn't like the sound, stopped.

No one likes a card sharp, so no one liked Louie, and no one talked. That was enough to keep the boy from getting life. It wasn't enough to stop them from withdrawing parole. The normal laissez-faire toward popular killings doesn't apply when you're inside. Nails. At first black humor, later just his name.

Cars whizzed by on the highway. Eddie watched them for a while, then gazed through the window of Dunkin' Dunuts where people sat at a counter, sipping, chewing, talking, doing the crossword. Then he noticed the bus station next door. A Greyhound Americruiser was scrolling through its destinations: Jax, Atlanta, Baltimore, Philly, NY. Eddie walked toward it. Ordinary walking. Didn't mean a thing. He just felt like going that way and he did. A long stretch, he thought. Comparatively, as Dr. Messer had said. Especially comparatively for an innocent man.

A red convertible stopped nearby. A woman got out. She had thick black hair, red lips, smooth double-cream-coffee skin, long legs, and a short black leather skirt. Eddie couldn't take his eyes off her. She was coming his way. Eddie forced himself to stop staring, turned toward the bus station.

"Hey you!"

Eddie kept going.

"Hey, you!"

Was she calling him? He turned back.

"Me?"

She laughed. She was close now, still coming toward him, her breasts jiggling under a little halter top, nipples protruding, hips swelling under the leather skirt: all these details spun through Eddie's mind in confusion. "Yeah, you," she said. "Wanna have some fun?"

Outside: Day 1

Chapter Three

Fun. Eddie stood in the glare under the madly chirping bird, his eyes on a vision of everything Prof's porno shot strove for (so unsuccessfully, he now realized): a vision of irresistible and available female sexuality. It wasn't just a function of those physical images still careening through his brain—hair, lips, skin, breasts, hips, thighs—but of the voice too. The voice especially. There was something arousing about the female voice, all by itself. Or was it just long deprivation of the sound that made him react like that?

She was looking at him funny. "What's the matter? You don't speak English?"

Christ, Eddie thought, I'm slow. Inside, fast, but out here, very slow. "Yeah. I speak English."

"Whoop-dee-do," said the woman. "We've got something in common already." She swung open the passenger door of the red convertible, her ass, solid and round, bunching slightly with the effort. "Let's roll."

Eddie's mouth was dry. He licked his lips. "Roll?"

She looked at him funny again. "You got a learning disability or something?"

"I'm a high-school graduate," Eddie said, inwardly cursing himself at once for the stupidity of the remark.

She laughed, not loudly, but the sound had magic—it drowned out everything: the traffic, the bird, the inarticulate warnings in

Eddie's mind. "Me, too," she said. "So let's go someplace and hit the books."

The words and the woman-voice fit together like the lyric and melody of a song no one can forget. Eddie took a step forward. His internal warnings grew louder and more articulate: What kind of someplace? The backseat of the car? The side of the road? Was she a hooker? Maybe not—he knew there'd been big changes with women, wasn't it possible this was some kind of casual pickup that went on all the time now? But if so, why him? And if a hooker, that meant money, but how much? He took another step. One more and he'd get a sniff of her—he was already getting the urge to inhale deeply, extravagantly, through his nose—and then the decision would be made.

Something flashed in Eddie's peripheral vision. The door of Dunkin' Donuts opened, catching the light. A cop came out, with coffee in one hand and a sugar donut in the other. He stuck the donut in his mouth, bit into it, saw Eddie. Red jelly spurted into the air. The cop looked hard at Eddie, lowered the donut, took in the car, the woman. Eddie thought: Is it a trap? What kind? Why? He didn't know. But he'd learned to sense them. He backed away.

"I don't think so," he said.

"You what?"

Eddie didn't answer. He had already turned and started walking toward the bus station. Slow down, he told himself, slow down. He got ready for a cry of "Halt!" or running steps or a bullet in the back. But there was none of that, just the woman saying: "What's the matter with you? You gay? Jesus H. Christ. A dyslexic fag. I can't take much more of this. Am I s'posed to kidnap the prick or what?"

Eddie stepped over a low wall that divided the Dunkin' Donuts lot from the bus-station lot and risked a glance back. The cop was moving toward a squad car now, still watching Eddie, but he was chewing on the donut again. The woman was in the red convertible. She slammed the door and sped away. Eddie walked into the bus station.

Inside was an ill-lit waiting room with rows of orange plastic seats, a ticket counter at the far end, a shop in an alcove on one side. Passing the shop, Eddie saw sunglasses in a rotating display case. He went in, spun the case. There were so many lens colors—

blue, green, yellow, rose, gray. He found a mirror-lensed pair, and there he was, reflected in miniature. He saw what everyone else must see: the shaven skull, the pale skin, and eyes they probably didn't like the look of; superficially nice, maybe, the whites clear, the irises light brown and speckled with coppery flecks, so the overall effect was close to bronze; but their expression, no matter how deep Eddie looked, was cold, wary, hostile. The woman must have been a hooker, and a foolhardy one at that.

"Looking for something?" said a voice behind him.

Eddie turned. A fat man in a sleeveless T-shirt had come out from behind the cash register. Now he took a step back.

"Sunglasses," Eddie said.

That reassured him. "For on the water, or just swanning around?" he said.

"For glare."

The man pointed a nicotine-tipped finger. "Try those."

"Yellow?"

"That's amber. Says antiglare right on them."

Eddie tried on amber sunglasses. They made everything yellow. "I'll have to look outside." He walked out of the shop, to the entrance of the bus station. The man followed, close behind. Eddie looked out. There was less glare, but everything was yellow, including the cop and his squad car, now parked in the bus-station parking lot. Donut consumed, but the cop was still watching him.

"Well?" the clerk asked, gazing up at his face. Eddie could smell him. "You want them or not?"

"Okay," Eddie said.

They returned to the shop. The clerk punched numbers on the cash register. "Twenty-four ninety-five," he said.

That seemed like a lot for sunglasses. Eddie took out the brown envelope, fished through for a ten and a twenty. The money hadn't changed at all. *It's expensive, outside these walls.* But you could buy things that changed the color of the view.

"I haven't got all day."

Eddie handed over the cash and put on the glasses. The clerk gave him $5.05 and came at him with a pair of scissors. Eddie jumped back.

"You wanna go around with that tag flappin' on your nose, fine with me."

Eddie let him cut off the tag. He joined the line at the ticket counter. In front of him stood a squat, olive-skinned woman with a baby in her arms and a restless little girl at her side. The little girl wore earrings, a frilly dress, and shiny black dancing shoes. She seemed too young to be turned out like that, but still Eddie couldn't take his eyes off her. She had skinny arms and legs and big, serious eyes, and she skipped around in circles, singing a Spanish song under her breath. Eddie had forgotten that such creatures lived, and lived on the same planet as the man with the ring in his tongue. He suddenly thought of the beautiful water snakes that saved the mariner's soul—"O happy living things!"—and understood them a little better. Then the girl saw him watching and buried herself in her mother's skirt. The mother turned, gave Eddie a hard stare and the girl a smack on the back of her head. Eddie, towering over them, tried to appear harmless.

"Where to, buddy?"

Then he was at the counter, facing the ticket agent. The ticket agent was an old man with hairs sticking out of his ears and nose and formless and faded tattoos on his shriveled forearms. He was a con; Eddie knew it at once.

"Where to?"

That was the question. The answer depended on his plans— *what you're going to do tomorrow, next week, next year*. Eddie scanned the destination board on the wall behind the agent. He thought of going down to the Gulf, finding work on a fishing boat. He knew, had known, a little about boats. There was a bus to Baton Rouge at four-thirty. Eddie moved to look at his watch, but of course it was gone. "What time is it?"

"Two hairs past a freckle," said the old man. "C'mon, buddy. We's on a tight schedule here." He tried drumming his fingers aggressively on the counter, but they were too arthritic for stunts like that.

Home, Eddie thought. That was a laugh; but why not? Had he known it all along? "Any buses going north?"

"All the ways to Beantown."

Close enough. "When?"

"Two minutes ago. You can catch it if you'll just kindly the hell move."

"How much?"

"One way or return?"

"One way."

The ticket cost Eddie almost a third of his gate money. He hurried out into the yellow, past the cop still watching from his squad car, and knocked on the door of the Americruiser. It opened. "Luggage?" the driver said.

"Nope."

"Lez go." The driver's hand was out, fingers gesturing for something to be laid in it. Eddie climbed on and gave him the ticket. Outside, in the real world, as the C.O. had put it, he was a step or two slow, like a visitor from another land.

The bus wasn't crowded. Eddie found a window seat halfway back. The bus rolled across the lot, past the squad car, onto the open road. Eddie watched the real world go by, all yellow. Then the motion got to him. I can't be tired, he thought, not after a lifetime on that bunk. But his eyes closed anyway.

He dreamed a familiar dream, of the banana-shaped island and the shed beside the tennis court. It was dark inside, despite the summer afternoon heat, and smelled of pig blood and red clay. Mandy smelled of red clay too, red clay and fresh sweat. Her tennis clothes clung to her body. She slipped her hand between his legs, under his shorts, around his balls. "Shh," she said. They had to be quiet. He couldn't remember why.

Eddie awoke with a dry throat and an erection. The bus was stopped and full of people moving around. A slight man in a cheap black suit said: "Excuse me, sir, is this seat taken?"

Eddie straightened, shook his head. The man sat in the aisle seat, opened a Bible. The bus started with a jerk and picked up speed. Eddie looked out. A long line of leafless trees went by, then a billboard that said "Christ Is Love" and pictured a garish Jesus on the verge of tears. Eddie glanced at the man in the black suit. With a kind of grease pencil Eddie hadn't seen before, he was highlighting a passage. Eddie leaned closer. "Whoever perished, being innocent? or where were the righteous cut off?" The man felt his presence and made a wall with his hand between Eddie and the text, like an A student stopping an unprepared one from cheating on a test.

Eddie gazed out the window. The sun was low in the sky now, everything still yellow. He removed the glasses to see if the glare had gone, but it had not. He put them on and was soon asleep.

When he awoke it was night and the man with the Bible was gone. Eddie felt in his pocket and found that his gate-money envelope and its contents, all but the $5.05 in change from the sunglasses, were gone too. He got down on the floor, peered under the seat, felt behind the cushion. He found Prof's cardboard tube, a book of matches, Kleenex, a used condom, but no gate money. He sat up, looked around. There was no one else on the bus, except the driver and a gum-chewing woman wearing hair curlers the same shade of green as his shirt. Not yellow: green. That's when he realized that the sunglasses were gone as well, snatched right off his sleeping face.

Eddie strode to the front of the bus. "Where'd the guy in the black suit get off?"

"Mind stepping back of the line?" said the driver. A new driver, Eddie saw: a woman. She had frosted blond hair and a strong jaw. No reason it shouldn't be a woman, but it stopped his momentum just the same. Eddie looked down at the white line in the aisle. "Do not cross when bus is in motion" was stenciled on the rubber. Eddie stepped back and repeated his question.

"Couldn't say," the driver replied. "I've got enough to do with this storm."

Eddie glanced out. Flying things swarmed all around, like insects. Snow. No reason there shouldn't be snow, but that threw him too, after fifteen snowless years. "Where are we?"

"Just across the state line," the driver said. She didn't say what state and Eddie didn't ask. What he wanted to do, at that moment, was get on a bus going the other way, back; back down south, to that shrimp boat. A much better idea. What the hell was he thinking, going home? Home was just snow, ice, a frozen river. Other than that, it didn't exist and never had. He came from somewhere, that was all. Everybody came from somewhere. It didn't mean a thing.

Eddie made his way to his seat, past the woman in green curlers who was now wearing earphones as well. He needed a smoke. Didn't have any, because that was one of the things he was giving up in his new life. What kind of a plan was that? These were his plans: 1) steam bath; 2) quit smoking; 3) take nothing with him when he went. So now he was hungry, hadn't eaten since yesterday, and was forced to ask others for the time. Fifteen years to think, and that was it?

Conscious of his hunger, Eddie wanted a cigarette all the more. But of course he had one: the cigarette El Rojo had given him. He reached in the pocket of his green shirt. Somehow the Bible man had missed it. Eddie stuck it in his mouth, took out the matches he'd found under the seat. On the cover was an eight-hundred number to call if you suspected child abuse. Eddie lit a match, held it to the tip of El Rojo's cigarette, inhaled. The tip flared and he sucked in smoke luxuriously. Then the woman in green curlers was standing over him, gesturing. From her earphones a tiny voice shrilled, "Dance, dance, dance." She mouthed something at him.

"I can't hear because you're wearing earphones?" Eddie said.

The woman didn't answer. She pointed to a sign on the wall: No Smoking. The women on this bus seemed to communicate with him through the written word. This one stood with her arms crossed, waiting for him to do the right thing. I killed three men, you stupid bitch, Eddie thought, but he butted out the cigarette on the plastic armrest. The woman went away.

Eddie was angry. In his anger he could have pounded the armrest, or ripped out a few seats, or smashed windows. Those images ran through his mind as he sat, motionless. His heart pounded like a war drum. He wanted to kill, not the woman in curlers, but whoever had ruined him. But there was no one to blame. It was just the way things were—the luck of the draw, bad break, Mother Nature's way, God's way; or the albatross's way, he thought suddenly. Maybe you were supposed to see the whole thing through the albatross's eyes. Maybe he'd read it totally wrong. Fifteen years, and he couldn't understand a simple poem.

Eddie saw his face reflected in the night and turned away.

He still had the cigarette in his hand. About to return it to his pocket, Eddie noticed a green corner sticking out of the burnt end. Pulling at it revealed more green. With his fingernails he tore through the cigarette paper, peeled it away. Underneath, wrapped tightly around the tobacco, was a bank note. Eddie unrolled it, scattering tobacco shreds in his lap, and found himself gazing at the face of Benjamin Franklin; an intelligent face, some-what amused.

A one-hundred-dollar bill. He held it up to the overhead light, turned it over, snapped it. It looked and felt like the real thing. No reason to think it wasn't.

Eddie smiled. He'd heard of people lighting cigarettes with hundred-dollar bills, but never smoking the money itself. El Rojo, Angel Cruz, whatever the hell his name was, had told him to smoke the cigarette later, on the outside. Kind of sentimental, but maybe it was a Latino thing. Save it for later, El Rojo had told him: *after you get laid for me*. Then Eddie remembered the woman in the red convertible and stopped smiling.

Outside: Day 2

Chapter Four

Eddie, with Prof's cardboard mailing tube in his hand and
$105.05 in his pocket, stepped down onto the bus-station platform
in his old hometown. The wind tore through his khaki windbreaker and green short-sleeved shirt. Snow was blowing, but not
in the form of flakes: they were too small, too hard, too gray.

Eddie had forgotten that wind. It made him think again of
shrimp boats on the Gulf, and getting back on the bus. This, after
all, was the town he had always wanted to get out of, wasn't it?
The door of the bus jerked shut behind him.

Eddie went into the station, thinking, I'll sit in here where it's
warm, order a sandwich and coffee, eat all by myself: luxury. But
the station was not as he recalled: the coffee shop, newsstand,
drugstore, were all gone. Time changes everything, as El Rojo had
said. There was nothing inside but vending machines, a ticket
counter with no one behind it, and a stubble-faced man mopping
the floor.

Eddie examined the vending machines. Coffee cost sixty-five
cents. He had the hundred-dollar bill, a five, and a nickel. "Got
change for a five-dollar bill?" he called to the man. Maybe he
should have just said, "Got change for a five?" Was that more
natural? He needed a phrase book.

Not looking up, the man replied, "Change machine makes
change." He spoke with the accent of the town, of the whole
river valley, a sound Eddie hadn't consciously associated with his
childhood until that moment. It didn't warm him.

Eddie found the changer at the end of the row of vending machines. "Insert one or five dollar bill," read the instructions. "This way up." He took out the five and was about to stick it in the slot when he noticed that someone had written in lipstick on the wall, "Does not work you assholes." He didn't chance it.

Eddie went outside. He remembered that wind but didn't remember it bothering him like this. Had he been weakened by fifteen years spent indoors? Or was it just his shaven skull that gave the wind its bite?

Hunched inside the khaki windbreaker, Eddie walked down Main Street. Downtown had been decaying when he left. Now it had decayed more. Shop windows were dusty, the goods in them yellowed, nothing had been painted in years. He moved on toward Weisner's Department Store, maybe to buy a hat, at least to have a sandwich at the U-shaped lunch counter. But Weisner's, with that U-shaped lunch counter, faded hardwood floors, scrawny-necked clerks in jackets and ties, was gone; just an empty lot, covered in crusty brown snow, littered with broken glass and windblown scraps.

Eddie turned onto River. A dog came trotting his way, a little spotted mongrel with pointed ears. Eddie remembered he liked dogs and made a clicking sound, hoping to draw it closer, maybe within patting distance. The dog heard the sound and without changing speed cut across the street. Eddie noticed the bone sticking out of its mouth; maybe the dog thought he was after it.

He walked onto the bridge and started across the river toward New Town. The river was frozen over, except for a narrow band in the middle where water ran black and fast. As Eddie watched, a mattress-size slab of ice broke loose from the New Town bank, spun slowly into the stream, picked up speed, came surging closer, vanished under the bridge. Eddie crossed to the other side and watched the ice slab bob down the river, past the limits of the town to where the woods began, and out of sight.

Two boys, Eddie and Jack, on a mattress in a darkened room. The mattress was the good ship *Fearless*, the room a storm-toss'd sea. Eddie was Sir Wentworth Staples, captain in the British Navy, on a mission to exterminate pirates on the Spanish Main, and Jack was One-Eye Staples, king of the buccaneers. Through a series of efficient coincidences, the long-separated brothers now found themselves alone on the *Fearless*, sailors and pirates all drowned, the ship sundered and foundering. The situation and characters came from a book the boys had found in a trunk in the basement of one of the rooming houses they'd lived in after their mother got fired: *Muskets and Doubloons*. They made up their own endings.

"By thunder," said One-Eye, because One-Eye had a salty way of talking, "we're in a tight one now."

"Aye, matey," said Sir Wentworth.

A mighty wave struck amidships. The brothers clung to the sheets to keep from being washed away. The wind moaned all around. After a while the brothers realized it was a real moaning, the moaning of a woman: Mom, to be precise. The sound came through the thin partition.

Then they heard Mel: "You like that, don't you, babe," he said.

No answer. The boys clung to the sheets.

"Say you like it. Then maybe I'll do it again."

Pause. "You know I like it."

"Say you like when I do that to you because you're such a hot slut."

Sir Wentworth tugged on One-Eye's pajama sleeve. "We'll have to make a raft," he whispered. "She's sinking." One-Eye didn't move.

"Say it," said Mel, on the far side of the wall.

"I like when you do that because I'm just a slut," said Mom.

"Good enough."

Sir Wentworth tugged again at One-Eye's sleeve. "Help me," he said.

"Help you what?" asked One-Eye.

"Build a raft. The good ship *Fearless* is going to Davy Jones's locker."

One-Eye pushed him away. "Stop being a jerk," he said. He rolled over and closed his eyes.

Sir Wentworth built a raft out of pillows. The *Fearless* went down. The storm moaned and moaned all around them, with two voices now, male and female. Sir Wentworth lay silent on the pillow raft until it passed, the body of One-Eye motionless beside him.

* * *

There had been a succession of Mels, each one harder to live with than the last. Maybe their own father had been just another Mel too; the boys didn't know. He'd checked out early, and Mom didn't talk about him. The last Mel liked to slap the boys around a bit. One day Jack slapped back. The scene that followed prompted Mom to farm the boys out to Uncle Vic, on the New Town side. She and the last Mel moved to California a few months later. That was that.

Eddie stood in front of 23 Turk Street, Uncle Vic's house in New Town. It wasn't much of a place; they'd known that even then: a shotgun house with wavy floors, depressing wallpaper, grimy trim. But Uncle Vic wasn't even their uncle, just some old friend of Mom's. He didn't have to do it. That was a plus. Another plus was that he kept his fists to himself.

Uncle Vic worked the night shift at Falardeau Metal and Iron. In the afternoons, he coached the high-school swim team. That had been the biggest plus of all: he had taught Jack and Eddie how to swim, really swim, and they had swum their way out of town.

Twenty-three Turk hadn't been much of a house then. Now, like the rest of the town, it was past saving. Eddie walked across the sagging porch and knocked on the door. No one came. He knocked a few more times, then put his ear to the door, listening for movement inside. Someone said, "Tonight at seven—nudist camp murders." Then came a Coke commercial.

Eddie knocked once more, harder. He was ready to do it again when the door opened. A tiny man with a matted beard and stringy white hair looked out, blinking. He shrank back a bit when he saw Eddie's hand, in knocking position. Eddie lowered it.

"Whatever you're sellin' I'm not buyin'," the old man said. Alcohol fumes drifted into the space between them.

Eddie didn't recognize the man at all, but he knew the voice. "Vic," he said.

The old man peered up at him. "Do I know you?"

"Uncle Vic," Eddie said.

The old man studied his face, then looked him up, down, up. "Shit," he said. "You still competin'?"

"Competing?"

"Is why you shaved your melon. Unless you've gone bald or some—" Vic remembered then, and his face, hard enough, hardened more.

"I got out yesterday," Eddie said.

"Just yesterday?" said Vic, puzzled. "Well, if it's money you want, I got none. Don't need no jailbirds around here. No offense."

The wind gusted across the porch, spinning a white cone before it like a seal toying with a ball. Vic, in a sleeveless undershirt and long johns, shivered.

"I don't want money," Eddie said. This wasn't what he'd expected. But what had he expected? An embrace? No; but a handshake, maybe.

"Good," said Vic. "'Cause I got none. Those fucking Falardeaus laid me off, laid off half the town. I suppose you didn't know that."

"I didn't."

Vic snorted. "Restructuring."

"What's that?"

"You tell me." Vic glanced up and down Turk Street. No one was out. He looked again at Eddie. "You don't want money?"

"No."

Vic opened the door wider. "Might as well come on in." Another gust ripped up the porch, blowing a tiny white storm inside before Vic got the door closed.

Same house, same layout: front room, stairs on the left, bathroom down the hall, but much smaller than in memory, and all comfort gone. The shag carpet, Vic's Lazyboy, framed photos of Johnny Weissmuller: gone. There was just the TV and a stained sofa sagging crooked on the warped floor. On the screen, a man in a party hat was jumping up and down. *Is this the hill? is this the kirk?* Eddie thought. *Is this mine own countree?*

"Bank's got the place now," Vic said, watching him. "So who gives a shit?"

They sat at opposite ends of the sofa. There was a half-full jug of wine on the floor. Vic pushed it around the side, where Eddie couldn't see. He gave Eddie a sidelong look, then fastened his eyes on the TV. The man in the party hat was laughing till it hurt.

"You were something in the pool," Vic said.

"Not that good."

"Yes you were. One hell of a swimmer." He turned to Eddie. "Not as good as Jack, but one hell of a swimmer."

Eddie said nothing.

"Go ahead. Say it."

"Say what?"

"That you were better."

"I wasn't."

"You beat him in the fly. Why don't you say it?"

The same old shit: trying to get him to rise to the challenge of Jack. A cheap coach's trick, and so long ago, stupid then, meaningless now. They'd already fallen into their old pattern. Eddie kept silent.

Vic began his rebuttal anyway. "So what if you did beat him in the fly? What does it prove? The fly is for animals. Freestylers need finesse."

The next moment Eddie was on his feet, standing over Vic. Just a stupid and meaningless trick, but he had a fistful of that stringy hair, slick and oily, in one hand and his other hand was cocked.

"I'm not an animal."

"Jesus," said Vic, "what did I say?" The good part was the lack of fear in Vic's eyes. Eddie realized that was as close as he was going to get to a homecoming. "I was talking about swimming, for Christ's sake. I didn't mean nothin'."

Eddie let go. Sorry. He almost said it. Vic was drunk. Eddie had seen him drunk before. Fifteen years had passed and now Vic was one, that was all. Eddie walked to the window. Wind and snow. Nice. He could just stroll out into it if he wanted.

Behind him, Vic reached for the bottle, took a swig. His hair stood up like a cock's crest. He held the jug out to Eddie. Eddie shook his head. He'd thought a lot about his first drink on the outside. He wanted a drink, but he wasn't sure he could stop at one, and that meant not now.

Vic took another drink, a long one. "It's all fucked up, isn't it?" he said.

"What is?"

Vic waved the jug around. "This town. Everything. You guys were great. Coulda gone to the Olympics, anything."

"We weren't that good."

"Good enough for USC." Vic's voice rose. "After that, who knows? You never gave it a chance." Vic rubbed his forehead with the back of his hand, hard enough to redden the skin. "Ah, hell," he said. "What's it matter anyway?" He picked up the remote control and snapped off the TV. When he spoke again his voice was quieter. "You never wrote, or nothin'. Or called. Can you call from a place like that?"

"Yeah."

"And now you just turn up." Vic stuck the remote in his shirt pocket. "Jack writes."

"He does?"

"Sure." Vic rose, a little stiffly—once his movements had been quick and smooth—and left the room. Eddie heard him go up the stairs, walk along the floor above. He got up, found the wine jug. It had a nice label—vineyard, wagon piled with grapes, setting sun. Eddie sniffed the wine, raised it to his lips, drank. It disgusted him, as though he was too pure or something. A laughable idea. But he spat the wine on the floor anyway.

Vic returned, saw him standing there with the jug. "Left over from a party," he said.

"I don't remember you as a party-giver, Vic."

"People change." He thrust an envelope in Eddie's hands. "Jack writes."

Eddie opened the envelope, unfolded the letter. The first surprise was the letterhead: J. M. Nye and Associates, Investment Consultants, 222 Park Avenue, Suite 2068, New York. The second was the date. The letter was ten years old.

Dear Uncle Vic:
Sorry to hear things aren't going so well. Here's fifty.
Hope it tides you over. We wouldn't want to make this a
habit, what with being "family" and all. Keep plugging,
as you used to say down at the pool.
                                                    Jack
JMM/cb

"I told you," Vic said.

"Told me what?"

"Jack writes."

"This letter's ten years old."

Vic snatched it out of his hands. "That's a crock." He stuffed it in his pocket, behind the remote.

Ten years old and a brush-off besides, Eddie thought. But he left it unsaid because of the expression on Vic's face: pissed off and crazy at the same time. He'd seen that expression often enough, not on Vic's face, but on plenty of faces inside.

"Sounds like he's doing all right," Eddie said.

"What's that supposed to mean?"

"Two-twenty-two Park Avenue. Investment consultant."

"I don't even know what that means," Vic said.

"Me neither. Maybe not much, or he would have sprung for more than fifty."

Vic glared up at him, more crazy, more pissed off; with the rooster crest Eddie had raised on his head, he looked like a fighting cock about to do something bloody with his talons.

Shouldn't have come, Eddie thought. He said, "I wanted to see how you were, that's all."

"Broke," Vic said. "Stony broke."

"And other than that?"

Vic blinked again. Eddie didn't remember that blinking. It was a sign of the loser, too slow to keep up. Vic had become a loser.

"Other than that, what?" Vic said.

"Nothing," Eddie told him. He extended his hand. "Take care of yourself, Vic." Eddie got his handshake. The old man's hand was hot and dry. Probably the drinking did that, Eddie thought, although he remembered an inmate whose hand had felt the same way. He'd died of brain cancer a few months later.

"You don't want any money?" Vic said.

"I answered that."

"Everyone's tryin' to put the touch on these days, with the way this lousy state's . . ."

Eddie went to the door, opened it.

"Where are you gonna go?"

"Out." Eddie stepped into the storm.

Standing behind him, Vic laid his hot, dry hand on Eddie's shoulder. "You were really something in the pool," he said.

Eddie walked away. "It's all psychological, this fuckin' life," Vic called after him. Eddie thought he heard the TV snap on just before the door closed.

Eddie walked back, down Turk, left on Mill, right on River, onto the bridge, toward the downtown side. His feet knew the way. It was colder now, snow thicker, blowing harder. Eddie felt the cold, but it no longer bothered him. The ice was spreading, narrowing the black band where the river ran free and fast in the constricted space. The fissure in the ice, bubbling and black, seemed to shrink even as Eddie gazed down into it. He pictured himself falling through the white air into black water, sinking. Why not? He was a free man.

The river was frozen all the way across. Eddie laced on his skates. He could never get them tight enough; they were Jack's old ones, still too big, and the plastic tips had come off the ends of the laces. He had to lick them, twist them, stick them through the holes, all with bare fingers getting colder.

"Is it safe?" he yelled.

Jack, stickhandling around some beer cans, made chicken noises. He could see Jack's breath rising in puffs of gray.

"I'm not chicken," Eddie said, but not loudly, more to himself: let your stick do the talking. If you win, say little, if you lose, say less. And there was another saying the hockey coach had told them, but he couldn't remember. Eddie tugged hard at the laces, quickly tying a knot, but not quickly enough to keep the laces tight. Then he took his stick, pushed himself off the bank, and skated out. The ice was gray and opaque under his blades, thick and solid. Mrs. Benoit had warned the class, that was all. She was just a worrywart.

"Pass, pass," he called.

Jack circled in that easy way he had, leaning into the turn, looked right at him, said, "Cluck, cluck," and fired a slapshot at one of the bridge supports. The puck rang off the steel, bounced back, slid across the ice toward Eddie.

He skated toward it, heard Jack's blades cutting snick-snick across the ice, skated faster, reached with his stick, lost his balance, touched the puck, tried to pull it into his skates; then Jack came swooping down, lifted Eddie's stick with his own, stole the puck, and whirled away, fast enough to flutter his Bruins sweater. Eddie saw that fluttering sweater just as he fell, hard, onto his back, losing his stick. He got up, picked up the stick, skated after Jack, out across the river, toward the New Town side.

"Pass, pass."

Jack slowed down, turned, skated backward, still stickhandling the puck. Eddie caught up to him. Jack smiled, pushed the puck toward him on the outside edge of his blade.

"Here you go, Chicken Little."

Eddie reached for the puck, but it wasn't there. It was sliding between his own skates; and before he could get his stick on it, Jack had skated around him, cradled the puck, snick-snicked away. Eddie's right skate slipped out from under him; he fought for balance like a cartoon character, almost stayed up. He rose, got his stick, skated after Jack.

"Pass, pass." He loved playing hockey.

Far ahead, Jack wheeled around, leaned into a figure eight, gathered speed, wound up, and passed the puck. Not a pass, really, more like a shot, but in his direction. Eddie took off, trying to intercept it.

He wasn't fast enough and the puck got by him. He chased it toward the New Town side, skating as fast as he could, expecting the snick-snick of Jack's blades at any moment, expecting the flash of that billowing Bruins sweater. But there was no snick-snick, no black-and-gold flash. Eddie caught up to the puck, out in the middle of the river, tucked it into the blade of his stick, and wheeled around like a defenseman gathering speed in his own end. His head was up in proper style. He didn't notice that the ice had changed from gray and opaque to black and translucent. He just heard a crack, and then he was in the water.

Eddie went right under, all the way to the bottom. First came the terror, then the shock of the cold, then the thrashing. One of his thrashing skates touched something. The bottom. Eddie pushed off. He must have, because the next moment he was on the surface. But only for that moment: the weight of his skates, the water saturating his thick clothes, pulled him back down. His eyes were open: he saw black, and silver bubbles, his own silver bubbles, bubbling out of him. He kicked his way up, got his hands on the edge of the ice, kicked, pulled. The ice broke off.

"Jack," he screamed, went under, swallowed icy water, came up gasping. "Jack."

He saw Jack. Jack saw him. Jack was standing still, his mouth open, a tiny breath cloud over his head. That was all Eddie had time to take in before he went under again.

Eddie hit bottom, pushed off, came up, looked for Jack. Jack was skating away, skating in a clumsy way he had never seen before. Eddie had that thought. Then he thought: he's going for help, and getting his frozen hands on the ice again, he kicked with his legs and tried to push himself up with his hands. The ice broke away, and Eddie started to go down again. Then something hit him in the face. His stick. He reached for it, got it in his hands. His hands were awkward things now, barely able to grip, and his shivers were beyond control.

Eddie took the stick, reached out as far as he could, scissored his legs with all his strength, tried to dig the blade into the ice. Pull. Kick. Pull kick. He flopped onto the ice, up to his chest. Some of it broke off beneath him, but not all. He kicked, pulled, wriggled, flopped up a little higher; and finally right out of the water. Eddie didn't get up, didn't skate, but crawled all the way to the river bank, frantic.

He was crying now, crawling and crying. "Jack, Jack." But Jack wasn't there. No one was there. He came to the bank on the downtown side, pulled himself up. The house was a block from the river. Eddie walked there in his skates. He didn't know what else to do.

The back door was always unlocked. Eddie pushed it open, called, "Mom, Mom." The house was silent. He had to tell someone, but there was no one to tell.

Eddie poured a steaming bath, lay in it, wearing his clothes and his skates; lay there until the shivering stopped. After that, he felt sleepy. He got out of the bath, unlaced his skates—that took a long time because of the wet laces and his sausage fingers— stripped, dried himself.

Eddie went down the hall to the bedroom he shared with Jack. The door was closed. He opened it. Jack lay in the bed, still in his Bruins sweater. He was doing the shivering now.

"I got scared," he said.

Jack was eight, Eddie seven.

Eddie, leaning on the bridge rail, looking down at the water, didn't hear the squad car stop beside him, didn't hear the door open and close. The wind was blowing harder, drowning out other sound, and his attention was elsewhere.

> The ice was here, the ice was there,
> The ice was all around:
> It cracked and growled, and—

A voice said: "You Eddie Nye?"

Eddie turned. A cop was standing there, all bundled up except for the bare right hand on his gun butt.

"Yeah," Eddie said.

"Just saying hi," the cop said. "Wouldn't want you to feel all— what's the word?—anonymous, or nothing." He waited, perhaps for Eddie to say something. When he realized it might be a long wait, too long in weather like that, he said, "Enjoy your visit," got in the car and drove off.

Eddie stood on the bridge. Snow collected in his collar and the tops of his shoes, and on his bald head. After a while he laughed, a little sound, lost in the wind. Vic had dropped a dime on him. Who else could it be?

Eddie walked quickly off the bridge, into downtown, amused. Good old Uncle Vic.

It was time for that steam bath.

Chapter Five

"You a member?" asked the man behind the counter at the Y. He had the valley accent too.

"No," said Eddie.

"Then it's three bucks. Plus fifty cents for a towel."

Eddie handed over the five, received lock, key, towel, change.

"Locker room's down the hall, second on the left," the man said. But Eddie knew that.

In the locker room Eddie stripped, stowed his clothes, his money, Prof's cardboard tube, and locked up. Hanging the key around his neck he went through the showers toward the steam room at the end. He hadn't thought about swimming; a steam bath was all he wanted. But the door to the pool was propped open with a bucket, and he couldn't help seeing the still blue quadrilateral in the door frame. He went back to his locker, dressed, returned to the counter.

"Rent swimsuits?"

"Used to. No demand now, not with this AIDS business. You can try the lost-and-found if you want." He pointed to a box by the scales.

Eddie looked through the box, found a faded Speedo that would fit. If AIDS spread through the lost-and-found, no one had a chance anyway.

A few minutes later he was standing by the pool at the deep end. Same pool. Twenty-five yards, eight lanes, no springboard. Eddie had it all to himself, except for a man sitting in a chair at the other end with a towel around his neck, talking on a portable phone.

Eddie stepped up to the edge in lane five. Lane five had always been his favorite, he couldn't remember why. Maybe there hadn't been a reason. Jack in four, Bobby Falardeau in three. Two high-school state championships, athletic scholarships for him and Jack—Bobby hadn't been quite good enough, hadn't needed the money anyway—if he had to sum it up, that would be it. But that left out the swimming itself.

Eddie stood by the pool, motionless, toes curled over the edge. He smelled the chlorine, felt cool air rising from the water. The man at the other end raised his voice, said: "Three is the final offer. They can take it or leave it."

Eddie dove in. Almost not registering on his consciousness was the impression that there was something familiar about the man's voice.

Eddie glided. The glide went on and on, slowed to the point of swimming speed. But Eddie didn't want to start swimming. He wanted to keep gliding through that cool blue, to feel it all around him. That was it: not so much the swimming itself as just being in the water. If there was a heaven, it must be a watery place.

"First time in the islands?" asked Mrs. Packer.

Eddie turned from the window of the little plane, turned from the sight of that clear blue-green sea with coral growing like forests on the bottom. First time in the islands, first time on a plane, first time he'd met a woman like Mrs. Packer.

"That's right, Mrs. Packer."

"Evelyn, please."

"Okay." But he didn't say her name. She was older, for one thing. Then there were her painted nails, her makeup, the smell of her perfume, her long tanned legs, her self-confidence.

"I could tell by the way you were making big eyes at the scenery," Mrs. Packer said. "Sometimes I think the planes should just turn back right about here and not bother landing."

"Why is that?"

Mrs. Packer laughed, laid her fingertips on his forearm. "I'm just being cynical."

She took her hand away, but he continued to feel the spot she'd touched, hot, like a local infection.

"Are you talking about the poverty?" Eddie asked, remembering something Bobby Falardeau had said; the Falardeaus went to the Caribbean every Christmas.

"There's worse poverty in Miami. I just meant tropic isles."

"Tropic isles?"

"And all that goes with them."

The plane rose suddenly, bumped back down like a car running over something in the road. Not a hard jolt, but enough to throw Mrs. Packer, half turning, onto his chest, with her hair, full of smells, all good, in his face.

"Sorry," Eddie said, disentangling himself. The infection began to spread all over.

"For what?" said Mrs. Packer, straightening, patting her hair.

Eddie could think of no reply, no way to resume the conversation. He gazed out the window again. The sea changed from opaque blue to translucent turquoise to transparent green. Then a round island went by and the sea colors passed under the wing in reverse order.

"You look like your brother," Mrs. Packer said.

"People say that," Eddie said, turning toward her. Face people when they talk to you: the job-hunting advice of Mrs. Botelho, guidance counselor.

Mrs. Packer took off her sunglasses for a better view. "Maybe not so . . . I don't know what the word is. Hard?"

"Jack's not hard."

Mrs. Packer put her sunglasses back on.

The plane banked, descended on an island shaped like a banana, a green island outlined in white sand. "Saint Amour," said Mrs. Packer. "You're going to have a great summer, if you do something about that hair. My husband has a thing about long hair."

The plane swooped down over treetops, so close Eddie saw a black bird, perhaps a buzzard or a vulture, on a branch, and touched ground, much too fast, Eddie thought, on a dirt strip. Only when the plane rolled to a stop did he glance at Mrs. Packer's unconcerned face and realize it must have been a smooth landing.

A jeep parked beside the plane. Jack and another man got out, rolled stairs up to the door. Eddie opened it, followed Mrs. Packer

out. The air hit him right away: hot, still, full of floral smells.
The blue of the sky was so deep and saturated it looked unnatural.
He was going to love it.

"Good news?" said the second man, helping Mrs. Packer off
the last step. He was as tall as Jack but broader: thick necked,
barrel chested, with wiry hairs curling up around the opening of
his short-sleeved shirt.

"I'll tell you all about it," said Mrs. Packer.

The thick-necked man held onto her arm. "Tell me now."

She didn't speak until he let go. "If their coming for a look is
good news, then it's good news," she said.

"It's great news." He tried to kiss her mouth, but she turned
her face and he got her cheek instead.

Jack threw his arm around Eddie's neck, gave him a hug. "Bro,"
he said. Jack looked great: browned, barefoot, strong: saturated
too, in some way. "Brad," he said, "this is Eddie, I've been telling
you about. Eddie—Brad Packer."

They shook hands. Packer's hand was huge, his grip powerful.
He squeezed hard, in case there was any doubt. Then he noticed
Eddie's hair. The grip softened; the hand withdrew.

"You didn't tell me he was a goddamn hippie."

Jack laughed. "Hippie? He's starting USC on full scholarship
in the fall. He's no hippie."

"What about that mop?"

"Needs a haircut, that's all. No objection to a haircut, is there,
Eddie?"

Eddie liked his hair the way it was. On the other hand, he
would have to cut it for swimming in a few months anyway. He
nodded, barely.

From the frown on Packer's face he could see that another
antihair remark was forming, but Evelyn cut it off. "That's settled,
then," she said. "Welcome to Galleon Beach."

"Resort, development, dive club, and time share," added her
husband, sticking out his hand. Eddie found himself shaking
hands with Packer once more. This time he was ready, or Packer's
grip had lost some of its power. "Dive club," said Packer: "That's
your line, correct?"

"Correct," said Eddie, smiling. He couldn't help smiling, not
with that air, that sky.

"Remember *Muskets and Doubloons?*" he said to Jack as they got in the jeep.

"Huh?"

Galleon Beach, resort, development, dive club, and time share: six cottages on the water, one with a broken window; a central building with office, kitchen, dining room, and the Packers' suite; a thatch-roofed bar; a floating dock; a fat folder of blueprints and architectural drawings. That afternoon, Jack opened it and showed Eddie the plans.

On paper, Galleon Beach had a two-hundred-room hotel, eight stories high; three restaurants—Fingers, the Blue Parrot, Le Soleil; two nightclubs—Mongo's and Voodoo Rock; box on box of time-share villas spreading back from the hotel, up into the hills and halfway across the island; an eighteen-hole championship golf course, tennis courts, two swimming pools; a fleet of boats on the water.

Jack was watching him, waiting for his opinion. Eddie leafed through them once more. "Mongo's—that's you."

"And Fingers. Evelyn came up with the rest."

Eddie studied an artist's rendition, not to scale. It showed a pink pavilion cut into the side of the hill. Pastel-dressed white people were dancing to the music of a bare-chested black steel band. Eddie said: "If someone has the money to build all this, why bother doing it?"

Jack put down his beer bottle. "No one uses their own money, Eddie. This is all about leverage. Leverage and operating in a tax haven with no unions and no bullshit. Brad's going to make a fortune. He's just lining up one more investor. We could break ground by the end of July, which is pretty quick considering we just got title three months ago."

Eddie said: "I thought you were in anthropology."

"What do you mean?"

"You sound like a business major."

Jack took a long pull from the bottle, wiped his mouth with the back of his hand. "Fact is," he said, "I'm not going back."

"Not going back where?"

"USC. I'm staying here. It's a chance to get in on the ground floor of something really big."

"What about your degree?"

"It's just a stepping stone to something like this. I'm already here."

"You want to work in a hotel?"

"I want to make money, jerk. You'll see when you get out there."

"See what?"

"How some people live."

A white bird dove out of the sky, splashed on the water, rose with something silver in its beak. "What's he paying you?" Eddie asked. He himself was supposed to get a hundred dollars a week, plus room and board.

"It's not what I'm getting now. It's what I'll be getting in the future—I've got a piece of the action."

"You bought into his company, or whatever it is?"

"GB Devco. Buying in was out of the question. That takes money, and we don't have money, you and I. It just hasn't hit you yet, that's all." Jack lowered his voice, although no one was around. "I own seven and a half percent of everything, all legal and binding. At least it will be in a few weeks."

"How did you manage that?"

Jack glanced around. "It's all part of the deal. That doesn't mean I won't have to work like a son of a bitch."

"Doing what?"

"Whatever it takes. Selling time shares, setting up the water-front program—you'll be helping with that—romancing travel agents, busting my ass."

There was a long silence. The sea shone like beaten gold. Eddie remembered that image from English class, but he couldn't place it. English was his worst subject. "What about swimming?" he said.

"Four hours a day in the pool? Who's gonna miss that?" Jack took another drink; his eyes rested on the dancing pastel people. "So: what do you think?"

Eddie didn't look again at the plans. He swiveled around on his stool. The bar had no walls, just a roof that seemed to be made of nothing but palm fronds. Up in the hills, a red-flowering tree blazed like the start of a forest fire.

"I like it the way it is," he said.

Jack snorted. "It's a dump the way it is. The last owner's selling pencils on the street."

Eddie looked into his brother's eyes for some sign that he was joking. All he saw was the shimmering of beaten gold.

Eddie gestured toward the hills. "Does Packer own all that land?"

"Not yet."

"But he can afford to buy it."

"Hell, no. I told you. He's got no money."

"Then how did he pay for the hotel?"

"Borrowed, except for the five percent that came from Evelyn's old man. And he got the place for a song."

"He tells you all this?"

"All what?"

"Borrowing from Evelyn's father. Isn't that embarrassing?"

"You've gone dainty on me, Eddie. There's nothing embarrassing about it. Got to have money in business. You get it where you can, at the lowest price."

"Did the plane come from Evelyn's father too?"

"Every dickhead developer in South Florida's got a plane, Eddie." Jack rose. "Enough theory. I'll show you the main attraction."

They walked down a path lined with sun-bleached conch shells to a shed by the beach. Jack came out with masks, fins, snorkels, tossed a set to Eddie, led him onto the dock. A silver-and-blue cruiser was tied up along one side; thirty-five feet or so, with tuna tower, portable compressor, dive platform. Eddie absorbed all that without really looking. What caught his eye was the name written on the stern in fresh black paint: *Fearless*.

Jack put his arm around Eddie's neck, squeezed hard. "Of course I remember, asshole. What do you take me for?"

Eddie put his arm around his brother, squeezed back.

They boarded *Fearless*. Jack led him below, pointing out the electronics, the tank racks, the twin Westerbeke diesels. Then they rode out half a mile and anchored. "Wait till you see this," Jack said. Eddie had done a lot of diving, but all in lakes and ponds. He donned his gear and followed Jack over the side.

First time in the islands, first time on a plane, first time on a coral reef. It lay on a bed of white sand about fifty feet below and sprouted up almost to the surface. Eddie took a breath and dove down, reached the bottom in eight or nine kicks. Even at fifty feet, the water was warm and shining with light. Tiny fish darted over the coral, wearing camouflage that would work only in a jewel box. Eddie took in a mouthful of salt water and realized he was smiling. He bit down on the mouthpiece.

They dove: two land creatures as at home in the water as land creatures can be. They didn't stop until the sun sank toward the horizon, first reddening the sea, then darkening it. After, in the boat, they watched the sun disappear, leaving radiant traces on the surface of the water, in the sky, on their retinas. Then, quite suddenly, it was night.

"Not bad, huh?" said Jack.

"Not bad."

"It goes on for miles up and down the shore. Sometimes better. Brad's got a big New York outfit handling the advertising. Every diver in the world's going to know about this place in six months. Nondivers, too. We're designing an underwater observatory—you won't even have to get wet."

Was this another joke? Eddie looked at his brother. It was too dark to tell.

The radio crackled. "Galleon Beach to *Fearless*. Come in, *Fearless*. Over." It was Evelyn.

Jack spoke. *"Fearless* here."

"You forgot to say *over*. Over."

"Over," said Jack, laughing.

Evelyn was laughing too. "Dinner is almost over. Over."

They ate sandwiches in the bar, Eddie and Jack at one table, the Packers at another. Baloney and cheese slices on white: the cook was arriving the next day. It didn't matter. Eddie ate until there was nothing left.

"Stay for a drink?" said Evelyn. The Packers had a bottle of Wild Turkey on their table.

"Or two," added Packer. "Then maybe Evelyn'll get out her scissors."

"Thanks," said Eddie. "Some other time."

Jack stayed for a drink. Eddie walked up the beach to the old fish camp—a go-cart track in the plan—where the previous staff had lived. There were a number of cabins but only two were habitable, Jack's on the beach, the other under a tall spreading tree farther inland. A light was on in the second cabin, and a human silhouette moved behind the shade. Eddie entered the cabin on the beach.

He felt for the light switch, switched on an unshaded ceiling bulb. It spread a weak yellow glow, almost brown at the edges but strong enough to illuminate the peeling paint on the walls, the pile of laundry on the floor, and the two beds, one with a bare mattress, the other unmade. Eddie went into the bathroom— sink, toilet, rusty shower stall—and splashed cold water on his face. He looked around for a towel and in looking glanced down at the wastebasket. There were crumpled papers inside. One crumpled paper with a USC letterhead caught his eye. Thinking, if at all, that it might have something to do with him, he picked it out, smoothed it.

Dear Mr. Nye:
This is to officially inform you of your permanent expulsion from the University of Southern California, effective today. You have the right to appeal to the Board of Governors. Appeal must be filed by the first day of fall term, September 3. As per our discussion with Dr. Robbins of the Ethics Committee and Mr. Morris, the A.D., your athletic scholarship is hereby terminated.
                    Sincerely,

                    John Reynolds
                    Dean of Students

Eddie recrumpled the letter, dropped it in the wastebasket. He sat on the bare mattress. After a while he shut off the light and lay down.

Through the window, Eddie could see the other cabin. From time to time, a human figure, female, moved behind the shade. Later something small and quick ran across his roof. Then there was silence, except for the quiet crashing of the waves on the beach.

The light in the other cabin went out.

Chapter Six

Thudding sounds, heavy and rhythmic. They grew louder and louder, then ceased with a slap like the closing of a screen door.

Eddie awoke. He opened his eyes and saw: the sun, glaring in the window over Jack's bed; Jack asleep in a beam of light, his forearm thrown over his eyes; a cockroach crawling through the laundry pile. He listened to the sea, quiet, yet making too many sounds to catalogue.

Eddie got up, went out the door, crossed the beach, already warm under his feet, and dove in. The sea bubbled around his body; he rolled in it a few times, swam a few lazy strokes, drifted. Waves bobbed him, up and down. He almost sank back into sleep.

A few minutes later, as he stood on the hard, furrowed bottom, making little whirlpools on the surface with his hands, a thought hit him: forget about USC. A crazy thought, and self-destructive. He knew it right away and was marshaling all the obvious counterarguments when the door of the second cabin opened.

Brad Packer came out. He wore running shorts and running shoes and carried a bottle of water, but none of that made him look like a runner. Packer didn't even glance at the ocean and so didn't see Eddie; he just walked quickly away on a path that led into the trees. Between their trunks, Eddie could see a dirt road that paralleled the beach. Packer turned onto it and began jogging, heavy-footed and slow, in a direction that would lead him to the hotel. He left behind dust clouds, brassy in the sunlight, and thudding sounds, heavy and rhythmic, that carried through the still air after he was out of sight.

Eddie stood at the waterline, back to the sea. Each retreating wave sucked his feet deeper in the sand. He was up to his calves when the cabin door opened again. A woman in bikini bottoms and nothing else came out, a woman of about his own age, perhaps a few years older. She was tall and muscular, with smooth round breasts, tanned as the rest of her. She closed her eyes, stretched in the sun, made a little sighing sound. Eddie stayed where he was, rooted. The woman opened her eyes, shook out her hair, took a step toward the beach, saw Eddie.

"Oh," she said, covering her breasts. At the same time her eyes looked him up and down, and it hit him only then that he wasn't wearing anything. Now, finally and too late, he was wide awake. Blockhead, he thought, found that his mouth was open, anticipating speech, the easy line that the situation demanded. The easy line didn't come. His only idea was to move deeper into the water, to waist level, say. Eddie tried, but his feet were stuck in the sand; he lost his balance, started to fall, caught himself, then decided that falling would be the best thing; and fell. He heard laughter as he went under, came up in time to see her diving into the water, arched like a dolphin.

The woman swam straight out, passing close enough to splash him with her kicks. She swam energetically, even powerfully, but not efficiently. Eddie, watching, had a notion to swim after her, to simply flash by; but realized just in time that it would not be cool. He was considering various lines of conversation, or perhaps going back to the cabin before conversation became necessary, when she circled, swam back, and stopped a few yards farther out, treading water.

The woman smiled. With her hair plastered to her head she looked younger, almost like a kid.

"Another nature boy," she said.

None of Eddie's lines adapted to that opening. He heard himself making some sound; she took it for incomprehension.

"Jack's brother, right?" she said.

"Right."

"Freddie?"

"Eddie."

"Much better. You don't look like a Freddie."

"What does a Freddie look like?"

"Stick-out ears. Goofy grin. Not you."

Something in the way she spoke those last two words, a deepening in the tone of her voice perhaps, unsettled him, delaying the arrival of the next obvious remark.

"What's your name?" It came at last.

"Mandy," she said. "Short for Amanda."

He nodded. Short for Amanda. Great. We could move on to surnames, he thought, or . . .

"What's Eddie short for?"

"Edward the Seventh."

She started to laugh, that same unrestrained laugh he had provoked by falling in. Eddie laughed too. Then came a silence, as though their conversation had run out of supplies, like an army advancing too rapidly into unknown territory.

"Going to be here long?" Mandy asked.

"The summer," Eddie said, thinking: maybe much longer. "What about you?"

"On and off. I work for Mr. Packer."

"What as?"

"What as?" Her voice was sharper.

"Your job."

"I'm his secretary." A wave came in, raised her above him. "Did you meet him yet?" she asked. The wave lowered her back down, a little closer to Eddie.

"Last night. I flew over with Mrs. Packer."

"What fun."

Eddie didn't know how to take that. He was forming a reply when another wave rose, bigger than the others, lifted Mandy up and threw her forward, against him; a lot like the way Mrs. Packer had fallen on him on the plane. Sea and air were conspiring to hurl women at him. For a moment he felt Mandy trying to squirm away. Then her body relaxed around his. She made a sound in his ear, much like the sigh he'd heard before, except now it was full of promise, like the introductory chord of a beautiful piece of music.

The plug was pulled at once.

"I see you two have already met."

Eddie jerked around, saw Jack standing on the beach.

"Adios," said Mandy, and slipped away.

Eddie swam in. Jack was smiling. "I've been waiting all my life to say that." He put his arm around Eddie's shoulders, walked him toward the cabin. Eddie glanced back, saw Mandy about twenty yards out, swimming parallel to the beach.

Jack said: "Bro?"

"Yeah?"

"Can I give you some advice?"

"Sure."

"Stay away from her."

Eddie didn't say anything: he wondered if Jack was interested in her himself.

"You weren't with her last night or anything, were you?" Jack said as they entered the cabin. The cockroach, or another one, was feeling its way across Eddie's pillow. He flicked it on the floor, raised his foot to stamp on it. The cockroach was too quick: it skittered under his bed, out of sight.

"Of course not," Eddie said. "We just went for a swim at the same time, that's all."

"Good," said Jack.

"Why good? Is there something wrong with her?"

"Far from it. She's taken, that's all."

"By you?"

"I'm not that dumb. She belongs to Brad."

That should have been obvious as soon as he'd seen them come out of the same cabin; for some reason the thought hadn't occurred to him.

"Don't look so surprised, Eddie. This is the grown-up world."

"You mean Mrs. Packer knows?"

"Not that grown-up," Jack said. He smiled to himself. "But close. The fact is, Evelyn doesn't know Mandy's here. Brad's careful. He hides her at the fish camp when Evelyn's on the island, moves her down to cottage six as soon as she's back on the plane to Lauderdale."

"How can he hide her? She's the secretary."

"Was. Evelyn fired her two months ago."

"Because she was suspicious?"

"Because she found a better typist. She said. The new one looks like that funny little actor. You know."

"Peter Lorre?"

"Yeah. Except Peter Lorre didn't have a mustache, did he?"

Outside, Mandy was still swimming, farther out now, probably pulled by the tide. Eddie watched until she looked up, saw where she was, swam in closer.

"Packer's not as careful as he thinks," Eddie said.

"No?"

"He wasn't careful this morning."

Jack's eyes narrowed. "Did he go jogging?"

Eddie nodded.

"One day Evelyn'll start wondering why he never gets in shape. That's the way this whole thing's going to unravel."

"What whole thing?"

"Galleon Beach. The treasure of."

"What treasure?"

"You saw the plans." Jack gazed out the window at Mandy. "No feel for the water," he said.

"She could be all right."

Jack turned, gave him a look. "He didn't see you, did he?"

"No. But what difference would it make? Does he know you know?"

The expression in Jack's eyes changed, as though he was thinking about something. "I don't know what he knows."

"How can he expect to keep it a secret, in a little place like this?" Eddie asked. "What happens when the staff gets here?"

"I guess he'll worry about that when he has to."

"That's tomorrow."

"Why tomorrow?"

"Isn't that when the cook arrives?"

"The cook won't be a problem."

"Why not?"

Jack didn't answer. Out on the water, Mandy kept swimming.

Chapter Seven

"Interested in herb, man?"

Eddie, screwing new planks on *Fearless*'s dive platform, looked up at the dock. A man on a bicycle was watching him, keeping his balance with one bare foot.

"No, thanks."

"With your hair like that, I could only aks myself."

"I'm not in the market."

"Market? Who be speaking of market? I just want to show you somet'ing interesting, man, if you be interested in herb. In the most friendliest way, since you and me be colleagues."

"Colleagues?"

"Sure. Meet JFK, the new cook."

JFK leaned down, extended his hand, fingers pointing up for a black handshake. They shook hands.

"I didn't hear your plane."

"Was no plane. I carry myself on this fine made-in-Japan bicycle."

"From where?"

"All the way down to Cotton Town, on the very tip of this earthly paradise," said JFK, waving toward the south. "The famous Cotton Town Hotel and Villas. Diving. Tennis. Sailing. Happy hour. Goombay smash. Push-push. When there be guests. Not now."

"You work there?"

"Formerly, man. Now Mr. Packer has sweetened my pot." He chuckled. "You Jack's brother."

"Right."

"I have two brothers. They both's in jail. Franco in Miami, Dime in Fox Hill."

"What did they do?"

"Lost their trials." There was a pause while JFK stared out to sea and Eddie waited for elaboration. Then JFK spoke: "Destiny, man. Destiny be rulin' the fates of humanity." He raised his hands slightly, as though summoning divine forces.

A black dot appeared in the northwestern sky, grew, formed the shape of a plane, turned white. It flew overhead, lost its whiteness, lost its shape, became a black dot again and disappeared.

"Don't trust no planes," said JFK. "Boats for me." He scanned the shoreline, taking in the six cottages, the thatched bar, the main building, the overgrown shuffleboard court.

"This place gonna make it, man?"

"It's a nice spot," Eddie said.

"Nice spot. These islands is not'ing but nice spots. Except no one be making it." He took a penny from his pocket, flicked it in the air, caught it. "Takes luck, man," he said. "Make a wish."

"You make it."

JFK shook his head. "You look lucky to me."

Eddie thought. He knew there must be things he should wish for, but all he could think was: fun in the sun.

"Ready?" asked JFK.

Eddie nodded. He wished for fun in the sun.

JFK spun the penny off the dock. It made a coppery arc and a tiny splash, then vanished.

JFK smiled. He had a big smile, with gaps here and there. "Maybe I can make your wish come true," he said.

"How?"

"Come. I show you."

Eddie tightened the last screw, climbed onto the dock. JFK made a wobbly circle on his bike—he had a big suitcase, tied with twine, on the rear carrier—and pedaled away. Eddie followed.

JFK rode at a walking pace, up the conch-lined path, past the cottages and the main building, onto the dusty road linking Galleon Beach to Cotton Town. "Feel the heat," he said. "We got nice spots. We got heat."

Eddie felt the heat on his bare shoulders, felt how it made him conscious of every breath.

"We got the heat here, that's for sure," said JFK after a while. "You got heat like this where you come from?"

"No."

"Where is that you come from?"

Eddie named the town.

"That be near L.A.?"

"No."

"I want to go to L.A. That my number-one goal in this earthly life."

"I'll be there in the fall."

The bike wobbled. "Whoa. You tellin' me the trut'?"

"I'm starting college—USC," Eddie said. He added: "That's the plan."

"Then what you be makin' wishes for? You already got everyt'ing a heart desires."

The road went past the fish camp, past a cracked, dried-out red-clay tennis court and its sun-bleached backboard, partly screened by scrub pines, then swung inland. The temperature rose at once; in seconds, a drop of sweat rolled off Eddie's chin, landed on his dusty sneaker, making a damp star.

"Easy, man," said JFK, pedaling more slowly; so slowly Eddie was surprised he could keep the bicycle steady. "You on island time now."

They came to a flamboyant tree—Eddie knew the name now—by the side of the road. Not far ahead lay the turnoff to the airstrip. JFK leaned his bike against the tree, set off on a narrow path through the bush. Eddie followed. Something bit him on the ankle. He slapped at it, received bites on the other ankle, back, and face.

"No-see-ums," said JFK. "Not'ing to be done."

The path narrowed; vegetation brushed Eddie's skin at every step. He began to itch all over. The sweat was dripping off him now. He thought of *Muskets and Doubloons*. Hadn't there been a scene where One-Eye's band of buccaneers chopped through the bush with cutlasses in search of buried treasure? The treasure chest had contained nothing but the severed head of Captain Something-or-other.

Ahead, JFK seemed to be moving faster. His thin calves knotted and lengthened in smooth motions, like water going back and forth in a tube. He began to sing.

> Gonna get some goombay goombay lovin'
> Gonna find a goombay goombay girl.

A no-see-um bit Eddie on the nose.

They mounted a long rise, came down in a clearing. It was filled with head-high plants growing in rows. JFK stopped, laid a hand on Eddie's arm. JFK wasn't sweating at all, hardly seemed to be breathing, but his pulse beat fast and shallow, like faraway tom-toms.

"You understandin' what you see?" he said.

"Marijuana," Eddie replied.

"You got a smart brain. A college brain. Only here we say *herb*. That's the friendly name."

A slow, heavy breeze blew through the clearing. The herb leaves rustled and then were still. The sun was high overhead. It seemed to have lost its shape, expanding to fill the sky, the way stars were supposed to do, Eddie recalled, at some point in their evolution. There wasn't a sound until JFK spoke again.

"I don't like no planes," he said. "Give me a boat every time."

"You said that before. Give you a boat for what?"

"A boat like *Fearless*. Best name I ever heard for a boat. Except maybe *Lot-O-Bucks*, and she be sinking off Bimini last year."

"*Fearless* belongs to Mr. Packer. Jack and I just have the use of it."

"Perfecto," said JFK. "If you want to be earnin' a little extra bonus."

"What do you mean?"

JFK smiled. He laid his hand on Eddie's arm again and was about to answer when something brown burst out of the clearing and crashed by. Too big for a dog: Eddie had time to think that thought. Then there was a blast that knocked the top off the marijuana plant beside him. JFK yanked him to the ground.

Eddie looked up in time to see the tall green plants part and

Brad Packer stumble out in front of them, a rifle in his hands. He saw them, saw, that is, living animals, and raised the gun.

"Boss!" said JFK.

Packer checked himself, lowered the gun. "Christ," he said, "I thought you were a fucking pig. What the hell are you two doing here? You're supposed to be working."

JFK picked himself up. "Looking for guava, boss. I be plannin' guava duff for dessert."

Packer glanced around the clearing. "There's probably some around. This island's a goddamn greenhouse."

"Plenty around boss, plenty," said JFK. "Mrs. Packer, I know she like it."

"She doesn't need it, not with those thighs. Neither do I, for that matter." Packer turned to Eddie. "Him I pay to look for guava. You I don't."

"He be helping me, boss," said JFK.

"Yeah? Well, he can help me now. There's a dead pig the other side of this clearing. They like it in here, fuck knows why. You can carry him back to the hotel while I go after the other one." He started for the path, stopped, indicated Eddie with the muzzle of his gun. "And get a haircut." Packer disappeared in the bush.

Eddie and JFK found the dead pig. It lay on its stomach in a circle of marijuana plants, legs splayed, bleeding from a hole in the side of its flattened snout.

"He be tense, man," said JFK.

"Rigor mortis," Eddie told him. "It's normal."

JFK laughed softly. "Too soon for rigor mortis. We know all about rigor mortis in these islands, my friend. But I be talkin' about Mr. Packer. He the tense one."

"Why?" asked Eddie. An ant crawled across the bared eyeball of the pig.

"The investor, man. Big investor coming from the giant to the north."

"To buy the place?"

"To supply the cash, man. Some friend of Mrs. Packer's daddy. Gonna make Mr. Packer's dream come true. The hotel eight stories, the restaurants, the condos, the time shares. Golf, tennis, a waterfall. Maybe Shecky Greene."

"Who's Shecky Greene?"

"You never been to Vegas, man?"

"Have you?"

"Not the question. The question be is I hip to Shecky Greene? And I most surely be. I plugged into the happenings of the world, man."

The ant stopped in the center of the eyeball, antennae trembling. JFK gazed down at the animal and sighed.

"I could handle it, man, but not on the bike."

"I'll do it," Eddie said, realizing that there was some presumption that if heavy work awaited, the black man was expected to do it. He squatted down, got a grip on one front and one rear foot, and rose, swinging the animal onto his shoulders.

"Ooo," said JFK. "Great white hunter."

"Packer's the great white hunter."

"He be white, white as white can be. No offense."

They walked back through the marijuana plants, Eddie carrying the pig. The coarse hairs of its underbelly prickled his bare skin; blood dripped down on his chest, diluting itself with his sweat. They found the path, mounted the rise. Eddie felt the burden now, not so much the weight of the pig, but the weight of anything in that heat. By the time they reached the flamboyant tree by the side of the road, his heart was beating the way it would in the last length of the four-hundred free.

JFK got on his bike. "Don't be calling it a pig if you run into any tourists. That be the famous wild boar of the islands. Ernest Hemingway he come to hunt them."

"Bullshit," Eddie said.

JFK laughed and started pedaling. Not slowly this time. Eddie realized that JFK wasn't intending that he keep up. "Where do I take it?" Eddie called.

The answer came back, faint: "The kitchen, man. You be bringin' home the bacon." JFK was soon out of sight.

Eddie started walking. There were no tourists, no people at all. There was just the sun, the dust, the pig, still warm. After a while it stopped bleeding and Eddie stopped thinking about how soon he could be in the shower. On that empty road on the edge of the banana-shaped island he lost his revulsion for the touch of the pig and began to enjoy what he was doing, began to feel strong— absurdly strong, like a white hunter, he supposed, master of the

wild. He ceased to feel the weight of the beast at all; by the time
he approached the dessicated clay court he was striding.

Eddie heard the thump of a tennis ball and looked through the
row of scrub pines. He saw a ball hit the backboard, bounce back,
saw a racket swing and meet it, saw a tanned arm. A tree blocked
his view of the rest of the tennis player's body, but he knew who
it was. He moved a little closer.

Mandy was working on her backhand. Eddie had played some
tennis, enough to know she was good. She wore a white T-shirt
and white shorts, both soaked, and white sneakers, reddened by
the clay. She grunted softly with every stroke. Without realizing
it, Eddie had drawn closer still. Soon he was standing at the side
of the court.

The ball took a bad bounce. Mandy stretched for it, saw him
as she swung. The ball flew over the backboard.

"Oh, my God," she said. "Look at you."

"Don't call him a pig," Eddie said. "He'd be insulted."

"I know what it is. Where's your gun?"

"I didn't shoot it," Eddie said, surprised. He'd never shot
anything, didn't want to.

"Who did? Br—Mr. Packer?"

"Yeah."

"Where is he?"

"Stalking another one."

Her gaze slid down to his chest, moved back up. "You made
me lose the ball."

"It's the pig's fault."

"You could help me find it. It's my last one."

Eddie hefted the animal off his shoulders and laid it on the side
of the court. They walked around the backboard, into a thicket of
sea grapes and low bushes. No ball in sight. Eddie raised a branch
to search the undergrowth, pricking his hand on a thorn. The
bugs, the thorns, the heat—*Muskets and Doubloons* had left all that
out.

"Forget it," said Mandy. "There might be balls in the shed."

The shed stood at the end of a short path that began on the far
side of the court. It had a window glazed with cobwebs and a
doorway with hinges but no door. Mandy walked ahead, her sweaty
T-shirt and shorts clinging to her body. Her calves, like JFK's,

bunched and lengthened with every step, but Eddie couldn't watch them in the same detached way. He felt a tightness in his chest that had nothing to do with the heat.

They went inside, out of the sun now, but Eddie felt no cooler. At first he couldn't see anything. He could hear Mandy breathing close by, and smell her too: fresh sweat, in no way repellent. His eyes adjusted to the darkness. The shed had an earthen floor; there was a heavy steel roller in one corner, a wheelbarrow and a mound of red clay in the other. On the walls hung wide brushes and wooden tennis rackets, warped in a way that reminded him of a bent pocket-watch in a painting he had seen somewhere.

"Don't see any," he said.

"No?"

There was a silence. Then her hand was between his legs, soft and gentle, but there. Eddie had had a few girlfriends, but none of them had ever reached for him quite like that, not even after they'd been going together for months.

No one said a word. Their mouths came together. They began to make a little world for themselves where the elements—their bodies, their sweat, pig blood—were hot and wet. It was a world dominated by rhythm but quiet, where sounds were moist and speech was monosyllabic and unrehearsed; a world full of irresistible animal smells. Eddie didn't resist. He sank down with Mandy on the mound of red clay.

After, they just lay there, bodies together but minds drifting apart. Their minds had to be drifting apart, because Eddie was thinking about *Muskets and Doubloons*, and how could she have read it? Today was a day for learning how much it had omitted about tropic isles. Then Mandy said, "I knew it would be like this," and Eddie thought that maybe their minds hadn't diverged very much after all: they were both thinking about what had happened and that it was good. He was trying to think of a way to convey this to her, to tell her about *Muskets and Doubloons* and maybe even other things from his childhood, when there was a tremendous boom in the sky, followed by the screaming of a low-flying jet.

"Jets can't land here, can they?" Eddie said.

"They'd better, nature boy," said Mandy. "That's the money man."

Chapter Eight

The wild boar, now minus its coarse hair and internal organs, turned on a battery-powered spit over a driftwood beach fire. JFK basted it with a paintbrush he dipped into a kettle of lava-colored liquid. His hands were long and delicate. Eddie stood beside him, tossing wood on the fire whenever JFK gave the signal. JFK was singing under his breath.

> Gonna get some goombay goombay lovin'
> Gonna find a goombay goombay girl.

Over the flames and across the beach, Eddie could see the dinner party, sitting in the thatch-roofed bar. They looked good, all fresh tans and white cotton, linen, silk. The dinner party: Packer, Evelyn, Jack; and Mr. and Mrs. Trimble, moneyman and wife. Their voices carried in the still air.

Packer said: "You've never seen it?"

Mrs. Trimble said: "No, but I'm looking forward to it, aren't you, Perry?"

Mr. Trimble replied inaudibly.

Packer said: "You've come to the right place, Mrs. T." He refilled their glasses from a chilled pitcher of planter's punch.

"They be talking about the green flash," JFK said to Eddie. "Biggest lie in the islands. Bigger than we gonna have jobs for everybody or I won't come in your mouth, baby."

"There's no green flash?"

"I be raised in this country, man. Seen so many sunsets to make me sick. But never not one time the notorious green flash."

The sun set. Colors appeared and disappeared, but there was no flash, green or otherwise, not that Eddie saw. He heard Packer.

"There! Right then! Did you see it?" He was on the steps of the bar, gesturing with his cocktail glass. Planter's punch slopped over the side, staining his white trousers; he didn't seem to notice.

"I—I think I did," said Mrs. Trimble, standing beside him. "I certainly saw something." She turned to her husband, watching behind them. Mr. Trimble: tall, beaky nose, concave chest, crewcut. "Did you, Perry?"

Mr. Trimble shook his head.

"Oh, come on now, Mr. T," said Packer. "Right there—" He pointed and slopped again. "As plain as the . . ."

Evelyn appeared. "I don't think so, Brad." Her voice was cold. "Not tonight."

"Jesus Christ, Ev, what do you—"

She cut him off. "Why don't you freshen our drinks, Brad."

"No more for me, thank you," said Mr. Trimble. He came down off the steps, over to the fire.

"Hello, gentlemen," he said. "Perry Trimble."

They shook hands with him, identified themselves.

"JFK," Trimble said. "An interesting name."

"That be my first name only," said JFK.

"And your last name?" asked Trimble.

"Never be usin' it," said JFK, and turned to baste the pig.

Trimble gazed at it. Overhead the sky was darkening quickly; the reflection of the fire danced in the lenses of Trimble's thick glasses. "Pig, I believe."

"Wild boar," said JFK. "Last of the big-game animals found in these islands. Ceptin' for in the water, of course. Down there we got more creatures than my wife got excuses."

"You're married?" said Eddie.

"Formerly," JFK replied, his eyes blank. "In the distant long long time ago."

Trimble was still examining the pig. "You don't mean to tell me someone shot it, do you?"

"Sure I do," said JFK. "Ernesto Hemingway himself the great

white hunter came to this very Galleon Beach fish camp to hunt the wild boar."

"But this particular pig. Did someone shoot it?"

"The boss. He did shoot it. Mr. Packer he a sportsman, and a dead shot with the three-oh-three."

"I don't call that sport."

"No?" said JFK. "What you be callin' it then?"

"Butchery."

JFK laughed. "Butchery be my job, man. Don't need no three-oh-three for that. Just a cutlass and a dog to lick up all the lickins." Still laughing, he dipped the brush in the kettle and swabbed lava-colored baste on the glistening carcass. The baste smelled of onions, garlic, pineapple, and something sweet and smokey that Eddie couldn't identify. He was going to ask what it was when he noticed that Trimble was staring at him; at least, the twin reflections of the fire were angled his way.

"You're Jack's brother."

"Yes, sir."

"He seems like a take-charge type. Not afraid of getting his hands dirty."

Eddie nodded.

"A project of this magnitude needs someone like that. Although a little seasoning doesn't hurt either."

Meaning he liked Jack or he didn't? Eddie wasn't sure and didn't know enough about the project, or any kind of business for that matter, to know whether Trimble's remark made sense. He said nothing.

"And how about you?" asked Trimble. "What do you think of it?"

"It's a beautiful place."

"I've seen better," said Trimble. "And worse. Beauty isn't really that high on the list of prerequisites. Ever been to Cancun?"

"No."

"Or Florida, for that matter. Complete absence of beauty. But I wasn't asking about the site. I was asking what you thought of the project."

"I'm no expert."

"I realize that. I don't need an expert. I was interested in your opinion."

"I've only seen the plans."

"And?"

"It looks very . . . grand."

There was a silence. Then Trimble nodded, the twin fires blurring in the darkness like taillights in a time-exposure photograph.

"In a well-chosen word," said Trimble. "And what's your involvement in all this grandeur?"

"I'm just here for the summer, helping Jack set up the waterfront program," Eddie replied. He had an idea. "Do you have time for a trip to the reef?"

"I wasn't planning on it. Should I?"

"I would."

"Why?"

"Hard to put in words. You really have to see it. Then the answer's sort of obvious."

The twin fires blurred again. "And after the summer?"

"I'm supposed to start college, at USC."

"Very wise," said Trimble.

A breeze stirred. The pig sizzled.

Eddie joined the others for dinner. They ate in the bar, sitting at a round wicker table. In the middle was a big glass bowl filled with sea water. Hibiscus blossoms floated on top and tropical fish netted by Eddie a few hours before—tangs, sergeant majors, royal grammas—swam below. Candlelight sparkled on the scales of the fish, the cutlery, the jewels on Mrs. Trimble's fingers. Packer poured champagne, then raised his glass.

"A toast," he said. "To our guests, Perry and the beauteous Mrs. T."

"Hear, hear," said Jack.

"And to this beauteous place," Packer added. "To the Galleon Beach Club, Hotel, and Villas."

"I'll drink to that," Jack said.

They raised their glasses, drank. Eddie, looking up, saw the moon over the water. He had never seen it so white, so defined, so clearly not a disc but a ball, massive, powerful, even dangerous in some way.

Mrs. Trimble, sitting beside him, followed his gaze. "Beauteous, isn't it?" she said, too quietly for anyone to hear but him.

Eddie smiled. Mrs. Trimble smiled back. She had platinum hair, an unlined face, plucked eyebrows, dark brown eyes. He couldn't guess her age. Her husband looked about sixty.

"I hear you're quite a swimmer," she said.

"Jack's the swimmer."

She studied his face for a moment, then glanced across the table at Jack. He was draining his glass. JFK, wearing a white shirt and black vest, arrived with the first course—spiny lobster tails, an hour out of the water.

"*Richesse de la mer*," he announced, in what sounded to Eddie like perfect, unaccented French.

They drank champagne. They ate lobster tails, conch salad, roast pig.

"The sauce is delicious, Evelyn," said Mrs. Trimble. "Do you mind telling me the ingredients?"

JFK was summoned. "Onions, garlic, pineapple, herb."

"Herbs?" said Mrs. Trimble. "What ones?"

Jack spoke before JFK could answer. "Lots of different herbs grow on the island. They've all got local names."

"How interesting." She turned to JFK. "Have you got an herb garden?"

"Many many," said JFK. "I could be carryin' you to one in the morning."

"Wonderful. Let's plan on it."

"Mind slicing me some more?" said Jack. JFK moved off to the cutting board.

Packer poured more champagne. Eddie noticed that Mr. Trimble laid his hand over his glass, wondered whether Packer might leave his own empty. But he filled it to the brim, gulped, said, "Evelyn's old man tells me you're quite the world traveler, Perry— if you don't mind me calling you Perry . . ."

Trimble nodded; now it was the candlelight that was reflected in his glasses.

"So tell me, Perry, in all your travels, have you ever come across a setting like the one we've got here at Galleon Beach?"

Trimble laid his fork and knife on his plate in the all-finished position. "I've seen some nice places, B—Brad. But as I was telling your able employee here—" He nodded across the table toward Eddie; Packer's eyebrows rose. "—it takes a lot more than setting to make a project like this work."

"He'd be a lot more able if he got a haircut," Packer said with a loud laugh. No one joined in. Eddie saw that Evelyn's fingers were wrapped tight around the stem of her glass, as though she were choking it.

"What does it take, Mr. Trimble?" Jack asked, pushing his own glass away.

"In a word? People. It all depends on the people."

"Christ, I'm glad to hear you say that," Packer said. "Hasn't that been my code since day one, Ev?"

Evelyn said: "What do you look for in people, Mr. Trimble?"

"Perry, please."

"Perry."

He gazed down at his plate. There was still a lot of roast pig on it, untouched. "Values, Evelyn. I look for values."

"Values?" said Packer.

"Honesty. Integrity. Loyalty. Reliability. Faith—in spouse, in family, in God." There was a silence, followed by a loud pop from the driftwood fire. Trimble looked up. "That's all. It's simple."

"What about imagination?" Jack asked. "Drive, determination, education, shrewdness, brains?"

Trimble smiled. He had big, uneven teeth, angled, jagged. "That's my end," he said. "The question was what do I look for in my people."

Packer checked his watch. "How about a snort of V.S.O.P.? Then we can take a gander at the plans, if that suits you, Perr."

"I'm anxious to see them."

Not long after, Packer and Trimble were sitting at the cleared table with the plans and a bottle of Remy. Evelyn and Mrs. Trimble had gone for a walk on the beach. JFK was in the kitchen. Eddie and Jack stood by the fire, cognac glasses in hand.

"What do you think?" Jack said.

"About what?"

"Everything. So far."

Everything was a lot: *Fearless*, JFK's herb garden, Packer's .303, the letter in the wastebasket, Mandy. "Unreal," he said.

Jack laughed. "That's what we're pitching, all right." He glanced up at the bar. Packer was leaning over the table, pointing out something in the plans. Trimble wasn't looking at whatever it was; he watched Packer's animated profile. "He's worth twenty mill, bro," Jack said.

"How do you know?"

"Evelyn. Her dad was Trimble's lawyer, when he was just starting out. Evelyn's dad is a very useful guy."

Something made a loud splash in the water, not far out.

"Fifteen footer," Jack said.

"Shark?"

"That's where they live. I've seen a dozen since I got here."

"You're going to need a special kind of tourist."

Jack checked the bar again. "We don't have to worry about it yet. Our worry is the shark over there." Trimble had his hand over his glass.

"How did you meet them?" Eddie asked.

"The Packers? It's a long story. And boring." Jack sipped some cognac. "I'm starting to like this stuff."

"Tell me about SC."

"What about it?"

"What was it like?"

"Hard to say. In a word."

"Did you like it?"

"Sure."

Down the beach, Evelyn and Mrs. Packer emerged from the darkness; or rather, their white dresses did, floating over the sand. Their legs, arms, heads, were invisible.

"Then why did you leave?" Eddie said.

"I told you already."

"That was it?" Eddie said, giving Jack a chance to bring up the letter.

"Sure. What else?"

There was another splash in the water, bigger, closer.

"But what if this doesn't work out?"

"It will."

"But what if it doesn't? What if Trimble turns him down?"

"Trimble's not our only shot."

"But what if everyone turns him down? What will you have to fall back on?"

"This island has a lot of resources."

"You mean you'd stay here?"

"Why not?"

"What kind of future is that?"

"You can be pretty dumb sometimes, Eddie." Jack took another drink. There were scratches on his hand and forearm.

Eddie walked away for a moment; he had to, when Jack made him mad. Soon he had a thought, came back.

"Jack?"

"Yeah?"

"Did you meet the Packers there?"

"Where?"

"SC."

Jack's voice rose. "You're full of questions all of a sudden. Like the caring mom we never had. Is that what your role's going to be?"

"Lay off," Eddie said. Packer and Trimble were watching them. "Why shouldn't I be interested in SC? I'm going to be there for four years."

An inward look appeared in Jack's eyes. "That's true," he said, quietly now. He took another drink. "I met Brad through SC, if you must know. It's not a secret."

"What's he got to do with SC?"

"He's an alum. Swim-team booster. Okay?"

Eddie nodded.

"He's not a bad guy, Eddie." Eddie said nothing. Jack punched him in the ribs, not hard. "Why don't you just cut your fucking hair?"

"You're joking, right?"

"Yeah, I'm joking."

The women were closer now; their legs, arms, faces took shape in the moonlight.

"Can you go back?" Eddie said.

"Back where?"

"SC."

"There's more than one bore here tonight. What's the matter? Scared to go away to school all by your lonesome?"

Now Eddie's voice rose. "I didn't mean now. Someday. Would you still have your scholarship?"

Jack looked up at the bar. Packer and Trimble were watching them again. "You don't get it, do you?" said Jack, keeping his voice down. "I've outgrown all that nickel-and-diming. School is a means to an end. I'm at the end already."

Chapter Nine

Champagne and cognac: a destabilizing combination, new to Eddie. It made him restless, made him want to move, to disconnect from the grown-up world. He didn't bother to say good night to the dinner guests; as soon as Jack returned to the bar, he just backed out of the fire's glow into the darkness and started down the beach, shoes in hand.

The moon was higher and smaller now, but still a massive ball circling close by. It shone on the surf, breaking in orderly lines along the shore like waves of white-horsed cavalry in one of his history textbooks. Eddie came to the fish camp, went by his cabin, paused outside Mandy's. It was dark and silent. He walked on, taking the path to the road, following it to the tennis court.

The backboard loomed in the silvery light, making Eddie think for a moment of JFK's imprisoned brothers, jailed for losing their trials. Dime and Franco. Eddie crossed the court, damp with dew under his bare feet. He found the beginning of the short path, kept going to the shed.

He looked in. Moonlight flowed through the cobweb window, gleaming on the steel roller. Eddie sniffed the air, smelled red clay. All the other smells were gone.

Eddie stood there for a moment, thinking about what had happened in that shed, confirming the details to himself. Under the influence of champagne, cognac, the night, its importance grew.

Eddie went back to the road. He could have turned left; that was the way to the fish camp, to bed. But he wasn't sleepy. He turned right instead and walked all the way to the flamboyant tree. For some reason—maybe it was simply the brightness of the moon—Eddie felt no unease at all about the night, as though he were in a place he knew well. He started up the path to JFK's herb garden.

The walk was easier this time, partly because it was cooler, partly because the path seemed wider: no plants brushed his skin, nothing made him itch. Eddie mounted the long rise, came down toward the clearing, singing to himself:

> Gonna get some goombay goombay lovin'
> Gonna find a goombay goombay girl.

He couldn't remember feeling like this, so elevated, so full of his own possibilities. Champagne, cognac, moonlight, banana-shaped tropic isle, Mandy. It was perfect. Then he saw that JFK's herb garden was gone. Not a stalk remained.

Something rustled in the bushes. The first pulse of adrenaline went through Eddie. A little form darted from the bushes, scuttled across his bare feet. Not a pig this time—just a crab, but the realization didn't come in time to block the second pulse. It washed the restlessness out of him. He wondered what crimes had sent Dime and Franco to jail.

Eddie returned to the fish camp, no longer singing. Both cabins dark. He entered his. Jack's bed was empty. Eddie undressed, lay down. A breeze curled through the screen window above his head, soft and smelling of the sea, sleep-inducing as the strongest potion.

Eddie dreamed of wild pigs swimming on a coral reef. Red bubbles streamed from their mouths. Something unpleasant was about to happen, but it never did. Instead there was a scraping sound, insistent. Eddie awoke, heard fingernails on the screen. He raised his head, saw Mandy's face, obscure on the other side of the screen. She didn't say a word. Eddie looked across the room, saw Jack's still form in the other bed, got up. He went outside, closed the door without making a sound, felt Mandy's hand in his.

Then her lips were at his ear. He heard her say, "I couldn't sleep without you." So quietly, she might have just mouthed the words.

Mandy led him into her cabin. He smelled ripe pineapple. Her body was a white glow in the darkness. She pushed him gently on the bed. The sheets were sandy. "So many things I want to do to you," she said. "I don't know where to start."

She found a place. Soon Eddie stopped having clear thoughts. He entered a sensory world, where surfaces were liquid and the atmosphere was full of breathing. She entered it too. He was sure she did; he could feel her doing it.

The moon sank behind the trees. In the darkness, almost complete, that followed, the bed seemed to move, to drift away, taking them on a journey, the way he and Jack had once sailed the Spanish Main.

After, they lay in twisted sheets, her head on his chest.

"I've died and gone to heaven," she said.

He stroked her hair, damp and grainy with sand. "No one's going to die."

"The pig died," Mandy said. "Just to impress a big shot."

There was a silence.

"What did it taste like?" she asked.

"Pork chops à la cannabis."

"Are you stoned?"

"Yes and no. Mostly no."

"Me too."

A breeze rose again, cooling them. They abandoned their bodies to it; this was luxury.

Then Eddie thought: Evelyn will be flying back to Florida soon; when she's gone, Mandy moves down to cottage six. Questions began forming in his mind. Why was she with someone like Packer? How did they meet? Did he pay her? He realized he didn't even know her last name. Eddie shuffled the questions, searching for a good way to begin. Finally, he said: "Where did you meet Brad?"

No answer.

"Mandy?"

She was asleep.

Eddie closed his eyes. There would be time for questions later.

*   *   *

Something thudded through his dream, heavy and rhythmic. The dream began reshaping itself to incorporate the sound. Then the screen door opened with a snick and slapped shut, snick slap, and Eddie awoke, too late.

Packer said: "You up, babe? We're gonna have to be quick."

There wasn't time for jumping under the bed, or into a suit of armor, or onto a greenhouse roof, or any of the other places they think of in funny movies. There was only time for Eddie to raise his head, time for Mandy to make a sleepy complaint into his shoulder. Then Packer, in singlet and jogging shorts, was standing in the middle of the room with his mouth open. Packer didn't say anything. He backed away, to the door, out.

"Oh, God," Mandy said, sitting up, covering her breasts although there was no one to see but him. "With those people here. I can't believe—"

The door burst open. Packer had found his voice, a yelling one. "You fuckin' little hoor." He came toward the bed, hands squared into fists, shaking. "You fuckin' little hoor."

Mandy sat there, covering her breasts.

"Don't say that," Eddie said, getting up.

Packer ran a furtive glance down Eddie's body, almost as though he couldn't help himself, then said: "You don't tell me anything, boy." He took a swing at Eddie, powerful, but long and slow. Eddie had been in a few fistfights: where he came from that was part of growing up. He leaned back. Packer's knuckles grazed his shoulder.

"Don't do that again," Eddie said.

"Who's going to stop me?" said Packer, getting ready to throw another one. But the way Eddie had moved made him pause. His eyes darted around the room, perhaps searching for a weapon. There was nothing obvious. That left his yelling voice.

"You're dead." Packer stormed out, banging the screen door shut behind him.

Mandy was up, tugging a T-shirt over her head. "You've got to get out of here," she said.

"Why?"

"Why? He's coming back with his gun, that's why."

"Over something like this?"

"What else?" She was looking at him in a way he didn't like, as though seeing him from a new angle.

"What about you?" he asked.

Mandy didn't answer. She went out the door; Eddie followed. Jack came hurrying out of the other cabin, zipping up his shorts. He saw them, glanced down the beach where Packer was running as fast as he could, ungainly, almost stumbling, toward the cottages; and understood at once.

Jack strode up to Eddie. Jack was looking at him in a new way too.

"Didn't I tell you?" he said. He said it again, louder. Then he hit Eddie across the face with the back of his hand. Eddie fell, partly because of the force of the blow, partly because it was Jack.

His brother stood over him. "You're a fuckup, you know that? You couldn't even cut your goddamn hair."

"Leave him alone," Mandy said.

Jack turned on her, raised his hand again, maybe to strike her, maybe just to threaten. At that moment the Trimbles walked out of the bush. They wore bermuda shorts and polo shirts, carried binoculars and butterfly nets.

"Oh, my goodness," said Mrs. Trimble, taking in the scene: Jack and Mandy, half dressed, Eddie, naked and bleeding on the ground.

Trimble stepped in front of his wife, raising his butterfly net like a symbol of office. "What's the trouble?"

Jack wiped his hands on the sides of his shorts, managed a smile. "No trouble, Mr. Trimble. Just a little roughhousing, that's all."

Trimble frowned. "Looks like trouble to me." He offered his hand to Eddie, helped him to his feet. "Get dressed."

Eddie went inside his cabin, threw on clothes. When he came out, Jack was saying, "Lepidoptery, isn't that the word?"

Trimble ignored him. He was looking at Mandy. "I've seen you before."

"Have you?"

"At the Pelican Club. You were waiting in the car for Packer after lunch. He said you worked for him, I don't recall in what capacity."

Mandy started to reply, but Jack interrupted. "She's no longer with the company."

"Then what's she doing here?"

Jack was still forming his answer when the sound of a revving engine came from the beach. Everyone turned, saw the jeep racing toward them, spewing rooster tails of sand. Packer was at the wheel, brandishing his rifle like a dervish.

"Run," Mandy said.

"What about you?"

"He won't hurt me," Mandy said, but her eyes weren't so sure.

Eddie grabbed her hand. "Where?"

"I don't know. Cotton Town."

"The commissioner lives there," Jack said. "That's all we need."

"Then what do you suggest?" asked Mandy, her voice rising.

"Anything else." The jeep fishtailed over the sand. Packer was shouting something at the top of his lungs.

Mandy glanced around wildly. Her eyes fastened on *Fearless*. "Who's got the boat keys?"

Eddie answered: "I do."

"Let's go."

"In the boat?" Jack said.

"Why not?" said Mandy.

"What do you mean, why not?"

Mandy looked at Jack. "Relax." She tugged at Eddie's hand.

Jack opened his mouth to reply, closed it.

"What the hell is going on?" said Trimble.

Eddie and Mandy started for the path.

"Wait," Jack said.

At that moment, the jeep came bouncing over a dune and into the fish camp. Packer saw Eddie, swerved in his direction. He roared right by Trimble, recognized him too late, glanced back to be sure, hit the brakes, and lost control of the jeep. It plowed into Mandy's cabin, flattening it like a dollhouse, and came to a stop at the edge of the bush.

Packer staggered out, bloody and dazed, but still holding the gun. He swung it in Eddie's direction.

"There's not going to be any violence," Trimble said, pointing at Packer with the butterfly net.

Mandy took off. It was all happening quickly, and Eddie was

only eighteen. He ran too. There was a cracking sound behind him. He ran faster.

The sea was calm, the charts clear, *Fearless*'s tank filled to the top. They sighted Bimini before noon. By that time, Eddie had the answers to his questions.

Her last name was Delfuego. She'd come to Packer as an office temp, been hired full time, gone out one night for drinks with the boss. He wasn't as bad as Eddie thought. His wife was a cold bitch, he had lots of worries, but he treated Mandy well and had big dreams that she was part of. Et cetera. The answers to his questions: he could have heard them on afternoon TV, but what did that mean? Packer was out of the picture now, wasn't he?

"Of course," Mandy said, wrapping her arms around him.

Fearless skimmed over a glossy blue sea. "I'm supposed to go to USC," Eddie said after a while.

"I know. You'll meet Raleigh."

"Raleigh?"

"Raleigh Packer. Brad and Evelyn's son. That's how they met, Jack and Brad."

"I thought they met through some kind of alumni booster club."

"Brad? He didn't graduate high school. That's what he's making up for now."

A voice came over the radio. "*Fearless*? That you?" It was JFK. "Come in, *Fearless*. Listen good. Don' you—" Then nothing.

"What was that?" Eddie asked.

Mandy stared out to sea. Eddie could feel her thinking, but she didn't answer. He repeated the question.

"I don't know," she said.

They waited for JFK to make contact again. He did not.

The sun was still high in the sky when the mainland came in view, at first not land at all, but the high-rises of Lauderdale floating on the horizon.

"Aim to the right of that pointy one," Mandy said.

Eddie turned the wheel. "What if he's waiting on the dock?"

"There're a zillion marinas here," Mandy said. "But he wouldn't come anyway."

"Why not?"

"He'll be too busy trying to pacify Evelyn." She was quiet for a moment. Then she said: "He's in love, you know."

"With Evelyn?"

"With her connections." Now they could see the land itself, a low brown hump; other boats appeared on the water. "Have you got connections, Eddie?"

"No."

"What about Jack?"

"Jack's not a connection. He's my brother."

She gave him a kiss. "I don't have connections either. But at least we'll be all right for money. We're going places, you and me." She took binoculars from under the console and studied the shoreline. "Make for that little gap."

Eddie steered for a gap between two buildings. A red, white, and blue cigarette emerged from behind a trawler and swung around in their direction. Mandy watched it through the binoculars for a few seconds, then focused on a seagull flying by with a fish in its beak.

"Going to the head," she told Eddie. "Back in a flash." She went below.

Eddie, one hand on the wheel, pulled out his wallet, counted what he had. Sixty-seven dollars. Why would they be all right for money?

When he looked up he saw that the red, white, and blue cigarette was much closer, moving very fast, coming right at him. Eddie was sure he had the right of way but changed course nevertheless. The cigarette changed course too, still coming at him.

Now it was near enough for Eddie to see that there were four figures on board, all dressed in orange. Eddie had heard stories of pirates in the islands, but he wasn't in the islands now, he was in sight of the mainland. He changed course again; the red, white, and blue boat mirrored his move.

And then it was on him, sweeping around *Fearless* in tight circles of spray. Four figures in orange jumpsuits: four men, all with deep tans and short haircuts. One was the driver, one had a bullhorn, two had rifles, pointed at him. Friends of Packer, Eddie thought at once: Packer had radioed ahead. Eddie considered turning, making a run for the open sea, but knew *Fearless* didn't have the speed.

"Mandy?" he called. No answer.

The cigarette pulled up alongside. The man with the bullhorn called out, "Cut your engine."

Eddie slowed down, but held his course. One of the riflemen stood up and fired a shot over Eddie's head. He throttled back to neutral.

"I said cut."

Eddie switched off.

"Hands behind your head."

Eddie put his hands behind his head. The two armed men climbed over *Fearless*'s rail. "Don't do anything stupid," one said.

"Packer's the one being stupid," Eddie said.

"Say what?" Eddie felt a rifle muzzle in his back, kept silent. "Let's go below," said the man.

Eddie twisted around. "You're going to kill me over something like this?"

"Who said anything about killing? It's not a capital crime, not yet."

They went below, Eddie and the four men. The men searched the berths, the engine compartment, the galley, the head. Eddie assumed they were looking for Mandy. She wasn't there. He noticed that his scuba gear, normally hanging on the wall by the galley, was gone. He said nothing, not wanting to give her away.

The men didn't seem discouraged. One returned to the cigarette, came back with crowbars and axes. They ripped up the deck boards. Underneath lay densely packed vegetation, tied in bales, looking so incongruous that at first Eddie didn't know what it was. Then he did.

Herb.

"You're under arrest," said one of the men. He took a file card from his pocket and read Eddie his rights.

Chapter Ten

If there was a heaven it was a watery place.

In lane five, his old favorite in the pool of his hometown Y, Eddie kept swimming. At first he'd had no rhythm, no technique at all, and had tired quickly. Weight lifting had made fifteen years go faster; it had also made him clumsy in the water. He thrashed up and down lane five for a dozen lengths, twisting around on the surface after each one like a beginner. His mouth filled with the taste of tobacco, nicotine-stained snot streamed from his nose. He decided to quit after ten laps—if he could swim that far. But on the very last length and without warning, his lungs suddenly cleared, the tobacco taste disappeared, the snot stopped flowing; and his body began to remember. On their own, his hands and forearms found the right angles, sculling, not pushing, and he felt himself rising higher in the water, going faster. He recalled the sensation of just skimming the surface that he'd felt when he'd been racing at his best; he wasn't skimming now, but he wasn't thrashing either. As he came to the wall, he piked, even remembering to spread his feet as they came over, touched, pushed off, streamlining himself in the thumb-hook position, then rolled as he slowed to swimming speed.

Flipped the turn, he thought, goddamn; and found himself smiling for a moment underwater. He kept going.

Eddie swam. Length by length, lap by lap, he watched the bottom tiles slide by, and his mind shut down, as though its power source was being diverted elsewhere. He stopped thinking, stopped remembering, stopped counting laps, strokes, breaths. His body took over. It swam him back and forth in the old hometown pool. Time shrank to the vanishing point, at last and too late. If there'd been a pool at the prison everything would have been all right. Eddie lost himself in that cool blue rectangle, and stayed lost until someone swam by him in lane six.

The other swimmer's body was unfamiliar: pale, thin-legged, with a roll of fat hanging over the drawstring of the swimsuit. But he knew that powerful, big-chested stroke, with its slightly too-strong counterbalancing kick. And now he could place the voice of the man who had been talking into a portable phone by the side of the pool when he'd come in.

Bobby Falardeau was waiting for him at the far end, treading water. Eddie pulled up, shaking droplets off his head. For a moment, Falardeau, studying his face, his shaved head, looked puzzled.

"Eddie?"

"Bobby."

"Son of a bitch. I knew it. I was watching you and I said to myself there's only one guy I know swims like that." There was a buzzing sound. "Just a sec," Bobby said, and climbed out of the pool. He picked up his phone, lying on a chair, and listened. "Dump it," he said, clicking off.

Eddie climbed out too. "Christ," said Bobby, "you're in shape." Pause. "That must be the silver lining they don't tell you about." He laughed.

"Silver lining to what?" Eddie knew the answer; he just didn't think it was funny.

"To going to—you know." Bobby leaned over the pool, blew out his nostrils. "But you're out now, right?"

"Went over the wall day before yesterday."

There was another pause; then Bobby laughed again. "That's a good one." His face grew solemn. "I got to tell you, Eddie, I feel really sorry—"

"Forget it."

"Right. Put it behind you. Look to the future." Bobby nodded to himself. "What're your plans?"

"Steam bath," said Eddie. "Take nothing with me. Quit smoking."

Bobby blinked. "I mean for what you're gonna do. That kind of thing."

"I saw Vic."

"Coach Vic?"

"What other Vic is there?"

"He's a sad case, Eddie."

"What do you mean?"

"If you saw him you know."

"His drinking?"

"He's a lush."

"He says you laid him off."

"Bullshit."

"You mean he quit?"

"I haven't got a clue what he did. We sold out in eighty-six. We had nothing to do with anything that happened after that."

"You sold Falardeau Metal and Iron?"

"BCC bought us out. One of those junk-bond things. You know."

"I don't."

Bobby shrugged. "Doesn't matter. Turned out they just wanted the railhead anyway. And the equity, of course. They sold off what they could, borrowed to the hilt, the usual."

"The usual what?"

"Procedure."

"But what happened to the plant? Vic's job?"

"I just told you." The phone buzzed again. Bobby answered it, listened, said, "and an eighth," clicked off.

"What about your job?" Eddie asked.

Bobby shrugged again. "Gone with the rest. It's business, Eddie."

"But what are you doing now?"

"I'm retired."

"Isn't it a little soon?"

"I keep busy," Bobby said. "We've got this investment company now. It's no picnic."

"You and your dad?"

"Me, actually. The old man's not really involved anymore."

"What happened to him?"

"Nothing. He's in Boca Raton."

Eddie nodded, but he wasn't getting it. He glanced at the pool, saw that the waves he'd raised had subsided to ripples; the surface would soon be calm again. He'd always liked that calm surface, liked being the first one in. Now he understood why:

> The fair breeze blew, the white foam flew,
> The furrows followed free;
> We were the first that ever burst
> Into that silent sea.

"You all right?" Bobby said.

"Yeah."

"Had a funny look there."

"I'm fine." He was hungry, that was all. When had he last eaten? He remembered: in F-block. Eddie walked to the other end of the pool to get his towel. Bobby followed.

"We had some times in this pool, didn't we, Eddie?"

"Yeah," Eddie said, toweling off.

"You were something. You had a scholarship offer, didn't you? Clemson?"

"USC."

Bobby shook his head. "Isn't that something?" he said. "I ended up swimming for Dartmouth. Just about my speed."

"That's nice," said Eddie, starting toward the locker-room door.

Bobby followed. "Best exercise there is," he said. "I'm still in here three, four times a week. Nothing strenuous. Long slow distance, keep some of this fucking fat off. But you know something, Eddie, I had an idea, watching you. A crazy idea."

Eddie stopped and turned.

"What's that?"

"It's kind of crazy, like I said." He looked Eddie in the eye; Eddie didn't remember Bobby having that look. "Thing is, I think I could beat you now."

"Do you?"

"Just a hunch," Bobby said. "You a gambling man, Eddie? I hear a lot of gambling goes on in . . . those places."

"I knew a bridge player once," Eddie said. "He liked to gamble."

"There you go. What do you say?"

"To what?"

"A little action. One-hundred free. How does that sound?"

"For money?"

"Just to make it interesting."

"How much?"

"You name it."

"A hundred," Eddie said.

"Dollars?"

"Dollar per yard," Eddie said. "Just for the sake of fearful symmetry."

Bobby stared at him for a moment, then laughed. "It's great you didn't lose your sense of humor," he said, holding out his hand. Eddie had been wondering when they would shake hands. They shook; in greeting, or simply sealing the bet?

They walked around toward the starting end, Bobby stretching his arms above his head, Eddie trying to remember where he'd read about fearful symmetry. It must have been years ago, long before he'd discovered "The Mariner."

Bobby took his place in lane six. "Do we need a starter?"

"No."

"We'll just use the clock, like in the old days." A big clock with a red second hand hung on the wall at the other end. "Second hand touches twelve, we go."

The water was still again, flat blue. The second hand rounded six, ticked up the other side. Eight, nine, ten. Bobby got into his crouch. Eddie had forgotten about that. He bent his knees, trying to find the right position. Eleven. One, two, three, fo—the red hand was a full click away when Bobby sprang off. Eddie followed, a hurried dive so steeply angled he almost touched bottom. By the time Eddie hit the surface, Bobby was half a length ahead. In seven or eight strokes, he stretched it to a full length.

Eddie had forgotten his racing dive. Now he forgot about sculling too, lost his feel for the water, fell into a crude imitation of Bobby's powerful stroke. He thrashed on, falling farther behind, thinking: What the hell are you doing, jailbird?

Bobby hit the first turn, flipped it well, smoother than in his racing days. That observation threw off Eddie's timing. He forgot to spread his feet, pushed off crooked, started his roll too soon, forcing himself to stroke too soon. Bobby gained another half length. Two days out of the pen, jailbird, and racing for all the money you've got.

Bobby gained another stroke or two by the second turn, flipped it nicely again. Eddie did better on his second turn, not perfect, but better. And in the calm of the glide, he realized he'd been thrashing. Like an animal: *a freestyler needs finesse.* Feel the water, feel how it gives against the palm, curls around the fingers. Feel it: an obvious psychological trick, but it worked on him. He began to scull, rising up in the water; not yet skimming, but moving faster. Bobby's big white kicking feet came back to him a little at a time: the one or two strokes he'd lost on the second turn, maybe more. He was about a length and a half behind when Bobby hit the last turn.

Eddie didn't see how Bobby handled it. No time. He came to the wall, piked, flipped, rolled, glided, stroked twice, breathed. Perfect. He glanced at Bobby. Half a length now, and closing. Stroke stroke stroke stroke breathe. Stroke stroke stroke stroke breathe. Eddie closed a little more, almost skimming now. Bobby glanced back; his eyes widened. Stroke stroke stroke stroke stroke—and then, in mid-pull, his body failed him, all at once, as though someone had switched him off.

How long had he been swimming before Bobby challenged him? He didn't know. It could have been twenty minutes, it could have been two hours. Enough so that now he was done, just like that. He almost stopped right there in the middle of the pool.

But he knew—there was no time to think, he just knew—that if he stopped it was over for him. So he kept making the motions of swimming; and at the same time a voice in his head, his own voice said: Go, Nails. Not yelling, not screaming, simply saying go, and calling him by that name.

My real name, Eddie thought: me. A surge of something— energy, adrenaline, endorphins, something—pulsed through him, lifted him. And then, at last, he was skimming. He didn't feel exhaustion, pain, fear, despair. He felt nothing but the cool blue, pushing him forward, helping.

Go, Nails. Go, Nails. The voice didn't stop until his hand smacked the wall, hard: he hadn't even seen it coming. He got his head up in time to see Bobby touch.

Bobby couldn't say anything at first. He just hung onto the edge of the pool, gasping. After a while he got his breath back. He said: "Fuck."

Eddie climbed out of the pool. His muscles ached, but he made sure he got out in one smooth motion.

"Very cute," said Bobby, still in the pool. He was smiling, but too broadly, and his voice was too loud. "The way I paid for you to get into that kind of shape."

Eddie turned. "How's that?"

There was a pause while Bobby made an effort to hold the words inside. They tumbled out. "You've been sucking at the public tit for the past fifteen years or whatever the hell it is, that's how, and I'm a taxpayer like you wouldn't believe."

Eddie came back to the edge, looked down at Bobby. Bobby's hair was plastered down on his forehead, his face was red. "If you win, say little," Eddie said. "If you lose, say less."

Bobby went redder, but kept his mouth shut.

Eddie walked away, into the locker room, showered, changed. He wrang out the Speedo, dried it under the blower, stuck it in his pocket. Another possession, added to his shades, the $1.55 left from the gate money, the $100 bill from El Rojo, and Prof's cardboard tube, which didn't belong to him. He went out into the lobby and sat in a chair. It was a wooden chair, hard and uncomfortable, but Eddie was almost asleep when Bobby appeared.

Bobby looked good. His hair, still damp, was slicked back; he wore a dark suit, glossy black shoes with little holes in them— Eddie knew they had a name but didn't know what it was—and had a glossy black fur coat over one shoulder. He walked over to Eddie. Eddie rose; it took a lot of effort, but he didn't want Bobby standing over him, not with all that wardrobe.

Bobby had recovered his self-confidence, or at least his composure. He took in Eddie's wrinkled trousers, the bright green short-sleeved shirt, the dirty prison sneakers. Then he reached in his pocket and pulled out his roll. It was a thick one, jammed into a gold money clip. He peeled off a hundred-dollar bill, one of many, and handed it over. Eddie found himself staring at it, like a bumpkin.

Bobby laughed. "You and Jack couldn't be more different, you know that?"

"What's that supposed to mean?"

Bobby stopped laughing, stepped back. "Nothing. He's at home with money, that's all. Big money."

"He is?"

"Sure. Who do you think sicced BCC on us?"

"Jack did that to you?"

"Hell, yes. It was brilliant. We're set for life."

"Who's we?"

"Dad and me. Who else is there?"

"Vic, for one," Eddie said. And the whole fucking town.

Bobby shrugged himself into his fur coat. "He didn't have any shares, Eddie. This is America."

They didn't shake hands again. Bobby went out. Eddie had a drink from the fountain and left soon after. He was almost at the bus station when he realized he'd forgotten his steam bath.

Chapter Eleven

The stubble-faced man had patterned the bus-station floor in dirty whorls and laid the mop aside. Now he sat behind the ticket counter, studying a magazine called *HOT! HOT! HOT!* He looked up as Eddie approached, spreading his hands over a picture of people having sex while watching a big-screen TV where people were having sex.

"When's the next bus to New York?" Eddie asked.

"Seven twenty-two, A.M."

"You mean tomorrow?"

"A.M.," the stubble-faced man repeated, his fingers stirring impatiently on the magazine.

"Where can I get something to eat?"

"Search me."

"But you live here."

The stubble-faced man snorted.

Eddie didn't like that. He leaned on the counter. The stubble-faced man drew away, dragging *HOT! HOT! HOT!* with him. Eddie laid his hand on the magazine; a page tore through a fat thigh. "Let's put it this way," he said. "Where do you go when you're hungry?"

The bus-station door opened and a cop came in, stamping snow off his boots; the same cop who had stopped Eddie on the bridge. The stubble-faced man smiled. "I go home, asshole," he said to Eddie.

"Everything okay, Murray?" asked the cop, looking hard at Eddie.

Eddie backed away from the counter.

"Best day of my life," said the stubble-faced man. "I just love this job."

The cop went over to the coffee machine, fed it change, pressed the button. Nothing happened. He slapped the machine with his palm.

"This thing on the fritz, Murray?"

"Guess so."

"I want my money back."

"Got no key," said Murray. "There's a number to call on the back."

The cop slapped the machine once more, then turned and walked out the door. Eddie and Murray stared at each other. Murray's lips twitched, as though he was fighting back a grin. Eddie didn't like that either. He grabbed *HOT! HOT! HOT!* and ripped it in half before leaving.

"Asshole," said Murray, but not too aggressively.

Outside it was colder, windier, snowier. Eddie walked up Main Street to the end, passing two diners on the way, both closed, and stopped where the state highway began. A car approached. Eddie stuck out his thumb. It kept going.

So did others. Time passed. Eddie didn't know how much time because he'd given his watch to Prof: part of his plan to take nothing with him. He got more tired, more hungry, colder. He wanted a cigarette, to fill his lungs with warmth, to hold a little fire in his hand. No cigarette: that was prong two of his three-pronged plan. But it was better than being inside.

"I'm free," he said to nobody.

There wasn't much traffic. After a while Eddie realized he was just watching it go by, without bothering to stick out his thumb. He stuck it out. A white car, pocked with rust, pulled over. Eddie opened the passenger door.

"Destination?" said the driver.

The driver was dressed in white: white trousers and a white tunic that came almost to his knees. Eddie noticed this in passing; his immediate attention was drawn to the man's head, shaved bald like his.

"New York," Eddie said.

"You've got good karma."

Eddie paused, his hand on the door, wondering if the man in white was gay and this was a come-on. His mind flashed images of Louie, the Ozark boys; and the man in white, lying by the side of the road while Eddie drove off in the pockmarked car.

The man spoke. "I mean you're in luck—that's where I'm going."

Eddie got in.

The man held out his hand. "Ram Pontoppidan."

"Nai— Ed Nye."

Ram checked the rearview mirror—a laminated photograph of an old Indian at a spinning wheel hung from it—and pulled onto the road. "Mind fastening your seat belt, Ed? It's the law."

Music played on the sound system, tinkling music full of rests. "Cold out there," said Ram. "Waiting long?"

"No."

"Nice and warm in here."

"Yeah."

Nice and warm; and smelling of food. The food smell came from an open plastic bag lying in the storage box between the seats. "Holesome Trail Mix," read the label: "Shiva & Co., Burlington, Vt."

"Try some," said Ram.

"No, thanks."

"Really. I'd like your opinion."

"About what?"

"The product. I'm the New York–New England distributor."

Eddie hadn't heard of trail mix, and was sure wholesome was spelled with a *w*, but he hadn't eaten since dinner the night before his release, and now the swim had left him ravenous. He dipped into the bag: nuts, and dried fruit in various colors. He tried it.

"Well?"

"Not bad."

In truth, better than not bad, much better. Eddie hadn't tasted anything so good since . . . when? In his case, he could fix the date: the night of spiny lobsters and champagne at Galleon Beach.

"Have some more," said Ram.

Eddie had another handful—"Don't be shy"—and another.

"That's what makes it all so gratifying," said Ram, handing him the bag: "customer satisfaction."

Eddie sat there with the bag on his lap.

"It's a sample," said Ram. "Enjoy and be blessed."

Eddie finished the bag.

After that he felt sleepy; his body came down from the swimming high. Outside it was bleak and raw, inside warm, the music soothing sound, with no rhythm or melody that Eddie could hear. He glanced at Ram. His eyes were on the road. Eddie let himself relax a little. He kept his eyes open but began to drift off, drawing out that time between wakefulness and sleep in a way he hadn't in fifteen years. In his cell, he'd always rushed to unconsciousness at night.

Ram spoke softly: "Have you tried spirituality, Ed?"

Eddie sat up. Ram was watching him from the corner of his eye. "What do you mean?"

"Love, to put it simply." Again Eddie's mind flashed images of Louie, the Ozarks, Ram by the side of the road. "The love that impels and compels the universe. The love that stands behind the food you just ate."

"It wasn't that good."

Ram smiled. "I'm talking about the spiritual power of Krishna consciousness, Ed. The path to inner peace and calm. Can you honestly say you are full of inner peace and calm?"

Eddie remembered his state of mind in the pool. "Sometimes."

The answer surprised Ram. "Then you've studied meditation?"

"I tried the F-Block system for a while."

Ram frowned. He had clear, unwrinkled skin, but suddenly appeared older. "I don't know that one. I've heard of beta blockers, of course."

"No drugs allowed on F-Block."

"Good," said Ram. "Although anything that leads to inner peace can't be rejected out of hand. It's so . . . hard, Ed. I know. I fooled myself into thinking I was at peace for many years. I had a wife, kids, tenure at SUNY, house, car, et cetera. All a sham. I simply wasn't very evolved at the time."

"You were a teacher?"

"Tenured professor of English literature. It wasn't the way."

Ram talked on, describing his spiritual crisis, how he'd left wife, kids, job, house, car, et cetera and found Shiva & Co. and inner peace.

Eddie waited till he finished and said: "What poems did you teach?"

"At SUNY?"

"Yeah."

"You name it."

" 'The Rime of the Ancient Mariner'?"

Ram wrinkled his brow, looked older; surprised again. " 'The Mariner'? Never taught it, per se—wanting to avoid the strait-jacket of the dead white male thing—but I know it, naturally. Are you taking an English course?"

"No."

A mile or two of windblown white scenery went by. Eddie took a chance. "And now there came both mist and snow / And it grew wondrous cold." He spoke aloud, but quiet, and to his ears dull and insipid too. Maybe it was a lousy poem after all.

"I'm impressed," said Ram. "You're not a poet yourself, by any chance?"

"No."

"What do you do, then, if you don't mind me asking?"

"I'm looking for work," Eddie replied, wondering if there was any truth in that reply.

"What kind?"

Eddie thought about that. Another white mile or two went by.

"None of my business," Ram said.

Eddie turned to him. "Tell me something."

"I'll try."

"Why did the albatross get shot in the first place?"

Ram's eyes shifted. Eddie realized that this man who'd evolved his way into an Indian outfit and a junk-heap car was beginning to fear he'd picked up a nut. He should have set up the question a little better.

" 'The Rime of the Ancient Mariner's' just a trifle, Eddie—like 'The Cremation of Sam McGee,' " Ram said. "I wouldn't get into it too deeply. Whatever you're searching for isn't there. That doesn't mean it isn't somewhere." Ram glanced at him to make sure he was listening. "What do you know about Krishna consciousness?"

Eddie didn't know much about Krishna consciousness and didn't want to. He wanted to know about "The Mariner," and here was someone who probably had the knowledge but wasn't going to tell. The image of Ram lying by the side of the road rose in his mind again. He made it go away.

They crossed a frozen river. Eddie drifted toward sleep once more. This time he didn't prolong the drifting but went quickly, like an inmate.

The walls of the visitor's room were gray and covered with signs. "Wearing of denim clothing by visitors is forbidden," "Female visitors must wear underwear," "No sitting on laps," "No loud talk," "Removal of any clothing prohibited," "Violators will be arrested and prosecuted to the full extent of the law."

There were two steel doors, both guarded by C.O.s. The first led to a strip-search area, a metal detector, and the cell blocks; the second led to a strip-search area, a metal detector, and the outside. Eddie was waiting on a bench when the second door opened and Jack came in.

Eddie hadn't seen Jack since the trial. He looked good: trim and tanned in a polo shirt and chinos. There were sweat stains under his arms, but that was understandable. Eddie was nervous too. He got up. Jack came to him, eyes filling with emotion. They embraced.

"Jesus, Eddie, you've lost weight."

"The food—" Eddie began, but knew he couldn't continue in a steady voice. He wouldn't break down, not in front of Jack, not in front of the four C.O.s sitting in the corners of the room.

They sat on the bench. Jack glanced around, took in the signs, the guards, the prisoner sitting on the other bench with a toothless old woman. He licked his lips. "Is everything okay?"

"Okay?"

"Besides the food, I mean. You're not being . . . mistreated, or anything?"

"I'm in jail for something I didn't do. Is that okay?"

"It's horrible—worse than horrible," Jack said, laying a hand on Eddie's knee. "But aside from that."

A C.O. got up. "Knock off the fag shit."

"We're brothers," Eddie said, raising his voice slightly, within the acceptable limit.

"So?"

There was no use arguing: Eddie had learned that in the first few weeks. Jack had already removed his hand anyway. He didn't look quite so good now, and the sweat stains were spreading.

The other prisoner was watching them. Eddie had seen him playing cards in the rec room. His name was Louie. He smiled at Eddie. Eddie ignored him.

Eddie and Jack lost the thread of the conversation, fell silent despite the wall clock ticking away the time they had together. After a while Jack licked his lips again and said: "There's nothing new, Eddie. I'm sorry."

Eddie had known that the moment Jack came in the room. Nothing new meant that JFK still hadn't been found. And finding him was only step one. Without a confession from JFK, without some statement that he was responsible and that Eddie had had nothing to do with the dope on *Fearless*, there was no hope of a retrial.

"Mandy?"

"Disappeared." Jack stared at the unpainted cement floor. "We still don't know if she was in on it anyway."

"Why else would she go overboard?"

"Maybe she just knew the load was there and took off when she saw trouble coming."

Without warning me, Eddie thought. The implication of that was clear, had been clear from the beginning, although it meant less and less as time went by.

"We've had this discussion," Jack went on, glancing at the toothless old woman and the prisoner named Louie before looking again at Eddie. "Mandy doesn't matter. What matters is JFK. No one saw him leave the island. Brice hasn't even been able to find out what his real name is, if he has one."

"Why did he try to raise us on the radio?"

"Because you were running off with his investment. We've been through this too."

"But he got cut off."

"Maybe he changed his mind."

"Why would he do that?"

Jack shrugged.

"The radio was in the bar. Someone must have seen him. The question is who."

Jack sighed. "The question is where did he go."

"Maybe he went to France."

"France?"

"He speaks French."

Silence. One of the C.O.s removed his glasses and rubbed his eyes hard. "Brice charges two hundred a day," Jack said.

"Borrow," Eddie said, his voice rising over the acceptable limit. "Borrow on your seven and a half percent."

The C.O. put his glasses back on, gave Eddie a red-eyed glare. Jack's voice rose too. "Seven and a half percent of what?"

"Fucking can it," said the red-eyed C.O.

"Galleon Beach," Eddie said, more quietly.

Jack shot Eddie a quick and angry glance. "The bank foreclosed last week." He looked away. "Packer's finished. Trimble, with his pious little scruples, finished him."

"He's a good man." Trimble had given Jack a thousand dollars to retain Brice.

"He fucked us," Jack said. "All because . . ." He went silent.

Eddie leaned forward. Their faces were very close. "Are you blaming me?" he said.

Jack didn't answer. The prisoner named Louie smiled at Eddie again.

"Are you?"

"Let's not argue," Jack said. Eddie smelled alcohol on his brother's breath.

"Get me out of here," he said.

"I'm trying, Eddie." Jack's voice broke.

They sat together on the bench while the hands on the wall clock circled toward the end of the visiting period. Jack shook his head. "Everything went to shit so fast."

The C.O.s rose the instant the minute hand touched twelve for the second time. "What's happening?" Jack asked.

"You have to go."

"God."

They got up, embraced again. "Hang on," Jack said. "At the very worst . . ."

"Say bye-bye," said a C.O., coming closer.

"At the very worst what?" Eddie said.

"Please take this the right way, Eddie. Five to fifteen, but at the very worst it means you'll be out in less than four, with time off for good behavior. It's bad, I know. But you'll only be—"

Eddie squeezed his brother's arm as hard as he could. "Get me out of here."

"I'm trying."

"Try harder."

Jack hadn't known the meaning of the very worst. Brice couldn't find JFK and sent his letter informing Eddie of the closing of the investigation a month or two later. By that time it didn't matter. Louie and the Ozark brothers got Eddie in the showers a week after Jack's visit. Less than four swelled to the full fifteen. Jack never returned to the visitor's room. He sent food packages at Christmas and Eddie's birthday for a few years, then just at Christmas, then not at all. That was understandable too.

"Where can I drop you?"

Eddie opened his eyes. Ram was looking at him. They were on a bridge, stuck in traffic. Ahead lay Manhattan. Eddie had never been there, but it couldn't be anything else. The tops of the towers were hidden in the clouds. The snow had turned to rain, steaming the windows of the cars.

"Two twenty-two Park Avenue," Eddie said.

"You live on Park Avenue?"

"That's where you can drop me."

"I'm not going uptown."

"Anywhere's fine."

"Washington Square?"

"Sure," Eddie said, although he had no idea where it was.

Ram drove across the bridge, got stuck in more traffic by a river. "It's funny," Ram said, "when I saw you shaved your head and all, I got the idea you'd been with us, maybe not too long ago."

"With you?"

"A convert."

"It's ringworm," Eddie said.

There was no further discussion until Ram stopped by a grassless park and said, "Okay?"

"Thanks."

Eddie got out. "Take this," said Ram, handing him another bag of Holesome Trail Mix. He drove away. There were two bumper stickers on the back of his car. One read: "Krishna & Co.—Food for the Soul." The other: "This car climbed Mt. Washington."

Rain fell, cold and hard. Eddie crossed the street. A woman was sitting on a scrap of cardboard with a baby and a sign: "Homeless and hungry. Please help." Eddie handed her the trail mix.

He had walked twenty or thirty blocks and was soaked to the skin before he realized that the description on the cardboard sign applied to him too. The thought had an odd effect: it filled him with a sense of well-being, made him smile. Everything was going to be all right—unlike the woman and her baby, he could always win money in swimming pools.

Chapter Twelve

Two twenty-two Park Avenue might have been one of the towers Eddie had seen from the bridge. It was all steel and glass, joined together at right angles, the top ten or twenty stories disappearing in the clouds. On the sidewalk below lay a man in a soggy blanket. He didn't have a baby, just a sign: "Please help." His eyes met Eddie's. The look in them was as bad as anything Eddie had seen inside. That puzzled him. Out of Holesome Trail Mix, he reached into his pocket and found the $1.55 remaining from his gate money. The man made no move to take it. Eddie laid the money on the blanket, leaving himself with the two hundred-dollar bills, and followed a woman wearing a trench coat and sneakers through a revolving door into the lobby.

The lobby was probably the grandest room he'd ever been in. It had a fountain with water spouting from the mouth of a bearded sea god; a marble floor, marble walls, and a huge chandelier hanging from a ceiling several stories high; and at the far side, gleaming banks of brass elevators. Men and women dressed in suits and carrying briefcases got on and off in a hurry, funneling through a gap between two velvet ropes. Eddie was almost across the lobby when he noticed the two men in chocolate-colored uniforms standing at a desk in the gap between the ropes and realized it was a security check. He stopped dead.

Relax, he told himself. He had passed through thousands of security checks, what was one more? And this one: like a child's notion of security, with the silly uniforms and velvet ropes. Besides, you're a free citizen, not an inmate. So: move. But he didn't want to go through that security check, had to force himself to take those last steps.

"Pass, sir?" said one of the security guards.

"What?"

The security guard's eyes gave him a quick once-over. Eddie understood how he must have appeared in his soaked windbreaker, chinos, sneakers: much closer to the man in the blanket than to the ones with the suits and briefcases.

"You need a pass," said the security guard, dropping the *sir*.

"Don't have one."

"Do you work here?"

"No."

"What's your business?"

Eddie almost replied, "I'm looking for work," before he realized the guard wanted to know what business he had in the building.

"I'm here to see my brother," Eddie said. "He's got an office. Suite 2068."

"One moment. Sir." The guard opened a book. "What name would that be?"

"J. M. Nye," said Eddie. "And Associates."

The guard ran his finger down a page, eyes scanning back and forth. "Don't see it," he said.

"It might be 2086."

"That's not the problem." The guard turned the page. "The problem is there's no J. M. Nye, period. Ring a bell?" he asked the other guard.

"Nope."

The first guard spoke into a portable phone, too quietly for Eddie to hear. He put down the phone, shook his head at Eddie. "Nope."

"I know he was here at one time," Eddie said. "Maybe he's left his new address."

"We don't keep information like that," the guard said, glancing over Eddie's shoulder. "Everybody's always moving. This is New York."

People in suits were jamming up behind Eddie. The chocolate guards, without being aggressive about it, were blocking his way. He wasn't going to get past this play-school security check.

Eddie went back through the grand lobby, through the revolving door, into the street. The man in the blanket noticed him, tried to make eye contact again. But this was New York, where everyone moved. Eddie would have to move too. He kept going.

Eddie had never been in a tower like 222 Park Avenue before, had seldom been in an office building of any kind, but he'd seen a lot of urban-drama type movies in prison, pseudo-experience he now relied on. He walked around the building until he found a parking garage, as he'd expected. He went down the ramp. A man in a glass booth watched him.

"Forgot my briefcase," Eddie said without stopping, the way some actor, Lee Marvin maybe, might have done it.

The elevator door opened just as he got there. A good thing, in case the man in the booth was still watching. Eddie stepped in and pressed number twenty. The door slid closed; the elevator rose, but only to G, where it stopped. The door opened. Two women got on. Beyond them, Eddie could see the security check. One of the guards turned and looked his way. He blinked as the door closed.

The women were well dressed, well groomed, angry inside. Eddie was good at knowing things like that; he'd had to be. The door opened at twelve and the women got out.

"The residuals are a joke," one said.

"No one's laughing," answered the other.

Eddie rode the rest of the way by himself, looking at his bald and damp reflection on polished brass.

Bing. Twenty. The door opened, not, as Eddie had expected, into a corridor, but directly into a reception area hung with paintings, full of flowers. Werner, Pratt, Olmsted, Larch and Groot, read a plaque on the wall, but Eddie had no idea what they did.

A man in a gray-flannel suit, yellow tie, and candy-striped shirt sat at the desk, tapping at a keyboard. "Sir?" he said.

"Is this twenty sixty-eight?" Eddie said.

"I'm afraid not."

"Or maybe twenty eighty-six."

"They don't exist," said the man. "This whole floor is Werner, Pratt. It's simply two thousand."

"My brother's office was here. J. M. Nye. And Associates."

The man looked blank. A phone buzzed. "Excuse me," he said,

picking it up. He was very polite. Eddie wanted to knock his computer off the desk, not hard, just a polite little toppling. Instead, he picked up a phone book lying on the desk, looked up J. M. Nye and J. M. Nye and Associates, found listings for neither. He closed the book. The man on the phone reached for it and tucked it in a drawer.

Eddie returned to the lobby, hopping over the velvet rope on his way out. The security guards didn't notice. Anyone already inside was presumed to be safe. That was another thing that differentiated this security check from the ones Eddie knew.

He stood outside the revolving door, lost in thought. He wasn't aware that he was standing over the man in the blanket until he felt a sharp kick against his ankle. He looked down.

"This is my spot," said the man, not seeming to recognize Eddie at all. "Fuck off."

Eddie didn't like the implication, even though he'd already made the comparison himself, and he didn't like being kicked. He recalled what he had done to the last man who'd kicked him. But Eddie did nothing this time. The man was protected by his blanket and his sign.

An hour and a half later, Eddie was in Brooklyn, standing outside 367 Parchman Avenue. It was a dirty brick building a few stories high, without a homeless man, revolving door, marble lobby, or security check. There was just an outer door and an inner door, with a row of buzzers in the square hall between them. Eddie checked the label on Prof's mailing tube and pressed buzzer three. Nothing happened. He pressed it a few more times, then tried the inner door. It opened.

Number three was at one end of the basement corridor. The corridor was dark and full of smells—fried food, spilled beer, cigarette smoke. TV voices came through the door of number three. Eddie knocked.

"Who is it?" A woman's voice, impatient.

"Ed Nye," Eddie said, and started to add, "a friend of Prof's." The door opened before he could finish.

"I know who you are." The woman was tall and lean. Eddie didn't recognize her at first. She wore a red terrycloth robe, not the reindeer sweater she'd had on in Prof's photograph. She'd also seemed rounder in the photograph, and darker of hair and complexion, at least the way he remembered it. But he wasn't sure how well he remembered it, especially since there'd been a little mixing in his mind of her image and the image of the woman in the porn shot that had been taped beside it.

"Tiffany?" he said.

"That's me." She had dark eyes, intelligent, alert, even excited, he thought, although he didn't know what there was to be excited about.

Eddie searched for some way to begin, found none, said, "Here," and handed her the cardboard tube.

"What's this?"

"From Prof. I said I'd mail it. But I was in New York anyway, so . . ." He took a step back, delaying his departure only to think of the phrase that would take him to *good-bye*.

Tiffany put a hand on his forearm, a long white hand, nails painted red. "You're not running off, are you? You've come all this way. At least I can give you coffee."

"No, thanks."

She didn't remove her hand. "Please. Prof would be really pissed if he found out I didn't even give you coffee."

"Okay," Eddie said. She let go.

He followed her inside. She locked the door, slid two bolts into place. That gave Eddie a bad feeling. Cool it, he told himself.

But the apartment did nothing to take the prison feeling away. For one thing, it was small. No hall, just a kitchen he was already in and a bedroom off it. For another, it had no windows. Light came from a fluorescent strip over the stove and the TV glowing by the unmade bed. It could have been midnight. Those reindeer sweaters had led him to expect something better. He glanced around for some sign of the two kids and saw none.

Eddie sat at the kitchen table. Tiffany boiled water, spooned instant coffee into unmatched cups, poured. Through the bedroom doorway he heard the TV voices.

"Milk and sugar?" asked Tiffany.

"No, thanks."

She came behind him, leaning over to put his cup on the table. He smelled her, felt her breast press lightly against the side of his head. "Back in a sec," she said.

She went into the bedroom, closed the door. Eddie sipped the coffee. That first sip was good. On the second he realized it tasted like prison coffee, the same brand exactly. He drank it anyway, listening to the TV voices, fainter now. He thought he heard Tiffany's voice too, maybe on the phone.

The door opened. Tiffany came out, her hair brushed, smelling of something floral.

"How's the coffee?" she said, sitting down on the other side of the table. It was small, about the size of a café table for two.

"Good."

She added three spoonsful of sugar to her own cup and stirred with her red-tipped finger. "This is great," she said. "I'm glad you came. Really. Having you here is almost like, having him. Isn't that weird?"

Eddie nodded.

"How is he?"

"Doing all right."

"But what's he doing, what's he thinking, what're his plans?"

"He wants to get into politics."

Tiffany started laughing. Eddie laughed too. He stopped when he got the feeling that she had spent some time behind bars herself.

"He's afraid, with you gone," Tiffany said.

"Why?"

"You protected him."

"I didn't."

"Just you being there protected him."

Eddie was silent.

Tiffany twisted in her chair, reached across to the counter for a pack of cigarettes. "Smoke?" she said.

"No, thanks."

"Fifteen years in the pen and you don't smoke?"

"Trying to quit."

She lit up, exhaled a blue cloud. The smell reached Eddie.

"Maybe I will after all," he said.

She regarded him without surprise. "Help yourself."

He lit up too. Big mistake: he knew that right away, but it went so well with the coffee.

"Habits are hard to break," she said. "I sure as hell hope Prof can break some of his."

"Like what?" Eddie didn't want to seem nosy, but he was curious: he'd lived with Prof for a long time. He and Tiffany had Prof in common. He started to feel a little more comfortable in the dark and tiny apartment.

Tiffany took a deep drag, blew smoke through her nose this time. "Like doing stupid things," she replied.

"You mean the documents and stuff?"

She squinted at him. "I mean getting caught. The documents and stuff are his job. How he supports us in the standard of living to which we've become accustomed." She stabbed her cigarette, still mostly unsmoked, into her coffee, still mostly undrunk. It hissed. Eddie couldn't imagine Tiffany in the reindeer sweater at all.

"He's afraid without you," she said, "but he was afraid of you, too."

"Prof?"

"He thinks you're crazy—reading books all the time and killing people."

Eddie felt his face grow hot.

She gave him that narrow-eyed gaze again. "You don't look crazy to me."

Eddie recalled his image in the polished brass of the elevator and realized he probably did look a little crazy. "I'm coming out of it," he said. "I've been in a crazy place for fifteen years."

"That's not the record," she said.

Eddie laughed, tried a joke of his own. "What's your personal best?"

Tiffany glared at him and didn't reply. She picked up the cardboard tube, lying on the table. "Let's see what this is."

She picked the plastic cap off one end, slipped her fingers inside, and withdrew a sheet of scrolled paper, about two feet long. She unrolled it on the table. He felt her go still.

It was a charcoal drawing of a nude woman. She was gazing right into the eyes of the viewer and was unmistakably Tiffany. She was sitting in a kitchen chair, very like the one she sat in now, legs slightly spread and pinching one of her nipples between forefinger and thumb. The drawing seemed professional to Eddie, even artistic. Prof's inscription wasn't in the same class: "To Tiff, from her dirty old man."

Eddie looked up from the drawing to find Tiffany watching him. Their eyes met. She licked her lips. "He'll always be an idiot."

"Is he an idiot?"

"Don't you think so?" In the silence that followed, Eddie and Tiffany didn't take their eyes off each other. "Don't you think so?" she repeated, and opened her robe, just enough to expose one breast. She took the nipple between her red-pointed finger and thumb and pinched, harder than in the drawing, much harder. At the same time she stretched her bare foot underneath that little café table and ran it under Eddie's khaki pants, up his leg.

"Come on, killer."

Tiffany rose, took him by the hand, led him into the bedroom. Eddie hadn't been with a woman in a long time, not since Mandy. The sex he had with her seemed so sweetly innocent now, compared to what was about to happen. It was going to happen. He couldn't stop it. The sight of Tiffany's breast, in life in color and on paper in black and white, the pinched erect nipple, the red fingernails, the knowledge that the cardboard tube he'd been carrying had had this power the whole time, like an amulet in a story or something: all that, combined with fifteen years of loneliness, the different kinds of loneliness, but especially the loneliness of a man for a woman, added up to much more than he could resist.

He went into the bedroom. She helped him strip off the clothes the state had given him. She looked him over.

"He's right to be afraid of you," she said. Even that couldn't stop him.

Outside: Day 3

Chapter Thirteen

Eddie awoke in complete darkness. The phone was ringing.

"Tiffany?" he said.

He felt the space beside him and discovered he was alone. The phone kept ringing. The sound came from somewhere on the other side. He crawled across the bed, reached down for the phone, and knocked the receiver out of its cradle.

A telephone voice, small and faint, spoke from down on the bedroom floor. "Hello? Tiff? Is that you? Tiff?"

It was Prof. Eddie could picture him, standing at the pay phone outside the rec room, other cons in line behind him waiting their turn, not patiently. Eddie fumbled for the receiver, got it in his hand.

"Tiffany?" said Prof.

Eddie hung up.

He got out of bed, moved through the darkness toward the kitchen, stepping over something that felt like satin on the way. He bumped into the stove, ran his hand along the control panel to the light switch, flicked it. The fluorescent strip buzzed on, radiating a tremulous blue-white light. It was an old stove; the clock had hands. They said ten to eleven, but Eddie didn't know if it was day or night.

There was a sandwich on the table and a note beside it. The note read: "Gone to work. Back at noon. Get some rest. You're going to need it. T. Oh yeah—I'm taking your clothes to the cleaners. Sit tight." His possessions—the two hundred-dollar bills and the Speedo—lay on the table too.

The sandwich—white bread, peanut butter and jelly—was not unlike a prison sandwich. Eddie opened the fridge. There wasn't much in it. Ultra Slimfast, a container of yogurt, a pint of milk, two lemons, an unopened bottle of maple syrup. Maple syrup from Vermont. Real. Genuine. Eddie opened it, poured some inside the sandwich. He sat down and ate. Delicious. He filled a table-spoon with maple syrup and had some straight.

The clock on the stove still said ten to eleven.

There was a tiny bathroom off the tiny bedroom, with toilet, sink, and shower stall all jammed together. Eddie had a shower, washing himself with a bar of soap that smelled like a freshly split coconut. After, he opened the bedroom closet. Women's clothes hung from the bar, women's shoes were scattered on the floor. At the back lay a cardboard box that had once contained a twenty-four-inch Gold Star TV. On top was an envelope. Eddie opened it, found ten or twelve blue Social Security cards with no names on them. Underneath were Prof's clothes.

Eddie tried on a blue shirt with yellow parrots, and a T-shirt that read "Rust Never Sleeps—Neil Young 1978," both too small. There was a pair of black Levi's he couldn't get into and baggy corduroys that he could fasten but were four inches too short. He settled for thick gray sweats that looked new—a hooded sweat shirt and drawstring pants with deep pockets at the front and a zippered one in back. Eddie put on Prof's sweats and a nice pair of wool socks he found at the bottom of Prof's box, laced on his own sneakers, stuck the Speedo in a front pocket and zipped the two hundred-dollar bills in the back, and sat down at the table to write Tiffany a good-bye note.

What to say? How to begin? Eddie didn't know. All he knew was that he couldn't stay. Not when the phone could ring at any time with Prof on the other end. What he'd done was wrong, even though Tiffany had been the one to start. All he had to do to know it was wrong was to put himself in Prof's position, and he could do that quite easily. Choosing the right words to tell her was the problem.

Eddie sat at the table, a blank sheet of paper in front of him, a pencil in his hand. He doodled. He doodled a flower, a burning cigarette, a bird. A big bird with an enormous wingspan, gliding over a calm sea.

"Dear Tiffany," he wrote. "I'm—"

There was a knock at the door. Eddie got up, sticking the sheet of paper in his pocket. It was probably noon—it could be anytime at all in Tiffany's little bunker—and that was probably her. Eddie opened the door.

A woman stood outside, but it wasn't Tiffany. This woman had thick black hair, red lips, smooth double-cream-coffee skin, and a voluptuous body under her short fur jacket and tight jeans.

"Whoop-dee-do," she said. "My long-lost high-school graduate."

He remembered her, remembered that mocking voice, remembered her red convertible in the Dunkin' Donuts parking lot and the red jelly spurting from the cop's mouth. But that was down south and now she was here. Meaning? His mind raced to find some meaning.

"Hey, graduate," she said. "You're forgetting your manners."

"Manners?"

"Aren't you going to invite me in? I don't want to stand out here—this place gives me the creeps."

Eddie stepped aside. She walked in. He closed the door.

"What a dump," she said, looking around. She circled the tiny space like a big cat. Prof's charcoal drawing lay on the kitchen counter. She examined it.

"Naughty, naughty."

Then she glanced into the bedroom at the unmade bed, smiled as though amused by some private joke, and said, "So, Mr. Eddie Nye, a.k.a. Nails—are you going to play ball this time, or hard to get?"

"What do you want?" Eddie replied, remembering the way Tiffany had gone into the bedroom soon after his arrival, and how he'd heard her voice mixed in with the TV voices. The prison, so rigid when he was in, reached out elastically when he was out.

"Dyslexic," said the woman with the double-cream-coffee complexion. "I forgot." She sat down at the table, brushed away crumbs with her beringed fingers. "We had a date, *chico*," she said, mouth smiling, eyes not. "Arranged by a mutual friend. Arranged and paid for, if you're going to make me spell it out, by this mutual friend. Blink twice if you get it."

Eddie got it. "It's the money."

"Wow. You're something, you know that? Yes, *chico*, it's the money. You weren't trying to abscond with it, were you, like some little sneak thief?"

Eddie didn't like that. She could see that, but it didn't seem to impress her at all. "I didn't even know it was there till I tried to smoke that cigarette. You and El Rojo or whatever he calls himself are the ones playing games."

She studied his face for a moment or two, then nodded. "That's what they thought."

"Who?"

"It was all a mistake. No rough stuff necessary."

"Rough stuff?"

"Nothing to worry about. Not necessary."

The phone rang in the bedroom. Eddie let it ring. The woman watched him letting it, the mocking look in her eyes. It rang for a long time. When it stopped she said: "Have you still got it?"

Eddie unzipped the back pocket of Prof's sweats and handed her one of his hundred-dollar bills. She stuck it inside her fur jacket.

"I love happy endings," she said.

"What's this all about?"

"You already know the answer. Money."

Eddie didn't believe that El Rojo would go to so much trouble over a hundred dollars. Some matter of principle was involved, macho Latin bullshit principle or crazy inmate bullshit principle.

"Just money?" Eddie said.

"That's right," she replied. "Now how about our date?"

"What date?"

"*Madre de dios.* The date that's paid for."

Eddie laughed. He was laughing a lot all of a sudden. "We didn't sign a contract," he said. "I'll let you wriggle out of it."

The woman wasn't laughing. "You're not very bright, for a high-school graduate. There's no wriggling out where our friend's concerned."

She paused to let this sink in. Eddie thought of their long-faced friend in the prison library pushing away the bloodied *Business Week* with distaste, and tried unsuccessfully to see the danger in him. Then he remembered how those liquid brown eyes had reminded him of maple syrup, and felt a tiny wave of nausea.

"So let's roll," the woman said. "I've got a car outside."

Eddie didn't want to go on a date; on the other hand, he had to get out of Tiffany's apartment, and a car was waiting. He turned over the sheet of paper with the doodles on it and wrote, "Thanks." What else? Didn't he owe Tiffany some explanation? Then he remembered her phone call, the one that had brought this woman. Maybe he didn't owe her anything.

Meanwhile the woman was on her feet. "There's nothing to say—don't you know that by now?" She dropped an envelope on the table. It was a thin-papered envelope; Eddie could see that there was money inside. "Let's roll," said the woman.

Eddie tore up the note, tossed it in the trash, and followed her out the door. They walked down the dark basement corridor, through the entrance hall, outside.

It was night. Late night, to judge from the quiet. Eddie was wide awake and disoriented at the same time. The state had regulated his sleeping patterns for fifteen years; now that he was on his own they were falling apart.

"God, you're slow," said the woman, crossing the street toward a silver sedan. She unlocked the door and they got in. "Ow," she said, reached into her waistband, pulled out a gun, and laid it on the seat between them. "These things are so uncomfortable." She started the car and zoomed away from the curb without looking. Eddie fastened his seat belt.

"Don't trust my driving?" she said, speeding up.

"I don't trust anyone with a gun."

She laughed. "You're going to be a very lonely guy."

She drove into a tunnel, emerged by a river, cut down a side street and double-parked outside a club called L'Oasis. The clock on the dashboard read two-ten, but twenty or thirty people who had given some thought to what they wore were waiting to get in. The woman went straight to the head of the line where a big man wearing sunglasses stood with folded arms. He smiled when he saw her.

"Well, well," he said. "Sookray. The night is young."

"Bullshit," said the woman. "And I'm freezing my ass off out here. Let me in."

The door was an elaborate affair of leather and studs. The big man swung it open, saw Eddie coming and held up a hand.

"He's with me," Sookray told him; and Eddie, in Prof's gray sweats, followed her inside.

They climbed over a furrowed sand dune and down to an oasis— date palms, soft breezes, a pool of still water. Chairs and tables ringed the pool. Beyond lay the casbah, with a bar at the bottom and a restaurant behind the battlements on top. There was a minaret too. An oil-smeared man wearing Ali Baba pants stood in it, swallowing fire.

Sookray sat at an empty table, kicked off her shoes, dipped her feet in the water. She patted the chair beside her. Eddie sat.

"Care for a swim?" she said.

"Had one."

A harem girl appeared with champagne. Sookray sent it back. The harem girl returned with a different brand.

"*Salud,*" said Sookray, raising her glass.

Eddie drank. It was bliss: more than the equivalent of Holesome Trail Mix, infinitely more. His mind returned at once to the dinner at Galleon Beach.

"We can have sex later, if you want," Sookray said. "It's all paid for."

"Thanks anyway."

"Really. I don't mind. You're kind of attractive, except for that shaved-head shit. I just hate that look. You might as well wave your cock around, you know?"

Caviar came next, followed by a spicy pie made with pigeons, and other dishes Eddie didn't know. He ate every scrap. Then there was more champagne. Music played, very loud. People danced on the battlements.

"Dance?" said Sookray.

Eddie shook his head. He had a good buzz going, but he was still too sober to want to shake around up there in gray sweats, next to all those fancy people. He refilled their glasses instead.

After a while the music stopped. The dancers returned to the restaurant, the bar, the tables around the pool. One of the dancers approached theirs.

He was a fat-faced man in a dark silk suit. He sat down uninvited and patted his forehead with a white handkerchief. A big diamond nested on his hairy pinky. Sookray took her feet out of the water and put her shoes back on.

"This is Señor Paz," she said. "Mr. Nye."

Señor Paz nodded but didn't offer his hand. He took out a cigar, cut off the end with a gold cutter, lit up with a gold lighter.

"Having a good time, Mr. Nye?" he asked after he had the cigar burning nicely.

"Till Rommel rolls through with his panzers."

The corners of Paz's mouth turned briefly up.

"Is that the new band?" Sookray asked. "I heard they were hot."

Paz ignored her. "Enjoy," he said, waving his hand around the oasis. "It will all be gone tomorrow, nothing more than an alcoholic dream."

"Why is that?" said Eddie.

"Business. We do a redesign every two years. Frankly, it can't come too soon. I'm so sick of climbing that dune I cannot tell you. We're going with virtual reality next time. The name will be either Synapse or Neuron, I can't decide."

"Do you run the place?"

"Own it, actually. Although I'm a surgeon by profession, training—and inclination."

Sookray frowned. Paz noticed and said, "You don't look well, my dear. Would you like to rest for a while? Some aspirin, perhaps?"

"I'm fine," said Sookray, sitting up straighter.

"Good. More champagne, then." He snapped his fingers. A harem girl arrived at once. "Champagne," he said. "Krug Grande Cuvée." She went off. "The only champagne worth drinking," he said to Eddie. "For a man. All the rest are just fizz, suitable for women and children." He looked at Sookray. She looked down.

The harem girl arrived with new glasses and a new bottle. She popped the cork and poured. Paz covered his glass when she came to him. He rose and knocked a cylinder of cigar ash into the pool.

"Glad to have met you, Mr. Nye. And glad we've cleared up our little misunderstanding." He started away.

"Who is *we?*" Eddie said.

Paz stopped, turned, smiled. "And especially glad it was just that—a misunderstanding." He went away.

Eddie emptied his glass. "He's right."

"About what?" said Sookray.

"Krug. It's the best." He refilled his glass. Two days ago—or was it there?—he'd been eating shit and drinking swill. Now he was eating caviar and drinking the best champagne in the world. A thrill went through him, strong and physical: he felt his freedom through and through. It made him want to move.

"Who are the Panzers?" asked Sookray.

"They were hot in their day," Eddie replied. "How about that dance?"

Sookray shook her head.

"I thought it was paid for."

"If you insist," she said.

Eddie gave her a closer look: he'd only been joking. He saw that the mockery had gone out of her eyes; they were dull and tired. Her body too had lost its vitality. She sagged in her chair.

"I don't insist," Eddie said.

Sookray smiled at him, a little smile, almost shy. "You can come home with me, if you keep it a secret."

"A secret from who?"

Sookray's eyes darted in the direction Paz had gone but she replied, "Just a secret in general."

Eddie smiled back. "Forget it."

"You don't want me?"

"It's not that."

"Because I'm a whore."

"No," Eddie said, although that was probably part of it. The rest of it had to do with Paz; and El Rojo.

"How do you know El Rojo?" Eddie asked.

Her eyes narrowed and all at once were wide awake. "Who said I knew him?"

"He's our mutual friend, remember?"

Sookray said nothing.

"What's his relationship to Paz?" Eddie looked around. "Does El Rojo own this place?"

Sookray bit her lip. "I don't feel very well," she said. "Do you mind if I go to the bathroom?"

"Of course not."

Sookray left. A harem girl arrived with more Krug.

"I don't think we ordered that," Eddie said.

"Drink up," said the harem girl. "It's all on the house."

Eddie drank up. Soon—at least Eddie thought it was soon—a beautiful woman—at least Eddie thought she was beautiful, although he wasn't seeing too clearly—asked him to dance and he said yes. He wanted to dance with Sookray, but more than that he wanted to dance.

Eddie and the woman went up on the battlements and danced. He forgot about Sookray. He and the woman—she had platinum hair and taut skin everywhere but under her chin—drank another bottle or two of champagne. After that they set out across the sand. They rolled around on the dune for a while. There was some kissing, some more champagne. A crescent moon floated over the desert and the sky filled with stars. The shadow of a huge bird passed overhead. The oasis grew darker and darker, the moon and stars brighter and brighter, the music louder and louder. The bass boomed through the earth with a seismic beat.

"I'm free," Eddie shouted into the woman's ear; taking up where he'd left off fifteen years before, having fun on the sand and winning races in the water.

She laughed hysterically. "Me too. We're both free, free as the fucking wind." She bit his ear.

Chapter Fourteen

Eddie awoke at the base of a date palm, his face in the sand. He felt like someone who had been wandering in a real desert: head pounding, mouth parched, cells dessicated.

He was alone. Sookray and Paz, the harem girls and the fire eater, the crescent moon and the skyful of stars: all gone. The dancers were gone too, and the music was over. The only light, an orange glow, came from inside the casbah. The only sound was the trickling of water. Eddie rose, steadying himself on the date palm. It tipped over and fell to the sand with a soft papier-mâché crunch. Eddie followed the trickling sound down to the pool.

The pool was round, with irregular edges that might have been found in nature, and muddy banks. The trickling sound came from a fountain in the shape of a silver breast that hung over the other side. Eddie walked around the pool, stuck his finger into the flow and tasted the water. Unlike the date palm, the water was real; cold and metallic, but drinkable. Eddie lowered his head and drank.

And felt a little better almost at once. He stripped off the sweats. Two or three cigarette butts floated in the pool, but it smelled clean. Eddie lowered himself in. The water came almost to his waist, just deep enough. He pushed off and began a slow lazy crawl.

The movement and the coldness of the water got his blood going. The fog of alcohol lifted from his mind, and the headache soon went with it. Eddie swam back and forth across the pool until he grew tired of making all the turns. Then he climbed out, dried himself with a cloth napkin from one of the tables, dressed. Time to go. He walked over the dune and onto the flat stretch of sand that led to the studded leather door.

It was locked. Locked from the inside, like a cell.

Eddie went back across the sand, past the pool, into the casbah. He entered a bar called Le Chameau Insolite. It had whitewashed walls, Persian rugs, plush divans, mosaic tiles. Behind the bar was a swinging door on which hung a calendar where the year was 1372. Eddie pushed through it, into a stainless-steel kitchen of his own era and civilization.

A man in coveralls was piling green-plastic garbage bags on a trolley. He saw Eddie and said: "Are you the new guy?"

"No."

"Then where the fuck is he?" The man waved his hand through the air, accidently striking the trolley. The bags slid off and tumbled on the floor.

"That's all I fuckin' needed," the man said, giving the nearest bag a murderous kick with his work boot. Lobster tails and champagne bottles sagged through the hole he made. The phone on the wall started ringing. He snatched at it, barked, "What is it?" listened for a few seconds, cried out, "That's what he always says," and banged down the phone. He glanced down at the garbage bags, stopped himself from kicking them again, turned to Eddie.

"Wanna make a quick twenty bucks, buddy? Or thirty?"

"Doing what?"

"My job. I've got to do some other asshole's."

The job: bagging the night's garbage, piling it on the trolley, wheeling the trolley out the kitchen, down a long hall, into a freight elevator, up to a loading bay, out to a gray-dawn street. It took three trips. When Eddie returned from the last one, the man, now dressed in a tuxedo, was on the phone again.

"All done," Eddie told him.

Without looking at him, the man offered a twenty.

"What happened to thirty?" Eddie said.

"Jesus," said the man. "No, not you, him," he said into the phone, adding a five. "Everybody wants everything," he said. He raised his voice. "Not you, I said. Him. Him. Him."

Eddie took the bills, zipped them into his back pocket next to the hundred, and left, out through the loading bay. "Out there you got to earn it," Dr. Messer, Director of Treatment, had warned. He was making it hand over fist.

A cold wind was snapping at the tops of the garbage bags and blowing scraps down the street. This wasn't the same street where Sookray had double-parked the night before, but a narrower, meaner one, lined with soot-covered buildings. Eddie raised the hood on his sweatshirt, tied it tight, and walked off with the wind at his back.

After a few blocks he came to a used bookstore. It had a faded sign, a dusty window, and a bin of twenty-five-cent paperbacks outside. Eddie paused and went through them. Westerns, science fiction, horror: all faded and yellowed, as though the paper were in the process of recycling itself. At the back of the bin, behind a copy of *We the Savage Reapers*, he came to a slim volume with a red-and-black cover. *Monarch Notes: "The Rime of the Ancient Mariner."*

Eddie took it inside.

A bell tinkled as he went in. The store was dark and narrow, lined with books from floor to ceiling. A boy stood on a stepladder at the back. Half-a-dozen books lay on the top step, waiting to be shelved, but the boy, balanced on the ladder, had his nose deep in another one: *The Codebreakers*. He didn't seem to have heard the bell.

The floor creaked under Eddie's feet. The boy heard that and looked up from his book. The sight of Eddie made his eyes widen; afraid simply of his size and appearance.

Eddie held up the book. "I'd like to buy this," he said, trying to make his voice sound gentle.

The boy climbed down off the ladder. He was short and thin, almost scrawny, and wore a skullcap.

"Twenty-five cents," he said.

Eddie gave him the five-dollar bill. The boy went to the desk at the front of the store, opened a drawer, and got change. He handed it to Eddie. Perhaps the fact that Eddie had turned out to be a customer rather than a hold-up man gave him the courage to say, "We've got the genuine article for a dollar, if you want it."

"The genuine article?"

"The poem. 'The Rime of the Ancient Mariner.' Paperback, but in good condition. What you've got there is just a crib."

"I know the poem already."

The boy blinked. "You know it?"

Eddie recited the first thirteen stanzas. For a few lines he was hesitant; then the story took over, using his voice but passing through him without any act of his own will. All fear, and even some of the shyness, left the boy's eyes. Eddie stopped after

> And ice, mast-high, came floating by,
> As green as emerald.

Not that it seemed a good place to stop. But it reminded Eddie of the ice on the river in his hometown, and broke the flow of the poetry through him.

"So what do you want the *Monarch* for?" the boy asked. His voice cracked.

"I've got some questions."

"Like?"

Like. Eddie recalled his unsuccessful discussion with Ram Pontoppidan, but he tried again. "Like why he shoots the albatross in the first place."

The boy didn't laugh at him. Instead he looked worried. "You won't find the answer to questions like that in the *Monarch*."

"Why not?"

"Because they just want to make sure you pass the test."

"So?"

"Questions like that aren't on the test."

"What kind of questions are on the test?"

"Show how Coleridge uses repetition in 'The Rime of the Ancient Mariner' to reinforce theme. That kind of thing."

Eddie knew he could think of many examples of repetition in "The Mariner"—"Day after day, day after day / We stuck, nor breath nor motion / As idle as a painted ship / Upon a painted ocean"—came to mind right away—but he didn't know what the theme was, wasn't even sure of the definition of theme. It was quiet in the bookstore; the books might have been silent living things, like plants.

The boy spoke: "It's about penance and redemption, right? I mean, he's not exactly subtle about it."

"Who isn't?"

The boy looked surprised. "Coleridge."

Another pause. Eddie had given a lot of thought to the Mariner's motives, but none to the poet's. He said: "Penance for killing the albatross?"

"Yes. But it didn't have to be an albatross, or killing at all, for that matter. It could be anything. The albatross is just a device, the MacGuffin."

"The MacGuffin?"

"Like in *Psycho*—the fact that the motel guy was abused by his mother or whatever it was. The secret that gets the plot going; useful, but not the reason you keep watching."

"Killing the albatross is just a device?"

The boy nodded.

Didn't that make the whole question of why the mariner did it irrelevant? There had to be more to the story than that. The boy was smart, much smarter than he was, but Eddie wasn't buying his explanation. He gazed out the dusty window, closing in on the thought that would show the boy he was wrong. Outside two men went by in a hurry. One was Eddie's employer in the tuxedo. The other was Señor Paz.

Eddie went to the window, looked down the sidewalk. The two men turned onto a busy street at the end of the block and disappeared in the crowd. For a moment Eddie had the crazy thought that they were looking for him. He'd drunk all that champagne, eaten caviar, and hadn't paid a bill. But there hadn't been a bill, had there? It was all on the house. Eddie relaxed.

The boy was sitting at the desk, tapping at the computer keyboard. After a few moments, the printer whined on, unscrolled two or three pages. The boy tore them off, handed them to Eddie.

It was a list of reference books on "The Mariner." "These might help," the boy said. "They're all in the library."

Eddie took the list, looked down at the boy. He had hollow cheeks, pimples, a wispy mustache, didn't even seem healthy. Eddie liked him more than anyone he'd met in a long time.

"How come you're not in school?" Eddie said.

All the talk had relaxed the boy. He blurted, "Are you the truant officer?"

Eddie laughed. "Do I look like a truant officer?"

The boy started to answer, stopped himself.

"Go on," Eddie said.

The boy licked his lips. "You look like a hit man."

"A step up from the truant officer," Eddie said. But he stopped laughing.

The boy saw that and quickly gave the straight answer. "No school today. It's a holiday."

"It is?"

"Purim," the boy said.

"I don't know that one," Eddie said.

"Esther saving her people," the boy said. "We bake these to celebrate." He picked up a bowl containing three-cornered pastries and offered one to Eddie.

Dry, and tasting of poppy seeds: not nearly as good as Ram's Holesome Trail Mix. Eddie ate it; he didn't want to hurt the boy's feelings. He was a smart boy, good with books; good at finding information.

"I'm looking for someone," Eddie said.

"To bump off? Sorry."

"You've been seeing too many movies."

"I don't see any movies. I'm not allowed."

"Why not?"

"Bad influence." The boy smiled to show he thought the restriction was silly but he wasn't chafing under it; a nice smile that made him seem stronger, less undernourished. Eddie pictured him for a moment in jail; the image turned his stomach.

"Maybe I could help," the boy said.

"How?"

"I've got access to all sorts of directories." He sat at the computer. "The phone book is primitive compared to what this can do. What's the name?"

"J. M. Nye. And Associates."

"Type of business?"

Eddie wasn't sure. They tried stockbroker, tax adviser, financial consultant, investment counselor. It took fifteen minutes.

The boy read from the screen. "J. M. Nye, president, Windward Financial Services." The address was a suite in the Hotel Palazzo. "Very upscale," said the boy, giving Eddie the printout.

"What do I owe you?" Eddie said.

"Nothing."

Eddie found himself wishing he had some Holesome Trail Mix to give him. But he didn't, so he just said, "Thanks," and walked to the door. He opened it, letting in a cold gust of wind, then paused.

"I've got an idea about the albatross," he said.

"What's that?"

"It doesn't ask anybody for anything."

"Go on," said the boy; there was excitement in his eyes.

"That's why he kills it."

"Very Christian," the boy said. He thought. Eddie watched him. The wind blew into the bookstore. After a minute or two, the boy shook his head and said, "The text doesn't support your theory."

"Meaning?"

"It's just the MacGuffin. Sorry."

Chapter Fifteen

The boy told Eddie how to use the subway. It was easy. You sat in a metal box packed with unhappy people. Eddie was an expert. The motion made it almost pleasant. He opened his *Monarch Notes*, and on a coffee-stained page found this:

> There is no explanation at all given of why the Mariner chooses the person he does to hear his story. In fact, the poem is full of actions and events that are left unexplained; indeed one may say that a principle theme in "The Rime of the Ancient Mariner" is the ambiguity and ultimate mysteriousness of motive. The central crime of the poem, the Mariner's killing of the Albatross, is a crime capriciously committed.

Eddie reread the paragraph twice. The boy had been right: he wasn't going to find the answer in the *Monarch*. Two things bothered him. One: Why should motives be ambiguous while consequences were so clear? That made it impossible for him to accept the *Monarch*'s explanation of the killing. Two: He didn't know the meaning of *capriciously*. He thought he had figured it out from the context but wasn't sure, and therefore wasn't sure he understood the passage.

Eddie turned to the woman beside him. She was reading a book called *Violence and Seduction: The Praxis of Patriarchy*.

"Excuse me," Eddie said. She'd have the definition on the tip of her tongue.

The woman looked at him.

"Can you tell me what *capriciously* means?"

She got up and moved to the other end of the car.

Wearing Prof's sweats with his lost-and-found Speedo, the *Monarch*, the boy's printout, and $124.75 in the pockets, Eddie walked into the Hotel Palazzo. He'd learned a little from his visit to L'Oasis, enough to understand this was just another stage set. But there was nothing papier-mâché here. The make-believe was as real as it could be, and the play promised to run forever.

Richly dressed people sat around the lobby in chairs almost as finely covered as they were. A Japanese woman in a black dress played the violin. Waiters glided by bearing trays of glittering glasses. Everything was lit with a golden light. A perfect world.

No one seemed to notice Eddie. Maybe they thought that just by being there he was perfect too, a millionaire returning from a morning jog, on his way upstairs where a wardrobe full of finery awaited. Eddie, in the role of the jogging millionaire, walked to the elevator as though he had a right to be there and rode up to the ninth floor.

He stepped into a hall that smelled of flowers. Sounds were muted, the carpet creamy and thick. As he moved along it, Eddie forgot how to play the jogging millionaire; he degenerated quickly into someone else, some lesser character, not even up to his own level, a short-of-breath character with a heart beating too fast and too light, like some cheap overwound tinny thing. A character who was light-headed when he reached his brother's door.

There was no sign saying Windward Financial Services, nothing but a number and brass knocker. Eddie stood outside the door in that hushed hall that smelled like a garden in spring, the sole sound the pulse in his ears. He faced the thought that had risen in his mind, demanding recognition: turn back. Eddie knew that turning back was the right thing to do. Fifteen years was too long, those fifteen years especially. The building itself sent the message. Leave it, leave town, leave the past completely: Eddie knew that with certainty. But his hand went to the knocker anyway, raised it and knocked. The tinny thing inside him was under the control of something more powerful than logic.

Ten or fifteen seconds passed. Maybe no one was inside, maybe the bookstore boy's information was wrong, maybe—

The door opened. On the other side stood a big man in a pinstripe suit. He wore half glasses, had graying hair, a fleshy face, a thickened body. It took Eddie a few moments to see Jack somewhere inside him.

"Yes?" Jack said.

"Jack." There was mist in the air all of a sudden, blurring his vision, the way it had blurred as the white station wagon drove him out of prison. None of that, Eddie told himself, and made it go away. "Jack. It's me."

Jack took off his half glasses and stared. "Oh, my God." He covered his heart. "Oh, my God."

And next? Eddie was ready for a handshake, an embrace. Neither happened. Jack looked over his shoulder. At a coffee table in the room behind him sat a blond woman in a gray-flannel suit, a little coffee cup in her hand; there was a French name for it that Eddie couldn't remember. She was straining to see who was outside.

"Eddie. Jesus." Jack turned to the woman. "One second, Karen," he said. Then he stepped out into the hall, half closing the door behind him.

Jack glanced up and down the hall. He had a little pouch of fat under his chin. "You're not . . ."

"Not what?"

"On the lam, or anything?"

On the lam. Was this an attempt to speak the language he thought Eddie's? The tiny and archaic phrase measured the enormity between them. Eddie almost laughed. "I've paid my debt to society," he said with a straight face. As long as they were going to talk silly.

Jack got it. He smiled. Jack had changed a lot, but his smile was the same: a flash that promised fun, lots of it and slightly dangerous. "You son of a bitch," he said.

Then came the embrace. They threw their arms around each other. Jack was still big and strong, but now there was some softness to his body. He shook a little. Eddie realized Jack was crying. Walking down the hall he'd been close to crying too. Now it was an impossibility.

They separated. Jack held him at arm's length. "You look good, Eddie."

"Yeah."

"How are you?"

"All right."

"You're in shape."

"Yeah."

"How are you?"

"All right."

"God, I'm glad to hear that." Jack looked into the room.

"Have I come at a bad time?" Eddie asked.

"So what's new?"

Jack laughed. Eddie didn't.

Jack wiped his mouth with the back of his hand. "I've got a client, that's all. Come in, if you don't mind waiting in the bedroom. I'd get rid of her, but I've been trying to sew this deal up for months. It won't be long."

"I can come back, if you like."

"Come back?" Jack said. "Bro!" And he wrapped his arm around Eddie's neck in that old familiar lock, half dragging him into the room.

"Karen," he said, letting Eddie go. "I want you to meet someone very special to me—my brother, Eddie. Eddie, Karen de Vere."

"A pleasure," the woman said. She wore tortoiseshell glasses; behind their lenses her eyes were cool blue.

"Eddie's just dropped in from out of town," Jack said. "Rather unexpectedly, but that's Eddie." He moved Eddie toward the bedroom. The *Monarch* fell out of Eddie's pocket. The woman leaned forward in her chair to see what it was. Eddie stooped to pick it up.

"Where do you live, Eddie?" the woman asked.

Jack was watching him. "Upstate," Eddie said.

"Whereabouts?" said the woman. "I'm from upstate myself."

Buffalo? Syracuse? Were those considered upstate, or did the term refer only to the towns near New York? Eddie wasn't sure. "Albany," he said.

"I've got a lot of friends there," the woman said. "I grew up on a farm near Troy."

Jack said: "It's a small world." Then, to Eddie: "We won't be too long. Help yourself to the minibar. Within reason." He smiled, to show the woman that it was a joke, and Eddie was a bit of a character.

Eddie went into Jack's bedroom. He heard the woman say, "He sounds just like you." The door closed behind him.

Except for all the electronic equipment, Jack's bedroom reminded Eddie of a movie he'd seen in the inmates' rec room, a movie where a bitter couple lived in luxury and said nasty things to each other. And then there was the equipment: four computer terminals, three phones, a printer, and what he assumed to be a fax machine; even as he watched, it dropped a sheet of paper into a tray. He glanced at it: all numbers and abbreviations, incomprehensible to him.

Eddie looked out the window. Jack had a view of Central Park. The landscape was brown, with a few gray patches of snow here and there. Rain was falling again, billowing past in long curving patterns. Down below, dull-colored people beetled along like characters in a computer game.

Warm and dry, all city sounds muffled, Eddie watched them for a while. This was nice. He opened the minibar, found beer and wine and a carton of orange juice at the back. "Not from concentrate. Shake first for better taste." He sat in a gilded chair, shook the carton, drank from it. Delicious. One of the computer screens flashed a message about Vestron dividends. The fax machine slid out another sheet. Eddie got up and looked at it. This one was from the Mount Olive Extended Care Residence and Spa in Darien, Connecticut. "Dear Mr. Nye: Please call re your account." Then came another fax full of numbers and abbreviations.

A copy of the *Financial Times* lay on the couch. Eddie picked it up and started reading. In this room it began to make sense. Eddie recalled El Rojo poring over *Business Week*. He and Jack could probably have found a lot to talk about. Eddie couldn't imagine Jack at the steel table in the prison library, but he could easily picture El Rojo in a room like this. El Rojo probably had whole houses like it in Colombia, or on the Riviera, or some other fancy place Eddie had encountered in his reading. That would make living in that cell in C-block all the more unbearable. Eddie recalled the picture of El Rojo's son, the dead shot in the cowboy outfit—Gaucho, wasn't it, and hadn't he had some other name too?—and found himself admiring El Rojo's stoicism, his self-control. Of all the inmates Eddie had known, he'd had the most to lose; and he'd lost it.

At that moment, Gaucho's real name came to him: Simon. After the Liberator.

Jack entered the room. "What's that?" he said.

Eddie realized he'd spoken "the Liberator" aloud. "Nothing."

Jack had a check in his hand. He stuck it inside his jacket pocket, gazed at Eddie, shook his head. "This is something," he said. "Really something. I'm having trouble believing it's true. That you're here, and everything."

"Me too."

Jack laughed. "The same old Eddie."

"No."

"No, of course not. Sorry. How are you, really?"

Before Eddie could reply, the fax produced another document. Jack went over, scanned it quickly—more than quickly, almost with the speed of a character in a silent movie—checked the other faxes in the tray, checked the computer screens, turned.

"Hungry? I'm going to order up some lunch. Or do you want to go out?"

Eddie wasn't hungry. The bookstore boy's little three-cornered pastry had somehow filled him up. "Whatever you like," he said.

"Let's eat in," Jack said. "Give us more time. There's so much I want to ask you. This is just so . . ." Words failed him. He smiled helplessly, then flipped Eddie a menu and sat down at the desk. "Just one sec." He began tapping on a keyboard.

"What are you doing?" Eddie asked.

"Hedging."

Eddie studied the menu. Many choices, many foreign words, prices he wasn't prepared for. "I'll have whatever you're having."

"Pasta salad okay?" Jack asked, reaching for the phone. It buzzed before he could pick it up. He answered, listened, then rose and began pacing back and forth as far as the phone cord permitted, as though it were a leash. "That wasn't our agreement," he said. "They're asking the impossible." He listened, paced.

"You'd better not be," he said, his voice rising. Eddie could hear a tiny voice protesting on the other end. Jack hung up.

He glanced at Eddie, stopped pacing, composed himself. "Everything you've read about those pricks is true," he said. "Just like bloodsuckers except they do it for pleasure. The money has nothing to do with it."

"What pricks?"

"Wall Street pricks." Jack snapped off his tie. He quickly undressed down to boxer shorts and knee-length socks, threw open a huge closet full of clothes. His body had grown top-heavy, his legs thinner. They were trembling slightly. He selected a new shirt, new tie, new suit, all of which looked almost identical to what he'd had on before, and began putting them on. Eddie followed every move, fascinated as a neophyte allowed in the master's studio; or like a boy watching his father.

"Got to pass on lunch," Jack said, knotting his new tie in a quick fluid pinwheel of navy and crimson. "Just order up whatever you want. Or call Hector, he's the concierge. I'll be back as soon as I can." He hurried through the bedroom door, came right back. "It's great to have you here," he said. "Just great. We'll celebrate tonight." He left, returned again. "Sorry I have to run off—I'm so excited about this I can't tell you." He went, came back once more. "Don't bother answering the phone—the machine'll take it." Then he was gone.

Eddie sat on the gilded chair in Jack's bedroom. He didn't order food because he wasn't hungry, didn't drink from the minibar because he'd drunk too much at L'Oasis, didn't go out because he was afraid he might have trouble getting back in. To make himself useful, he picked Jack's suit off the floor and carried it to the closet. He folded the pants, hung them on a wooden hanger, slid the jacket on top. He was about to hook the hanger over the rail when he remembered the check Jack had stuck in the inside pocket. He reached for it out of curiosity, just wanting to see.

It was a check drawn on the Banque de Genève et Zurich, made out to Windward Financial Services, signed by Karen de Vere. The amount was $230,000. Eddie put it back.

The phone rang. Eddie didn't pick it up. A voice said: "Mr. Nye. This is the billing department. Please call to discuss your account at your earliest convenience." Eddie returned to the closet and looked at the check again.

He went into the sitting room, sat down on the couch where Karen de Vere had been. The cushions were still warm from her body; very slightly, but he could feel it. There were a lot of papers spread out on the coffee table. Some bore the letterhead of Windward Financial Services, some were the prospectuses of companies listed on the stock exchange, some had nothing on them but more numbers and abbreviations. Going through them, Eddie discovered a glossy brochure with Jack's picture on the cover.

Jack was standing in front of 222 Park Avenue: the number was visible behind him. His hair was a little darker and thicker, his face a little darker and thinner, and he was smiling his smile. Eddie opened the brochure and began reading.

He learned a lot about his brother: how he was the president and founder of Windward Financial Services, one of the top-ten small financial consultancies in the nation, according to *Crain's New York Business* (1990); how before that he had been the president and founder of J. M. Nye and Associates, a private investment firm that had specialized in trading high-yield bonds in the eighties, and had been acquired by a Belgian conglomerate (1988); how he had houses in Connecticut and Aspen; how he and his wife were skiers and golfers; how he'd graduated from USC with a degree in engineering.

Eddie stopped right there. He checked the graduation date: three years after the summer at Galleon Beach, which was when Jack would have graduated had he stayed in school.

But he hadn't, had he? He'd left during his freshman year. Maybe he'd gone back, somehow made up the work he'd missed, graduated on schedule. Then Eddie recalled that Jack hadn't left USC, exactly. He remembered the letter he'd found in Jack's cabin at Galleon Beach, remembered what he hadn't understood at the time and had almost forgotten: Jack had been expelled, permanently.

Meaning what? He didn't know; didn't know enough about how the world worked to even guess. He flipped on the TV. Wile E. Coyote lost his balance and fell off a cliff.

Chapter Sixteen

Although he had never been to France, Eddie dreamed he was in a French café. The elements of the dream: a little cup of the type Karen de Vere had held in her lap—in his dream he remembered it was called *demitasse;* snails dripping with garlic butter; blue smoke. He smelled smoke—even as he smelled it wondering if the smell had triggered the dream: didn't dreams pass in seconds?—and opened his eyes.

It was dark. He lay on the couch in the sitting room of Jack's suite at the Hotel Palazzo. The night glow of the city came through the window. The only other light was a red cigarette end moving back and forth along the opposite wall.

"Jack?"

The tiny red light was still. "Did I wake you?"

"What time is it?"

"Late. Sorry."

"No problem. Did you sort out whatever it was?"

"Partly."

The red light began moving again, back and forth.

"Do you live here, Jack?"

"It's where I lay my weary head." No mention of Aspen or Connecticut.

Eddie sat up. The smell was irresistible. "Got another cigarette?"

"You smoke?"

"Trying to quit. It's prong one of my three-pronged plan."

There was a soft smack on the coffee table—the cigarette pack; and a softer one—the matches. Eddie lit up.

"I give up," said Jack.

"About what?"

"Prongs two and three."

"Steam bath, which I haven't had yet. And take nothing with me."

"Did you?"

"I took my sneakers," Eddie said. But he knew the break hadn't been as clean as that. There was El Rojo's hundred dollars, for starters. That had led to Sookray and Señor Paz. Then there was Prof's charcoal drawing. That had led to Tiffany, who was in contact with Sookray. He hadn't made a clean break at all; his old community reached out for him.

"Still wear a ten?" Jack asked.

"Yeah."

"There're boxes of tens around here somewhere. Jogging, tennis, loafers, Christ knows what else. I've got this personal shopper, don't ask me why. Take what you want."

The red-tip glow kept moving, back and forth.

Eddie said: "You got rich."

Jack made a sound, half laughter, half choking on cigarette smoke. "Rich? What's rich?"

"This place. Boxes of shoes. Personal shopper, whatever that is." A check for $230,000 left in a jacket on the floor.

"That's not rich, Eddie. Rich is never having to worry about money. Never having to think about it. Just living in it, like the air you breathe."

"Is Bobby rich?"

"Bobby?"

"Falardeau. He says he's set for life."

The red light stopped, brightened, moved on.

"You went home?"

"Yeah."

"Saw Bobby?"

"And Vic."

"What made you do that?"

"Bobby I ran into. Vic . . . I don't know."

"He's a pathetic drunk."

"The whole town's kind of pathetic now."

"It was always pathetic. How about a drink?"

"What's BCC?"

"Mining and metals."

"They fired Vic."

"That's such a loaded word," Jack said. "I wish people would stop using it. Firing's just an expression of socioeconomic forces. You can't fight forces like that. All you can do is get on their backs and ride them."

"I'll tell Vic that the next time I see him."

Jack laughed again, this time without choking. "How about that drink?"

"Okay."

The red light went out. Then came bumping sounds and clinking sounds.

"You like Armagnac?"

"What is it?"

"Cognac, but snobbier."

"That's me."

Jack appeared in the pool of pink-orange night glow, sat across the table with brandy snifters and a bottle. His half glasses were up on his forehead; there were deep pockets under his eyes, garish pits in the city light.

"Bobby's set for life, all right," said Jack as he poured, "but I wouldn't call him rich. He could have been rich, but he didn't have the balls."

"Didn't have the balls?"

"To hold out for what he could have gotten. I wasn't surprised. You remember how he was in the pool."

"I raced him yesterday. One-hundred free."

"You're kidding."

"His problem was technique, not character." But even as he said it, Eddie wasn't sure.

"That means you beat him."

Eddie didn't say anything. Jack brought the snifters together with a ping, handed one to Eddie. "Bobby in good shape?"

"He still works out in the pool."

"Maybe. But he must have had delusions. Look at you. I wouldn't stand a chance either."

"I never beat you, Jack. Not in the free."

"Let's leave it like that." Jack raised his glass. "Here's to you, bro."

They drank. Eddie didn't know about the snobby part. He just knew the Armagnac was good, and said so.

"A present from Karen, actually. She brought it back from Paris."

Eddie thought of his French café dream right away. "She's a client?"

"Right."

"What does she do?"

"Manages a family trust."

"Her family?"

"One half of it. The poor half. They came over with Peter Stuyvesant and split in two. Her half sat on their little acre for three hundred years. The other half started General Brands."

"Is she good at it?"

Jack smiled. "Good enough to come to me." He took another drink.

"What do you do, exactly?"

"Investment research. Analysis. Counseling."

"You invest the money for them?"

"Some clients have commission accounts with me, yes. Others pay a straight fee, plus a percentage bonus if earnings targets are reached."

"How did you learn all this stuff?"

"Picked it up on the fly. That's how everyone does it. They may tell you different, but it's the only way."

"So you didn't go back to school?"

"School?"

"After Galleon Beach."

Jack's eyes went to the papers scattered on the table; at least Eddie thought they did: the light wasn't good enough for him to be sure.

"I did, in fact."

"USC?"

Jack nodded. "But that's not where I learned this business."

"Did you swim?"

"Swim?"

"At USC."

"No." There was a silence. "I got bored with it. All those hours in the pool. I wasn't really that good."

"You were."

"I wasn't going to get any better, then."

I was.

Jack lit another cigarette. It glowed in the space between them.

"How did you manage?"

"College? It's not so tough, Eddie. Like high school, except you get laid more."

"I meant without a scholarship."

Jack took a drag. The red tip brightened. "Waiting tables, loans, scrounging, the usual."

Someone screamed, faint and far away, down in the park.

"Did Bobby tell you how to find me?" Jack said.

"I saw your letterhead at Vic's. Your old letterhead."

Jack refilled their glasses. Eddie's didn't need refilling, but Jack poured anyway. He swirled the liquid in his glass, staring into the tiny whirlpool he'd made.

"What happened to J. M. Nye and Associates?" Eddie said.

Jack made a sound, not a laugh, more like a snicker. "It was an eighties thing. The climate's changed."

"How?"

"Like the ice age." He took another drink, a big one, as though to fend off the cold.

"So Windward Financial Services is something different?"

"Leaner. I don't know about meaner. We were mean from the get-go."

"You're talking about the associates?"

"Right."

"Who are they?"

Jack shrugged. "What you'd expect. It doesn't matter. They're gone."

"You're on your own?"

"Thank God."

"Why do you say that?"

"Because now I don't have to worry about a bunch of fuckups fucking up. One of my beloved associates is still in the hoosegow."

Hoosegow. One of those words that was supposed to be funny. Eddie didn't find it funny at all. He said nothing.

Jack misinterpreted his silence. "He didn't do anything sinful," he said. "In this business the line between making a killing and breaking the law can be very fine."

"So people can end up in the hoosegow just by accident."

There was another silence, much longer than the last. Jack laid down his drink. He put his hands together, almost in the attitude of prayer; his fingernails glowed pink-orange in the light flowing through the window.

"I'm sorry, bro," he said.

"For what?"

"For not . . . keeping in touch. It was inexcusable. But—" His voice broke. "—I couldn't stand to see you like that. That goddamn visitor's room. That was hell, Eddie. I won't forget it till my dying day."

"I don't blame you."

"Yes, you do. I took the easy way."

"What do you mean?"

There was wetness on Jack's face. "It was easier to forget," he said. He picked up his glass and drained it. "To try to forget."

"You're being too hard on yourself."

"No, I'm not." Jack took out a handkerchief and wiped his face.

He drank more Armagnac. So did Eddie.

"Eddie?"

"Present."

"How are you? Really."

The phone rang. Jack answered it. "Send it up," he said. Then he turned to Eddie. "I want you to stay here. I mean that. As long as you like. Don't worry about anything, anything at all. Understand?"

"Sure." He understood the concept of not worrying. He was free. What was there to worry about?

"Do you need any money?" Jack asked.

"Got some. I've been making it hand over fist."

"Here." Jack laid some bills on the table.

"No, thanks."

"Just take it. Get yourself some clothes. See the sights. I'm not going to be around tomorrow."

"No?"

"Business trip."

"Where?"

"Nowhere interesting. We'll come up with a plan when I get back."

"What kind of plan?"

"To get you back on your feet."

"I'm on my feet."

"I know. I can't tell you how impressed I am." Jack poured more Armagnac. "But what do you want to do, Eddie? Or is it too soon to say?"

Eddie thought it over. "Go for a swim."

Jack laughed. "Same old—" He cut himself off. His eyes were pink-orange in the light. Someone knocked on the door.

Jack went to it. A bellman held out a silver tray bearing an envelope. Jack took it and returned to the couch.

"You can swim anytime you like at my club," he said. "Although that wasn't what I meant."

"Is it too late to get into junk bonds?" Eddie said.

Jack smiled his smile. "They're making a comeback already." He had one more shot of Armagnac, then rose, stretching. "You can sleep on the pullout," he said.

"I'm fine here."

"Pullout's more comfortable." Jack went into the bedroom.

Eddie finished what was in his glass, put it down. His eyes rested on the envelope the bellman had brought. It wasn't sealed. He peeked inside, saw a plane ticket, slipped it out. Jack was taking a return flight to Grand Cayman, first class.

"All set," Jack called.

Eddie went into the bedroom. Jack was spreading a quilt on the pullout. He gave the pillows a little pat and went into the bathroom.

A few minutes later they were in their beds. The pullout was comfortable, but Eddie couldn't sleep. He lay in it, feeling the Armagnac tingling inside him. He'd had too much, on top of too much the night before, and nothing for so many nights before that. The room began to spin, just a little. He watched it spin for a while, listening to Jack's breathing. He knew that sound.

He spoke. "What happened to *Fearless?*"

"Confiscated." Jack replied immediately, wide-awake.

"How did Packer take that?"

Eddie heard a little laugh. "Brad? I don't think he cared much by then. The bank owned the boat anyway."

"It did?"

"Sure. Packer was just a nobody with a two-bit dream. The world's full of Packers."

Eddie had only met one, and Galleon Beach hadn't seemed two-bit to him. The room spun a little more.

"Did you ever go back?" he said.

"Back where?"

"To Galleon Beach."

"Why would I have done that?"

"It was a nice place."

"It was a dump, Eddie. You'd be disappointed now. Some things only work when you're young."

Eddie knew that last part was true. That was what was killing him.

"Did JFK ever turn up?" he said.

Pause. "If he had, we'd have gotten you out."

"He must be somewhere."

"He could be dead. And even if he isn't, does it matter anymore? You're here. From now on things are going to be good for you. I'll see to that."

Eddie said nothing. He heard Jack roll over.

"Big day tomorrow," Jack said. "Better get some sleep."

A big day for you, maybe, Eddie thought. He stared at the ceiling. It was moving. He listened to Jack's breathing, that same breathing he'd heard when they shared a bed in their little room.

"Do you remember Mom?" he said.

"A little."

"What was she like?"

"Who knows?" There was a long silence before Jack said, "Christ, Eddie, we were living like shit the whole time."

"No, we weren't."

"You're wrong."

But Eddie knew he was right, knew now what living like shit was about. There was another silence. It went on and on. Eddie occupied himself with the tingling of the Armagnac, Jack's breathing, and the slowly spinning room. Time passed. Then Jack spoke once more, soft and gentle.

"Good night, Sir Wentworth," he said.

That brought the mist to Eddie's eyes, but of course no one could see, so it was almost all right. He pretended to be asleep.

Good night, One-Eye.

Outside: Day 4

Chapter Seventeen

Eddie awoke with a question on his mind: Did it matter if JFK was alive? was somewhere? He didn't know the answer.

Jack was gone. He'd left a note on the coffee table, beside the bills he'd laid there the night before.

"Bro—here's the card that opens the door and a pass for the health club. Did I mention the concierge? Hector? Don't tip him—the fucker's already taken care of. Back in a day or two. Get some clothes. Have a swim. Boogie. J." At the bottom was a map showing the location of the health club, near Grand Central Station, and of Macy's.

Eddie counted the money—$350—and left it where it was. He dressed in his sneakers and Prof's sweatsuit, pocketed the note, the cards, and his Speedo, and started for the door. His hand was on the knob when he turned back, went into the bedroom, and opened the closet.

The suit Eddie had hung up for Jack was still there, between two pinstripes, one charcoal, one navy. Eddie checked the inside jacket pocket. The check for $230,000 was gone. He returned to the sitting room, came close to picking up the $350—it was just about equal to his take for the past fifteen years—and went out.

It was cold and rainy again, and everyone on the street looked pained. Not Eddie: just being outside was enough to make him happy. The rain fell in icy little pats on his bald head, like some exotic form of massage.

The Midtown Athletic and Racquet Club had everything Eddie's hometown Y did not—a juice bar, fluffy towels, rows of the latest Nautilus, StairMaster, and LifeCycle machines, a cushioned track, men and women in fancy outfits, squash and tennis courts—everything but swimmers of Eddie's class, or even Bobby Falardeau's; or so he thought, watching the slow passage up and down the lanes. He dove into an empty one.

Right from the start he felt much better than he had in the hometown Y the day before; now he was a fluid being in a fluid medium. He swam for about an hour, just stretching out, listening to the water go by. He barely noticed when someone came up in the next lane, passed him with an easy fluttering kick. Eddie would have let him go, except he was curious about the ease of that kick.

He let loose a little, drew close on the next length, cruised half a body length behind, studying the other man's technique. Not bad: he was swimming about fifteen stroke cycles per length, riding high in the water, keeping his head still; and he had that easy kick.

Eddie swam on, losing himself in the water, forgetting the other man. Forgetting, until the other man shot by him, passing him again. Shot by. And not because of an increase in arm speed. The other swimmer had decreased his arm speed, if anything; it was the underwater acceleration he'd speeded up.

Eddie did the same thing, felt himself surge. He was swimming beautifully, skimming, fluid and strong and fast. But the other swimmer drew farther and farther ahead. After three more laps, Eddie had lost sight of him. In ten more, he passed Eddie again. Eddie climbed out of the pool on his next touch.

The other man swam another lap, then fell back in the water, stretching. He looked up at Eddie and smiled. He was very young.

The young man climbed out, pulled on a Columbia sweatshirt. Columbia. Eddie didn't remember it as a swimming power.

"You must have been really good," the young man said. "Where'd you do your swimming?"

"Alcatraz," Eddie replied. He'd learned something: It mattered whether JFK was alive, and where he was. It mattered a lot.

He went into the weight room. Eddie always started at the squat bar, but a woman in sheer tights and a pink leotard was there already. He waited until she finished her set and hoisted the bar back on the rack. She'd been lifting fifty pounds. Eddie added four hundred more, got under the bar, set his feet, got his grip, shouldered the bar, squatted, thrust himself back up. Usually he did three sets of ten, sometimes four. Today, feeling strong, he knew he could do five or even six. But after just that one lift, he lowered the bar back in the rack. He didn't want to lift. Lifting was for making time go faster, a prison thing. Why would he want time to go faster now? He was free, free not to do something a little too much like breaking rocks in the hot sun. He walked away from the bar.

The woman in pink was chalking her hands and watching herself in the mirror at the same time; she was watching him too.

Eddie went into the showers. He was drying himself with one of the fluffy towels when he saw a sign: Steam bath: Co-Ed— Please Cover Up. He wrapped the towel around himself and went in.

Eddie had the steam bath to himself. It was small, with wooden benches lining three sides. He sat at the back, leaned against the tile wall. Steam hissed out of a nozzle in one corner, filling the room with wet heat, wonderful wet heat that reminded him right away of the shed by the red clay court.

I need more memories, he thought. He got hotter; sweat poured off him. Eddie forgot about the shed and simply felt his body relax, relax as though gravity had failed and all the muscles, ligaments, and tendons could finally stop straining to hold his bones together.

"Tell me your plans," El Rojo had said.

And he'd answered, "A steam bath. After that I'd only be guessing."

There was nothing wrong with the steam-bath part. It was a good plan. He wished he'd carried it out sooner. As he sweated he imagined that all the foulness, dirt, and corruption of the past fifteen years was seeping out of him, leaving him clean, pure, untouched.

Time passed. A man with a sandy mustache peered through the window of the steam-bath door but didn't come in. Eddie grew thirsty, but he was so calm, so detached from everything outside that steam bath, that he made no move to leave. Even his thirst was strangely pleasant, perhaps because he knew he could slake it at will. Slake: he liked the word. It had lake in it, so it meant an endless supply of drinkable water. It was also good for rhyming.

> With throats unslaked, with black lips baked,
> We could nor laugh nor wail;
> Through utter drought all dumb we stood!
> I bit my arm, I sucked the blood,
> And cried, A sail! a sail!

Arm biting, bloodsucking: Eddie had seen crazy things like that. He was remembering some of them when the door opened and a woman with a towel wrapped around her body materialized in the clouds of steam. She sat down on one of the side benches, sighed, and leaned her head against the wall.

The woman had a trim body, nicely cut hair, cool blue eyes. Because he didn't think New York was the kind of place where you ran into people you knew, and because she wasn't wearing her tortoiseshell glasses, it took Eddie a few surreptitious looks before he was sure he recognized her: Karen de Vere.

"Hi," he said.

She gave him a cold glance, said nothing.

Karen? Miss de Vere? He wasn't sure of the proper form. Ms. de Vere? Ms. sounded funny to him; he'd never used the word in conversation and it brought to mind eye-rolling black servants in old movies, but he had a hunch it was the right choice.

"Ms. de Vere?"

"Excuse me?"

"You're Karen de Vere, aren't you?"

She squinted at him. "Do I know you?"

"Ed Nye. Jack's brother."

"Oh, my God. I'm sorry. I'm blind as a bat without my glasses." Her towel slipped slightly, exposing the tops of her breasts. She hitched it back up.

"Jack's a member here, isn't he?" she said.

"Yes."

"I never see him. I do aerobics and he's into squash. The two crowds don't mix. I suppose you're a squash player too."

"No," Eddie said, trying to imagine Jack on a squash court. Even with the added weight, he'd probably be good. There wasn't a game he couldn't play.

Karen was starting to sweat too. Her skin shone; a drop rolled down her neck, disappeared between her breasts. Her eyes went to the "Yeah?" tattoo on Eddie's arm, then up to his face.

"What do you do to keep in shape, Eddie?"

"Swim."

"Do you belong to a place like this in Albany?"

"Albany?" said Eddie, and then remembered. "I use the Y."

Karen's towel slipped again. This time she didn't bother adjusting it. "What do you do up there?"

"Nothing too hard," Eddie said. "Just stretching out a little."

She laughed. "I didn't mean in the pool. I meant for a living."

Why not tell her the truth? Eddie thought of a reason immediately: Jack did business with her, and knowing his brother was an ex-con might give her second thoughts, especially if Jack had spun some cover story about him last night. On the other hand, Jack might have told her the truth. "Didn't Jack tell you?"

"He was very mysterious."

"There's no mystery. I'm looking for work."

"In what area?"

"The junk-bond revival."

Karen laughed. Jack had already prepared her for the fact that Eddie was a bit of a character.

"It's tough out there, I know," Karen said. "Any leads?"

"Plenty. I've got friends in low places."

Karen laughed again and the towel slipped some more. Eddie didn't think there was anything to it: this was just big-city sophistication.

"But at least you're taking courses in the meantime," Karen said. "That's smart."

"Courses?"

"That *Monarch* you dropped. Don't worry—I won't snitch to your prof."

"Prof?"

"I had one who confiscated any crib she saw. Like it was smuggled dope or something."

Eddie's muscles, tendons, ligaments, didn't feel so relaxed anymore, and he was very thirsty. "It's just for pleasure," he said.

She smiled. "Dope?"

"The *Monarch*."

"I'm teasing. What kind of *Monarch* does anyone read for pleasure?"

For some reason, Eddie didn't want to tell her. He could see no way to avoid it. " 'The Rime of the Ancient Mariner.' "

"You're kidding."

"I guess it's just a trifle," Eddie said, recalling Ram's opinion; a trifle like "The Cremation of Sam McGee."

"I hope not," said Karen. "I wrote my senior thesis on it. 'The Cruciform Bird: Christian Symbolism, Coleridge, and the Fate of the Mariner.' "

Karen laughed. Eddie laughed too. This was fun—fun to sit in the steam bath with this beautiful woman, wrapped in fluffy towels, throwing words around. The man with the sandy mustache peeked through the window again and went away.

"If it's for pleasure, why not just read the poem?" Karen asked.

"I know the poem," Eddie said. "It's just that—"

"What do you mean, you know it?"

"By heart."

"The whole thing?"

Eddie nodded. She looked at him, bathed in sweat now. "I don't believe you."

Eddie could have recited the beginning, as he had for the bookstore boy. Or he could have recited the arm-biting stanza, since it had just been on his mind. Instead, he began:

> Her lips were red, her looks were free,
> Her locks were yellow as gold.

His voice dropped.

"Go on."

He didn't want to go on. The sentiment was crude, the comparison inappropriate, applying to Sookray, maybe, but not to this woman.

Karen, in a low voice, finished it for him:

Her skin was as white as leprosy,
The nightmare LIFE-IN-DEATH was she,
Who thicks men's blood with cold.

There was silence, except for the hissing steam.

"What does your crib make of that?" Karen said.

"I don't know," Eddie said. "I got it to find out something else."

"What's that?"

"It's kind of stupid."

"I doubt it."

They looked at each other through the steam. Her legs had parted slightly. Her left knee was almost touching his right. His whole right leg tingled, as though it were being acted upon by some force.

Eddie cleared his throat. "I'm trying to find out why the Mariner shoots the albatross in the first place."

Karen didn't smile, didn't laugh. He started to like her. "There are only two explanations I can see," she said.

"What are they?"

"The first, less supported by the text, is the Everest explanation."

"Because it was there?"

"Check. And the second, which fits much better, is the apple-and-Eve explanation."

"Meaning?"

"Original sin."

Eddie didn't like that one. He preferred some of his own devising—such as the Mariner was afraid of sailing fast, or jealous that the bird could fly.

"Doesn't grab, huh?" said Karen.

"No."

"I didn't believe in original sin either for the longest time. My work has convinced me otherwise."

What had Jack said? She managed family money. "You're an investor?"

"Right."

Eddie didn't see how that would give her special insight into original sin, and she offered no elaboration.

"I'm going to melt," Karen said. She stood up, leaving a sweaty imprint of her sex on the bench. "And I've got to give your brother a call, as a matter of fact."

Eddie rose too. "He's out of town."

Her voice grew sharper. "Where?" She hitched up her towel.

Eddie paused. They were very close. The heat, the nearness of their almost-naked bodies: what would happen if he just put his arms around her? He had no idea. He looked down into her eyes. There was something odd about them, but he couldn't place it.

"I can't believe he didn't tell me," Karen said, backing away. Suddenly she was angry. "That's so sloppy of him. He knew this was rollover day. We discussed it last night. This is going to cost—him and us."

Eddie didn't know what *rollover day* meant, or how missing it would cost anyone. But it all sounded probable. "He's gone to Grand Cayman. I don't know where he's staying."

"Thank Christ," Karen said. "I know where he stays. You just saved him a bundle. And me."

Eddie was pleased, and more pleased when she smiled and said: "Now I owe you one."

"You don't."

"I do. And I'm free for dinner tonight."

"Me too."

She laughed. He felt her breath on his face, cool in the atmosphere of the steam bath. "Pick you up at six," she said. "Dress casual."

And then she was out the door, trailing steam. For a moment Eddie was breathless, and not just because of the heat.

It wasn't until later, in the shower, that he realized what had been odd about Karen's eyes: he'd seen the circular outlines of transparent discs floating on her cool blue irises. How could she be blind as a bat when she was wearing contact lenses?

Chapter Eighteen

Dress casual: what did it mean?

Eddie wandered around Macy's, checking out the clothes and lots of other things, even trying on a blue blazer in front of a three-way mirror. He noticed stubble on his head. He hadn't shaved it for a while, no longer had his Remington, of course; that was one of the gifts he'd left for Prof. The stubble had a tarnished sheen. Eddie stepped closer to the mirror, and saw that his hair was growing in gray.

"Fabulous," said the clerk. "It fits you like a glove."

Eddie left Macy's without buying the blazer or anything else, and returned to Jack's suite at the Palazzo. Jack would know how to dress casual. In the bedroom, he opened drawers full of stuff, better than anything he'd seen at Macy's. There were all kinds of colors and textures. Eddie had worn denim so long he'd forgotten what matched what. He began putting on and taking off clothes, reminded of a scene in a book about Marie Antoinette.

Some time later he was standing in front of the mirror again, wearing a black cotton turtleneck, a blue wool sweater, gray corduroy pants rolled up an inch or two and held in place by a tightly cinched woven-leather belt, gleaming loafers with tassels on them.

He studied his reflection. A clever trick, like the photographic blending of ruffian's head on Ivy Leaguer's body. Fabulous. Fit like a glove, but someone else's. He stuck his hands in the pockets, trying for casual, and withdrew a half-full pack of Camels. He came close to lighting one, came close to throwing the pack away, ended by putting it back in his pocket.

At six o'clock the phone buzzed. "I'm downstairs," said Karen de Vere.

Karen did look fabulous: her hair was swept up, revealing the substructure of her face, at once strong and fine. She wore jeans, leather boots, a leather jacket; and her tortoiseshell glasses. She offered her hand. He shook it: warm, dry, not without power.

"You look so much like your brother," she said, "except for the hair. But I guess everyone tells you that."

"We don't hang out with the same people," Eddie replied.

Karen almost laughed; but how could she have gotten the joke? Eddie saw the laugh coming in her eyes; then she stifled it.

"Did you get in touch with him?" Eddie asked.

"Everything's fine."

Karen had a car outside, a low Japanese two-seater. "Not too hungry, I hope," she said. "It takes about an hour."

"Fine."

They drove out of Manhattan, onto a bridge, headed north. She stuck a cassette into the tape player. "Like jazz?" she said. "I'm sick of rock."

A bass played a bouncy line that made Eddie think of hippos, then came a trumpet, soaring above. "Me too." He'd heard nothing but rock blasting out of the cell blocks for fifteen years.

Karen drove fast, cutting from lane to lane. She watched the road ahead. From time to time, he watched her. The clouds darkened and darkened, and then it was night.

"Funny thing," she said, as they crossed the Connecticut line. "I've known Jack a number of years. Business, but we've had lunch a few times, went to a hockey game once, if I recall."

"You like hockey?"

"Just the fighting," said Karen. "The point is, in all the time I've know him, he never mentioned you."

"I'm the black sheep."

"How so?"

"You know how families are," Eddie said, although his own didn't deserve the name.

"I know how mine is—completely screwed up," Karen said.

She glanced at him; oncoming headlights glared on the lenses of her glasses. "What makes you the black sheep?"

Eddie shrugged.

"Jack did make an animal analogy last night about you, now that I think of it, although it was to a bird, not a sheep."

Eddie waited.

"The albatross, specifically. Odd, given our earlier conversation about 'The Mariner.' "

An icy wave flowed across Eddie's shoulders and down his spine. He hadn't felt anything like it since the moment in the shower room when he'd come to and realized what Louie and the Ozark brothers had done. Icy: because Jack considered him an albatross; because Jack would tell someone; because of what it said about his own obsession—yes—with the poem.

Karen was looking at him again. This time there was no headlight glare, and her eyes were nothing but black sockets. The trumpeter began something that sounded like "Where or When" and quickly lost its wistfulness. Karen said: "Sometimes there are coincidences that don't mean anything—like when you're reading a word and someone says it on the radio at the same time. But some coincidences mean a lot."

"Do they?" Eddie said.

"If you believe that things go on under the surface."

"I wouldn't know," Eddie said.

"I don't believe you."

"Why not?"

"Because you're smart, and you know something about life. Anyone can see that."

"Not Floyd K. Messer," said Eddie.

"Who's he?"

"An old colleague."

"In what business was that?"

"Warehousing."

Karen turned off at an exit, drove through a prosperous town and onto a country road. The headlights picked out details in the darkness: the white fence of a stable, reflective tape on the heels of a jogger's shoes, a sign that read "Antiques" in Gothic letters, to prove how old they were.

"That's to prove how old they are," Eddie said.

Karen laughed. "I was thinking the same thing."

Some coincidences mean a lot. The icy feeling subsided.

In a few miles they came to the restaurant, Au Vieux Marron. Outside it looked like a barn; inside like a French country inn, or what Eddie imagined a French country inn to be. The maître d' welcomed them in French. Karen answered him in French. She said something that made him laugh. He showed them to a table by a window overlooking a pond. A waiter arrived.

"Something to drink?"

"Kir," said Karen.

"Monsieur?"

Eddie didn't know what kir was, thought that beer might not be fancy enough. "Armagnac," he said.

"Prior to the meal, monsieur?"

The waiter was watching him; so was Karen. "With ice," Eddie said. The waiter withdrew.

Drinks came, and later food. Eddie ordered *canard* because it was the only word he knew on the menu. He'd never had duck like this—thin underdone slices of breast served with a sauce that tasted like raspberries, only more tart. The name of the recipe seemed to have something to do with Inspector Maigret; Eddie had read several books in the series, liking them mostly for their descriptions of food and drink, and the relish with which Maigret consumed them.

"Good?" said Karen.

"Good."

She was eating something Eddie couldn't identify from the menu, still couldn't identify when it arrived. It didn't matter. The food was delicious; she had another kir, he had another Armagnac—she taught him how to order it *"avec glaçons,"* and how to say several other things in French, such as, "I'm going to call the cops," and "Take it or leave it." Eddie caught a glimpse of what life could be like at the happy-go-lucky end. Under the table their feet touched; Karen waited a few moments before shifting hers away.

It was all false, of course. He knew that deep down the whole time, knew it up front between courses, as soon as Karen looked at him over the rim of her glass and said, "So tell me about yourself, Eddie Nye."

"There's not much to tell."

"I can't believe that."

"It's true."

"It can't be. You're between jobs, for instance."

"Right."

"Tell me about that."

"It's the same old story."

"What did you do before?"

Why not just tell her the truth? He knew it wasn't simply to protect Jack. He didn't want to tell her because he didn't want to see the expression that would come into those cool blue eyes when she found out.

"I was involved in a resort development."

"Was this after the warehousing business?"

"The warehousing business doesn't count."

Karen stabbed a strange-looking mushroom. "Where was the resort?" She popped it in her mouth.

"In the Bahamas."

"Which island?"

"The banana-shaped one."

Karen laughed, but only for a moment. He was starting to like that laugh—it was loud and came from deep inside—and was trying to think of a way to trigger it again, when she said: "What's this banana island called on the map?"

"Saint Amour."

"It's lovely."

"You've been there?"

"Sailed by a few years ago. I hope you didn't spoil it."

"Spoil it?"

"With your development."

"It wasn't my development. I just worked there."

She stabbed another mushroom. "Was Jack involved?"

"Yes."

"Funny."

"Funny?"

"He never mentioned that either."

"He went on to bigger and better things."

"Don't I know," said Karen.

Soon the waiter arrived with coffee. "Another Armagnac, monsieur?"

"Okay," Eddie said, although he was suddenly conscious of how much he'd been drinking since he'd found Jack.

"*Avec glaçons?*"

"Now I can have it *sans*, can't I?" *Sans*—it came to him from his reading: "La Belle Dame Sans Merci," whatever the hell that was about. Karen laughed; even the waiter smiled.

Karen stirred her coffee. "So Windward wasn't involved in the resort."

"No."

"J. M. Nye and Associates?"

"It was before all that."

Karen shot him a quick glance. It said: You've been out of work for a long time.

The waiter laid the bill in front of Eddie. It came in a leather folder, as though there was something to hide. "Why don't I take that?" Karen said. "I invited you."

"I ate the most," Eddie said, opening the folder: $107.50. That surprised him.

"I insist," Karen said.

"Next time," Eddie said. She smiled. He laid down the $100 bill and the rest of his money, making $124.75. Not enough tip. He remembered the $350 sitting on the table. Jack's $350.

They went outside. The sky had cleared. There was a moon and stars. The trees were black, the pond silver. Karen took Eddie's arm. "Let's go for a walk."

They walked around the pond, following a footpath of crushed stone. Karen still held his arm. "You don't know much about your brother's business, do you?" she said.

"Should I?"

"You were involved in it."

"What do you mean?"

"At that resort."

"It wasn't Jack's. We were just employees."

"Who owns it?"

"I don't know who owns it now."

"Who owned it then?"

"People named Packer."

She stopped. "You don't mean Raleigh Packer?"

"No," Eddie said. But then he remembered Brad and Evelyn's son, the one Jack had met at USC. "Who's Raleigh Packer?"

"One of Jack's associates. Former associates."

Eddie made another mental leap. "The one who went to jail."

Karen let go of his arm. "So you do know something about Jack's business."

"That's all I know."

Karen was silent. Eddie picked up a flat stone and skipped it across the pond. It left footprints of quivering silver in the moonlight.

"What jail is he in?"

"Raleigh Packer? He's in a halfway house somewhere. He only spent a few months in jail. Jail of the country-club type."

"What for?"

"Stealing. The indictment was complicated, but it came down to stealing."

"Stealing from who?"

"Investors."

"You?"

"No. I just signed on with Jack last night, as a matter of fact."

"So why do you know all this?"

"I do my research."

Eddie scaled another stone. It bit into the water and disappeared on first contact. "I'd like to see Raleigh Packer."

"Why?"

"Just to find out how he's doing."

"Did you know him?"

"I knew his parents."

"We have something in common, then, besides Jack," Karen said. "I've met his mother."

"Where is she?"

"In the area." Karen picked up a stone. "Try this one."

Eddie whipped it over the pond. It skipped once off the silvery surface, rose, and disappeared into the night, as though launched into space.

Eddie stared out over the water. Karen moved close to him. "I like you, Eddie," she said. "I think you should go back to Albany or somewhere similar."

"I don't understand."

"Just to be on the safe side."

"The safe side of what?"

Karen didn't answer. She just took his face in her hands and kissed him on the mouth. "I'm attracted to you," she said. "And I haven't been attracted to anyone in a long time. Remember that, no matter what happens."

"What could happen?"

"Anything."

Anything could happen when you were free; even getting kissed by a woman like this. Eddie took Karen in his arms, kissed her. She responded, even moaned, very low, but he heard it. The sound thrilled him, spurring his imagination. It rushed ahead, much too far, developing snapshots of a wonderful future: he and Karen, a house, even children. She pushed him away. "Let's go," she said.

"I like it here."

"So do I, believe me. But I'm insane." She walked toward the parking lot. He followed.

Karen drove. Eddie sat beside her. Jazz played. He wondered if she would reach out for him, touch his knee, hold his hand. She didn't. After half an hour or so, she slowed the car and turned into a lane marked by two gateposts with carved owl heads on top.

"I just have to drop in on someone for a few minutes first," said Karen, "if that's all right with you."

"First before what?"

"Before we go on."

It was all right with him.

At the end of the lane was a big stone house with three chimneys. Karen parked in front of it. Her spine straightened, as though she was steeling herself for something unpleasant.

"Do you want me to wait in the car?"

"No."

They got out, walked to the front door. Karen rang the bell. There was a small bronze plaque under it, very small, considering the size of the door, the house, the grounds. Eddie read it: "Mount Olive Extended Care Residence and Spa."

The door was opened by a woman in a nurse's outfit. Karen gave her name.

"This way, please," said the nurse.

They followed her down a long parquet hall, past many rooms, into a library at the end. The room was furnished with leather chairs and couches, a Persian rug, and books from floor to ceiling. There was no one in it except a woman sitting at a table near the fire, bent over a jigsaw puzzle that was mostly open spaces.

"You have visitors, dear," said the nurse.

The woman looked up. She had stringy hair, a gaunt face, unfocused eyes. Was there something familiar about her?

Karen approached the woman and took her hand. "Hello, Mrs. Nye," Karen said.

The woman stared up at her. "Do I know you?" Her voice was familiar too; Eddie remembered a plane ride long ago, over an emerald sea. The woman had lost her tan and her self-confidence, but she still had her makeup and her painted nails. She looked at Eddie and smiled.

"Is this your husband?" she said to Karen.

It was Evelyn Packer.

Chapter Nineteen

"On second thought," said Evelyn, picking up a puzzle piece, "he couldn't be your husband—he looks like someone I know rather all too well." She studied the piece for a moment, then slipped it down the front of her blouse.

"Now, now, Evelyn," said the nurse: "We'll never finish our puzzle that way, will we?"

"It's not *our* puzzle," Evelyn said. "It's mine."

The nurse started to say something, but Karen interrupted. "Thanks for showing us in."

The nurse closed her mouth and backed out of the room, shutting the door behind her.

Karen pulled up a chair and sat at the table opposite Evelyn. Evelyn picked out another puzzle piece and tried it in several spaces. The borders of the puzzle were done—they were black—and there were clusters of black pieces here and there, some of them silvered. There was also a white shape, somewhat triangular, that might have been a mountaintop. Evelyn's piece wouldn't fit. She handed it to Karen and said: "Did you know my father?"

"I never had the pleasure."

"Don't be smarmy. Just yes or no."

"No."

"You-know-who killed him. He was a fine man. A good man. He never abused me in any way, not the mental way or the physical way or the sexual way. Unlike a certain aforementioned I could mention." Her gaze rose, fastened for a moment on Eddie. Then she looked quickly away and whispered to Karen, a symbolic whisper, audible to anyone in the room: "Who is he?"

"Don't you know?" said Karen.

"Whisper."

Karen lowered her voice. "Don't you know?"

"How would I? I'm not exactly in circulation. What's the date today?"

Karen told her. Evelyn nodded, as though receiving news at once bad and unsurprising, then found the thread of the conversation. "I don't even know you either, although you've been visiting lately."

"Karen. Karen de Vere."

"Evelyn. Evelyn Andrea Manning Packer Nye. Looks like hell, wants to die."

"Don't talk like that, Evelyn."

She brightened. "*No problemo.* What ax are you grinding, Karen? Or is that just the sound of your teeth?" She started laughing, with the expectation that others would join in. None did.

"No ax, Evelyn," Karen said. "But your father died of heart disease, according to the hospital records."

"Driven to it," said Evelyn, "by the aforementioned unmentionable."

"Driven to heart disease?"

"You've never heard of stress?"

Eddie had been standing by the door, perfectly still on the outside, reeling within. He spoke: "Karen."

Both women looked up at the sound of his voice. There was fear in Evelyn's eyes; perhaps it wasn't entirely absent from Karen's either.

"I want to talk to you."

Karen rose.

"Oo," said Evelyn. "Big manny-man." Then she had another look at Eddie and said, "Sorry." Karen followed Eddie to the door. As they went out, Eddie heard Evelyn murmur, "Mental, physical, sexual."

Eddie and Karen stood in the hall outside the library. "What's going on?" Eddie said.

"In the old days they called it madness. Now we say dysfunctional."

"'That's not what I meant. I meant what are you doing? Why did you bring me here?"

"I thought you could help me."

"Do what?"

"Shed some light on her situation."

"Why would I be able to do that?"

"Because you're her brother-in-law."

"I don't know her."

"How is that possible? She's been married to your brother for fourteen years. Besides, you already said you did."

Eddie looked down into Karen's eyes, saw complexity. Bits of information—Evelyn's father and his connections, her madness, the $230,000 check—popped up in his mind but refused to cohere. All he knew was that he was being set up. He didn't know how, why, or by whom, he just knew it was happening.

Karen put her hand on his arm. "Whatever you're thinking, stop," she said. "I meant what I told you at the pond."

"Did you?" Eddie said. "I think you were pumping me."

"No."

Eddie shook off her hand. "And I don't think Jack called me what you said he did. You invented that, just to divide us."

Karen's voice rose. "Think what you want."

Down the hall a door opened. A man came out. He had a sandy mustache. Eddie recognized him from the health club: he'd peeked twice through the window of the steam bath, once before Karen entered, once after. Now he was here, living proof. Karen waved him away, too late.

"Where's the woman in the pink leotard?" Eddie said.

"What are you talking about?" Karen said, but her eyes shifted.

"And next time you're pretending to be blind as a bat, don't let anyone see your contacts."

"Everything all right?" said the man with the sandy mustache, coming down the hall.

"Please, Eddie," Karen said, "I've got to talk to you."

"I don't talk to cops."

"I'm not a cop."

"He is."

One of the mustached man's hands disappeared inside his jacket.

Arrest, Eddie knew, was next. Arrest, trial, prison. He knew the drill.

Eddie didn't think. He just let things happen. Things like snatching the tortoiseshell glasses off Karen's face and flinging them at the mustached man.

"Hold it right there," the man said.

Things like moving, the way he could move. The mustached man had time to get his gun out, but not raise it, before Eddie hit him. The mustached man went down. Instant disorder. Eddie ran from it, down the parquet hall, past many rooms, to the front door, out. He kept going, down the lane, through the gateposts with the carved owl heads on top, into some woods across the road. There he stopped, listened for sounds of pursuit. Hearing none, he stayed where he was.

Through the trees Eddie could see lights in the windows of the Mount Olive Extended Care Residence and Spa. He felt like a barbarian coming upon an outpost of civilization: much safer where he was. A few minutes later clouds slid across the moon, blackening the night. Eddie felt safer yet. Then it began to rain. He didn't care.

Not long after that, headlights appeared in the lane. Two cars drove out, the first a sedan, the second Karen's Japanese two-seater. They turned onto the road and sped away. Eddie waited until their taillights vanished before leaving the woods.

He recrossed the road, went back through the gate, cut over the lawn to the library end of the house. He peered through a mullioned window.

Evelyn was sitting in the chair by the fire, shaking her head no. The nurse was standing over her, saying something Eddie couldn't hear. They went on like that, the nurse talking, Evelyn shaking her head. After a while the nurse took Evelyn's hand. Evelyn snatched it away. The nurse took it again, this time in both of hers. Evelyn tried to free herself, but failed. The nurse pulled Evelyn to her feet and led her from the room.

Eddie backed away from the house. Soon a light went on in an upstairs room, directly over the library. The nurse appeared in the window. She drew the curtains. A few seconds passed, long enough for her to cross the room. The light went out.

Eddie moved under a tree. Rain fell on him through the leafless branches. He wiped the top of his head, felt the stubble. Gray stubble: that made him mad.

Room by room, the house darkened. Eddie waited until every light had gone out except the one in the front hall. He approached the library and examined the windows. Casement windows—he remembered the name from one of the Inspector Maigret books— hinged on the outside, opening in the middle. He put his hand in the middle and pushed, not hard. The window didn't budge. Eddie pushed harder, then much harder. The window gave, not without a splintering sound. Eddie stood still, waiting for an alarm, running footsteps, an anxious voice. There was none of that. He placed his hands on the sill and climbed into the library.

The fire in the grate burned low. It gave off enough light for Eddie to see that the jigsaw puzzle was finished. The black pieces were the night sky, the silvered ones were moonlight on the sea, the white triangle was the tip of an iceberg, the great blank space was now filled with the *Titanic*, steaming across the puzzle toward its doom. Only one piece was missing: the red base of the *Titanic's* foremost smokestack.

Eddie walked out into the darkness of the corridor. The tassel loafers clicked on the parquet. Eddie took them off. Light glowed in the entrance hall. He moved toward it, soundless in his stocking feet.

Eddie reached the entrance hall. To his left was a desk. A man in a security-guard uniform had his head on it. To Eddie's right, broad stairs led up into darkness. Eddie climbed them to the top.

The second-floor corridor was carpeted and lit with dim ceiling lights every ten or fifteen feet. Eddie walked past closed doors toward the end. Through one of them he heard a man muttering about Jesus.

The door to the last room, over the library, was closed too. Eddie put his hand on the knob and turned it. The door opened. Eddie went in.

The room was dark. Eddie couldn't see a thing. He advanced with little sliding steps across the floor, his hands out in front of him, until he touched the wall. Then he felt along it for the curtains, found them, drew the string. Moonlight flooded in; the sky had cleared again. Eddie turned to the bed. Evelyn was lying in it, her eyes open, reflecting back the moonlight.

Eddie spoke quietly. "That was a good job you did on the puzzle, when no one was watching."

Evelyn spoke quietly too. "Thank you, manny-man."

"Don't you know me?" Eddie said.

"Sure. You're the new inmate."

Eddie felt that chill again, across his shoulders, down his spine. He sat on the bed. She went still. "Evelyn, what happened to you?"

"Since when?"

"Since we knew each other."

"When was that? I've forgotten so many memories. It's all because of the brain-loss diet they've got me on."

"We met at Galleon Beach," Eddie said.

There was a silence. Evelyn's eyes moved, changing the angle of reflection of the moonlight. "I remember Galleon Beach," she said.

"Then you remember me."

She looked at him. "You're the unfortunate bro."

"Why do you say that?"

"Because of what the pigs did to you."

"What pigs?"

"The wild ones. They've got wild pigs down there. You know that, if you are who you say you are. I was married to one. Then I married a much wilder one."

"Jack?"

"The aforementioned. He had designs on me. The same designs as Pig One, only bigger."

"What designs?"

Evelyn sat up. "You're a spy. Like Ms. de Cool."

"I'm not. I just want some answers, that's all."

"Then you've got to ask questions, silly." She lay back down. "Pharmaceuticals kicking in," she said, and closed her eyes.

"Evelyn?"

"I hear you loud and clear. Over."

"I've got a question."

"Shoot. Over. And say *over*. Over."

"Why did Jack get kicked out of USC?"

She opened her eyes. "Raleigh should have been kicked out too."

"What did they do?"

"Does it matter now? Except that it's how he got his foot in the door. In retrospect, if you take my meaning. He was clever. He knew how to sacrifice the pawn to topple the king."

"What door are you talking about?"

"The same door Brad stuck his stinky foot in—the door to my father's influence. Did you know him?—Daddy, I'm talking about, not Stinky."

"No. What kind of influence did he have?"

"Contacts. From his practice, from Yale, from Groton. How do you think the aforementioned got started in the fleecing business?"

"Tell me."

She started talking faster. "And it wasn't enough. He wanted money too. Well, the joke is, Daddy didn't have a lot of money, not the kind of money the big dreamers call a lot. Brad got himself punched by that punch line too. But it served him right for all his unfaithfulness." She began to laugh, harsh and unpleasant. "I owe you thanks."

"For what?"

"For fucking his little fuckee. Pardon my French." She stared at Eddie. "But they made you pay. I forgot. So what good are thanks?"

"What do you mean—they made me pay?"

"Click," said Evelyn. "Channel change. I'm tired of all your questions. Here's one for you—why can't men be faithful? Answer me that."

"Were you having an affair with Jack at Galleon Beach?"

Evelyn's voice rose. "What a nasty suggestion. I couldn't help myself. Now go away."

"Not till you tell me who made me pay."

She thought. He could feel her thinking, feel her giving up. "The details are sketchy, like all details. Why not ask the cook? Or should I say *aks*?"

"The cook in this place?"

"What would he know? I'm talking about JFK."

"That's a good idea. Where is he?"

"Don't take that patronizing tone."

"Where is he?"

"Around. He showed up for money, like a lot of jetsam in the aforementioned's glory days."

"Around where?"

"Try the hospices."

"What hospices?"

"In the city. Or ask the aforementioned." She laughed the harsh laugh again. "On second thought, don't do that."

"Why not?"

Footsteps sounded outside the door. Eddie froze. Evelyn smiled at him, moonlight gleaming on her teeth. "You're gonna get it," she said.

Eddie put his finger to his lips. She grew solemn, then quickly pressed something into his hand. Eddie dropped down on the floor, rolled against the wall.

The footsteps came closer. The nurse said: "Can't sleep, dear?"

"Yes, I can. I'm very good at it."

"Then why don't you, instead of talking to yourself?"

"I'm not talking to myself."

"I could hear you all the way down the hall."

"That doesn't prove your insinuation in all its particulars."

"And how do you expect to sleep with your curtains open?"

"I like the moonlight in Vermont, or anywhere in the lower forty-eight, for that matter."

Footsteps. The snick of the curtain string being sharply tugged. Then darkness.

Footsteps, back to the bed. "I'm going to give you just a little something to help you sleep."

"I don't want a little something. I want to get intimate with manny-man."

"A little something will help."

"Don't talk to me like I'm Winnie-the-Pooh."

A rustling of sheets. "This won't hurt," said the nurse.

Pause. "It did."

"Sweet dreams."

Footsteps retreated. The door closed. Footsteps faded away.

Eddie rose, sat on the bed, felt across the covers, found Evelyn's hand, took it. She groaned.

"Evelyn?"

"Get me out of here."

Eddie didn't know what to say. He'd made the same plea to Jack, long ago.

"Get me out," she said again. There was a long pause before she added, "of here." The words came slow and sleepy.

She squeezed his hand, much harder than he would have thought she could. "I've done that puzzle . . ." Another long pause. Her hand relaxed, fell away. When she spoke again her voice was weaker. "A thousand times. Can you grasp that?"

"Yes."

"So get me out." Silence.

"Evelyn?"

"So get me out."

"I'll try, but first I want to talk to you."

No response.

"Evelyn?"

She was asleep.

Eddie rose, shoes in hand, and left the room. He walked down the carpeted corridor, down the stairs. The desk in the hall was deserted. He followed the parquet to the library. The fire in the grate was almost out, but there was still enough light to see the puzzle. Eddie went to it. He knew what Evelyn had put in his hand. He took it now and fitted it in place: the red base of the *Titanic's* lead stack.

Eddie slipped on the tassel loafers and climbed out of the casement window, closing it behind him.

Chapter Twenty

Quietly, because of the possibility that Karen and the mustached man might be inside, Eddie let himself into Jack's suite. Someone was slouched on the sofa watching a James Bond movie, but it wasn't Karen or the mustached man. The man on the sofa had a beer in his hand, and there were empties all around. Bond said something funny and shot an Oriental gentleman in the balls. The man on the sofa laughed, unaware that he was no longer alone until Eddie stepped in front of him. The sight displeased him.

"Who the fuck are you?" he said. He was a broad, thick-necked man of about Eddie's age and reminded Eddie of someone, although he couldn't think who.

"I'm not in the mood," Eddie said.

"Not in the mood for what?" The man rose, to show Eddie how big and tough he was.

"Any bullshit." Bond climbed into bed with a big-breasted blonde. He stuck his gun under the pillow. She purred.

The thick-necked man stepped forward, close enough to jab his finger in Eddie's chest. He jabbed his finger in Eddie's chest. "The bullshit's all coming from you, pal," he said.

Then the man was on the floor with a bloody face and a nose that wasn't quite straight.

Bond said something insouciant. Eddie said: "Who are you?"

"I asked you the same question," answered the man, getting up and dabbing his face with his sleeve.

"But not politely."

The man gave him a hard look but kept his mouth shut. How familiar, thought Eddie, that sudden violence. He got the funny feeling that the thick-necked man had spent some time inside. His mind skipped a few steps and he said: "Out on a pass, Raleigh?"

The man frowned. "Do I know you?"

"Everyone keeps asking me that," said Eddie. "I'm Ed Nye."

There was a pause. Then Raleigh Packer said: "You could have mentioned that a little earlier."

"We'd have missed the benefit of all this exercise."

Raleigh dabbed at his face again, sat down on the sofa. Eddie noticed his anklet. Raleigh saw that he noticed. "Not a pass," he said. "Parole." He raised his pant leg a little more, revealing the lightweight plastic ankle bracelet with the box transmitter that allowed a computer to monitor him. "I'm on a beeper, just like the gofers on Wall Street."

"Could be worse," Eddie said.

Raleigh gave him a long look. "Where were you?"

Eddie named the prison.

"For ten years or something?"

Eddie corrected him.

"How did you stand it?" Raleigh wasn't a tough guy: Eddie had known that from moment one.

"You can get used to anything."

Raleigh dabbed at his nose again. "Bullshit," he said, but not in a challenging way.

"Why don't you go clean up?"

Raleigh went into the bathroom. Water ran. James Bond's parachute failed to open. He pretended to look scared but there was a twinkle in his eye. Eddie noticed that the $350 was no longer on the coffee table.

Raleigh came back into the room, holding a towel to his nose. "I think it's broken."

"Noses are vulnerable," Eddie said. "Where's the three-fifty.?"

"Huh?"

"Do I have to go to a whole lot of trouble to find it?"

"Is it yours?"

"It's Jack's."

"Then consider it a down payment on what he owes me."

"What does he owe you?"

"That depends on my billing rate, but the hours are twenty-four times three sixty-five."

"Just the same," said Eddie, "I'd better hang onto it till he comes back."

Raleigh handed over the money in the resigned way an inmate would after the pecking order had been established. "You're just like him."

"Like who?"

"You know who. Where is he?"

"Out of town."

"Out of town where?"

Eddie didn't answer.

Raleigh glanced around the room. "Maybe he's not coming back."

"Of course he is," Eddie said; but he wondered.

Raleigh touched his nose delicately with the tip of his finger.

"Let me see that," Eddie said, went close to Raleigh, examined his nose, saw that he was making a fuss about nothing, saw too how much he resembled his father, the way Eddie remembered him. "You're going to live," Eddie said.

Raleigh snorted. That started the bleeding again. "On what?" he said.

"Your inheritance."

"Is that a joke?"

"I thought your parents were rich."

"What do you know about my parents?"

"Not much," Eddie said, thinking of the *Titanic* plowing through the night. "How are they doing?"

"Just great. Dad's dead and Mom's in the nuthouse."

"See much of her?"

"I've been out of circulation," Raleigh said; almost his mother's exact words about her own condition.

Eddie said: "Did you go to Groton and Yale and all that too?"

"What do you mean, 'too'?"

Eddie didn't answer.

"My grandfather went to Groton and Yale, if that's what you're referring to. But how did you know that?"

"Lucky guess."

Raleigh studied him for a few moments in a way that again reminded Eddie of Brad Packer: not quite smart enough. "Groton yes, Yale no," said Raleigh. He picked up his beer, drank.

Eddie went to the sideboard, got the Armagnac bottle, poured himself a glass. "Ever had Armagnac?"

"Of course."

"Every night in the dining halls of Groton," Eddie said.

"If you want to think in stereotypes."

"I wouldn't want to do anything like that." Eddie was starting to feel manic, as though something exciting were about to happen and he couldn't wait. He raised his glass.

"Here's to USC," Eddie said.

"What's that supposed to mean?"

"It's a toast, to a fine institution."

Raleigh took a sip. "That's where I went to college."

"I almost went there myself."

"Did you?" Raleigh took another sip, bigger this time.

"Things didn't work out. There was a whole chain of events, if you follow me."

"I don't think I do."

"Would it help if I said that the first link in the chain was something that happened between you and Jack?"

Raleigh was still. "What do you mean?"

"You tell me."

"Tell you what?"

"What happened between you and Jack."

Raleigh took a big drink. "Why don't you ask him?"

"He's not here."

"Where is he?"

"I told you—out of town."

"Out of town where?"

Eddie was silent.

"Why are you covering for him? You should be on my side. He's such a bastard."

"Watch it." The warning came from Eddie's own lips, but it took him by surprise.

Raleigh looked surprised too. "Watch what?"

"Watch what you say about him."

Perhaps this time he didn't say it with enough conviction. Raleigh started to laugh. He was still laughing when the door opened and Jack walked in.

He had on a long coat of somewhat Western cut—the kind a rich cattleman might wear—and he was smoking a cigar. "What convention is this?" he asked.

"Convention?" said Raleigh.

Eddie wasn't sure what the remark meant either, but if the reference was to ex-cons he didn't like it. Jack took off his coat. Underneath he wore faded jeans, a polo shirt, and Topsiders with no socks.

"Been away, Jack?" said Raleigh.

Jack didn't answer the question. Instead he eyed Raleigh's face and said, "What the hell happened to you?"

"Nothing."

Jack's gaze went from the pink-stained towel on the table to Eddie. Eddie smiled a noncommital smile.

"Been away?" Raleigh repeated.

"Away?"

"Your brother here mentioned you were out of town."

"You said that, Eddie?"

Eddie nodded.

Jack puffed his cigar. "Does Brooklyn count?"

Raleigh stood up. "I want to talk to you, Jack."

"Talk."

"In private."

"How ill bred." Jack smiled around his cigar. Eddie could see he was in a good mood. Jack came over to him, gave his shoulder a little squeeze. "You don't mind, bro?"

Eddie shook his head. Bond peered doubtfully at a glass of red wine. Jack picked up the remote and switched him off.

Jack and Raleigh went in the bedroom. The door closed. They talked in low voices for a few minutes. They came out. Now Raleigh was smoking a cigar too.

"How about a celebration?" said Jack.

"Of what?" Eddie asked.

"You being here. Good enough?"

"Isn't it a little late?"

"In this town? Let's show him the kind of fun you can have in the city that never weeps."

"Whatever you say," said Raleigh.

"As long as we don't leave your ankling area," Jack added. Eddie saw that his brother was a bit manic too.

Raleigh almost managed a smile. He drained his glass and said: "Let's go."

"This is supposed to be the latest," said Jack, as they entered a club; so new that the sign was still clad in protective canvas.

Inside was a world of light, without fixed boundaries or dimensions. Floors, walls, ceilings didn't exist; there were only curves, rounding into one another. And everything had a glow: pearly in the lower regions, shading up through greens and blues to indigo above.

A man dressed in a silver space suit greeted them. He spoke through a speaker in his helmet. "Welcome to Brainy's," he said. "Fifteen-dollar cover, two-drink minimum. The official opening's not till tomorrow, so please bear with us."

He led them to a table with a translucent surface that flickered in black and white, like snow on a TV screen. They sat in almost invisible clear-glass chairs. Mounted on the tabletop were concave viewers, the size of a human head. "Look in those," said the man in the space suit. "Maneuver by sticking your right hand in those slots and experimenting. The waiter will be around to take your orders." His gaze lingered on Eddie for a moment before he left.

"What the fuck is this?" said Raleigh.

"Five-million dollars' worth of software," Jack replied.

Eddie put his face in the viewer. It was more than a viewer; it wrapped around his ears as well, covering them with perforated foam pads. He was in a place of total darkness, total silence. Nothing happened. He felt for the slot in the side of the table, stuck his hand inside a hand-shaped hole that felt like rubberized plastic. He fitted his fingers in the right openings. Something happened.

First came a strange noise, an eerie whine, like interstellar wind. It filled his head. Then the sun rose, so bright it hurt his eyes.

He moved his fingers. That turned him slowly around, and away from the glare of the sun. Now he was soaring through a blue sky. He tried pressing his thumb on the rubberized plastic. That tipped him forward, made him look down, down at a green jungle. He fell toward it with sickening speed. He moved his hand again, pressed with different fingers. That slowed his descent. He drifted down, closer and closer to the trees, then right into them, through a gap, down, down. Below was an emerald-green pond with a waterfall cascading into it. It roared in his ears. He fell into the emerald-green water; the roaring turned to pounding. He fell deeper and deeper, down to the gurgling dark bottom, toward a pool of light. In the pool of light was a bare-breasted mermaid. She smiled and said, "May I take your order, sir?" He shifted his hand to try to get a little closer. Everything went black.

Eddie drew back from the viewer. The mermaid was talking to Jack: "Heineken, Beck's, Beck's Light, Corona, Sam Adams, Moosehead, Bass, Grolsch—"

"New Amsterdam."

"We don't carry it."

"Bass, then."

"And you, sir?" she said, turning to Eddie.

Not the mermaid, of course, and not bare-breasted and fish-tailed, but the woman who had played the mermaid, if *played* was the word, down in the emerald-green pond. She wore a tiny silver space dress but no helmet.

"I'd like water," Eddie said, wanting all at once to be sober.

"Evian, Perrier, Volvic, Contrexéville, Saratoga, San Pellegrino, Ramlösa, Poland Spr—"

"It doesn't matter."

She went away. "Mine was the wild west," said Raleigh. "What was yours?"

"Skiing in Zermatt," said Jack. "Eddie?"

"Falling."

Jack glanced into his viewer. "There's a pissload of money to be made in this, if you knew who to back."

"To be made in what?" asked Raleigh.

"Virtual reality."

The words almost triggered a memory in Eddie's mind. He

came close to dredging it up, a worrisome, champagne-drenched memory, but Raleigh broke his concentration by getting up to go to the bathroom. Eddie found himself gazing at his brother.

"Something on your mind, bro?"

"I don't know. Does an albatross have a mind?"

Jack smiled; that flashing smile, but his eyes were blank. "Run that by me again."

"I've got lots on my mind," Eddie said.

"Like what?"

Where to begin? Karen? Evelyn? JFK? Galleon Beach? Grand Cayman? It all began at USC, didn't it? Eddie rose. "Tell you in a minute." He went off in the direction Raleigh had gone.

The bathroom was part of the experience. It was all pearly light and rounded surfaces. For a moment, Eddie thought it was supposed to be a giant urinal. There was a female attendant, dressed in a little space skirt and halter top. Eddie, trying to take her presence in stride, said, "All it needs are holes in the floor."

"Everyone says that," said the woman, toying with the change on her plate.

Eddie found Raleigh soaking his nose on a wet towel. Their reflections studied each other in the mirror.

"Now would be a good time," Eddie said.

"For what?"

"For telling me what happened at USC."

Raleigh zipped up. "Ask Jack. Didn't I say that already?"

"I want to hear it from you."

"No can do." He faced Eddie. "You're going to beat me up in here, aren't you? That would be the inmate thing."

It was true, both parts. Eddie backed away. "You did something and Jack took the blame."

"Keep guessing," Raleigh said and walked out the door, passing the attendant without leaving a tip. Her eyes were on Eddie.

"He didn't even wash his hands," Eddie said.

"Ninety percent of them don't," the attendant replied. "I wrote a poem about it."

"I'm listening."

"It's long," said the attendant, "but it starts, 'You stupid fucking fuckers / with piss-dripping dicks / and silver-dripping pockets / divine Manhattan Judases, artists of betrayal / so careful with every scheming breath / why do you forget to wash your pissy digits?' "

Quite different from the poem Eddie knew best, but he liked it. "I like it," he said.

"You do? You're not in publishing, by any chance?"

"No."

"Maybe you know someone in publishing? A university press will do."

"Sorry."

"Shit."

The door to one of the toilets opened. A man came out, short and fat, wearing a dark suit. It was Señor Paz. He went to the sink beside Eddie, washed his hands. They were plump pink hands with manicured nails; not what Eddie pictured as a surgeon's hands. Eddie started to back away, thinking that Paz hadn't recognized him. Then Paz spoke.

"Young lady," he said, "will you leave us for a moment, please?"

She went out. Things came together in Eddie's mind, and he realized where he was.

"I thought you were calling it Neuron."

Paz smiled. "Or Synapse. But our consultants on Madison Avenue came up with Brainy's. More impudent, they said, as though impudence were somehow desirable. What do you think?"

"I like Neuron better."

"As do I," said Paz. "You strike me as an intelligent man." He sighed—theatrically perhaps, yet what wasn't theatrical in a place like this?—and looked melancholy. "But isn't there an English expression about being too smart for one's own good?"

"Meaning what?"

"We'll explore the subject of what it all means in good time," said Paz. "Let's just say some of us are very disappointed." He glanced over Eddie's shoulder.

Maybe it was the pearly light, or possibly the rounded surfaces. Both disorienting: dulling the fifteen-years-honed edge on Eddie's alertness. He didn't spin around, or start to spin around, until it was too late to avoid the first blow, that brought him to his knees, and the second, that sent him into unconsciousness.

Outside: Day 5

Chapter Twenty-One

A woman said, "One-twenty over eighty."

Eddie opened his eyes, looked up into a blue-white glare. He saw a white ceiling with powerful lights hanging from it. He tried to turn his head to see more but couldn't. He couldn't move his head, couldn't move any part of his body. He started to say something stupid, like "What the hell?" but found he couldn't open his mouth. Something was clamped tight under his chin. All he could do was make an angry noise in his throat. He made it.

Soothing music played in the background. Massed violins. The woman's face came into view. She wore a surgical mask. Her eyes looked into his. There was something familiar about her.

"Pulse—eighty-two," she said.

"Remove the gown," said a man he couldn't see.

Eddie recognized the speaker: Señor Paz.

The woman's face withdrew, and Eddie found himself looking again into the blue-white glare. He felt a draft around his groin. Then something sharp and silver came gleaming into view: a scalpel. It came close to his eyes. The hand holding it was pink and plump, with manicured nails.

Eddie tried to get up, tried to move, tried to struggle against whatever bound him. He couldn't even squirm. He made a noise in his throat, a raw noise, as loud as he could. The soothing music played on. The scalpel turned, inches from his eyes. Even as it did, he recognized the tune: "Malagueña."

The scalpel moved away, down across his chest and out of sight. After a few moments, he heard Paz say, "Right there."

Eddie tried to make a noise in his throat. Now he couldn't even do that, although nothing was stopping him. Time passed. He didn't feel anything, didn't see anything but blue-white glare, didn't hear anything but "Malagueña" played soothingly on countless strings; yet he sensed work going on around him.

He heard Paz grunt. Then the pink, plump hand swung up into his view; the pink, plump hand now spattered with blood. In the manicured fingers dangled a little pouchlike object Eddie couldn't identify at first. And then he did: it was a severed scrotum, with testicles still inside.

Something stung his arm. Everything went white, then black.

Eddie awoke in a pleasant room. There were books, soft lights, pictures on the walls. The curtains were drawn. It might have been any time at all, but it felt like night.

He lay on a hospital bed. He couldn't move his arms or his legs, but he could raise his head. He raised it, looked down at his body. He was naked except for the bandages wrapped around him from just below the rib cage to mid-thigh. His wrists and ankles were bound to the safety bars along the sides with hard rubber restraints. He felt no pain, but he remembered everything. He lost control of his face. It began to crumple, like the face of a baby about to bawl.

The door opened. Señor Paz came in, glancing at his watch. "How's the patient?"

Without thinking, Eddie tried to burst up off the table. He didn't budge. At least he got control of his face.

"Quite pointless," said Paz.

Eddie spat at him, a gob of spit that landed far short.

"I wish you wouldn't do that," said Paz. "Apart from the vulgarity, it's unhygienic."

Eddie tried again to burst free, tried even harder. Again, he got nowhere with the restraints; but he felt the end of one of the safety bars, the end near his right hand, giving slightly. *Be smart.* He stopped struggling. He couldn't possibly free himself while Paz was watching.

"That's better," said Paz. "It won't do any good, you know."

Be smart, Eddie told himself, but he couldn't stop his voice. "I'm going to kill you," it said. "And the nurse and anyone else I can find."

Paz nodded. "Understandable. The pity is you brought it all on yourself. You didn't factor in the sort of people you were playing your little tricks on. I find that strange, considering that you must be some kind of survivor, given your history."

"What are you talking about?"

Paz sucked impatiently on his teeth. "I can't believe you still want games. I'm talking about the C-note, of course."

Eddie's voice took off again, up and out of control. "I gave it to you, you stupid fuck."

Paz shook his head. "You gave us one hundred dollars. But it wasn't the right bill. How did you imagine you'd get away with that?"

It wasn't the right bill? What did that mean? He'd had two of them, of course, the first rolled in El Rojo's cigarette, the second won from Bobby Falardeau.

"It wasn't the right bill?"

"Don't pretend you haven't known that all along," said Paz. "It was never a question of the money. We wanted the bill itself. As I'm sure you know."

Eddie's voice rose once more. "You . . ." He couldn't say it, couldn't make it real with words. "You did that to me because I mixed up two bills?"

"Mix-up?" said Paz. "I don't think so. Now, to prevent additional . . . procedures, why don't you tell me where to find the C-note Señor Cruz gave you?"

Eddie felt a laugh, wild and insane, building inside him. He didn't let it out because he was afraid of the pain that might come. He squeezed all that wildness and insanity into contempt, and said: "I used it."

Paz came closer. His hands curled around the safety bar.

"A lie, and not particularly inventive."

Eddie was silent. Paz slapped him across the face with the back of his hand; the way Jack had long ago at Galleon Beach. Then he took a deep breath, as though trying to compose himself. "More games," he said. "You used the money. Where?"

Eddie remembered where: at the restaurant in Connecticut

where he'd eaten with Karen. He even remembered the name: Au Vieux Marron, although he didn't know what it meant. But why tell Paz the truth? Why give him a chance to recover the bill? He wasn't going to let Eddie out alive, no matter what happened.

"Suppose," said Paz, "you really did spend the money. If you tell us where, you can leave."

Eddie let some time pass, as though he were making up his mind. Then he said: "Do I have your word on it?"

"I give you my word."

The insane laugh rose again. Eddie stuffed it back down and said: "Grand Central Station."

Paz grasped the safety bar. A vein pulsed in his forehead, jagged, like a lightning bolt. "Grand Central Station?"

"At the newsstand."

"You're lying. You don't believe I'll keep my word."

"I know goddamned well you won't. Because if you do I'll come back and kill you, and the nurse, and whoever else I can find."

Paz smiled. "I don't think you'll want to do that."

"Are you crazy?"

Paz leaned closer. Eddie could smell his breath: it smelled like meat going bad. "Just for the sake of argument, what did you buy?"

"Cigarettes."

"With a hundred-dollar bill?"

"It didn't bother them."

"What kind of cigarettes?"

"Camels."

Without another word, Paz left the room. Eddie knew what he was doing: searching through his clothes for corroborating evidence. It was there: the half-full pack left in the pocket of Jack's corduroy pants.

Paz returned in less than a minute with the cigarettes. He shook them out of the pack; some fell on Eddie's chest. He even peered inside, as though the bank note might be there. Then he studied the writing on the outside of the pack. Eddie foresaw the direction Paz's thoughts would take. If he could prove that the cigarettes came from the newsstand at Grand Central, then Eddie was probably telling the truth and the C-note was gone, back in circulation. If he could prove that the cigarettes hadn't come from there, then

Eddie was lying and he probably still had it. There was also the possibility that he couldn't prove it either way.

Eddie reached that point a half second before Paz. Paz frowned, slipped the empty pack inside his jacket, and said: "We shall see." He went out.

Eddie lay still for a few moments. Then he threw up all over himself.

Rage began to grow inside him, so fast and strong he felt his chest would split. He wanted to release some huge sound but couldn't, not without bringing Paz. Control, Nails, control. That's how you got Louie and the Ozark brothers, that's how you'll get him. Nails. Yes. Now there was no escaping that identity. The future was clear: red and short.

Eddie pushed against the safety bar with his right arm, pushed as hard as he could. Something slipped a little inside the joint where the bar met the bed frame. He pulled back the other way, suddenly and with all his might. That brought the sound of shearing metal and then a clink, as though a bolt had fallen down a hollow tube. Eddie jerked against the safety bar. The end sprang out of the bed frame.

He slid the restraint off the bar, reached across to the restraint on his left arm and unbuckled it. A few seconds later he was free.

Eddie sat up and put his feet on the floor, but he didn't get up right away. He was afraid of igniting the pain. *Move, Nails.* Slowly, pushing off with his hands like an invalid, Eddie rose. He felt no pain at all. The painkillers were still working.

He used the sheets to clean himself, glancing down at his bandages as he did. The sight of them made him light-headed; he had to bend down, hands on knees, to keep from fainting.

Eddie went to the door, listened, heard nothing. He opened it and looked out. He was at one end of a corridor. There were several doors leading off it; at the other end, stairs. He stepped silently into the corridor. Paz. Then the nurse. Then anyone he could find.

The first door on the right was open. Eddie looked in, saw a simple room with no one in it. It had a bed with a bare mattress; wheeled up beside it was a metal device that resembled a dentist's x-ray machine. On a radiator in the corner lay the clothes he'd borrowed from Jack; the corduroy pants had slid to the floor.

Eddie moved toward the radiator. On the way he passed the

metal device, saw that there was no x-ray tube suspended from it, but a metal helmet with a chin clamp at the bottom. He stopped, examined it. Then he swung the helmet around and stuck his head inside. It fit him perfectly.

First there was only blackness and silence. Then a woman spoke. "One-twenty over eighty," she said. After that came a blue-white glare. Through the glare he saw a white ceiling with powerful lights hanging from it. Music played: "Malagueña." He saw a woman's face. She wore a surgical mask, but he recognized her: the mermaid-waitress from Brainy's.

"Pulse—eighty-two." Her voice sounded in his ears.

"Remove the gown," said Paz, somewhere out of sight.

Then came the blue-white glare again, the scalpel, the pink and plump hands with the manicured nails. The scalpel rotated, giving him a good look at it, then disappeared from view.

Paz again: "Right there."

Pregnant pause.

Blue-white glare.

"Malagueña."

Paz grunted. A nice touch. Then up came the pink, plump hand, red with blood or dye number two, with the dangling pouch in the manicured fingers.

A prop, or a cadaver's pouch, or a live one, but not his. Eddie ripped off the helmet, tore at the bandages. *Not mine, not mine, not mine.* Eddie's mind repeated those words, but he couldn't be sure, wasn't sure, until the bandages fell in a heap and he saw himself, intact.

Intact. Relief flooded through him like the best drug on earth. Intact.

Eddie got dressed. He went into the corridor, walked to the end. All the doors were open, all the rooms empty. Eddie went down six flights of stairs, all the way to the bottom. He found himself in a big basement; naked bulbs spread pools of yellow light. There was a steel door at the far end. He went toward it, passing mounds of sand, stacks of plush divans, Persian rugs, papier-mâché date palms, and a disassembled minaret made of whitewashed plywood.

Eddie opened the steel door. It led to a short set of cement steps, smelling of stale beer. At the top was a bulkhead door, locked from the inside with a bolt. Eddie slid it back, pushed open the door, and climbed out onto the street.

He'd been wrong about the time. It was day. A cloudy day, dreary and dark, probably, but bright enough to make him blink. Eddie let the bulkhead door fall shut and started to move away. A woman on a mountain bike screamed, "You fucking idiot," and almost ran him down.

Chapter Twenty-Two

"Bonjour, monsieur," said the maître d' of Au Vieux Marron. *"C'est fermé jusque à cinq et demi."*

"Knock it off," said Eddie.

"Pardon?"

They stood in the doorway of the restaurant, Eddie outside in the cold rain, the maître d' inside, warm and dry. It was about three o'clock and the restaurant was empty. The maître d' hadn't yet put on his jacket and tie. He wore a white shirt, black pants, black vest, and a puzzled smile.

"Is it part of your job, speaking French all the time?"

The maître d's smile changed to an expression that reminded Eddie of Charles de Gaulle. "I am in the food business, monsieur. French is the language of food."

"I'm not hungry."

"Then may I ask to what we owe this visit?"

"I was here last night," Eddie said, thinking that the maître d' spoke better English than he did.

"Armagnac, avec et sans glaçons," said the maître d', recovering his smile; a knowing one.

"That's me," said Eddie. "I want my C-note back."

"Pardon?"

"C-note. It means—"

"I know the meaning of C-note. What was your complaint?"

"No complaints," said Eddie. "I don't want the actual money.

Just the C-note." Eddie produced the $350 roll and peeled off two fifties. "Here."

The maître d' eyed the money but made no move to take it. "It's a rare bill, perhaps?"

"No. Call it a lucky charm."

The knowing expression grew stronger. The maître d' began to resemble Claude Rains. "The tables?" he said. "Or the horses?"

"You're reading my mind."

"I am something of a gambler myself," said the maître d'. "Have you been to Atlantic City?"

"Not yet."

The maître d' was shocked. "Not yet! And so nearby!" He shook his head. "Atlantic City, *quel* . . ." Words failed him in two languages.

The maître d' led Eddie past the kitchen, into the office. A framed autographed photo of Julia Child hung on the wall. The maître d' removed it, revealing a small safe. He glanced at Eddie, smiled again, then turned to block his view as he spun the dial. On the desk lay a half-eaten hot dog with ketchup and relish.

The maître d' took out a cash box, carried it to the desk, opened it. Inside were checks, credit-card slips, money. The maître d' fingered through it. He picked out a hundred-dollar bill. Then another. And another. He laid the three of them on the desk, Benjamin Franklin side up, flipped them over, then over again.

"Which is the lucky charm?"

Eddie studied the bills. There had to be a reason why Paz wanted the bill, had to be a reason why El Rojo had tried to smuggle it to him; something that made it different from the other bills. Invisible ink? Should he take all three, examine them under ultraviolet light? Eddie doubted that El Rojo had that kind of writing material in his cell.

One of the bills was crisp and unwrinkled; as though fresh from the mint. Eddie concentrated on the other two, holding each up to the light. He looked for clues in Franklin's prosperous image, in the leafy scene on the back, in the clock tower of Independence Hall, where the time appeared to be 1:25. He checked the margins and the other open spaces for handwriting, but found none. None, unless you counted the tiny numbers inked here and there on the more wrinkled of the two bills.

Eddie had another look. He located the numbers one through fourteen, all on the Franklin side, inscribed in black ink. Some of them were written under individual digits of the serial number, B41081554G. The *one*, for example, appeared under the *four*. Other numbers were elsewhere: *ten* in the borders of the *S* in "ONE HUNDRED DOLLARS."

"This is it," Eddie said.

"How do you know?" asked the maître d', peering over his shoulder.

"By the cigarette smell."

The maître d' sniffed the air. "You have a good nose, monsieur."

"Armagnac lovers. We're all like that." Eddie handed over the two fifties.

The maître d' looked at them doubtfully, tried snapping one of them between his fingers.

"That doesn't prove a thing," Eddie said. He'd known a few counterfeiters.

Eddie took the bus back to New York. On a pad of paper he realigned the printed letters and numbers on the bill according to the order suggested by the inked-in numbers, one through fourteen. That produced the following sequence: 46505719 14THST

Meaningless. Eddie knew nothing about codes. He made the obvious move, assigning a letter value to each number, governed by its place in the alphabet: *four* becoming *D*, *six* becoming *F*, and so on. The only problem was the zero. He decided to substitute the letter *O* for now, and change it later if needed. Soon he had a line of fourteen letters: DFEOEGAIADTHST

He played with those letters all the way to the city. The best he could manage was this: DIE SAD THEFT AGO

Eddie stared again at the original line: 46505719 14THST. He began at the letter end. *ST*. *TH*. *TH* was short for Thursday. It also made the sound *th*. *ST* could be short for Saturday. It was also short for saint and street. Thursday Saturday. Thursday Saint. Thursday Street. Was there a Thursday Street? He hadn't heard of one. He had read and half understood a yellowed paperback called *The Man Who Was Thursday*, but he recalled no Thursday Street. *TH ST*. *TH* Street. His gaze slid back into the numbers. *14 TH ST*.

14th Street.

Fourteenth Street.

There were certainly 14th streets. Were there 914th streets as well? Probably not. So stick with fourteenth.

Eddie went back to the beginning. He now had this: 46505719 14THST

Was it an address? 9 14th Street? 19 14th Street? 719 14th Street? 5719 14th Street? And if so, in what city? It suddenly occurred to him to check what Federal Reserve Bank the bill had come from.

B. New York.

He dropped 5719 because he didn't think street numbers went that high in New York; high street numbers meant out west. So, it was 9, 19, or 719. Then what were 46505 all about? He tried to fit them into some form of address and couldn't.

A voice spoke, "Let's go bud. Haven't got all day."

The bus driver was standing over him. They were in the station and the bus was empty. Eddie rose, but slowly, the driver's words lingering in his mind.

"What's the date?"

"The sixth. All day."

"Of April?"

"Yeah. Where you been?"

Eddie got off the bus. April 6. 4/6. 4/6 505 719 14th St. 4/6 5:05 719 14th St. 5:05.

5:05. A.M. or P.M.?

Eddie checked the clock in the terminal: 4:15.

He went outside, stuck up his hand at a passing cab. It passed, as did several others. Then one stopped, but a woman with a shopping bag jumped in ahead of him. When the next one stopped, Eddie jumped in ahead of someone else.

Eddie gave the driver the address and asked, "Is it far?"

"No far."

"Can you get me there by five?"

"Fi dollar?"

"Five o'clock."

"Eas' or wes'?"

"What?"

"Eas' or wes' fourteen?"

Eddie didn't know. They tried west, but found no 719. There was a 719 East Fourteenth. The driver dropped Eddie outside it at ten to five, by the clock hanging in the window of Kwik 'n Brite Dry Cleaners next door. It was impossible to see into 719 itself. The windows had been painted red to eye level. The neon sign said: "Adult Books, Mags, Videos, Peeps." A secondary, hand-lettered sign added: "Male-Female, Female-Female, Male-Male, More."

Eddie went inside. There were two men in the store. One wore a ponytail and a Harvard sweat shirt. He stood behind the counter, inhaling nasal spray. The other wore a stone face and a suit. He browsed in the all-amateur section of the video department. Neither looked at Eddie.

He left the store, crossed the street, waited with his back to a florist's shop. The rain had softened to a light drizzle. It glistened on the flowers in their bins outside: tulips, roses, others Eddie couldn't name. He smelled their smells and kept his eyes on "Adult Books, Mags, Videos, Peeps."

The browser came out, a plastic shopping bag in his hand. A woman in a black sombrero walked quickly past. A young man, not much older than the bookstore boy, went by the door of 719, turned, passed the other way, glanced around, saw Eddie, checked his watch as though he were on a schedule, and slinked inside the store. Then came a woman with a leashed mongrel that pissed against the wall of the store, a bare-chested man on roller blades, and an unleashed mongrel that sniffed the wall and raised its leg in the already pissed-on place.

At 5:04, by the clock in the Kwik 'n Brite window, a taxi stopped in front of 719 and a man got out. He wore a trench coat and a hat, the kind of hat men wore in old movies—a fedora maybe, Eddie didn't know much about the names of hats. He had fat cheeks reddened by the sun, curly graying hair, a trim gray beard: a potential department-store Santa. Eddie couldn't name him at first. That was partly because of the coat and hat, mostly because the man was so far out of context. But Eddie knew him, all right. How could he forget a man who had taken a gram of muscle from his forearm with a big square-ended instrument for some drug company, who had labeled him an inadequate personality, who had predicted that Eddie would be back in prison soon? It was Floyd K. Messer, M.D., Ph.D., Director of Treatment.

The taxi drove off. Messer stood on the sidewalk. He glanced around, his gaze passing over Eddie, not ten yards away, with no sign of recognition. Eddie ducked into the florist's, watched Messer through the window.

Messer looked behind at 719, saw the sign, and moved in front of Kwik 'n Brite. He checked his watch. Cars went by. Messer eyed every one.

"Can I help you?"

Eddie turned and saw a little Asian girl—Korean, he supposed: hadn't he read somewhere about the coming of Korean shopkeepers?—gazing up at him. He remembered the olive-skinned girl in the dancing shoes at the bus station down south; and the water snakes: "O happy living things."

"I'm just looking," Eddie said.

"We've got some nice iris." She brandished purple petals at him. "Special—five dollars a dozen." An old woman watched from behind the cash register.

"I'll take a dozen," said Eddie.

The girl withdrew. Eddie looked out the window. Messer was pacing now. The Kwik 'n Brite clock read 5:11. The woman with the leashed mongrel came by, going the other way. The dog sniffed the still-damp stain on the wall, pissed again. The girl returned with a bouquet.

"How about these?"

"Fine."

She left, busied herself with wrapping paper. The door of 719 opened and the young man came out, red-faced, with a plastic shopping bag. The unleashed mongrel appeared, sniffed, pissed. Messer checked his watch. The Kwik 'n Brite clock read 5:20. Messer kept pacing.

Rain fell harder. The old Korean woman went outside, began bringing in the flowers. The girl left her wrapping to help. A passing car splashed Messer's shoes. Messer said, "Shit." Eddie couldn't hear him, but he could read his lips.

At 5:29 the Korean girl said, "Here you go, mister," and handed Eddie the bouquet wrapped in green paper. As he took it,

Eddie saw an empty taxi come up the street. Messer saw it too. It was almost past him when his arm shot up. The taxi stopped. Messer got in. The taxi drove off. Eddie ran into the street. The old Korean woman ran after him.

"Fi dollar," she cried. "Fi dollar."

Chapter Twenty-Three

One door down from the Korean flower shop stood the Café Bucharest. The table in its front window commanded a good view of Kwik 'n Brite Dry Cleaners and 719: Adult Books, Mags, Videos, Peeps. Eddie sat at the window table, checking out the posters on the walls of the Café Bucharest—rugged mountains, green valleys, crumbling castles, Bela Lugosi as Dracula—and drinking a steaming cup of espresso. His first espresso; Eddie didn't like it much. He kept his eye on 719 and resisted the urge to buy cigarettes.

Night fell. The rain slanted down out of the darkness, shimmered through the yellow cones of street light, disappeared. Not a good night for the pornography business. In an hour, three customers—all of them male, all of them alone—entered 719. One came out with a plastic shopping bag, the others empty-handed.

Eddie ate a thick sandwich of roast beef on black bread, served with a strange orange pickle, and imagined he was getting the feeling of Bucharest. A cigarette, unfiltered, Turkish, would make it perfect. Brightly colored packs of them, all with foreign names, were displayed beside the cash register. Eddie ordered another cup of espresso instead.

"Some strudel?"

"No, thanks." Dessicated pastries posing under that name were served in the cafeteria shared by E and F-Blocks every Sunday night.

Eddie began to like espresso. He was taking his last sip when a truck, rusty and dented, bearing the words "Simon Poultry Farms" on the side, parked in front of 719. The store's neon sign flashed off, glowing dully for a few moments, then fading to darkness. Eddie rose, laid some money on the table.

The ponytailed man in the Harvard sweat shirt came out, rolled down a steel door that covered the entire front of the store, locked it in place. Then he climbed into the truck on the passenger side and started arguing with the driver. Eddie left the Cafe Bucharest.

The truck pulled into traffic, headed down Fourteenth Street. Eddie followed, first walking on the sidewalk, then running on the road, as though connected to the truck by an unseen force. The truck picked up speed. It had an unroofed cargo space, surrounded by slatted wooden sections about five feet high. Running at full speed, Eddie caught up to it and leaped, grabbing the top of one of the wooden sections.

He hauled himself up. A slat cracked under his weight. Eddie got his feet on the edge of the steel platform and vaulted over. The slat snapped. He lost his balance and landed hard on stacks of wire cages, knocking some loose. Chickens began squawking all around him.

The truck swerved to the side of the road, skidded to a halt. Eddie crawled over the cages, dropped into a small space against the back of the cab. He lay down in it. A chicken pecked his hand through the wire.

Eddie heard one of the doors of the cab open. Then came a grunt of effort, followed by the sight of the ponytailed man leaning over the side, squinting into the back of the truck. If he had glanced straight down, he might have seen Eddie, but he did not.

Eddie heard the driver call, *"Que pasa?"*

"The fucking *pollos*," replied the ponytailed man.

At that moment there was a tremendous burst of rain. "Fuck the fucking *pollos*, Julio," yelled the driver.

Julio ducked out of sight. The door slammed shut. The truck jerked back out into the street.

Rain lashed down on Eddie and the chickens. The chickens went quiet. Eddie felt around for a tarpaulin. Wasn't there always a tarpaulin in the back of a truck? Not in this one. He sat huddled between the cab and the cages. Rain swept down, cold and hard.

Eddie bounced around on wet steel. None of that bothered him. The espresso was still warm inside him, and if he tilted his head back he had a wonderful view of skyscrapers rising into the night. It reminded him of a line from his reading: "Alps on Alps arise." That was the city of Karen de Vere, champagne and Armagnac. He lost his enthusiasm for the view.

The rain stopped abruptly; the skyscrapers vanished. They were in a tunnel. The chickens shifted nervously. Newspaper rustled on the floors of their cages. Eddie made a clicking sound. It failed to soothe the chickens. He was struck with the mad idea of opening the cages and letting them all out.

Then he was back in the rain. The truck swung onto a ramp, halted soon after at a toll booth, then sped off on a turnpike under sodium-orange skies. The rain stung. Eddie got his back against the cab, hunching below the window; the chickens tucked their heads under their wings and endured. They all did it, even though the only ones getting wet were in the top row.

The truck seemed to be heading south. Eddie confronted the possibility that while there had to be a connection between Dr. Messer, Señor Paz, El Rojo, and the hundred-dollar bill, the ponytailed man might have nothing to do with it. Why would he, especially since Messer hadn't even entered 719? Maybe it was only the outside of 719 that mattered. Julio could be on his way home to the wife and kids, or to a bowling alley, or, more probably, to a second job at a meat packer's. A beer can flew out of the cab, and then another.

Eddie was soaked and shivering by the time the truck left the turnpike. They followed a two-lane road, going more slowly now. The sky lost its orange glow, went black. The only light came from headlight beams that flashed from time to time across the cages. Eddie caught glimpses of the chickens; they appeared headless, as they soon might be. More beer cans flew by, faint whizzing shadows in the night.

Time passed, how much time Eddie didn't know. His watch was on Prof's wrist, locked up in F-block. Eddie was wet, cold, unsure; but free, and therefore happy, right?

The truck slowed, down to a speed where Eddie could have jumped off safely. He considered it, and was still considering it when they turned onto a dirt road and bumped through a wooded flatland. The trees stretched overhead, catching some of the rain. Under their shelter, the chickens came to life, shifting around in their cages, nervous again. Just like inmates: catatonic when things were at their worst; agitation always following slight improvements.

They were alone on the dirt road. Five or six miles passed before the truck came to a stop. Eddie rose, peered over the side. The headlights shone on a fence, not especially high but made of barbed wire, stretching out of sight in both directions; a closed gate on which hung a sign—"Simon Poultry Farms"; a gatehouse with a motorcycle parked inside; and a man standing in the road with an automatic weapon over his shoulder and a shotgun in his hands. He approached the truck.

The man spoke in Spanish. "Late," he said.

"You drive in this piss," the driver told him.

"Try standing in it all fucking night," answered the man with the guns. He opened the gate, backed into the shadows. The truck rolled through.

The truck mounted a long, low rise, turned right off the main road, came down in a clearing. In the changing angles of the headlights, Eddie picked out an old two-story farmhouse, a barn, outbuildings. The truck passed the barn, turned toward the house, slowed. The door of the house opened, framing a short, round man in a yellow rectangle of light. Eddie hopped off the truck, slipped on wet grass, came up running. A fruit tree, gnarled and bare, grew between the house and the barn. Eddie crouched behind it.

The short, round man unfurled an umbrella and walked to the truck. Julio and the driver got out. The driver was a big man, perhaps six and a half feet tall. The short, round man went as close to him as the umbrella would allow.

"You're late," he said. He spoke Spanish, but Eddie recognized his voice: Señor Paz.

"It's the weather."

"And you've been drinking."

"Just one beer on the way."

Paz reached up from under the umbrella and slapped the driver's face with the back of his hand, the way he'd slapped Eddie.

"Sorry," said the driver.

Paz wasn't listening. He had moved in front of Julio. "You too," he said. "I can smell it."

"Not me."

Paz spoke to the driver. "Hit him."

The driver threw a punch at the ponytailed man's head, knocking him down.

Paz said, "Now get busy," walked back into the house, leaving the door open.

The driver helped Julio to his feet. "Did it have to be that hard?" asked Julio.

"Just doing my job," the driver replied.

The driver went around to the back of the truck, climbed up, began hoisting off the rear slatted sections and stacking them to the side. Julio went into the house, returned with an empty cardboard box. The driver opened one of the cages, tossed the chicken and the newspaper flooring onto the ground, picked up the cage and dumped it out into the cardboard box. The chicken skittered across the grass and into the barn.

The driver opened another cage and went through the same routine, tossing out the chicken and the newspaper, dumping what was left into the cardboard box. He kept doing that until Julio said, "Enough," and carried the box into the house. He came back with an empty one, and they did it all again.

And twice more. The last time the driver followed Julio into the house and closed the door. Eddie came out of the shadows.

He made a wide circle around the house, approached it from the back. Lights shone through the windows on both floors. Eddie dropped to the wet ground and crawled to the nearest one, raised his head above the sill.

He looked into a big kitchen, saw a cozy rural scene. Julio and the driver sat in front of a stone fireplace, roasting marshmallows over a snapping four- or five-log fire. A glossy German shepherd lay beside them, staring into the flames. At one end of the long table in the center of the room sat Paz, reading a newspaper and eating vanilla ice cream; pure white against his olive skin, his red tongue. Three old women in kerchiefs and shawls sat along the far side of the table, facing Eddie, chatting to themselves.

While they talked, the old women busied themselves with the cardboard boxes Julio had brought in. The first two emptied them, spilling paper money across the table. Then they sorted it into piles by denomination, banded the bills in stacks, dropped the stacks into a canvas bag. The third woman made entries on a laptop and called to Julio when the bag was full. He got up from the fire and added the bags to a mound of others near the door. The women filled three canvas bags while Eddie watched; their knobby hands never stopped, working together like giant inhabitants of an insect colony.

Suddenly, the dog's ears rose. Eddie sank down, listened, heard nothing. He crept along to the next window, looked in.

A bedroom. The only light came from a TV on a corner desk. On the screen a hideous man with four-inch nails was tiptoeing toward a car parked in a lovers' lane. The only viewer was a dark-haired boy of about ten or eleven lying on the bed, but he wasn't paying much attention to the show. He was more interested in the gun in his hand.

It might have been a toy, but to Eddie it looked just like the nine-millimeters worn by the C.O.s in the towers. The boy spun it around on his index finger like a quick-draw artist, jabbed it at the man with four-inch nails, at a teddy bear against the wall, at the window where Eddie watched.

Eddie dropped to the ground. He was quick, surely too quick for the boy to have seen him. But the next moment came an explosion, and the window blew out over Eddie's head. He scrambled away, dove among the nearest trees.

Voices rose from the house. Shadows made wild gestures in the blue light of the boy's window. Then Paz poked his head out, peered around. Rain fell steadily and the night was quiet, except for the beating of Eddie's heart against the earth.

"It's just his imagination," said Paz in Spanish, holding his ice-cream spoon. "All that TV."

"That's not the point," said one of the old women in the room behind him. "He shouldn't be playing with guns."

Then came the high voice of the boy. "It's mine," he said. "And I saw someone out there, whether you believe me or not."

"What kind of someone?" asked Paz, turning back to the room.

"All white. Like a ghost."

Paz sighed. "Bedtime," he said. He glanced outside again,

picked a shard of glass out of the frame, withdrew. "Back to work," Eddie heard him say. "And one of you get this fixed."

The shadows moved out of the blue light. Eddie stayed still. The boy's head appeared in the window. Eddie recognized him from the photograph on the wall of El Rojo's cell. Simon Cruz, known as "Gaucho"—a fine boy and a dead shot, according to his proud papa.

Gaucho aimed his gun at the forest and said, "Pow, pow."

Julio taped a piece of cardboard over the window. The farmhouse grew quiet, the lights went out. Rain began again, just a drizzle at first, then harder. It dripped down off the leafless branches onto Eddie. He circled the house, crawled under the truck and waited, listening to the rain.

It was still dark when he heard the door of the farmhouse open. Eddie rolled over, saw the glare of a flashlight, its beam zigzagging over the ground on an unsteady path toward the truck. For a moment it rested on Julio, carrying canvas bags over his shoulder.

"When is this rain going to stop?" he said in Spanish.

"All you do is complain," answered the other man; Eddie recognized the voice of the driver.

"I hate this country."

"So go home."

Julio snorted.

The driver pointed his light at the truck. Eddie stayed still. With a grunt, Julio slung the canvas bags over the side, into the cargo space.

"I mean it," he said. "What's so good about this country?"

"The women," replied the driver. They started back toward the house.

"The women? Are you joking?"

"They fuck like crazy."

"So?" said Julio. "They hate men. At least our women like men. The women here piss me off. Sometimes I feel like just taking one, you know? One of those cool ones."

They went into the house, came out with more canvas bags, tossed them into the truck. Then they climbed into the cab. The doors closed, the engine started, the truck vibrated above Eddie.

He slid out from under, got a grip on the edge of the platform, and climbed up and over the side just as the truck drove away.

They mounted the rise, turned right on the main road, away from the gate. Eddie sat on the canvas bags. After a mile or two they took a narrow track, followed it through the woods. Eddie couldn't see much but knew they came to a stream because he heard water flowing, knew they crossed a wooden bridge because he heard it creak. Not long after, they came to a clearing, a charcoal-colored opening in the night. The truck slowed. It hadn't quite stopped when Eddie vaulted over the side, landed on all fours on hard-packed dirt, ran low into the woods. The driver cut the engine; headlights and brake lights flashed out.

They waited, Julio and the driver warm and dry in the cab, Eddie cold and wet in the trees. Eddie didn't know what they were waiting for; he was waiting for Floyd K. Messer, although he couldn't have given a logical reason why.

The night lost its blackness. Shadows firmed into solid shapes— the trees, the truck, the driver standing beside it, pissing against the wheel, a small car parked nearby. The eastern sky turned silver for a moment, then settled on dark gray. In the growing light, Eddie saw that the truck was parked at one end of a long, narrow dirt strip cut through the woods.

The driver, on his way back to the cab, went still, his head tilted up. Then Eddie heard it too, a plane coming from the south. Julio climbed from the cab into the cargo space, tossed the canvas bags onto the ground.

A white plane with green trim burst out of the clouds, very low, buzzed over the truck and landed not far away. It rolled down the strip, slowed, turned, rolled back. Eddie could see no one inside but the pilot, and he looked nothing like Messer. The pilot was wearing sunglasses. Maybe the sun was shining somewhere high above.

The plane halted beside the truck. The driver ran to it, swung open a compartment near the tail. Julio threw the canvas bags inside. The plane was already moving again by the time the driver closed the compartment. No one said a word.

The plane sped down the runway, lifted off, rose into the clouds, went silent, vanished.

"What a prick," Julio said in English.

"They're all like that," the driver replied.

"Monday?" said Julio.

"Monday."

The driver got into the truck, Julio into the car. They drove away.

Outside: Day 6

Chapter Twenty-Four

"How do you want to play this?" said Max Switzer, picking at his sandy mustache.

Karen de Vere hated when he did that, hated working with Max at all; he had no touch. Drawing his stupid gun on Eddie Nye, for example. He reminded her of her ex-husband, making his insufferable way up the ladder of Whiteshoe and Silverspoon, or whatever the hell it was. "It's a no-brainer," she said, with an edge in her voice; she heard it and sharpened it as she continued. "I say I've changed my mind."

"And ask for the money back?"

"Bull's-eye. It's called a sting."

"Then what happens?"

"Everyone fucks up in his or her own way, as always."

Eddie entered Jack's suite at the Palazzo. No one was there. Raleigh's beer cans, the empty glasses, the pinkened towel, the cigar ashes; all gone. Tidy, quiet, peaceful; like the hotel room it was, ready for the next guest. Eddie searched for a note Jack might have left him, found none. He went into the bedroom, checked the fax, read a page about an engineering company in Dubai that wanted investors. "Jack—thar's gold in them thar sands," someone had scrawled at the bottom.

Eddie opened the closet. Jack's suits still hung there by the dozen; shoes for every occasion lay in formation on the floor. He was out, not gone. Eddie kicked off the tassel loafers, chose a pair of sneakers. Lacing them up, he remembered that most inmates only tied their shoes tight when there was fighting to be done; it was one of the little things you looked for.

Eddie walked into the sitting room, looked out the window at a low sky of unbroken cloud. The first drops began to fall as he watched, thin streaks like scratches on gray slate, almost invisible. Down in the park a jogger in blue passed a jogger in red, was passed in turn by a jogger in green. Then a black dog trailing its leash zipped by all of them.

Eddie left the Palazzo and took a cab to Brainy's. Brainy's was closed, as he had expected. He walked the nearby streets in the rain. Everything looked different: because it was day, because he was sober, because he had a purpose. Not to take up where he'd left off; he knew he couldn't do that. But he also knew he had to go back fifteen years, to revisit his life—as a spectator, perhaps, or an investigator. There were questions that had to be answered, questions raised by Evelyn Andrea Manning Packer Nye; partly by what she'd said, partly by how she'd ended up.

Eddie found the used bookstore. This time he noted its name: Gold's Books—Fine, Used, and Rare. The paperback bin was empty because of the rain. Eddie went in. The bell tinkled. The boy in the skullcap was reading at the desk. He looked up. There was a pimple on his forehead, making Eddie think of those high-caste Indians.

"Another holiday?" Eddie said.

"It's Sunday."

He would have to learn to keep track of the days again.

"We're not really open," the boy went on. "I just come here because it's . . . quieter."

Eddie listened. The sounds of the city were barely audible, as if all the books could somehow muffle them.

"What's your name?" Eddie said.

The boy hesitated.

"Mine's Ed. Ed Nye."

"Pinchas," said the boy, and again Eddie imagined what would happen to him in prison, again felt his stomach turn.

"I need some help," Eddie said. "I'll pay you for it."

The boy closed his book: *The Comedians.* "I'm not really an expert when it comes to poetry," he said.

"This isn't about poetry."

"Is it legal?"

Eddie laughed. "Why do you ask that?"

The boy bit his lip.

How to put him at ease? Eddie didn't know. He smiled. "Go on," he said.

"Don't take this personally."

"I won't."

"But you do look like someone who might do something illegal."

"Like a hit man, you said."

"Maybe not so much like a hit man, the way your hair's growing in."

Gray. "I'll tell you something," Eddie said, perhaps more forcefully than he'd intended, because the boy shrank in his chair: "I've never done anything illegal in my life." In his mind it was true: the three men he'd killed had been in self-defense, and he hadn't known what had been hidden away on *Fearless.* He'd done nothing illegal, but the look had rubbed off on him anyway.

"Nothing?" said Pinchas. His Adam's apple bobbed, as though a bubble that couldn't be suppressed was on its way up. "I've broken the law myself."

"You have?"

Pinchas looked down, nodded.

"What did you do?"

"I shoplifted . . . an object."

"What was it?"

The boy was silent. From outside came the strangely muted noise of the city. Pinchas spoke. "You won't tell anybody?"

"Except the FBI."

Pinchas didn't laugh, but he got up, moved into the shadows at the back of the store, climbed the stepladder, and reached up to the top of the highest shelf. He returned with something wrapped in tissue paper.

What? Surely not a watch, or jewelry, or an electronic gadget. A rare book, maybe? Or something Jewish that Eddie knew nothing about. That would be it.

Pinchas unwrapped the tissue paper. Inside was a brand-new Minnesota Twins baseball cap. Pinchas didn't touch it. Slowly his gaze came up, met Eddie's.

"You stole it?"

"From Herman's. I walked in, stuck it under my jacket, and walked out. Like I was an automaton or something. I couldn't help it."

"But why?"

Pinchas stared down at the cap.

"Couldn't you have asked your parents to buy it for you?"

"You don't understand."

Was the boy poor? Eddie saw nothing to indicate that. "What about saving your own money?"

"It wasn't the money," Pinchas said. "It was the act of buying I couldn't do. That would make it official. Like I consciously made a decision to . . . possess it. This way it's just something that happened. The will of . . ." His voice trailed off.

Eddie picked up the cap. It was made of wool, just like the real ones, but smaller. "Let's see it on you."

The boy's eyes widened. "I can't."

"You mean you haven't tried it on yet?"

Pinchas shook his head quickly from side to side.

Eddie held it out. "Just slide into your automaton mode."

This time a smile appeared on Pinchas's face; but quickly vanished. He didn't move for a few moments. Then, slowly, he took off his skullcap, laid it gently on the desk; it left a circular imprint on his hair. He accepted the Minnesota Twins cap from Eddie in both hands and put it on. It was too big for him, made him appear even younger, nothing like a ball player.

"How do I look?" Pinchas asked.

"Just like Canseco," Eddie said. He'd watched a thousand games in the rec room.

"I don't like Canseco," Pinchas said. "Kirby Puckett's my favorite." He went to the dusty window, bent forward, peered at his reflection. He tilted the cap at an angle and came back. He was walking differently, perhaps in imitation of Kirby Puckett or some other slugger.

"What position do you play?" Eddie asked.

"Play?"

"In baseball."

"Oh," said the boy, "I've never actually played. There's no time, with the store, and Yeshiva, and Talmud-Torah at night. And even if there was, my parents . . . they want the best for me. That's the beauty of this country for them. They're free to live a life that has nothing to do with it."

Eddie wasn't following this too well. "You look like a second baseman," he said.

"I do?" Pinchas smiled. This time it stayed on his face a little longer. He tugged at the bill of his cap, making a small adjustment. Then he shot Eddie a glance. "I'm sorry for saying you looked like a criminal."

"A natural mistake," Eddie said. "I did the penance first, that's all."

Pinchas frowned. "Before the crime?"

"The crime that happened had nothing to do with me," Eddie said. "That's where I need your help."

"Help you do what?"

"Find a hospice," Eddie said.

"Where people go to die?"

"Is there another kind? The problem is I don't know which one this person is in."

"Are you going to do something to him?"

"Would that make sense?"

Pause. Then Pinchas started laughing. Eddie laughed too. Pinchas turned to the computer, switched it on. "What kind of hospice?" he said, tapping the keys. "AIDS, cancer, normal dying?"

"We'll have to try them all."

Ten minutes later, Pinchas tore off a two-page printout and handed it to Eddie. He picked up the phone and dialed St. Sebastian's Home, the first one on the list.

Eddie: "I'm trying to find an old friend of mine who's not well. I thought he might be with you."

Woman: "What's his name?"

Eddie: "JFK. That's what he called himself."

Woman: "I'll need his real name."

Eddie: "I don't know it."

Woman: "Sorry."

Eddie went through similar conversations eight times. The ninth time, a man answered. "The Caring Place," he said.

Eddie went through his spiel.

"Do you mean Mr. Kidd, by any chance?" asked the man.

"Possibly."

"We had a Junior Fairbanks Kidd," said the man. "At least that's what it said on his passport."

"A Bahamian passport?" asked Eddie.

"That's right."

"You said *had*."

"Mr. Kidd left last week."

"Where did he go?"

"He said he was going home."

"Does that mean he was better?"

"Better? More reconciled, perhaps. More in tune with the end rhythms of his life."

Eddie hung up.

Pinchas was watching him from under the bill of his Twins cap. "You've seen the world, haven't you?" he said.

"Parts."

"That's why you're interested in 'The Mariner.' All that sailing."

Eddie shook his head. "I'm interested in it . . ." He paused. Why? An answer came: "because it's a beautiful thing that doesn't make sense."

"Doesn't make sense?"

"Because the punishment doesn't fit the crime. How can it when the nature of the crime's a mystery?"

The boy looked puzzled. "Have you read the Bible?" he asked. "I'm talking about the Old Testament."

"No."

"That's why you can ask a question like that."

They looked at each other for a few moments. Eddie laid the printout on the desk. "What do I owe you?"

"For what?"

"The computer time."

"Not a thing."

Pinchas took off the Twins cap, put on the skullcap. He was rewrapping the Twins cap in tissue paper when Eddie left.

Chapter Twenty-Five

Now when Eddie walked into the suite, Jack was there, pacing by the window, smoking a cigarette. He wore a double-breasted suit, a white shirt, and a silk tie, but his feet were bare.

"It's you," he said. "Where'd you fuck off to?"

"Just taking a virtual-reality check," Eddie said. "Not my thing."

Jack nodded, but absent, blank. He paced, glanced out the window, let cigarette ash flutter down to the rug.

"What's wrong?" Eddie said.

"Nothing."

Eddie noticed that Jack's feet, once high-arched and strong, had changed. They were almost flat now, and the toenails were thick and yellowed with fungus.

"I don't believe you," Eddie said.

Jack rounded on him. "Nothing's wrong that you can help with. Let's put it that way."

Eddie nodded. He took out what was left of the $350 and laid it on the TV. "I'll send you the clothes." He moved toward the door.

Jack bounded toward him, spun him around, held him by the shoulders. He was still strong.

"I don't need any shit from you, bro."

For a moment Eddie just stood there, like a rabbit mesmerized by a predator, like an inmate who knew the pecking order. Then he raised his hands, placed them on Jack's chest, and pushed him away. Not too hard—Jack was his brother; but he didn't want to be handled.

Not too hard, maybe, but it was hard enough to send Jack to the floor. He bounced up, came at Eddie with his hand raised for a backswing across the face. Eddie was tired of that; he caught Jack's wrist in midair and held it. Jack wasn't like Raleigh. He was much stronger, much tougher. Still, he couldn't move his arm at all. When he saw that, he showed he was much smarter too—the resistance went out of him completely and at once.

Eddie released him. Jack gave him a long look. "You've changed."

"That's a pretty stupid thing to say."

"I know. Shit. I can't think straight." Jack rubbed his forehead with the heels of both palms, as though that might unscramble whatever was going on inside.

"What's the trouble?" Eddie said.

Jack sighed, turned to the window, glanced out. "When's this fucking rain going to stop?" He picked his smoldering cigarette out of an ashtray and started pacing again. He took powerful strides, three or four one way, three or four back. Rain made spidery streaks on the window, arpeggios to his rhythm section. "Money trouble, Eddie. What other kind of trouble is there?"

Eddie knew lots. "You're talking about Windward Financial?"

"What else?"

"I thought it could be your personal money or something."

Jack laughed; an unfunny two-track sound, harsh and ironic. "Other people are likely to make the same mistake. And when they do it's finito. I'm not just talking about fines I can't pay, I'm talking about jail, bro. Is that clear enough?"

Jail was clear enough to Eddie, but he still didn't know what Jack's problem was. "Explain," he said.

Jack took a deep drag of his cigarette, deep enough to burn off half an inch of it. Eddie felt a strong desire for a smoke himself, suppressed it. "The way this business works," Jack said, "I make money for people. I invest what they give me as I see fit, within parameters we establish at the beginning. Follow?"

Eddie nodded.

"In addition, Windward has its own account."

"Meaning you."

Jack squinted at him through a cloud of smoke. "Yeah, meaning me. Sometimes, just for simplicity—you wouldn't believe how complicated this can get—money from the investor accounts gets pooled for a while with Windward money. Nothing wrong with it, as long as everything's kosher by the time the quarterlies go out. Sometimes mistakes happen."

"Like with J. M. Nye and Associates?"

Pause. "That's right. Raleigh fucked up, but it was just a technicality. If it hadn't happened when it did, at the end of the eighties when everybody got so righteous all of a sudden . . ." He took another drag, and then a deeper one, as though he couldn't get enough smoke inside him. "And of course we were an easy target. A boutique, right? Not Drexel or some big dick like that. So they got in a pissy mood and took a swing at us and now Raleigh's the way he is. But it wasn't the end of the world. There was still lots of money around, money to cover. Now there isn't."

"Where did it go?"

"It didn't go anywhere. That's the point. There's this flow of money, Eddie. You've got to tap it—like maple sap up at the sugar bush when we were kids. Remember?"

"No."

"Maybe you weren't there that time. It must have been with Mom." Jack's eyes assumed an inward look for a moment. "What I'm saying is that the money's not flowing anymore," he continued. "There are a lot of reasons—you can find them in the part of the paper that interesting people don't read. I got into a situation where I couldn't wait anymore. I tried a few things—copper futures, that was one." He paused, took another drag, resumed pacing. "Copper futures. It's all controlled by three or four ball busters in London. I got in a hole. It led to some . . . maneuvering in the accounts. Technical stuff. The quarterlies were coming up and I was going snake."

"What about selling the houses in Aspen and Connecticut?"

Jack's gaze went to the coffee table, where the Windward brochure had lain the night of Eddie's arrival. "They're gone, bro. They were mortgaged right down to the Jacuzzis anyway. I tried everything, even the banks, that's how bad it was." He looked out the window. "I hate this city now. If I get out of this . . ." His cigarette was burned down to the nub. He lit a new one off it, kept smoking, staring out at the rain. "Then you know what happens?"

"What?"

"Karen de Vere calls, out of the blue. Potential investor from upstate. I'd heard of the family. Potential, that's all. Meaningless. But two days later she's here with a check in her hand, big enough to get me through the quarterlies. She'd heard good things about me, blah blah blah. Looks like a Manhattan she-wolf who knows her stuff, but she's just an upstate girl with a lot to learn. No matter. To me she was Jesus Christ, in his role as savior."

Eddie thought: What about the hockey game you and Karen went to? One of them was lying. He said: "So what's the problem?"

"She called last night. She's changed her mind. Wants to close her account."

"Meaning what?"

"Meaning take back her goddamn two hundred and thirty grand. What could be clearer?"

"You'll have to give it to her then, won't you?"

Jack turned. "You know something, Eddie? You're slow."

"Out here, maybe." In the real world. It hit Eddie then that prison, an unreal world, was like virtual reality. Instead of sticking your head in a helmet you stuck your whole body behind walls. "I'm quick in the VR world."

Jack shook his head. "You didn't lose your sense of humor."

"I keep hearing that. Tell me why you can't give Karen the money."

"Because it's gone, most of it. That's why. I had a lot of debt, the kind that couldn't wait."

The Mount Olive Extended Care Residence and Spa? The Palazzo bill? What else was there? Eddie didn't know enough about Jack's world to even imagine. Raleigh: how much was he owed? He remembered the way Raleigh had emerged from his talk with Jack behind the closed bedroom door, smoking a cigar.

"What was left over I stuck in a really hot thing in Singapore that's going to earn it all back by the next quarter," Jack went on. "It's locked in till then, of course." He made a fist again, stared at it, then hit himself in forehead, hard.

"Don't," Eddie said.

"Why not?" A welt rose on Jack's forehead; his whole face reddened. "It's all over."

"I don't see that."

"Don't you? Karen wants her money back. I don't have it. She'll call her lawyer. He'll go right to the SEC, the D.A., everybody. Then it's what I told you—fines I can't pay and jail. I'm talking about prison, Eddie."

That had no shock value for Eddie. He felt the balance shifting between his brother and himself. It had begun to move when he'd caught Jack's arm and stilled it. Now what had always been static was suddenly in motion.

"What was her reason?" Eddie said.

"For what?"

"For wanting the money back."

"She doesn't have to give a reason. It's her money."

"But she gave one anyway."

Jack looked at Eddie, nodded. "She said there was a family emergency."

"Whose family?"

"Hers, of course. Do you find something funny about this?"

Eddie almost did, felt that if he could see a little better he surely would. Or maybe if he could see it from Karen's point of view. "When do you have to pay her?"

"Yesterday, today, tomorrow. Now. She wants it. I can stall for a day or two, that's it."

"How much do you need?"

"The whole bundle. Two thirty. I told you already. And that's just to get to next week. To get out of this hole, I need twice that. And I could have made it in Singapore. It was a sure thing." Jack formed another fist but this time did nothing with it.

The phone rang. Jack picked it up. "Hello?"

The person on the other end spoke. Jack flinched. Eddie had watched a lot of men go down without letting it affect him; but he was having trouble watching this.

"There are a few technicalities, Karen, that's all. Paperwork. We're going as fast as we can."

Karen said something that made him flinch again. She wouldn't make it easy, Eddie knew that from those cool blue eyes. He knew too that Karen had lied about that hockey game, just so she could get in that line about Jack never mentioning him, in the hope that Eddie would reveal something damning.

"I will," Jack said. "You have my word." He put down the phone.

"Just an upstate girl with a lot to learn," Eddie said.

Jack glared at him. "You're taking some pleasure from this, aren't you, bro?"

"No," Eddie said. "But it's worse than you think."

"How can it be worse?" Jack said, with contempt in his tone but fear in his eyes.

"She's a cop," Eddie said.

"What the hell are you talking about?"

"Or something like it," Eddie continued. "You can trust me on that. We ran into each other at your health club. Actually, it was a setup. We talked. This and that. Your business came up, but of course I knew nothing about it. Then she took me to see Evelyn."

Jack sat down on the couch. It was more like subsiding, as though his legs couldn't support him any longer.

"She's not in good shape," Eddie said. "My long-lost sister-in-law." Jack flinched again. "When did you two get together?"

Jack took a deep breath. "After the Galleon Beach fiasco. She left Packer, and I couldn't stick around. Brad blamed me for what you—for what happened. Didn't she tell you all about it?"

Eddie remembered that Evelyn had placed the beginning of her relationship with Jack a little earlier: *What a nasty suggestion. I couldn't help myself.* But he let it go. "She didn't make much sense," he said.

"No. She doesn't. I did everything I could for her, Eddie, believe me. The best shrinks, the latest medications, you name it. Nothing did any good."

"She wasn't like this before."

"It was there. I just didn't see it." Jack closed his eyes. Eddie saw the exhaustion on his face, digging out an engraving of how he would appear as an old man.

"What happened to your seven and a half percent of Galleon Beach?"

Jack's eyes opened. They gave Eddie a look that revealed noth-

ing. "Seven and a half percent of zilch is zilch." Jack untied his
tie, unfastened his belt, loosened his pants. "What does any of
that matter now? Nothing matters. They've got me by the balls.
It's a sting, Eddie. I can trace it back to the Associates thing.
They wanted me, not Raleigh."

"Why didn't they get you?"

"I told you—it was just a bullshit technicality."

"But Raleigh took the fall."

"I wouldn't put it that way."

"Why did he do that?"

Jack didn't answer.

"It goes all the way back to USC, doesn't it?"

Jack shook his head. "USC's like some dream place to you, El
Dorado. It's just a school in a bad part of town. Drop the subject."

"I can't do that," Eddie said. The balance had shifted between
them. It opened a new way of talking. "You and Raleigh got into
some kind of trouble there. They kicked you out. A few months
later you were a partner at Galleon Beach. Fill in the blanks."

"Blanks are what you're firing, bro. I didn't get kicked out of
USC. I left because I wanted to."

Eddie crossed the room, stood over his brother, lowered his
hand, laid it on Jack's cheek, just touching him. "Don't call me
bro," he said.

Jack jerked his head away. "You've turned into a fucking crazy
man, you know that?"

"A crazy man who doesn't like being lied to," Eddie said. "I
know for a fact you were kicked out. I've known it all along. Now
tell me why."

He didn't want to hit Jack. Jack wasn't some degenerate in the
next cell, some rapist, murderer, thief. He was his brother. But
now, with the balance shifting, he could do it if he had to.

Perhaps Jack realized that. He sighed and said, "All right. Why
not? I'm in the toilet anyway." He lit another cigarette, inhaled.
The smoke puffed him up a little, restored some of his confidence.
"It was just child's play, really. Raleigh and I started a little
business. Raja Research. Raleigh and Jack, get it?"

"What kind of business?"

"The essay business. We sold essays. In a gray area, I suppose,
but so are *Cliffs Notes* and *Monarch*, right?"

"*Monarch*'s all right."

Jack looked puzzled for a moment. "We bought product from fraternities all over the country," he went on. "Brad lent us a grand to get our library stocked. We paid him back in a month. Everything was going great. We had a sliding price scale, depending on subject, difficulty of the course, length of the paper, all that. Then one day Raleigh sold one to the wrong guy. They took it so seriously, threatened to take us to court, held an investigation. Brad was afraid his name was going to get dragged in—they wanted to know where the start-up money had come from."

"So you blackmailed him for the seven and a half percent."

"That's a prejudicial way of putting it, br—Eddie. I'd decided by then, this was February or March, that college wasn't for me. I knew what I wanted. The opportunity presented itself. I kept Brad out of their tinpot investigation, made them think that Raleigh was just an underling who didn't know what was going on, and got on with life." Jack paused; he watched Eddie. "There. The whole truth and nothing but. Is that so bad?"

"What about swimming?"

"Swimming's not a life, Eddie. I wanted to get started."

"Started at what?"

"Making money. Besides, the practices were endless and I wasn't getting any better. Up and down those lanes for hours—it's pretty dumb when you think about it."

"The point is not to think about it."

"Ah," said Jack with a little smile, "the Zen approach. That's not me."

Eddie liked that smile. It almost distracted him. "And now Raleigh's taken a fall for you."

"More or less."

"What deal did he make?"

"That's a moot point now. He's not going to be happy. That's about the only satisfaction I'll be able to salvage from this."

"How much did you offer him?"

"A hundred grand."

"Did he really do a year?"

"We didn't expect anything like that. Three months at most, maybe even a suspended sentence."

"I'd have been rich at the same rate."

"A million five? That's not rich."

"What's rich, Jack?"

"We've been through that."

"You want to be rich, don't you?"

"Who doesn't?"

Eddie had never thought much about money. Was there any mention of money in "The Mariner"? No.

Jack rose from the couch. It took some effort. He fastened his pants, buckled his belt, went to the window. Eddie was reminded of Karen steeling herself before the visit to the Mount Olive Extended Care Residence and Spa. Jack held up his finger and thumb, spaced about an inch apart. "I came this close. That's what kills. It's not failure, it's getting so close you can smell it and taste it. That's what kills." Rain ran in sheets down the window. "Did you have much rain . . . down there?" Jack asked.

"The weather wasn't a factor."

Jack nodded. He looked at the phone. "What's the best way of doing this?"

"Doing what?" Eddie said. This was the first time Jack had ever asked him for advice, with the exception of play conversation in their pirate games.

"Surrendering to the inevitable. What do you think—call my lawyer, call Karen, call the SEC?"

"Are we at that stage?"

"Thanks for that *we*," Jack said. "Christ, I can't get used to you with no hair."

"I'm growing it down to the ground."

A smile crossed Jack's face, almost too quickly to see. He stubbed out his cigarette hard, against the window. "Yeah, we're at that stage. Where are we going to find two hundred and thirty grand?"

"Funny thing," Eddie said.

"Funny thing?"

Eddie didn't reply at first. It was justice, in a logical sort of way. He had done penance for a crime he hadn't committed. Punishment without crime left a void, waiting to be filled. And if that was just a debating trick, then he could always say that what he was about to propose wasn't criminal at all, that the money belonged to no one. And if that too was tricky in some way, he could call it reparation, the way the Japanese had been compensated for their internment, and the Jews for the Holocaust. The idea took hold of him. It was right.

Jack was staring at him. "What funny thing?" he said.

Eddie smiled. "We're going to shoot the albatross," he said.

Outside: Day 7

Chapter Twenty-Six

Monday.

Jack dressed for the occasion. He came out of the bedroom wearing a black turtleneck, black Patagonia jacket, black jeans, black high-tops. He was carrying a black gym bag.

"What's in there?" Eddie said.

Jack unzipped the bag, showed him the contents: two handguns, clips of ammunition. "One for you, one for me," Jack said.

"You're a gun owner?"

"Lots of gun owners on Wall Street," Jack said. "You'd be surprised."

Eddie shook his head. "No guns."

"No guns?"

Eddie had heard hundreds of robbery stories, most of them robberies gone wrong. Guns didn't help. They made people overconfident and careless. That was the opinion of Jonathan C. McBright, former cellmate and a pro. "It's not that kind of thing," Eddie said. "No one's even going to see us." The sign of a good job, Jonathan C. McBright liked to say, was when no one knew he was being jobbed.

Jack returned the gym bag to the bedroom, came out rubbing his hands together. "Jesus," he said, "this is exciting."

Eddie didn't like that. Excitement was one of the common elements of robberies gone wrong. "Let's go," he said.

Jack's car was waiting in front of the hotel. All the new equipment, paid for in cash, was in place. The two mountain bikes were locked onto the rear carrier, the large capacity, lightweight EMS backpacks lay on the backseat, the ax was in the trunk. Jack took the wheel. They drove out of the city. The rain stopped and the setting sun poked through a hole in the clouds, casting a coppery glow on the river, on the bridges, on every puddle, windshield, pane of glass.

"Sun at last," Jack said. "I was giving up hope."

A few minutes later it went down, sucking away the coppery glow and all other color. Jack turned up the heat.

"Nice car," Eddie said.

"Never use it," Jack replied. "It just sits in the garage."

"What's it worth?"

"It's leased, Eddie. Not really mine, so I couldn't get anything for it, if that's what you're thinking." He stopped at a toll booth, took a ticket from the dispenser, drove south on the turnpike. "There's a bottle of something in the glove compartment," he said.

Eddie shook his head. Alcohol was another factor in robberies gone wrong.

"You'll never guess what I'm thinking," Jack said.

"Plundering the Spanish Main," Eddie replied.

Jack took his eyes off the road for a moment, looked at Eddie. He reached over, squeezed Eddie's knee. "You know me, bro," he said. "Don't take offense. Just an expression. You're my brother. It's something special, right?"

"Yeah," Eddie said. It meant you had the same mother and father. After that, it was what you made it. He left the thought unspoken; this wasn't the time for introducing complications.

"Know something?" Jack said. "You're a smart guy. I deal with smart guys all the time and you're a smart guy. In a little different way maybe, but you really could have been—" Jack stopped himself. A mile or two went by. "Still, everything's going to change now, isn't it?"

"In what way?"

"In what way. Shit. In a material way. What are you going to do with all that money?"

Eddie hadn't thought about that, had no desire to. "Take the next exit," he said.

Jack took the next exit, drove west on a two-lane state road.

For a while they had it to themselves. Then taillights appeared in the distance. Jack was driving fast. The taillights grew bigger and brighter. Then Eddie saw a beer can rolling beside the road.

"Slow down," he said.

"Slow down?"

"That's them."

Jack took his foot off the gas. The taillights dimmed and shrank, finally disappearing. Jack turned down the heat. He was sweating; Eddie could smell it.

There was a long silence. Then Jack said, "What are they like?"

"It doesn't matter what they're like," Eddie said. "They're not going to see us."

"Right. That's key, isn't it?"

"If we want to live," Eddie said.

Jack laughed, high and tight.

"Are you sure you want to go through with this?" Eddie asked.

There was a buzzing sound.

"What's that?" Eddie said.

"The phone."

Jack reached into the console between them. "Hello?" he said. His voice was low, as if someone nearby might overhear.

"Jack?" It was Karen on the speaker phone. "I can hardly hear you."

"I can't talk right now," Jack said. "I'll call you tomorrow."

"That's not good enough. I'm concerned about my account. Extremely. I spoke to my lawyer about it this afternoon. She's extremely concerned too. I don't want this to get messy, Jack, but I'm afraid—"

Jack's voice rose. "Tomorrow. You'll have it tomorrow."

There was a pause. Then Karen said, "Where are you?"

"I'll call you by noon," Jack said, and clicked off.

He turned to Eddie. "And don't you patronize me," he said. Again Eddie was conscious of the shifting balance between them. "I may not have your experience in these matters, but I'm used to managing risk." He drove on; in the glow of the instrument panel Eddie could see his hands tightening around the steering wheel.

"Then take the next right," he said.

Jack turned onto the dirt road. "Besides," he said. "What choice have I got?"

"Cut the lights."

Jack slowed down, switched them off. A half moon hung just above the trees, lighting their way. Big clouds drifted across the sky like continents. "My night vision has gone to shit," Jack said.

"We're not in a hurry."

Eddie checked the odometer. The road ran straight through the woods. The moonlight glistened on the wet branches, on a pond in the distance, on the eyes of a small animal that ran across the road. Good things happened under the light of the moon, at least in "The Mariner."

> The moving moon went up the sky,
> And nowhere did abide;
> Softly she was going up,
> And a star or two beside.

Eddie looked up through the windshield for a star or two, saw none.

Three miles passed, three and a half, four. Eddie wanted to make their exit as fast as possible, but he didn't want to take the chance of being heard from the gate.

"Stop the car," he said.

Jack stopped the car.

"Turn it off."

Jack switched off the engine. Eddie got out, listened. He heard nothing but the wind rising in the trees. A cold wind: he looked up at the sky and saw that more cloud continents had appeared. Those near the moon had white trim, like beaches. Eddie got back in the car.

"Next place you can pull off to the side, do it."

Jack drove on. There was a small clearing a few hundred feet ahead, an opening in the shadows.

"Back in," Eddie said.

Jack backed in, parked behind a screen of trees. Eddie walked into the road. A ray of moonlight caught the antenna; otherwise the car was invisible. Good enough. Eddie glanced up at the gathering clouds: there wasn't going to be moonlight much longer.

They took the bikes off the rack, the ax from the trunk. Eddie put it in one of the backpacks and strapped it on. Jack strapped on the other, locked the car, pocketed the keys.

"Is there another set?"

"Why would we need another set?"

Eddie didn't want to let his imagination go on that one. "Someone I knew did six years because his keys fell through a grate at the worst possible moment."

Jack smiled; that old smile, flashing in the moonlight. "There's another set under the floor mat in back."

Eddie smiled too.

They got on the bikes.

"I feel kind of silly," Jack said.

But bikes were perfect for what Eddie had in mind, faster than a man could run, and silent. They peddled off on the dirt road, side by side.

The wind whistled in Eddie's ears, cold, exhilarating. Wind, like the moon, was a good omen. Eddie felt excitement rising inside him and stilled it. Omens, exhilaration, excitement: these were the stuff of ballads, and of robberies gone wrong.

"I haven't been on a bike since we were kids," Jack said.

"Sh."

Ahead, Eddie saw a metallic gleam. He braked, at the same time reaching across the space between them and touching Jack's arm.

"What?" said Jack.

"Sh."

Jack halted a few yards ahead, came back, walking his bike. "What is it?" he said in a low voice.

Eddie pointed. In the distance he could see moonlight on a steel gate, and beyond it a shadow that might have been a man.

"I don't see anything," Jack said.

Eddie didn't explain. He turned and started walking his bike the way they had come. Jack followed. After a few hundred yards, Eddie cut into the woods at a right angle.

The treetops filtered out the moonlight. Eddie couldn't see the branches that reached out to snag the backpack, or the rocks the tires bumped against. He bumped against a few things himself. The ax in his backpack shifted into an uncomfortable position. Behind him, he heard a soft crash.

"Shit," Jack said.

"Quiet."

Eddie listened, heard only the wind.

They went on for a while, made another right-angle turn. Five or ten minutes later, Eddie caught another gleam through the trees. A few more steps and they were at the fence: four horizontal strands of barbed wire extending into darkness in both directions. A rural fence, meant for marking boundaries and containing livestock, not for keeping out determined people or attracting the curiosity of law-abiding neighbors. Eddie raised the lowest strand. Jack crawled through, dragging his bike behind. Then he held the wire up for Eddie.

"It's like that old punch line," Jack said. "So far so good."

Eddie didn't know the joke that went with it.

They moved into the woods on the far side of the fence, turned right, and came to the dirt road sooner than Eddie had expected. They must have gone through the fence much closer to the gate than he'd intended. He'd have to remember that on the way back.

They remounted their bikes, rode on, over the rise and past the turning to the farm. The wind blew harder now, and colder. Above, the clouds thickened, crowding the half moon on all sides. Eddie pedaled faster; without moonlight there might be trouble spotting the track that led to the airstrip. Jack was quiet except for his breathing, which grew heavier. He began to fall behind.

Eddie was almost past the track before he saw it: a narrow opening in the darkness. He halted, waited for Jack. He heard the crunching of a fat tire on pebbled earth, Jack's breathing, and then Jack was beside him.

"How much farther?" he asked.

"Not far," Eddie replied. "And keep your voice down."

"When this is over, I'm going to get in shape," Jack said, more quietly. "Maybe you and me'll do some swimming."

"At Galleon Beach," Eddie said.

Pause. "Why there?"

"It's a nice place."

"There're lots of nice places."

They rode up the track. Eddie wasn't sure of the distance. It seemed like a long time before he heard water gurgling, came to the wooden bridge.

"Here?" Jack said.

Eddie nodded. He examined the bridge. It was about two car lengths long, surfaced with worn planks that weren't laid flush to each other. The downstream side sagged slightly. Not a sturdy structure: that was good.

Eddie walked his bike down the bank of the stream, laid it on the dry earth under the bridge supports. There were four of them, two on each side of the stream, wooden posts almost twice the diameter of telephone poles. He took off his backpack, removed the ax, unclipped the leather blade-cover.

Jack, laying his bike beside Eddie's, said, "What about the noise?"

"That's why I didn't bring a chain saw," Eddie said, and swung at the downstream support. High to low on the first cut; the blade sank into the wood with a thunk that didn't sound especially loud to Eddie but made Jack suck in his breath. Low to high on the second cut. Again the blade bit deep; the wood was half rotten. This time Jack made no sound.

Eddie cut a deep notch, then stepped around the support and cut a second notch on the other side, leaving a core of wood about six inches in diameter. It didn't take long; he had chopped lots of firewood as a kid, and the occasional tree in the forest, just for fun.

A beautiful night. Moonlight shone on his breath and Jack's, rising above them, on the flowing water, on the silver blade of the ax. The stream bubbled at their feet. Everything was going to be all right.

Eddie spoke:

> A noise like of a hidden brook
> In the leafy month of June,
> That to the sleeping woods all night
> Singeth a quiet tune.

"What's that?" Jack said.

" 'The Ancient Mariner,' " Eddie replied. "Ever read it?"

"Haven't had much time for reading," Jack said. "Heard of it, naturally." He checked his watch. "It doesn't sound like much from that bit."

"No?"

"Moon-June stuff—no edge."

Eddie replaced the leather cover on the blade. He looked at his brother. Jack was studying him, a complex expression in his eyes. Then the clouds finally closed over the moon, and Eddie couldn't see Jack's eyes at all, couldn't see anything until his own pupils widened in the darkness. "What's the time?" he said.

"Four forty-two, a minute ago."

Eddie nodded. "I'd better get started."

"I'm all set."

"Any questions?"

"Just one—how come you know poetry by heart?"

"I had the time."

Eddie waited for Jack to say something. When he didn't, Eddie said, "Stay out of sight," climbed up the bank and began walking back the way they had come with the ax on his shoulder, leaving his brother under the bridge with the bikes and the backpacks. He should have said good luck, or shaken hands, or something, he couldn't think what.

Something cold landed on his nose and melted there.

"It's snowing," Jack called after him in a stage whisper. "Is that going to make a difference?"

"They don't follow FAA regulations," Eddie called back.

He counted his paces, three hundred. Enough? He counted fifty more. He studied the trees that grew near the track. Snow was falling steadily now, brightening the night. Eddie chopped a thick branch off a hardwood tree—a beech, he thought, from the smoothness of the bark; there had been a lot of beech in the woods behind New Town—and dragged it into the track. He laid the branch at an angle, as though the wind had brought it down, making sure that the biggest clump of sub-branches covered the track, then walked a few steps away to check his work. He returned, dropped wet leaves on the scar the ax had made in the wood, and moved out of sight.

Eddie clipped the leather cover back on the blade, stuck the ax in the back of his belt, sat on a log. Snow fell silently through the trees. He waited.

Jonathan C. McBright, professional robber specializing in banks, had said: "It's like any challenging work—details, details,

details. You've got to picture everything before it happens. Even then, there's always the unforeseen." Eddie tried to picture everything: a white plane with green trim, somewhere above the clouds; an alarm ringing in the farmhouse, a few miles away; Jack waiting under the bridge, three hundred and fifty steps up the track. He could summon up those images, but no feeling of reassurance accompanied them. Had he forgotten something? He tried to figure out what it might be, and was still trying when he heard an engine sound, distant and muffled by falling snow but growing louder. He crouched behind the log.

Headlights appeared on the track, two yellow cones filled with snowflakes that blackened in their glow. Eddie recognized the outline of the poultry truck. It was going fast, maybe fast enough to plow right through the branch or sweep it aside. Details, details, details. There was nothing he could do but watch.

The headlight beams reached the branch, snow-covered now, blending with the track. It wasn't going to work, Eddie thought. But then the horn honked and the wheels locked. The truck went into a skid, sliding along the track, the rear end swinging around. It struck the branch sideways and came to a stop.

The passenger door opened and Julio stepped out, wearing a ski jacket and a tuque with a tassel dangling from the top.

"What the fuck?" he said, walking into the headlight glare. "It's a goddamn tree."

"Move it," called the driver from the cab.

"Sure," said Julio, switching to Spanish, "move it." He approached the branch, grabbed a small stem, tugged. His feet slipped out from under him and he fell hard on his back. Eddie heard the driver laugh.

"Fuck you," said Julio.

"Watch your language," the driver told him.

Julio got up, muttering to himself in Spanish. Eddie caught only one word: "chiropractor."

Julio reached into the tangle again, pulled. The branch shifted a few inches. The driver came down from the cab to help him. Someone else got out too. A much smaller figure, who hopped down, landed lightly: Gaucho. He wore a cowboy hat, vest, chaps, a gun belt.

"Are we going to be late?" he asked.

"Don't worry," the driver answered.

Gaucho stood in front of the truck, watched Julio and the driver drag the branch to the side. The cleaved end passed right by his feet. Eddie could see the marks of the blade, straight, gleaming, unnatural. Gaucho stared at them. Then he bent down, picked up a handful of snow, tried to make a snowball, failed.

"How come I can't make a snowball?"

"Too dry," said the driver. "Let's go."

"Snow," said Julio, as they got back in the cab. "This country. I wish I was going with the kid."

"Stop whining," said the driver. "You're making more money in a month than your father made in his life."

"My father was an idiot."

The doors slammed shut. The driver straightened the wheels, inched forward, the tires spinning in the snow. Squealing conveniently, Eddie thought, as he came out of the woods, got his hands on the edge of the cargo floor that protruded beyond the slatted sides, and pulled himself up. As the truck picked up speed, he climbed over and down into the cargo space.

He got on his hands and knees, crawled along the floor. The chicken cages were gone. There was no cargo but the canvas bags, about a dozen, piled against the rear of the cab, and a small suitcase nearby. In the light reflected off the falling snow, Eddie could see the Mickey Mouse decal glued to its side.

He rose, picking up one of the canvas bags. Over the top of the cab he saw the bridge, snow-covered and deserted. He dropped the canvas bag over the side, picked up another, dropped it out too, and then the rest. He counted them: eleven.

The truck slowed as it came to the bridge. Eddie crawled to the back, climbed over, jumped down. He lost his balance, fell, rolled to the side of the track, the covered blade of the ax digging into his back. Other than that, everything was perfect. So far so good— punch line to a joke he didn't know. Jack could tell him on the way back.

The truck kept going. It rolled across the bridge, making a loud creaking sound, then went around a bend. For a few moments its taillights blinked through the trees; then they vanished. Eddie rose, ran to the stream, down the bank, under the bridge.

He heard a footstep behind him, felt something hard prod his back. "Don't move," Jack said.

"For Christ's sake."

"Sorry. I thought they'd got you. That honking."

"They're not going to honk us to death. And I said no guns."

"That didn't seem prudent," Jack replied. "How many?"

There was no point arguing. "Eleven," Eddie said. "We don't have room for them all."

"I'm a good packer," Jack said, strapping on one of the backpacks. Taking the other, he wheeled one of the bikes up the bank.

Eddie unhooked the ax from his belt, unclipped the blade cover. He felt for the notch in the downstream bridge support, then stood back and chopped at the remaining core. In six swings he was through. The bridge made a creaking sound.

Eddie wheeled the other bike up the bank, onto the track. Jack was kneeling there, transferring banded wads of cash from a canvas bag into one of the backpacks.

"Just throw the whole bag in," Eddie said, taking the other backpack and sticking the ax inside.

"Can't fit as much in that way, bro," Jack said. "Should have brought bigger packs."

"How many have you done?"

"This is the first."

Eddie looked down the track, saw the dark forms of the bags lying here and there like boulders. "Hurry," he said.

"How much time have we got?"

Eddie glanced up, saw no lightening of the sky, heard no engine from above. At the airstrip, they would sit in the shelter of the cab until they heard the plane. That was when Julio would climb into the back and see the Mickey Mouse suitcase lying there all by itself. "Just hurry," Eddie said.

He walked the bike down the track, counting bags and stopping at the last one, planning to work his way back. He removed the backpack, put the canvas bag inside, went on to the next one. The second bag fit comfortably, but he had to take out the ax to jam in the third. Enough.

He looked toward the bridge. Jack was kneeling in the snow, stuffing money into his backpack, a handful at a time.

"Jack. Let's go."

"Almost done," Jack called. He rose, buckled the flap of the backpack, swung it on. He moved toward his bike, noticed another canvas bag, paused over it.

"Jack."

Jack bent down, opened the bag, grabbed a handful of cash, stuffed it in the pocket of his jacket. Then he filled the other pocket and was shoving more money down the front of his shirt when a light shone on him. He froze in it.

"Jack! Move!"

The truck came barreling around the bend in the track, straight at the bridge.

Eddie swung a leg over his bike. "The bike, Jack."

Jack took a step toward his bike, then another. He bent, righted it with one hand. The other still clutched a wad of bills. Eddie started toward him.

The truck hit the bridge, moving fast. It was halfway across when Eddie heard the crack, a loud crack, like the sound just before the boom in thunder, and the bridge gave, planks flying through the air like loose piano keys. The truck flew too, but not high enough. The right side of its front bumper caught the top of the bank. The truck flipped, skidded on its side, knocked down a small pine, and came to rest at the edge of the woods, one headlight out, the other shining at a low angle on Jack and the bridge.

Jack gazed at it, raising a handful of money to shade his eyes from the glare. Except for popping-metal sounds, it was quiet in the woods, as though nothing had happened. Things started slowly, slowly enough for Eddie, standing outside the pool of light, to record all the details, details, none of them foreseen.

First Gaucho stepped out of the woods, no longer wearing his cowboy hat but otherwise unharmed. He glanced at the remains of the bridge, at the empty money bags on the road, at Jack. His hand dropped down to his holster.

Eddie shouted, "Shoot him, Jack."

"Huh?"

"Your gun."

"He's just a kid," Jack said, "playing cowboy."

Then Gaucho had his pistol out, pointing at Jack. "Pow pow," he said.

Jack started to smile his smile. Gaucho pulled the trigger. Jack spun around, coughed, coughed again, this time a bloody one, fell and lay still.

Things speeded up. Gaucho turned in Eddie's direction, fired into the darkness. Something roared from the other side, and a single headlight came into view. The gateman: he'd heard the bridge collapse, heard the crash, heard something. Eddie slipped back into the edge of the woods. Gaucho fired another shot. The bullet smacked into a trunk, not far away. Gaucho on one side, the gateman on the other. Then Julio came limping out of the shadows, carrying a shotgun and changing the geometry.

"He's dead," he said in Spanish, thumbing back at the cab.

"So's this guy," said Gaucho. "And there's another—"

The rest was drowned out by the motorcycle, flying toward them. At the last moment, Eddie stepped out of the woods and swung the ax, butt first, into the visor of the driver's helmet. The impact tore the ax from his hand and knocked him down. He caught a glimpse of the gateman spinning in the air, his machine gun strapped to his back, and the motorcycle somersaulting down into the stream.

Gaucho fired another shot into the darkness.

Then came a blast from the shotgun.

Eddie, the pack on his back but forgotten, jumped on the bike and pedaled away as fast as he could.

The tires squeaked in the snow. That was the only sound Eddie heard. He concentrated on it all the way to the end of the track and onto the dirt road that led to the steel gate, listening to that squeaking in the snow, shutting out everything else, every sickening image and second thought that tried to force its way into his mind. He almost didn't see headlights rounding the turn that led to the farm, almost didn't get off the road and into the trees before a car sped by, with Señor Paz behind the wheel, his round face almost touching the glass. And then, pedaling on, he didn't immediately notice the milky tones in the sky, or hear the airplane flying in from the south.

He reached the steel gate, tossed over the bike, the backpack, then climbed over himself, strapped on the pack, rode on. The sound of the plane grew louder.

A few minutes later, just as the airplane sound ceased abruptly,

Eddie came to Jack's car. It was easy to see now in the gathering light, backed in between some skinny pines. He got off the bike, threw it in the woods.

Is there another set?

Why would we need another set?

Eddie kicked in one of the rear side windows, opened the door, yanked up the floor mat, found the keys. He unlocked the trunk, dropped the backpack inside, closed it. Then he got behind the wheel, started the car, drove out, onto the dirt road.

He drove. That was all he did. Dirt road to paved two-laner, paved two-laner to the turnpike; where he lost himself in the traffic, flowing slowly in the falling snow. Once or twice he glanced in the rearview mirror, saw only the sights of normal commuting life.

Cold air blew in through the smashed window. Jack's car had a good heater, and Eddie cranked it up to the max, but there was nothing he could do about that icy feeling on the back of his neck.

Outside: Day 8

Chapter Twenty-Seven

The clouds disappeared, just like that. The sun came out. The skies were blue. The snow melted. It was spring.

Eddie was too busy to notice. He lit a fire in Jack's fireplace and burned every scrap of paper in the suite. When the fire was at its hottest, he added all the computer disks. Not knowing how to erase the computer's internal memory, he unplugged it, unscrewed the back panel, tore out everything that would tear out, and tossed it in the fire too.

The rest—clothes, books, pictures, office equipment—he packed in boxes addressed to Uncle Vic. Then he phoned the desk.

"Mr. Nye is checking out," he said. "What's the bill?"

"Checking out? But he just paid his account to the end of the month."

"Change of plan."

"I'm afraid we have no prorating mechanism for situations like this."

"Meaning there's no checking out?"

Tentative laugh. "Meaning there's no refund. Regrettably."

Eddie called the Mount Olive Extended Care Residence and Spa.

"The account," he was told, "is paid up to the thirtieth."

"What's the monthly rate?"

"Three thousand dollars."

"Mr. Nye would like to pay for a year in advance."

"I'm afraid we have no discount mechanism in situations like that."

Eddie waited for her to add "regrettably." When she did not, he said, "Cash a problem?"

"Cash is never a problem, sir. Checks are the problem."

Then there was nothing unburned or unpacked but the phone and the bottle of Armagnac. Like cognac, Jack had said, but snobbier. Eddie sat by the fire with the bottle in his lap, facing away from the window. He had noticed those blue skies. He didn't drink, just sat with the bottle in his lap.

The phone rang.

"Hello?" he said.

"Jack?" It was Karen.

"No."

"Eddie. You sound so much alike." There was a pause. He could feel her thinking, as though the electric impulses in her brain were somehow feeding into the wire. "Is Jack there?"

"No."

"When will he be back?"

Eddie searched for the right sort of lie, settled on one, opened his mouth to utter it only to find he physically could not. Something was choking him. He was all right as long as he didn't speak about Jack. He saw himself in the mirror, completely distorted.

"Eddie?"

"Yeah."

"I think you and I've had a little misunderstanding."

"Have we?"

"I'd like to clear it up," Karen said. "Maybe I could see you."

Eddie said nothing.

Karen said: "Could I come over?"

It hit him then: the desk clerk had called her, told her that Jack was checking out. Why not? She was some kind of cop, and it was an obvious cop move.

"Why don't I come over there?" Eddie said.

"Over here?"

"What's your address?"

She gave it to him.

"See you in an hour," Eddie said.

*   *   *

Eddie called down for a cardboard box, wrapping paper. He opened one of the canvas bags and counted out $230,000. There was a knock at the door.

He opened it. The bellman. "Can you wait a minute?" Eddie asked him, taking the box and the wrapping paper.

"Certainly, sir."

Everyone was calling him sir all of a sudden, as though money had a smell. Eddie closed the door, leaving the bellman in the hall. He put the $230,000 in the box, wrapped it, wrote Karen's address on the front, adding, "From Windward Financial Services," gave it to the bellman.

"I'd like this delivered right away," Eddie said. "By you." He gave the bellman fifty dollars.

"Right away," said the bellman, but there was no "sir." Maybe fifty wasn't enough.

The bellman left. Eddie counted out another $36,000, for the Mount Olive Extended Residence and Spa, dropped it in a shopping bag. What else? He remembered Raleigh, and then forgot him.

He counted the rest: $488,220.

Eddie stuffed it into the backpack, threw the canvas bags on the fire, slung on the pack. He looked around the room. He had taken care of Jack's obligations and destroyed the records of any possible financial impropriety. That didn't make him feel any better. He hadn't belonged in Jack's world and Jack hadn't belonged in his. Bringing them together had been a mistake. He toyed with the idea that the two worlds had come together within him, due to circumstance, and therefore it was no one's fault. A bad idea. Jack was dead and the fault was his.

Eddie picked up the Armagnac bottle and was on his way out when he noticed the *Monarch* lying by the couch. He tossed it in the fire. Then he went down to the street, where Jack's car was waiting. A uniformed man held the door for him. Eddie gave him money.

"Nice day, isn't it, sir?"

Eddie glanced up at the blue sky. It hurt his eyes. He drove away from the Palazzo with Jack's heat on full blast and the icy feeling on the back of his neck.

He was out of the northeast and out of Armagnac before the obvious lines lit up in his brain.

> The man hath penance done,
> And penance more will do.

Then he couldn't get rid of them.

Chapter Twenty-Eight

Karen de Vere knelt in front of the fireplace. She saw a half-burned canvas bag, warped computer disks, ashes. Mostly ashes. She pinched some in her fingers and sniffed them.

"Smell anything?" asked Raleigh Packer.

"The end of your parole."

"What does that mean?"

"You're going back to finish your sentence. What else?"

He reddened. "Why? I cooperated, didn't I?"

Raleigh was whining. Karen didn't like whiners. "With no result."

"I did everything you asked. I tried."

"Try harder."

"How."

"Think of where he might have gone. You know him."

"Yeah, I know him. He's out romancing a prospective client, or sucking around for tips, or having a few down at the Seaport or some place like that. He'll be back soon."

Karen blew the ashes off her hands. Raleigh was wrong. Jack Nye was gone, period. She was left with a fireplace full of ashes, $230,000 in well-used currency, and no case against him. And a question: why had he run? She could understand running and not paying, or paying and not running; she couldn't understand running and paying.

No explanation. No note with the money, not even his business card. Just a scrawl on the wrapper: "From Windward Financial

Services." Karen had compared it to samples of Jack's handwriting, found it didn't match. She wished she had a sample of Eddie Nye's handwriting too.

"Are you trying to tell me that he's taken off?" asked Raleigh.

"No interpretation required," Karen said. She poked at the ashes with the toe of her shoe, saw something red and charred. She picked it up: a fragment of the cover of the *Monarch Notes* guide to "The Rime of the Ancient Mariner."

"Taken off?" said Raleigh. "And not coming back, you mean? The fucking bastard." He pounded the wall, although not hard enough to hurt himself.

"I'm sure it's nothing personal," said Karen, dropping the fragment in her bag.

"The fucking bastard," was Raleigh's only reply.

Karen waited on a bench. A guard in a gray uniform sat at the other end, glancing at her from the corner of his eye. Through the closed office door across the room came a laugh that made her think of crows. Then the door opened and a red-haired man in denim came out. He reminded her immediately of Goya's portrait of Charles IV of Spain. The guard rose. The red-haired man nodded toward her—it was almost a bow—and smiled. He had beautiful teeth but was missing a canine. He left the waiting room with the guard following close behind.

The receptionist said: "You can go in now."

Karen entered the office, smelled a piney smell she didn't like. She handed her card to the man behind the desk. He studied it. She studied him. He looked like Santa Claus gone sour.

"Take a pew, uh, Miss de Vere," said Floyd K. Messer, M.D., Ph.D., sliding her card across the desk. "I haven't heard of this agency of yours, but I made some calls and apparently it's legit."

"Glad to hear it."

Messer blinked, sat farther back in his chair. "I'm a little pressed for time," he said, "what with this bit of business we've got lined up for tonight. So if you'd tell me how I can help you."

"What bit of business?"

Messer looked surprised. "Wasn't there a lot of media outside when you came in?"

"I didn't see any."

Messer checked his watch. "They'll be along. Just like vultures. Execution tonight, Miss de Vere. We'll be going into a precautionary lockdown in forty-five minutes."

"Who's being executed?"

She'd surprised him again. "You haven't heard of Mister Willie Boggs? I thought he was a national figure by now."

"What did he do?"

"Found a way to wrap a lot of bleeding-heart lawyers around his little black finger."

"I was referring to his crime," Karen said, noticing the photographs of Messer posed with dead fish on the walls.

"Killed a liquor-store clerk in a robbery," said Messer. "Or was with the guy that killed him. Or drove the getaway car. Can't remember. It was a long time ago, Miss de Vere. Now how can I help you?"

"I'm looking for a former inmate of yours."

"Name of?"

"Eddie Nye."

Messer went still.

"What is it?" Karen said.

"Nothing."

"You recognized the name."

"Oh, sure," said Messer. "I was thinking, is all."

"Thinking what?"

"Thinking—that was quick."

"What do you mean?"

"Ol' Nails's been gone hardly more'n a week and he's screwed up already, otherwise you wouldn't be here. Not a record, fifteen minutes is the record, but quick just the same." Messer glanced at the closed office door. "I take it you don't know where he is."

"That's why I'm here."

"You think we know where he is?"

"Any information might help."

Messer nodded. "What's he done?"

"Nothing that I'm aware of. Why do you call him *Nails?*"

Messer smiled at some memory. "It's a long story," he said. "If he hasn't done anything, why are you looking for him?"

"The investigation concerns his brother."

"Didn't know he had one." Messer swiveled around to a computer, tapped at the keyboard. "He a jailbird too?" Words popped up on the screen. Messer scrolled through them. "Here we go. Nye, J. M. Residence: Galleon Beach Club, Saint Amour, the Bahamas. Fancy-dancy. One visit and one visit only, and that was fifteen years ago." Messer looked up. "What's he done?"

"He's suspected of various securities infractions."

"Can't picture Nails involved in something like that."

"Why not, Mr. Messer?" Karen said, realizing as she spoke that she was coming to Eddie's defense in some way, and not stopping herself.

"Doctor, if it's all the same to you," said Messer. "I've got a doctorate in psychology."

"Doctor," said Karen, very distinctly, not mentioning her law degree from Harvard or her Ph.D. in economics from Penn.

"Thank you," said Messer. "See, Nails is a criminal, all right, but not the white-collar type." He glanced at the computer screen. "He got himself in here on a dope-smuggling conviction, five to fifteen, should have been out in three and a half, four, but then he killed three inmates and ended up pulling the full load. Not the white-collar type, if you see what I mean."

"He killed three inmates?" She'd known about the dope conviction ninety minutes after Eddie had first knocked on Jack's door.

"Not that we could ever prove in a court of law. No one's going to talk for the record, right? Or he would've been here forever. But we didn't need that shit to deny parole. Excuse my language."

"Of course, doctor. Could you tell me more about these killings?"

"Like what?"

"The motives, for example."

Messer turned to the screen, scrolled through. "The usual initiation thing, I guess you could say. Only he took revenge. Successfully, you might say. That hardly ever happens."

"Initiation thing."

"This isn't summer camp, Miss de Vere. How specific do you want me to be?"

"They raped him, is that what you're pussyfooting around?"

"One way of putting it," said Messer. "You've got to look at it in context."

"Context?"

"It wasn't an attack on Joe or Joanne Normal. Ol' Nails is a violent guy."

"I've seen no sign of that."

Messer leaned forward. "You've met him?"

"More than once."

"In New York?"

"That's right."

There was a silence. "But you've got no idea where he is."

"That's why I'm here," Karen said. "As I mentioned."

"No idea at all."

"That's what I said." Karen got the odd idea that Messer shared her interest in Eddie's whereabouts.

Messer shot her a quick, angry glance from under his Santa Claus eyebrows. Then he heaved a deep sigh. "Sorry if I'm a little distracted today. These executions are a nuisance, if you want my frank opinion."

"You're against them?"

"Against capital punishment? Just the reverse. For all the usual reasons. Plus it just feels right, morally speaking."

"To whom?"

He yawned, stretched. There were sweat stains under both arms of his short-sleeved white shirt. "I'm sure you didn't come all this way for a philosophical discussion, Miss de Vere. Have you got any other questions relating to Mr. Nye?"

"I could use a list of all his visitors over the fifteen-year period, but if that's too much trouble, the last two or three will do."

Messer turned to the computer. After a moment or two he said, "You've already got it."

"I don't understand."

"There was just the one visit. His brother, two months after processing day."

"That can't be right."

"It's all in the computer," said Messer. He checked his watch. "Now, if there's nothing else . . ."

Karen rose, extended her hand. That took some effort. He shook it. "Good luck," he said.

She was almost at the door when she had a final thought. She stopped, turned.

"Did Eddie know Willie Boggs?"

"All those longtimers know each other, more or less."

"Did they spend time together?"

"The death-row boys don't do much circulating. About the only place they might have run into each other was the library. That's where Mister Willie Boggs went when he wanted to play lawyer."

"And Eddie Nye spent time in the library."

"Oh, yes, he was quite the reader."

Karen drove away from the prison in her rental car. A crowd of people stood in a dusty field by the side of the road; a woman in black held up a sign: "Stop the Murder of Willie Boggs." Karen pulled over and got out.

She walked through the crowd. She saw a priest, a nun, a Buddhist monk; a woman in business dress, a leathery man wearing nothing but cutoffs, a baby in a stroller; a cameraman, a soundman, a reporter fixing her lipstick. She didn't see Eddie Nye.

That didn't mean he wasn't coming. She glanced in her bag, saw the red fragment of the *Monarch*. Maybe Eddie and Willie Boggs had had long discussions in the library. Maybe he would want to be here.

The sun was setting, but the air was still warm. In the middle distance, the prison rose like a castle in the kind of bloody fairy tales that have been dropped from the anthologies, its stone walls reddened by the last rays of the sun. A breeze stirred, raising dust off the field. When a vendor came by pushing a cart, Karen ordered a diet soda, just to wet her throat.

"I've got beer too," said the vendor. "And wine coolers."

"No, thanks."

The leathery man bought a can of beer with change dug from the pockets of his cutoffs and sat down cross-legged to drink. Night fell. Lights shone on the walls of the prison, as though a *son et lumière* show was in the offing. A few more people arrived, none of them Eddie. The reporter interviewed the nun and a man with a bottle sticking out of his pants, then went into the TV truck with her crew. Karen could see them passing around cartons of food.

She found herself standing next to the woman with the sign. The woman had a milk-white face, bony arms, hair as black as her dress.

"They don't interview me anymore," she said.

"Did they use to?"

"Every time. Now they say they want a fresh point of view. Just when it's most vital that I bear witness."

"Aren't you bearing witness anyway?"

"It's hardly the same if the camera's not running." The woman, who had been gazing at the prison, glanced at Karen. "Everyone knows that."

"What's special about this time?"

"Willie Boggs."

"I don't know much about him."

"Willie Boggs is a great man," the woman said. "I've written him hundreds of letters. I mean that literally. Hundreds. He's a wonderful human being, and now they're going to murder him, when they should be setting him free at last. He could do so much good, out here in the world."

"Did he ever write back?" Karen asked.

The woman closed her eyes. "Once," she said. "He wrote me a beautiful letter." Her eyes opened. "He writes like an angel, you know. If he'd written a book, it would have been published. I guarantee."

"What did he say?"

"Say?"

"In his letter."

The woman reached into the pocket of her dress, pulled out an envelope. "I'll let you read it, if you want."

"Not enough light," said Karen.

The woman had a pencil flash. She stood close to Karen, aiming its beam. Karen could smell her breath. She read:

Dear Luanne:
Thanks for your letters. It is good to get letters in here as you can imagine—or maybe you can not. Of course it is not always easy to anser every one. My time for such activities is limited and most of it I spend on my case, as I am sure you understand.
                    Sincerely,
                    W. Boggs

"Very sensible," Karen said, handing back the letter.

Luanne shone the pencil flash in her eyes. "But doesn't he write beautifully?" she said.

Karen shielded her eyes. "He writes well," she said, "based on this sample." But she'd noticed the single spelling mistake in the letter, like the flaw that had made him kill the liquor-store clerk, or be present at the killing, or drive the getaway car for the killer.

Luanne snapped off the light, said, "He's a great man," and moved away, holding up her sign.

Three or four more people appeared; but not Eddie. The vendor returned, sold another beer to the man in cutoffs, a hot dog to the nun, coffee to the TV crew, another diet soda to Karen. The air was dusty and her throat dry.

The reporter approached her.

"Are you going to be here till the end?"

"When's that?"

"Midnight," the reporter said. "They always do it at midnight, for some reason."

"Like Cinderella."

"That's good," said the reporter. "You're articulate. We need someone for a short interview after it's over."

"Try Luanne," Karen said.

As midnight approached, the priest led most of the vigilants in prayer, while the Buddhist monk and a few others went off by themselves to chant. Karen participated in neither ceremony.

The distance to the prison, so brightly lit in the night, seemed to have shrunk, and it kept shrinking all the way to midnight, the prison seeming to come closer and closer. "Give us a miracle," said a man, raising his arms to the sky like Moses in a painting.

After that there was silence. Plenty of *lumière*, Karen thought, but no *son*.

Midnight brought *son*. "No, no," someone screamed at the prison walls. The baby in the stroller awoke and started to wail. The man in cutoffs hurled a beer can in the direction of the stone walls and yelled, "You fucking no-good faggot butchers."

"I beg of you," the priest said to him.

The reporter said, "Remember to edit that out."

The woman in business dress began to cry.

Someone turned up a portable radio. At twelve-fifteen it passed on the official pronunciation of death. Then there was more crying, more praying, more chanting.

Ten minutes later, the TV truck was gone. The Buddhist monk soon followed, and after him the priest, the nun, the others. The vendor sold one more beer to the leathery man in cutoffs, then locked up his cart and pushed it away. The leathery man wandered into the night.

That left Karen and Luanne. "He's a martyr now," Luanne said, still holding up her sign.

"To what cause?"

"You're pretty cynical, you know that? Why did you even bother coming if you don't care?"

Karen looked around, saw that the only car still there was hers. "Can I drop you somewhere?" she said.

Luanne shook her head. "I'm not going anywhere till he comes out. I always stay till I see them free."

"What do you mean?"

"They'll be taking him to the county after the show's all over. You'll see if you stick around."

Karen stuck around. The night was pleasant, the moon was up, the prison glowed like an anti-Xanadu. Karen found herself thinking about Coleridge, "The Rime of the Ancient Mariner," Eddie Nye. Jack had got his hands on a bundle; it would probably take her months to discover how. Then he and Eddie had taken off; she might never find out where. Coming here had been a long shot. What next? She had no idea. She searched her mind for one; Luanne stood beside her, silent, holding up her sign.

An idea did come to Karen, but it was fuzzy. Something to do with bananas. Before she could bring it into focus, headlights appeared, and Luanne said, "Here he comes." She hurried to the side of the road. Karen followed.

The headlights came closer. An ambulance. It wasn't sounding the siren or flashing the light display. It wasn't even going fast. There were two men in the front; Karen thought she recognized the one in the passenger seat. As the ambulance went by, Luanne stepped onto the road and cried, "Willie Boggs. Willie Boggs." It almost hit her.

The ambulance drove on, rounded a bend, disappeared. Luanne dropped her sign where she stood, turned to Karen. "That's it," she said. "There's nothing more I can do."

They got into Karen's rental car and drove off. They passed signs in the night: Motel 6, Mufflers 4U, Lanny's Used Tires, Bud Lite, Pink Lady Lounge, All the Shrimp You Cn Eat $6.95, XXX Video, Happy Hour.

"Where can I drop you?" Karen said.

"There's a Dunkin' Donuts up ahead."

Taillights shone in the distance, shrank quickly and vanished; someone going very fast. Then Karen noticed a second set of taillights that seemed not to be moving at all. They grew bigger, sharper. Karen sped up a little. She saw a car parked on the shoulder of the road at a funny angle. Not on the shoulder, actually, but in the adjacent field; and not a car but an ambulance.

Karen pulled off the road, got out of the car, walked toward the ambulance. Lights on, engine off, no sign of an accident. She looked in the front. The driver was alone, slumped forward on the wheel, as though he'd grown too tired to go on. Karen opened the door. The interior light went on, illuminating the bullet hole in the left side of his head.

Karen walked around to the back, tried the handle on the big door. It turned. The door swung open. No interior light went on; she saw shadowy forms.

"Luanne," she called.

But Luanne was right beside her. "I'm here. What's happened?"

"Give me your flash."

Luanne handed her the flash. Karen switched it on, shone it into the back of the ambulance. There was a man-sized bag on the floor, of the type the bodies came home in from Vietnam. A man slouched against the wall beside it, a piney-smelling man who was staring at nothing.

"Mr. Messer?" Karen said. No answer. "Doctor?"

She climbed up, bent over him. Messer had a hole in his head too, but in the back. She felt his neck for a pulse. There was none.

Karen knelt by the body bag, found the zipper, pulled it down, shone the pencil flash inside. The body bag was empty.

"Oh, God," Luanne said. "He got away. He's free, free, free." She reached in for the bag, held it to her face.

"Don't be stupid," Karen said, moving into the front of the ambulance to call the police.

Luanne wasn't listening. She was standing by the road, peering into the night for some sign of Willie Boggs, the body bag trailing behind her.

A few hours later they found Willie's body, singed on the temples, wrists, and ankles from the electrodes, jammed into a locked supplies closet in the prison infirmary. The inmates were rousted and counted. All present, except for the occupant of cell 93 on the third tier of C-Block: Angel Cruz, known as El Rojo. The picture of the boy in the cowboy outfit that had been taped to the wall of C–93 was gone too.

Outside: Day 9

Chapter Twenty-Nine

Eddie parked Jack's car outside 434 Collins Avenue. He remembered the address, remembered word for word the letter that had lain in his locker for almost fifteen years. One third of his accumulated correspondence: not hard to remember.

Wm. P. Brice
Investigation and Security
434 Collins Ave., Miami

Dear Mr. Ed Nye:
As I informed your brother, all our best efforts to locate the individual known as JFK have to this point in time been unsuccessful. Lacking further funds to continue, we are obliged to terminate the investigation.
                    Sincerely,
                    Bill Brice

Four thirty-four Collins Avenue was a faded-pink office building with a Space Available sign on the roof. Eddie got out of the car, taking the backpack with him. The sky was blue, the sun gold, the air hot. Hot to Eddie, at least, still wearing Jack's wintertime clothing. He went inside.

The lobby was small and dark. There was a single elevator with graffiti scratched on its steel door, and a black office-directory board with white rubberized letters and numbers, some missing.

Brice and Colon Security, he read, number 417. Eddie took the elevator to the top floor.

"Ring and Enter, *Pujar y Entrar*," was written on a plastic strip taped to the door of 417. Eddie rang and entered.

A brassy-haired receptionist looked up from her magazine. She raised what was left of her eyebrows.

"I'd like to see Mr. Brice," Eddie said.

"Name?"

"Ed Nye."

The receptionist picked up her phone. "A Mr. Ed Nye to see you." Eddie heard a voice on the other end: harsh, loud, metallic. The receptionist hung up and said: "Very last door on your right."

Eddie went past her, into a short corridor. There were only two doors to choose from; perhaps the receptionist fantasized herself part of a big operation. The first was closed and had "Señor Colon" on the front. The second was open. Eddie walked in.

An old man was sitting with his feet up on his desk. The soles of his shoes were worn; so were the carpet, the desk, his face, his eyes. A white-mesh screen covered his throat.

"Mr. Brice?"

The old man took his feet off the desk, tugged at the mesh screen, and replied. At least, his lips moved and sound came from him, harsh, loud, metallic. Eddie understood none of it.

The old man pointed to the white mesh and spoke again. His mouth, lips, tongue, all moved to shape words, but the sound came from whatever was under the mesh screen. This time Eddie caught most of it. "Sawbones took my larynx, Mr. Nye. Got to listen close."

Eddie nodded.

"Siddown."

Eddie sat, laying the backpack on the floor.

"What can I do for you?" the old man said. The voice was amplified, mechanical, like a robot's; at the same time, there was something disembodied about it, which made Eddie think of the oracle in a book of Greek legends he'd read.

"You're William Brice?"

"I am."

"My name's Ed Nye."

"That's what she said."

"Does it mean anything to you?"

"No. Should it?"

"Maybe not," Eddie said. "It was a long time ago."

"How long?"

"Fifteen years. My brother hired you to find someone."

Brice wore thick glasses. Behind them were little brown eyes that watched Eddie's face. He inhaled sharply, like a singer getting ready for a hard note. "And did I?" he said.

"No. But I'd like to know how far you got."

"Why?"

"I'm still looking for him."

"Your brother should have anything like that. I always send a case summary, win or lose." Brice took a raspy gulp of air, short of breath, as though the machine in his throat was exhausting his supply.

"I'd like a copy of it," Eddie said, "if your records go back that far."

"I got records of every case. Thirty-six years." Brice sucked in another deep breath. "But I don't give them away."

"How much?"

The little brown eyes looked Eddie up and down, as though assessing his net worth. Eddie's net worth was right there on the floor of Brice's office: $488,220.

"Fifty bucks," Brice said.

"Okay."

"What's your brother's name?"

"J. M. Nye. Jack."

Brice picked up his phone, held the speaker halfway between his throat and his mouth. "Rita? Bring me the file on Jack or J. M. Nye." He hung up, leaned back in his chair. "So who are you looking for?"

"A drug smuggler from the Bahamas."

"No shortage of those. What's special about this one?" Another raspy breath.

"He committed a crime that someone else paid for."

There was a pause, but brief. "Someone else like you?"

Eddie nodded.

"Thought so. Moment you came in." The words, amplified and mechanical, had an official sound, like an announcement over a loudspeaker. "How much time did you do?"

"All of it."

"How much was all."

"Fifteen years."

This pause was longer. "That means you just got out."

"Right."

"Maybe I could take a gander at the fifty bucks."

"First we'll see if you've got anything," Eddie said.

"I got something. I got something on every case." Brice glanced down at the backpack. "What's this drug smuggler's name?"

"Kidd," said Eddie. "But we didn't know that at the time. All we knew then was his nickname."

"What was it?"

"JFK."

Brice sat straighter in his chair, just a little, and lowered his gaze. His hand went to the desk drawer, opened it, took out a pack of cigarettes. He lit one, inhaled deeply, blew smoke. Some came through his nose and mouth, some through the white-mesh screen.

"Now do you remember?" Eddie said.

Brice shook his head. "Kind of a funny nickname, that's all."

The brassy-haired woman came through the door carrying a file, stopped dead. "God in heaven," she said. "Look what you're doing."

Brice glanced down at the cigarette in his hand, then glared at her. "I got a client in here, Rita." A blue wisp curled through the mesh screen. She dropped the file on the desk and left without another word.

"Not married, are you?" Brice asked.

"No."

"Neither's Rita, soon as her next divorce goes through." Eddie didn't respond. Brice opened the file. There was a single sheet of lined yellow notepad paper inside. Handwriting filled the top third. The rest was blank. It didn't seem like a lot for Mr. Trimble's thousand dollars.

"That's it?" Eddie said.

Brice looked up from the file. "The investigation was unsuccessful, as you said."

"You must have discovered something."

Brice closed the file. "Not a thing."

"Or eliminated some possibilities. Even that could help." Eddie dug some bills out of his pocket, counted out fifty dollars, laid it on the desk.

Brice put his hand on the file. "Does your brother know you're here?"

"No."

"Plan to see him?"

"No."

"Know where he is?"

"I don't know what's on your mind, Brice. My brother's dead."

"You kill him?"

The next thing Eddie knew he was on his feet, standing over the old man.

"Don't," said Brice. The tone was harsh and commanding, but that was just the machinery; his eyes were full of fear.

Eddie didn't touch him. He just picked up the file and took it to the window. Down on the street a cop was tucking a parking ticket under the windshield wiper on Jack's car. Eddie withdrew the single sheet of paper from the file and read it.

The date was on the top line. Then:

Nye, Jack. Intview #1.
Retainer $250—bank check.
Brother—Eddie (Edw. Nicholas) 5–15 drugs (mj)
Atty.—Glenn Weems, Smith & Weems, Ft. L. (who $$$?)
Nds. dvlp. new evdnce re: "JFK"
Bahamas—Saint Amour—Galleon Bch.
DEA—tip? Eddie N.—enemies? J. N. says no.
What about "JFK" as poss. enemy? Doesn't kn.
"JFK" had mj patch.
But

That was all.

"Where's the rest of it?" Eddie said, moving in front of the desk.

Brice shook his head.

"But these are just your notes from the first meeting. It doesn't say what you did or where you went."

"I didn't do anything, didn't go anywhere."

"Why not?" Eddie ran his eyes over the page again. "And I know he paid you a grand, not two-fifty."

"Maybe I shouldn't tell you this."

"But," Eddie said. The word that closed the file.

"But your brother's dead, so maybe you have a right to know."

"Know what?"

"That I was just following his directions."

Eddie didn't understand; all the same, the icy feeling crept across his back and up his neck.

"And two-fifty was all he gave me, I don't know about any grand."

"Gave you to do what?" Eddie said.

"Nothing. He said money had been raised and it had to be spent"—Brice gasped for air—"but that you and this JFK were partners—he grew it, you ran it—and you were as guilty as he was. So no confession from him would do you"—another gulp of air—"any good."

Eddie backed into the chair in front of the desk, almost sat down.

"You're lying," he said. His legs didn't want to hold him up. He made them.

Brice shook his head. "When you mentioned JFK it all came back. I couldn't forget a thing like that." Pause for breath. "Only time it happened in thirty-six years." Brice's gaze went to the fifty dollars on the desk, then to Eddie. "JFK was lying low in Nassau, according to your brother. I guess your fifty buys that much." He took another deep breath, but said no more.

Eddie folded the sheet of yellow paper, stuck it in his pocket, picked up the backpack. He remembered Brice's letter—"our best efforts to locate the individual known as JFK have to this point in time been unsuccessful"—and didn't think he owed Brice a penny, but he left the money where it was. He didn't want to touch it.

Rita looked up from her magazine as he went by.

"Can you believe him?" she said. "I tell him, 'Pa, how can you still smoke after everything that happened to you?' He just ignores me. He's such an idiot, sometimes."

"That's one of his minor flaws," Eddie said.

Chapter Thirty

Do most lives turn on one crucial event? Eddie didn't think so. But some did—the Mariner's for one, and his own for another. Now, after talking to Brice, Eddie knew that he didn't understand his own crucial event any better than he did the Mariner's. His imprisonment wasn't simply the result of bad luck and a twisted chain of circumstance, as he had always thought. That left a lot of questions, questions that Jack could have answered.

The twin-engine Piper followed its shadow southeast across a sea smooth as Jell-O. Blue marked deep water, green the sandy shallows, red-brown the coral heads. A long white cruiser cut across the surface on the same course as the plane, like a tab opening a zipper. The shadow of the plane darkened the boat and left it behind.

"There's beer in the cooler," the pilot called from the cockpit.

"No, thanks," Eddie said.

"Mind grabbing one for me?" Pause. "Little joke."

The pilot looked back at Eddie to see if he got it. He had watery eyes and a puffy face; perhaps the cooler was for the return trip, solo.

"Good thing," Eddie said. "I'm with the National Safety Board."

There was no talk after that. The Bahamas appeared like emeralds on blue velvet, and soon came Saint Amour, as he remembered it, banana shaped and outlined in white. The pilot descended, banked, flew so low that Eddie could see a manta ray gliding below the surface, then skimmed down over pine tops and touched down on the strip, now paved, bounced a few times, and rolled to a stop.

Taking the backpack, Eddie got out. He felt the heat right away. It opened his pores, worked itself deep inside, slowed him down. *You on island time now.*

He looked around. Except for the pavement on the strip, nothing had changed, not the scrub forest, the still air, the floral smells. The strip was deserted but for a single crab sidestepping down the center. Eddie hoisted the pack on his back, crossed the strip, and started down the dirt road. Behind him, the plane gathered speed, roaring as it rose into the sky, then throbbing, then buzzing, then making no sound at all. A big brown bird rose from the trees, orange legs tucked up against its tail. Eddie could hear the heavy wings beating the air.

In five or ten minutes, he came to the flamboyant tree that marked the path leading to JFK's marijuana patch. The path was gone, lost in a coiling growth of creeper and bush. But the flamboyant tree seemed much bigger, its red-flowered branches now reaching across the road, dappling the sun. He had a strange thought: *This would be the place to bury Jack.*

Eddie walked on, and a verse of the poem came to him, as though his mind were a CD player programmed on shuffle.

> The many men, so beautiful!
> And they all dead did lie:
> And a thousand thousand slimy things
> Lived on; and so did I.

But Jack, it turned out, hadn't been beautiful, and he himself didn't feel slimy. Where were all these beautiful dead people? Louie? The Ozark brothers? Paz's driver? All dead, none beautiful. Killing might be wrong, but not because of some inherent beauty in the species. Where was it? In Tiffany? Sookray? Paz? El Rojo? No. Not in Gaucho either. Childhood and beauty were not the same; he remembered how he had fallen through the ice in his hockey skates. Then he thought of Karen, how she had kissed him and said, "I'm attracted to you, and I haven't been attracted to anyone in a long time. Remember that, no matter what happens."

And despite what had happened, despite the fact that she'd been working to bring his brother down, Eddie couldn't fit her into this new and dismal scheme of things.

The road swung right, toward the sea. He could see patches of it framed by the trees, flashing shapes of blue and gold, like abstract art on the move. He was sweating now; it dripped off his chin the way it had the last time he'd walked this road. The dead pig had weighed much more than $488,220, but he hadn't been wearing Jack's winter clothes. He stopped, took off the sweater, rolled up the shirt-sleeves, kept going.

A salty breeze curled across the road. Eddie still hadn't seen anyone. The island might have been deserted and he a real-life equivalent of Sir Wentworth Staples, watching for a galleon through the trees. The illusion grew stronger and stronger, and with it came the idea of making a life here. Then he heard the thwack of tennis balls.

Eddie shifted the pack on his back, walked a little faster, recalling the red clay court that lay ahead, with its sun-bleached backboard and damp and dark equipment shed. Just ahead: behind that line of scrub pines.

But as Eddie drew closer he saw they were all gone: the dried-out clay court, the cracked backboard, the tumbledown shed. Instead there was an arched gate with a sign: "Pleasure Island Tennis Club"; and through it the sight of a dozen green all-weather courts, a clubhouse with a deck, and suntanned people in tennis outfits. Lots of them: lounging on the deck with drinks, drilling with the pros on the center courts, playing doubles on the side courts.

Eddie didn't enter the gate. He stayed on the road, paved now and hot under his shoes, as it angled closer to the sea. He knew he was near the old fish camp, close enough, he thought, to hear the ocean. But all he heard was the whine of high-pitched engines. Then he came to the row of casuarinas that shielded the fish camp from the road. He walked through them and saw that the fish camp too was gone. In its place was a go-cart track. Three white kids fishtailed around the far turn, not far from the spot where Jack's cabin had stood. A black man gassing carts at the side of the track glanced up at Eddie.

Eddie followed the road to its end at Galleon Beach. The beach itself was the same, if you ignored the ranks of glistening bodies flopped on chaises longues. But where the six waterfront cottages, thatch-roofed bar and central building with office, kitchen, dining room, and the Packers' suite had been, there now stood a slab hotel eight stories high. Behind the hotel Eddie saw fairways, sand traps, greens, and in the distance clusters of white squared-off villas like a hard-shelled growth on the hillsides. Brad Packer's blueprint had come to life.

"Take your bag, suh?"

A boy in a blue polo shirt with the words "Pleasure Island" on the chest was beside him.

"I'm not staying," Eddie said.

"Land-crab race tonight, suh." The boy looked up at him with unblinking eyes.

Eddie smiled. "Who owns this place?"

"Big, big company." The boy spread his hands.

"What's it called?"

The boy thought. "United States company," he said.

"You from this island?" Eddie said.

The boy nodded.

"Know a man named JFK?"

The boy took a step back.

"He's an old friend," Eddie said. "I'd like to see him."

"Ol' frien'?" said the boy, backing away some more.

"What's wrong?" Eddie said.

"He got AIDS."

"I know."

"You got it too?"

"No."

The boy relaxed a little.

"Where is he?" Eddie said.

"Down to Cotton Town." The boy pointed south.

"How far is that?"

"Far," said the boy, "except when the jitney carry you."

"Where do I get the jitney?"

The boy pointed his chin at the hotel.

Eddie went inside. There was a newsstand, a gift shop, a bar. A big-bellied man wearing nothing but a bathing suit and a straw hat sat on a stool with a drink in his hand. "I'm gettin' smashed on Goombay smash," he said to the bartender. "Is that funny or what?"

The bartender smiled, but her eyes were expressionless.

The big-bellied man leaned over the bar. "What's your name, sweetheart?"

Eddie, walking to the reception counter, missed her reply.

No one was at the counter. Eddie rang the bell. A door opened and a woman came out. She was a big woman, perhaps twenty pounds overweight, with short frosted hair, plucked eyebrows, and a face that had spent too long in the sun. She wore a name pin on her white blouse: "Amanda," it said, "Assistant Manager."

"Checking in?" she asked, noticing the backpack.

"No," Eddie replied. "When's the next jitney to Cotton Town?"

The woman didn't answer. She was staring at his face. "You look like someone I used to know," she said.

"Yeah?" Eddie said, feeling in his pocket for money to pay the fare.

"And sound like him too." She tilted her head to one side, revealing a wrinkled line at the base of her neck. "I couldn't forget those eyes. You're Eddie Nye, aren't you? Jack's brother."

"That's right," he said, looking at her face again, hardened and thickened by the sun, and not placing her.

"Have I changed that much?" the woman said.

His eyes went to her name pin: Amanda. "Mandy?"

"The one and only." They looked at each other. "My God," she said, "isn't this something? I mean, what goes around comes around."

"I've got a bad memory for faces," Eddie said, thinking that a chivalrous phrase might be required but doubting that that was it. He searched her face for the features of the Mandy he had known, and found some; but smudged, blunted, coarsened. Like the others—Jack, Evelyn, Bobby Falardeau—she had aged more quickly than he, as though prison, with its bad food that kept him from eating too much, and its absence of sunlight, which had kept his skin unwrinkled, had slowed the life clock inside him. A nice thought; but it left out his hair, growing in gray.

"Of course I remember you—I never forget anyone I sleep with," Mandy said, verifying Eddie's doubt. "There haven't been all that many, considering."

The office door opened again and a little man came out, carrying a briefcase. "Not all that many what, dear?" he said.

"Requests for the Cotton Town jitney," said Mandy. "Say hi to Eddie, an old acquaintance of mine. Eddie—my husband, Farouz."

They shook hands. Farouz's name pin read "Manager." "Gotta run," he said, and went out.

Mandy's eyes were on him again. "You're lookin' good," she said. "Stayed in shape, unlike yours truly. I don't have the discipline." She raised her arms hopelessly. "That's my sad story. What have you been up to?"

A routine question for most people, but not for him. Had he heard it right? "What have I been up to?"

His tone surprised her. "Since I wimped out on you that time up in Lauderdale," she explained.

"Wimped out?"

She lowered her voice. "When the cops came. You don't have much of a memory for anything, do you? I heard them come aboard and just grabbed some gear and jumped off. I didn't mean to leave you hanging and all, but what could I do? Especially since I was hip to what was on board and you weren't. I just knew you'd be okay."

"Okay?"

Mandy glanced around to see if anyone was watching. "I know you were pissed off. But you could have answered my letters. After all, there was no harm done." Eddie was silent, but something in his expression made her say, "What? What is it?"

"You'd better explain," Eddie said.

"About what?"

"About no harm done."

Mandy shrugged. "You know. Nothing came of it."

"Nothing came of it?"

"Brad lost everything to the bank, of course, but I meant nothing came of it in terms of you. I was back at my parents' in Wisconsin by that time—classic move, right?—but when they dropped the charges I wrote you, more than once, and you didn't write back."

"Wrote me where?"

"Care of your brother in Lauderdale. I kept in touch with him for a while. That's how I knew you got off."

Eddie leaned on the counter, not trusting his legs to hold him up. "Jack told you I got off?"

"In a postcard or something. That's when I started writing you. I gave up after a few months. I'm the kind who carries a torch, but not forever."

Eddie didn't say anything. He just stared at her, looking for some sign that she was lying. He saw none.

She misread whatever expression was on his face. "Hey! You really couldn't expect me to, now could you? I mean, you didn't even answer my letters."

"It's all right," Eddie said. His legs felt a little stronger now; he stepped back from the counter.

"Whew," said Mandy. "I thought you were going ballistic there for a second." She looked him up and down. "How about a drink?" she said. "On me."

"I've got to get going."

She reached across the counter, touched his forearm. "What's the rush? You're on vacation, right?"

They went into an air-conditioned bar overlooking a heart-shaped swimming pool. It had green-glass floats hanging from the ceiling, fishnets and harpoons on the walls, and a neon name glowing over the rows of bottles: "Mongo's." Jack's suggestion, outliving him like the work of some great author.

"Do you own this place?"

Mandy laughed. "Are you kidding? It's owned by AB Gesselschaft. They bought it from the bank, way back." A waiter arrived. "What'll it be?" Mandy said. "Cecil makes the best damn planter's punch in the Bahamas."

Two planter's punches arrived, in tall frosted glasses with pineapple wedges stuck on the rims. Mandy raised her glass. "To old times," she said, taking a big drink.

Eddie drank too; the glass trembled in his hand. It was too bitter.

"We were so young," Mandy said. "And what a place. Undeveloped then, but still. Irrestistible, I guess. At least, I couldn't resist it."

"When did you come back?"

"After the bank took over. I kind of drifted down. It was closed, but they needed someone who knew the history. When the Germans took over I stuck around, answering the phone, working my way up. Then Farouz arrived." She took another drink. "Jesus, that's good. You like?"

Eddie made himself drink some more. She watched him, watched his face, his hand, his throat as the liquid went down. "I've got a confession to make," she said. "Promise you won't tell a soul?"

Eddie smiled. It was such a childish idea. "Promise," he said.

Mandy smiled too. "Remember that shed by the old tennis court?"

He nodded.

"I still think about it." Her voice grew husky. "I mean a lot. When I'm in bed, kind of thing." She tried to meet his gaze boldly, but couldn't. "With Farouz, I mean. As soon as I start getting all hot, or if I'm not, I just think of that time, and then I do." Her face, dark and leathery as it was, reddened. She gulped her drink. There was a pause. She leaned toward him. "Are you married?"

"No."

"Girlfriend?"

"No."

"I find that hard to believe." She leaned a little closer. "Do you think about it?" she asked.

She didn't have to say the shed. He knew. In his cell in F-Block he'd thought about it a lot, not as a hormone booster to get him in the mood for someone else, but just because it was one of the best memories he had. Now he knew he would never think about the shed again, not in the same way. "It's gone now, isn't it?"

She leaned back. "What's gone?"

"The shed."

She looked at him. Her eyes grew cooler, businesslike. "We've got twelve Deco-Turf courts and an outstanding program, if you'd like a lesson sometime." She glanced at his drink. "You don't like Cecil's creation?"

"I do." He took another sip. "But I've got to get going."

*   *   *

The jitney left from the dock. Eddie sat alone at the back, waiting for the driver to finish saying good-bye to his girlfriend and climb aboard. He kissed her, patted her shoulder, patted her rump, kissed her again, answered a question, then another. Out on the water, a cruiser slowly approached the dock: long, white, multidecked, topped with rotating antennae and satellite dishes; possibly the boat he had flown over. It was much too big to cross the reef. Even as Eddie had the thought, the cruiser swung round, slowed some more, dropped a bow anchor. Eddie could read the name on the stern: *El Liberador*. Men appeared on deck, began winching down a Boston Whaler.

The driver hopped on the jitney, cranked up his boom box, shot away from the dock. "Cotton Town and all points in between," he said. "Which is nowhere. Va va voom."

Chapter Thirty-One

Cotton Town was an hour away. In that hour, the road degenerated to a rutted track, and Western civilization, except for flattened beer cans flashing in the sun, disappeared. Eddie caught a glimpse of one house along the route, standing on a bluff over a quiet bay. It was white with closed shutters, a verandah, and a peace sign painted large on the slanted roof.

"Who lives there?" Eddie asked.

"In the old gin house?" said the driver, turning down his boom box. "Nobody now. The hippies they crash in it when there was hippies."

"Does anyone own it?"

"Everything be owned," said the driver, "even the mangoes hanging from the trees." He glanced at Eddie in his mirror. "You in the market for a house?"

Eddie looked down at the bay, sheltered by two curving arms that ended in sandy points about half a mile apart. He could picture himself swimming back and forth between them. "How much would it cost?"

"The old gin house? Thousands and thousands."

He had thousands and thousands. Why not? Then he thought of Mandy. Would he want to settle in so close to her? There were other islands, with other bays perfect for swimming.

"That be the problem, man," said the driver. "Where to get those thousands and thousands."

*   *   *

The road ended in front of a pink church the size of a two-car garage. "Cotton Town Tabernacle Kirk of Redemption," read big blue letters on the wall.

"End of the line," said the driver. "Tipping permitted."

Eddie gave him five dollars—too much? he didn't know, not having been in many tipping situations—and got off the jitney, carrying the backpack. The jitney backed, turned, departed. That left Eddie alone with a brown chicken, pecking at the dirt outside the open door of the church.

Music came through the doorway, one of those familiar pieces that appear on classical-highlight records not sold in stores. Eddie went inside.

A little girl with a bow in her hair sat at an upright piano, her back to the door, her eyes on the sheet music. She sensed his presence; her hands flew off the yellowed keys and her head snapped around.

"I didn't mean to interrupt," Eddie said.

She stared at him.

"I'm looking for a man named JFK."

"You the doctor?" Her voice was so soft he could barely hear her.

"Just a friend."

The girl stared at him. It was quiet in the church; he heard something land with a thump outside, a coconut perhaps. Just when he'd decided she wasn't going to respond, the girl said, "The house after the Fantastic."

"Where's that?"

She pointed with her skinny arm.

Eddie went outside, slipped on the backpack, and set off on a path that led beyond the church, in the direction the girl had pointed. He went past an overgrown garden, a half-built cinder-block house with weeds growing through the holes in the blocks, and a lopsided dwelling with an open window through which he saw a woman slumped forward at a table, her head in her arms. He came to an unpainted wooden structure with a sign over the door in big childish letters: "Fantastic Bar and Club." He heard a man hawking inside, saw a gob of spit fly out a side window.

The path led through a grove of four or five sawtooth-leaved palms to a small house painted in broad vertical stripes of red, green, and black. A curtain hung where the door should have been. Eddie knocked on the door jamb.

The house was silent. Eddie knocked again. "Hello?" he called. "Anyone here?"

No answer. He brushed the curtain aside and went in.

He was in a small room with a cement floor and unfinished wooden walls. There was nothing in it but an icebox, a card table, two card-table chairs, and a rusty bicycle leaning against the wall. "Hello?" he called again. Silence. He opened the icebox. It was empty except for an oblong yellow-green fruit of a kind he didn't know.

Eddie crossed the room, entered a short hall with two doors off it, both closed. He opened the first. A bathroom; he shut the door, but not before the smell reached him. A ball of nausea rose up inside him. He stood in the hall, took a few deep breaths, kept it down. Then he opened the second door.

He looked into a darkened room. A strip of tar paper hung over the single window, but there were coin-sized holes in it, and golden rays of sunshine poked through, spotlighting a Bob Marley poster taped to the wall, an L.A. Lakers sweatshirt rumpled on the floor, and a man lying on a bare mattress, eyes closed. A fly buzzed in the shadows.

Eddie had seen AIDS before. There was lots of it inside, although the victims were usually removed by the time they reached the point that the man on the mattress had come to. Eddie went a little closer, gazed down at him.

Was it JFK? Eddie couldn't tell. The image of JFK in his memory was blurred, and what was left of this man bore it no resemblance, other than in race and sex. The man wore only a pair of white briefs; on the mattress near his still hand lay another oblong yellow-green fruit, with one piece bitten out. As Eddie watched, a shudder went through the man. The expression on his face, which had been peaceful, grew anxious. His eyes opened.

He saw Eddie. "I in a dream about L.A., doctor," he said. "Universal Studio, Disneyland, Knott's Berry Farm—I be knowing all these places in my past traveling life."

It was JFK.

"I'm not a doctor," Eddie said.

JFK looked him over. "No problem," he said. "Intern? Resident? Fellow? I got it all down, *toute* that jive, the hospital jive, man. Fellow the best. You looks like a fellow."

"You don't remember me?"

The eyes, big as a child's in that hollow face, gazed up at Eddie. "What hospital you be from?"

"No hospital," Eddie said.

"No hospital?"

Eddie shook his head. "Maybe you remember the wild pig."

Pause. Then JFK smiled. "Boar, not pig," he said. "Hemingway himself, he come to hunt the wild boar on this very island." JFK's teeth, probably just normal teeth, looked extra-big, extra-healthy. That they would long survive him, Eddie knew, was only a function of the hardness of teeth; but there was something macabre about that smile, as though JFK's teeth were mocking the body they lived in.

The smile faded. When JFK spoke again, his voice was quiet. "I remember that creature. Cook him up real nice. Onions, garlic, pineapple, herb. The herb what does it." He paused, then spoke again, quieter still. "I remember you. You done lost all that hippie hair, but I remember you."

JFK turned his head away, toward the tar-papered window with the rays shining through like the blades of gold swords. The room was silent, except for the buzzing of the fly. Then JFK spoke: "Don't be having the idea JFK is a gay man. Needles. Needles be the source of my disease."

"I don't see what difference it makes," Eddie said.

Slowly his head turned back. "No difference?" he said.

"No."

There was another card-table chair in the corner. Eddie pulled it up, sat by the mattress. The big child-eyes watched him. "You lose your trial, man. That right?"

Eddie nodded.

"Same thing be happening to my brothers. Dime he die in Fox Hill. Franco he get shot in Miami. And me . . . soon I shuffle off this earthly skin." His eyes went to the Bob Marley poster, lit with golden rays. The words on the poster read: "One World." There was a long silence. JFK's eyes closed.

"Can I get you anything?" Eddie said.

"Water," JFK replied. "For my thirst."

Eddie went into the stinking bathroom. A dirty glass sat on a shelf above the sink. Eddie turned on the tap. Rusty water trickled out. After a minute or so it cleared slightly. Eddie washed the glass, rubbing it clean inside and out with his fingers, then filled it.

He returned to the bedroom. JFK's eyes were still closed.

"Water," Eddie said.

Not opening his eyes, JFK said, "You know we all ninety-nine percent water? All humanity? So it be the water have this disease, not me. All I be needing to do is piss out that sick water and fill up with clean. Abracadabra—problem solve." His eyes opened. "You believe there truth in that?" he said.

"I'm not a doctor," Eddie replied, coming to the side of the mattress and extending the glass.

JFK tried to sit up, could not. He raised his hand. It shook. "So weak, man," he said. "I was never in this life a big strong white hunter like you, but . . ." His hand flopped down at his side.

Eddie sat on the mattress. He put his hand behind JFK's head, feeling the dampness in his tightly curled hair and the fever in the scalp beneath. He raised the glass to JFK's mouth. JFK's lips parted. Eddie poured in the water, slowly. JFK's Adam's apple, prominent in his fleshless neck, bobbed up and down. He drank half the glass, then grunted and shook his head. Eddie lowered him back down.

JFK breathed rapid, shallow breaths. "Down to ninety-eight percent now, man. Maybe ninety-seven." His breathing slowed. "Water, water everywhere," he said. "How true it be, those things they say in church."

"Water, water everywhere's not from church," Eddie said.

"Sure it is," said JFK, "sure it is. The gospel truth I strayed away from all my born days. Like my brothers, Franco and Dime." His eyes shifted to Eddie. "You be different from your own brother."

"In what way?"

"Not the same." He licked his lips.

"More water?"

JFK shook his head. "Too hard," he said. His eyes closed.

"You were in New York," Eddie said.

JFK nodded, barely.

"You saw Jack."

He nodded again.

"Why?"

"Old times," said JFK. "And him so rich, I be wondering if he could spare a little material advance for old JFK."

"Did he?"

"Fifty dollars. U.S." A faint smile appeared on JFK's face.

Fifty dollars: exactly what Uncle Vic had got. It must have been Jack's standard handout. "When was this?" Eddie asked.

The smile vanished. "Two years ago. Maybe three. The sickness already have me in its coils then, but not so strong." He opened his eyes, looked at the Marley poster, then at Eddie. "You be in Switzerland at the time."

"Switzerland?"

"Doing finance."

"Who told you that?" said Eddie, rising.

JFK shrank back on the mattress. "Your brother. I aks about you. Feeling bad about how you lose your trial in the distant past. And that what he say. Switzerland."

Eddie reached down and took JFK's head in his hands; not hard—at least, he didn't think it was hard. "Are you listening to me?" he said. "I want you to listen carefully."

JFK licked his lips. "I be listening," he said, almost too softly to hear.

"Then get this straight. I just got out. I did fifteen years for a crime I knew nothing about. Your crime."

"Fifteen years?"

Eddie took his hands off JFK, rose, walked to the tar-papered window, peered through one of the coin-sized holes. He saw a goat straining its tether to get to the leaves of a dusty bush just out of reach.

There was a noise behind him. Eddie turned, saw JFK crawling desperately off the mattress. He got hold of the chair, pulled himself up, his movements weak and agitated at the same time; trying to reach eye level with Eddie. He gasped for breath: "But I tries to warn you, man. On the boat radio."

"Warn me about what?"

"Mr. Packer he call ahead to the harbor police in Lauderdale, man. For reporting a stolen boat. No problem, except I know what be on this stolen boat, man. I get on the radio in the bar, to be warning you don' go to no Lauderdale. But Mr. Packer he come in the bar, see me, shut off the radio."

"Did he know what was on board?"

"No, man. It be just the three of us know."

"The three of you?"

JFK held up three fingers, long and delicate, counted them off one at a time.

"Me."

Eddie nodded.

"Mandy."

Eddie nodded again.

JFK touched his third finger. "And Jack."

"Jack?"

"Jack your brother."

"Jack was in on it?" An image came to him, lit by a beach fire: Jack's hands and forearms, scratched as if by heavy gardening.

"Equal partners," said JFK. "I the owner of the ganja, Mandy she have the buyer in Miami, Jack have the boat. I be aksing you first, but you was saying no to me." JFK's body, supported by his grip on the card-table chair, began to tremble. The feet of the chair rattled on the floor.

Jack had been in on it. That explained why the search for JFK had been a sham—a real investigation would have implicated him too—but it didn't explain everything. "Did Jack know Packer called the harbor cops?"

"Sure he know. We all right there in the bar—me, Packer, Jack."

"And Jack didn't try to stop him?"

"He try. He say why be making it police matters? Packer he say to teach you respect for property. Not just the boat—the girl too, that be his system of thinking. They argue back and forth."

"But Jack didn't tell him about the dope?"

"How he do that without he incriminating hisself? Instead he tell Mr. Packer come out on the beach, for talking private. That give me the chance to call you. But Mr. Packer he smart. He come running back in, rip the plug out of the wall."

"That was all?" Eddie said.

"All?"

"All it took to stop my brother?"

JFK thought for a moment. "Like he could hit Mr. Packer on the head or thing like that?"

"If he had to."

JFK shook his head. "No way," he said. "Mr. Packer he use his hold on your brother."

"What hold?"

"He say one more trick and you don' be gettin' the seven and a half percent."

"That stopped him?"

"Seven and a half percent of everyt'ing, man. The hotel, the time share, the golf, the marina. Could have been millions, maybe. Millions. You understand the forces of the situation?"

Eddie understood. Understanding had a physical component; at first it was all physical: a light-headedness, as though he were much too tall, and fragile, like some strange bird. Then came the mental part, the fact of what Jack had done to him and the way it had happened. But not how Jack could have done it to him. He wanted one thing: to ask Jack that question.

Eddie stood motionless in JFK's hot room, unconscious of passing time. His mind was far away, in a cold northern place of pirate games, of hockey, of falling through the ice. He thought of all that, and more, but failed to find the reason why. Just the MacGuffin, the bookstore boy had said, a device. There was no explanation. Would he have to accept that, in the poem and in his own life? Silence thickened, tangible, immobilizing. JFK broke it by saying, "Hey! You all right?"

Eddie grew aware of JFK leaning on the card-table chair across the room, separated from him by golden bars of light. The light burnished all his bony parts, as though they were already exposed.

"You better lie down," Eddie said.

JFK nodded, made his way to the mattress, sat, used his hands to pull up his legs, lay down. Eddie could hear him breathing, fast and shallow. After a few minutes he groaned, then breathed more slowly. He looked at Eddie.

"Too weak, man. But I be wanting you to know."

"Know what?"

"That it wasn't me."

Eddie nodded. "More water?"

"Not a drop to drink."

"Why not?"

"Too far to go, all the way down from ninety-seven percent. Nine or ten, maybe. I could reach it from there. But not ninety-seven."

Eddie opened the backpack, took out a wad of bills, put them in JFK's hand.

"What this?" said JFK.

"For medicine, the doctor, whatever you need."

"Your brother's money?"

"Mine."

"You got money? That be something, anyway." JFK's eyes went to the Marley poster: "One World." "I be wanting to make a little confession," he said.

Eddie waited.

"JFK no be a gay man."

"You said that."

"But he be doing some gay things at one time, despite his own self."

"So what?" Eddie said.

There were no buses in Cotton Town, no jitneys, no taxis. Eddie borrowed JFK's rusty bicycle, promising to send it back from Galleon Beach. In fifteen years he had made no plans other than to quit smoking, to take nothing with him, to have a steam bath. He had realized all of them, not hard to do. The hard part was knowing what you wanted. And now Eddie knew. He wanted a house on a bluff and a bay for swimming. There were other islands. He bicycled north, toward the airstrip and a flight to the next one in the chain.

It was hot, the road bumpy, the pack increasingly heavy on his back. Eddie was aware of all those things, but they didn't bother him. He was alive, he was free, he had money, all he would ever need. He tried dividing fifteen into $488,220. Thirty-two thousand and something per annum, as though he had spent those years teaching high school: not an excessive return.

Eddie pedaled JFK's bike. The track widened slightly, grew

smoother. Soon he would see the white house on the bluff, the hippie house with the peace sign on the roof. Five or ten minutes had passed without a single thought of Jack. That was good. That was the way it would have to be. He came to the bluff, saw a lane leading up to the house, paused.

A dust cloud rose in the distance, over the treetops. It drew closer, like a small approaching storm. A car appeared beneath the dust cloud, sunlight glinting off the windshield. It topped a rise a few hundred yards from Eddie, going fast, much too fast for the road. He pulled to the side, got off the bike.

The car roared by, so quickly and spewing so much dust that Eddie didn't see the driver at all. He pushed JFK's bike back on the road, adjusted the backpack, got ready to remount. Then the car made a shrieking sound. Eddie looked in time to see it skidding sideways, wheels locked, on the edge of control. But not out of it: the car spun around and came toward him, slower now. The dust began to settle, leaving a little smudged dome across the sky.

The car stopped beside him. The door opened. Karen got out.

Chapter Thirty-Two

"The world is much smaller than you think," Karen said.

They stood on the Cotton Town road, Karen beside her car, Eddie at the head of the lane leading to the hippie house.

"I'm familiar with the concept," Eddie replied.

Karen laughed, a complex sound and not particularly friendly. "Maybe it's Jack who's not."

He saw himself reflected in her sunglasses, two uncertain little Eddies, leaning on their bikes.

"I'm going to disappoint you this time," Eddie said.

"In what way?"

"If you've come to pump me about my brother."

Karen took off her sunglasses. There were shadows under her eyes and her face was pale. "We're just like an old couple," she said, "picking up the conversation in mid-fight."

A breeze stirred in the trees, clearing away the dust, blueing the sky. Karen looked up at the hippie house. "Why don't we just go up and talk to him?"

"He's not there."

Her eyes went to Eddie, and then to the backpack. "Aren't you the loyal little brother."

There was no reason to be loyal, now that he knew what Jack had done. Still, Eddie replied: "You're a cop."

"Not exactly," Karen said. "And he's no longer the subject of an investigation."

"Why is that?" Was it simply the returning of the $230,000,

or did she know Jack was dead? Had his body been found and identified? Eddie couldn't think of any reason why Señor Paz would let that happen.

"Lack of evidence," Karen replied.

"And you've come to dig up more."

"I told you—the investigation is over."

"Then why are you here?"

"I just want to talk to him."

"About what?"

Karen didn't answer right away. Her eyes weren't quite the same now. Same shade of blue, of course, but because of her fatigue, or the heat, or something else, not as cool as before.

"You," she said.

"You're investigating me?"

"In a sense."

"Meaning what?"

"In the broadest sense. I'm interested in you. In what happened to you."

"For your thesis?"

"If you like." Karen put her sunglasses back on. "I've read the transcript of your trial. You denied knowing the marijuana was on board. I found myself inclined to believe you."

"That's nice."

There was a long pause. Then Karen said: "They executed Willie Boggs last night." She waited for Eddie to speak. He watched his close-mouthed reflection in her sunglasses and said nothing. "Some odd things happened," Karen went on. "First I spoke to a man named Messer. He seemed very curious to know your whereabouts. Not long after that, not long after Willie died, in fact, Messer died too. Bullet in the head. I found him in the ambulance that should have been carrying Willie. Willie's body bag was empty. They counted the inmates. One was missing. Can you guess who?"

"No." But he could.

"Angel Cruz. The one they call El Rojo. Did you know him?"

"We'd met."

"And?"

"And what? Are you suggesting I helped him escape?"

"No. I'm just wondering if you can explain what happened."

"Why would I be able to do that?" Eddie said, and Karen

didn't answer. But he could explain it, all right. He understood everything: how El Rojo must have gotten to Messer, how, fearing surveillance, he had tried to set up the payoff rendezvous using the hundred-dollar bill, how Eddie had interfered with the plan, first by not giving the bill to Sookray in the Dunkin' Donuts lot, later by handing her the wrong one. El Rojo had found another method, proving his resourcefulness and Messer's naivete. He'd be in Colombia by now, lying low on one of his ranches.

"Come up with it yet?" said Karen.

Eddie saw that her face had paled more, wondered if she was running a fever. "What does your friend with the gun think?"

"Forget him. Max errs on the side of error." The angle of her sunglasses dipped, as though she was looking him over. "Your appearance made him cautious."

Caution; not a bad idea. Eddie moved closer to the car, checked inside, saw no one lying on the backseat or crouched on the floor.

"Want me to open the trunk?" Karen said.

Eddie shook his head.

Tiny beads of sweat appeared on her upper lip. She brushed them off with the back of her hand. "You won't mind if I see for myself," she said.

"See what?"

"If Jack's up there." She got in the car, waited for Eddie to join her. When he did not, she turned the key and drove up the lane. Eddie stood for a minute or two by the side of the road. Then he mounted JFK's bike and followed.

The lane rose steeply up the bluff, so steeply that Eddie had to get off and walk the bike most of the way. He rounded a bend, passed another tree bearing the small yellow-green fruit, and came to her car, parked beside the house. From there, at the top of the bluff, he could see to the horizon where an invisible line segregated sky-blue from sea-blue. Closer in, perhaps a mile offshore, waves broke over the reef. Not far beyond them the long white cruiser he had seen at Galleon Beach glided south.

There was no sign of Karen. Eddie walked to the screen door at the side of the house. Near the handle the screen was bent back from the frame, leaving a fist-sized hole. Eddie opened the door and went in.

Kitchen. Discolored rectangles imprinted on the linoleum

marked the spots where the appliances had rested. Nothing remained but a wine bottle with a candle in it, upright on the floor, and a simple wooden table, painted yellow. An enormous toad squatted on it like a centerpiece in a restaurant destined to fail. For a moment Eddie wasn't sure whether it was alive. Then its long tongue flicked out and caught an ant crawling across the table.

Eddie went through the kitchen to the living room, the toad's eyes following him the whole way. The living room had a fraying sisal carpet on the floor but no furniture. A screened porch with a rusted kettle barbecue and another endless view ran the length of the room. The long white cruiser had moved farther south. As Eddie watched, it turned out to sea, away from the reef, circled, and started coming back.

At the far end of the room was a narrow staircase. Eddie went up. There were words on the wall, painted in faded rainbow colors:

Whoever loved that loved not at first sight?

The stairs led to the single room on the top floor. A bedroom, with bed still in place. Too hard to move: an ancient and massive four-poster, probably shipped from Europe generations ago, carved with roses and hung with mosquito netting. What the bed might have implied the walls and ceiling clearly stated. Every inch of whitewashed space was covered with rainbow-painted inscriptions:

Forever wilt thou love, and she be fair!

And this maiden she lived with no other thought
Than to love and be loved by me.

'Tis better to have loved and lost
Than never to have loved at all.

I wonder by my troth, what thou, and I
Did, till we lov'd? were we not wean'd till then?
But suck'd on country pleasures, childishly?
Or snorted in the seven sleepers' den?

They do not love that do not show their love.

Is it, in Heav'n, a crime to love too well?
To bear too tender or too firm a heart,
To act a lover's or a Roman's part?
Is there no bright reversion in the sky
For those who greatly think, or bravely die?

Western wind, when wilt thou blow?
The small rain down can rain, —
Christ, if my love were in my arms
And I in my bed again!

Cross that rules the Southern Sky!
Stars that sweep, and turn, and fly,
Hear the Lovers' Litany: —
"Love like ours can never die!"

That out of sight is out of mind
Is true of most we leave behind;
It is not sure, nor can be true,
My own and only love, of you.

And dozens, perhaps hundreds more, crowding out any blank space. Karen stood with her back to him, head tilted to read the one about out of sight and out of mind, written on the ceiling.

"Arthur Hugh Clough," she said without turning: "the Leo Buscaglia of Romantic poetry."

"Never heard of him," Eddie said. "Either of them."

"You're not missing anything." She faced him. "Coleridge is your man, isn't he? Or have you chucked him?"

"Why do you say that?"

She reached into her bag, removed a charred red scrap. He recognized it: the remains of the *Monarch* he had thrown in the fire at the Palazzo. He didn't reply.

Karen glanced around the walls. "Nothing here from your Mariner. I guess he doesn't fit the theme of the room."

" 'A spring of love gushed from my heart,' " Eddie said, the words coming of their own accord. " 'And I blessed them unaware.' "

Karen smiled. "You're something, you know that? But whoever wrote all this didn't have that kind of love in mind." She looked out the window. The sun was low in the sky now, flabby and red. The long white cruiser lay at anchor, outside the reef.

She gazed at it for a few moments, then said: "No Jack."

"That's right."

Behind Karen, the sun kept sinking, reddening, fattening. She ran her finger through the dust on the sill. "What is this place?" she said, turning to him.

"They call it the hippie house."

"Hippies with a Ph.D. in literature."

"Or dropouts with a Bartlett's."

Karen laughed. "Does it matter?" She looked around. "They were besotted, that's what counts."

He stared at her.

"That surprises you, doesn't it, coming from me?" she said. She waved her hand at the room. "Can't you just picture it? The candles, the dope, the long-haired boy and girl, the moon shining through on all this poetry?" She swallowed.

He could picture it. The image brought to mind another: the tennis shed, damp and dark, with the warped racquets on the wall and the mound of red clay. Perhaps the hippies had been on the island at the same time, just miles down the Cotton Town road.

Karen moved away from the window, took a step toward him. "I was wrong, Eddie."

"About what?"

"The world. It's not small. It's a big, big place, and right now we're far away."

"From where?"

She came nearer. "From anywhere." She was close enough to touch him. She did, resting her fingertips on the side of his face. Behind her, the sun sank into the sea, filling the room with garish light. There was even a flash of green.

Eddie thought: What does she want? Jack? The money? Evidence to tie him to Messer, El Rojo?

Those were important questions, but Karen's breasts pressed

against him, and her tongue was searching out his, and his mind refused to deal with questions, refused to acknowledge them, threatened to forget them entirely. He let the backpack slip off his shoulders. It fell on the floor and he put his arms around her. She moaned.

Soon they were on the four-poster bed, inside the mosquito-net cocoon. Outside the netting bloomed the last rays of the sun, lighting all the words of love in pulses of wild color. Inside Karen moaned and didn't stop. Eddie lost himself in her sounds, her rhythms, her smells. Pressure built inside him, built and built, passed the point of explosion, kept building, demanding his all, forcing him to abandon self-consciousness, self-control, self-defense. She called his name. Not Nails, his prison name, his animal name, but Eddie; him. At that moment he would have done anything she wanted, but all she wanted was to call his name.

Darkness fell.

Some time later a breeze sprang up, blew through the hippie house, stirred the mosquito net.

"Jack's dead," Eddie said.

There was no answer. Karen was asleep. He felt her beside him, still hot, damp with sweat.

Her body cooled. The sweat dried. Eddie got up, went to the window, saw the lights of the cruiser, yellow and white, glowing in the air, sparkling on the water. Two other lights, much duller, one red, one green, separated themselves from the cruiser, grew bigger and brighter.

Eddie returned to the bed, lay down. Karen rolled over, her arm falling heavily across his chest. He liked the feel of it. The night made soothing sounds—insect sounds, bird sounds, wave sounds. Soon he was sleeping too.

Something crashed. Eddie sat up, not sure if he had heard a noise or dreamed it. Karen's arm slipped off his chest. She made a sighing sound and lay still. Eddie listened, heard nothing. His mind, still half asleep, offered a dreamy explanation from the two known elements, toad and wine bottle. He almost accepted it.

Eddie drew back the mosquito netting and rose quietly, without disturbing Karen. There was moonlight, enough to differentiate the shadows. Eddie entered the square shadow that marked the top of the stairs, went down. The last footboard creaked beneath him. The moon shone through the window on his face.

There were more shadows in the living room. One was bigger than the rest. The big shadow moved, eclipsing the moon. A man spoke.

"Surprise."

Jack.

Chapter Thirty-Three

A surprise? Not really.

Eddie had buried deep in his subconscious the idea that Jack might have survived, too deep for his thoughts to reach, but not deep enough to keep it from giving off a faint miasma of anxiety, anxiety that had stayed with him all the way to Saint Amour. Now unfettered it ballooned inside him. He had abandoned not a dead body but his brother, bleeding on the chicken-farm road.

"Say something, bro."

A horrible betrayal. But since that night on the chicken-farm road, he had learned what Jack had done to him. That was the first complicating factor. The second was that Jack couldn't have survived alone, couldn't have gotten away by himself: who had helped him? The third complicating factor was Karen, sleeping upstairs.

"Eddie? You awake?"

"Yeah," Eddie said in a low voice. "I'm awake."

"Got a babe upstairs? The jitney boy said something about that."

"She's gone," Eddie said, moving toward the screened porch. He saw the overgrown lawn, trees, more shadows. They could have been the normal shadows of night. Out on the water, the lights of the cruiser still shone. *El Liberador. His real name is Simon, after the Liberator.*

Eddie went into the kitchen, looked out the door. There was a shadow in the front seat of Karen's car.

"Gave me up for dead, didn't you?" Jack said, following him. "But I'm a tough old nut. They fixed me up real good."

"Who is they?"

A geometry problem, as on the chicken-farm road: Jack down here, Karen upstairs, something else outside. This one he couldn't solve.

"The doc, of course," Jack said.

"What doc?"

"It was just superficial. Lots of blood, but once they stopped it I was fine." Jack's voice broke, as though he was about to sob.

Eddie went past him, to the foot of the stairs.

"Where're you going?"

"Getting my stuff," Eddie said.

"Why?"

Without replying, Eddie climbed the stairs, opened the netting, leaned in. His lips touched Karen's ear. "Karen," he said, barely mouthing the words: "Don't speak. Don't move until you hear noise. Then climb out the window and run."

Karen lay still, but he sensed the sudden tension in her body, knew she was awake.

Eddie picked up the backpack, started down. Jack was waiting at the bottom. He wore something white around his neck.

"Wouldn't have a gun in there?" he said.

Eddie brushed past him.

"You don't seem happy to see me," Jack said.

"I'm happy you're alive. But it gives you the chance to do it to me again, doesn't it, Jack?"

"Do what?"

"Your seven-and-a-half-percent trick."

Pause. "You lost me."

"You can stop lying to me now," Eddie said. "I've talked to a few people—JFK and the detective, Brice. I know everything. I just don't know how you could have done it."

Eddie stepped onto the screened-in porch. A massive, silver-edged cloud slid over the moon, darkening the night. The wind was rising. He picked up the rusted kettle barbecue. There wasn't going to be a better moment.

Jack came closer. "Don't be like this, bro. I was just a kid. I got scared. I panicked."

Panic. That had been Mandy's excuse. Did panic justify anything that came after? Eddie turned on him. "What about Switzerland?" His voice shook.

"Switzerland?" But Jack knew what he meant.

"You weren't a kid then."

Jack was silent. There was just enough light to illuminate his teeth and the bandage around his neck.

"But that's history now," Eddie said. "What's your reason this time?"

"This time?"

Something thumped outside. It could have been another coconut falling; it could have been someone stubbing his toe. Eddie said: "And don't call me bro." Then he hurled the barbecue through the screen and dove out after it, the backpack in his hand.

He hit the ground hard, lost his grip on the backpack, lay there for a moment waiting for the sound of gunfire, running men, clubs swishing through the air at his head. All he heard was his own heart, beating against the earth. He got up, shouldered the pack, and started running.

Eddie ran away from the house, away from the lane. He came to the edge of the bluff, saw the road, a faint charcoal strip in the blackness below. No lights shone on the water. That didn't mean *El Liberador* was gone. Eddie turned and crawled feet first over the edge.

The bluff was steep but not sheer; Eddie found tree roots and toeholds in its face. He could hear nothing but the wind, blowing harder now, and the falling pebbles he dislodged. No gunfire, no shouting, no running men. Maybe he was wrong, maybe Jack had escaped somehow and come to the island by himself, and *El Liberador* was just a businessman's pleasure boat. He was beginning to consider going back when he heard a woman scream, somewhere above.

Eddie lost his grip on the face of the bluff, fell ten or fifteen feet to the road. He got up, took a first running step in the direction of the lane that led back up to the house. Just one step: then a light glared in his eyes, blinding him, and a heavy collar landed on his shoulders. He ripped off the backpack, swung it toward the light, hit nothing. The collar tightened around his neck, hard and itchy, tightened and tightened more. He dropped the pack, clawed at the rope cutting off his air. He could do nothing.

A voice spoke. "Be very careful with this one." Eddie knew that voice, a cultured voice that reminded him of maple syrup.

"Believe me, I know," said another voice. Señor Paz. The rope tightened more around Eddie's neck.

The first man laughed. There was nothing cultured about that sound, harsh and crowlike: El Rojo's laugh. *Be seeing you.* A joke after all; too late, Eddie got it.

He lay on his back in wet sand. He could feel it in his hair, feel windblown grains against his face. Jack was crying. "You promised I could go. You gave your word."

No one answered him. Eddie couldn't see. He realized his eyes were closed, and opened them.

Flashlight beams shone at different angles in the night. Eddie caught glimpses of men standing above him: several big olive-skinned ones he didn't know; Paz, holding the rope; El Rojo, wearing the backpack; Jack, with tears on his face.

"Where the hell is Julio?" Paz said to one of the olive-skinned men.

The man pointed to the bluff.

Karen was up there somewhere. Eddie started to rise.

"Jesus," said Paz, "he's come to already." The rope tightened around Eddie's neck, then jerked him back down, flat on the sand.

"You don't have to do that," Jack said.

No one answered him. The rope remained tight around Eddie's neck. Jack moved closer, loomed over him, looked down. A light shone on his face, exposing every line, making him look much older, old enough to be Eddie's father.

"Brought them to our little island, Jack?"

Tears filled Jack's eyes, overflowed them. "They made me."

"You get to keep the money, is that it?"

"Money? They cut off my balls, Eddie." His voice broke again; this time he couldn't hold the sob inside.

"For Christ's sake," Eddie said. "They were just trying to scare you. It's a computer trick, like at the nightclub."

El Rojo stepped onto the beam of light. "Computer trick?" he said. "Show him."

Jack pulled down his pants. A bloody bandage covered the flatness where his scrotum had been.

A killing urge flooded through Eddie, raw and animal. He rose again, grabbing at El Rojo's legs. Paz yanked him back down. Then El Rojo came forward and placed his foot on Eddie's face, slowly increasing the amount of weight he made Eddie take.

"Would a computer trick be adequate punishment for murder and armed robbery?" he said. "You know the way punishment works, Nails. That's one of the things I liked about you, why I offered my friendship." He leaned harder on Eddie's face. "You repaid me by scheming, robbing, killing."

"That was bad," said Paz.

"But not the worst."

"No."

"The worst was what you did to my little boy. He has dreams about you, every night. He thinks you're in the closet and wakes up screaming. How can I forgive that?" He peered down at Eddie. "How?" Eddie didn't make a sound. El Rojo lifted his foot from Eddie's face. "Answer."

"He belongs in a nightmare," Eddie said.

El Rojo's features—eyes, nostrils, mouth—all seemed to expand at once, replacing his civilized look with something wilder. He stomped back down on Eddie's face.

"What are we going to do about poor Gaucho?" he said, grinding his heel as though to put out a stubborn little fire.

"Devise a program of therapy for him," Paz said.

El Rojo smiled, revealing the blank where his canine had been. The wild look faded.

"We'll have to take him with us for that," Paz said.

"We'll take both of them," El Rojo said. He raised his foot from Eddie's face. Eddie, finding he couldn't breathe through his nose, opened his mouth. Blood trickled in.

"You promised I could go free," Jack said.

No one answered him.

"You gave your word."

Eddie spat out some blood and said: "Shut up, Jack."

El Rojo nodded. *"Hombre,"* he said to Eddie, "explain to your brother here that it's simply a matter of protecting my business reputation, like filing a suit."

"Tell him yourself," Eddie said.

El Rojo laughed his crow laugh. "I feel wonderful."

Julio moved into the circle, wearing his Harvard sweat shirt, holding a gun.

El Rojo frowned. "What kept you?"

"Sorry, señor," he said, unable to restrain a smile. "He had a girlfriend up there. I got to know her a little bit."

Eddie kicked out at Julio, striking him in the side of the knee. Julio cried out, lost his balance, fell. Eddie rolled on top of him, got a hand on Julio's ponytail, a thumb in Julio's eye. Then the rope dug deep into his neck and something hit his head. He got lost in a fog.

For a while he was aware of nothing but the wind and the sea, both growing louder. Then Julio was screaming, "I can't see, I can't see."

Paz said: "Quiet. You're all right."

Julio screamed: "I can't see."

El Rojo said: "Control yourself."

Julio went silent. Eddie, still in the fog, saw him glaring down, blood seeping from the corners of his eye, saw Julio's foot draw back, saw the kick coming, waited. It came. The fog went red.

The sea was angry. It put on a spiky face and tried to toss the speedboat away. Eddie, sprawled over the transom between two outboards, with the rope around his neck and his face almost in the water, felt the power of the sea. The sea was his friend. It slapped his face, stinging and cold but friendly, driving away the red fog.

In Spanish, someone shouted, "I don't see it."

"They've moved farther out," El Rojo said, "because of the weather."

"I don't like it," said the first man. "How will I find the cut in this?"

"Steer," said El Rojo.

A wave lifted the boat high, banged it back down. Eddie fell on something hard-edged. The fuel tank. Hoses dug into his chest.

The next wave was bigger still. It raised the propellers out of the water and almost threw Eddie overboard. Only the rope around his neck kept him in place. In the weightless moment before the stern dropped back down, he glimpsed two plugs in it, one above the deck line, for drainage, and the other about a foot below, indicating a double hull.

The boat rose again, swung sideways. The engines stuttered, the props came up, whining in the air, someone heavy fell on Eddie's back. The rope tightened around his neck. Then the boat crashed down in the trough, the heavy weight slid off, the rope slackened.

"Where the fuck are they?" said the man at the wheel, raising his voice over the storm.

"Radio them," El Rojo replied. "Tell them to turn on the lights and move in."

"*Liberador, Liberador*," called Paz. "Come in, *Liberador*."

Someone moaned, close by. Jack. "It hurts," he said, but not loudly. "It hurts."

Double hull. That meant an airspace, didn't it? Eddie reached one hand below the waterline, felt for the bottom plug. Why not? The sea was his friend, and the alternative was being part of Gaucho's therapy.

He found the plug. It had a metal-ring handle, snapped tight to the hull. He unsnapped it, pulled. Nothing happened. He tried rotating it, first one way, then another. The ring turned, counterclockwise, releasing tension in the rubber plug, shrinking its volume. It popped out. Eddie let it go.

A wave tossed the boat up again, and he saw the round hole in the stern. Then came the fall into the trough, and the hole sank from view.

"Lights at two o'clock," shouted Paz.

"Those?" said another. "So far?"

"Steer," said El Rojo.

"It hurts," said Jack, close by.

Eddie lay slumped over the transom, waiting for the hull space to fill with water, waiting for the boat to turn heavy and sluggish, to go down. But the boat didn't turn heavy and sluggish; it pounded on, into the waves. Why? Some time passed before Eddie figured it out, time that took them farther out. It was simple: forward motion kept water from entering the hole. Forward motion would have to be stopped.

Eddie felt for the fuel hose under his chest, ran his hand along it to the coupling with the starboard engine, saw that a second hose connected the starboard engine to the port. The sole feeder of fuel was the hose that ran from the tank, under his chest, to the starboard engine. Eddie reached for the coupling, unsnapped it, and hung the hose over the stern.

The engines roared on. Maybe he had miscalculated, maybe there were factors he knew nothing about. He pushed himself up on hands and knees, and had his hand on the clamps that fastened the starboard engine to the hull, when both engines coughed and died.

There was a moment of quiet. Then sound poured in: the sea, the wind, raised voices from the cockpit. Eddie turned, saw a wave looming over the bow, saw El Rojo, Paz, Julio, and the olive-skinned men, all gazing at the engines, saw Jack sitting doubled up, his back to the hull, saw that the other end of the rope around his neck was tied to a cleat.

The front slope of the wave raised the boat high; the back slope crashed it down. This time cold water swept over the transom, and the stern swung heavily in the wash.

El Rojo said: "Julio."

Julio made his way to the stern.

"We're sinking," cried a man in the cockpit.

"Silence," said El Rojo.

Water ran across the deck. Julio slipped in it as he reached the stern. He rose, kicked Eddie out of the way, examined the engines.

"The fucking hose," he said. He looked down at Eddie. The boat rose, fell, crashed, settled lower in the water. "I can't swim," Julio yelled to no one in particular. He seized the hose.

Eddie got to his feet. "Anyone can learn to swim," he said. He lifted up the fuel tank, raised it high over his head, and heaved it overboard. One corner of it caught Julio on the shoulder. He lost his balance, slipped again on the watery deck, now ankle-deep, and fell backward over the transom, sinking out of sight in the black water.

The men in the cockpit froze. El Rojo was the first to move. He reached into his pocket, was still reaching when the boat swung sideways and yawed until the sea slopped over the edge, knocking everyone down.

The boat slowly righted itself; much lower in the water now.

Half crawling, half sliding across the flooded deck, which reeked of gasoline, Eddie made his way to the cleat where the noose was tied. Paz arrived first.

Paz unfastened the rope, jerked it hard, cutting off Eddie's air. But Eddie got his hands on it too, gathered his legs beneath him, and sprang over the side.

Paz was strong enough to keep his hold on the rope but not strong enough to stay on board. He fell in after Eddie. The rope loosened around Eddie's neck.

They went down together, tangled in rope. Ten, or fifteen, or twenty feet below, the water was almost calm, and not particularly cold. Eddie had no fear of it at all. He felt tugging around his neck, reached out and wrapped his arms around Paz. Paz wriggled, struggled, gouged, but couldn't get away, couldn't go up. When the wriggling, struggling, and gouging stopped, Eddie released Paz and kicked his way up to the surface, alone.

He broke through on a rising wave, striking his head on something. The backpack. He slipped the noose off his neck and swam toward it. He was a stroke or two away when it went under.

As the wave carried Eddie higher, the moon shone through a break in the clouds. Eddie looked around. In the southwest he saw the lights of *El Liberador*, not far away. In the east, much fainter, glimmered the lights of the island. The speedboat was gone. There were only two men in the water, one in the trough beneath him, the other on the crest of the next wave. The man in the trough was Jack; the man on the crest was El Rojo.

El Rojo's eyes, silver in the moonlight, fastened on Eddie. "You will never be safe." Then he turned and started swimming toward *El Liberador*, his stroke smooth and strong.

Eddie dipped into a trough. When he rose again El Rojo was out of sight, but Jack was much closer. Eddie swam to him, touched him.

"You all right?"

Jack nodded. The dressing had slipped off his neck, revealing the black stitches across his skin.

Eddie pointed toward the lights of Saint Amour. "It's nothing, Jack, just a training swim. We'll be fine."

"Never."

The wind whipped off the top of a wave and flung it in their faces. Jack gasped, choked, went under for a moment, came up coughing.

"Let's go," Eddie said.

"Sharks are down there."

"They won't bother us."

"They can smell blood, Eddie. For miles and miles."

"We'll be fine. Come on."

To set an example, Eddie turned toward Saint Amour, stretched out, swam. He found his rhythm at once, easy and powerful, slashing through the spikes, climbing the crests, sliding down into the troughs. The ocean might have been rough, but all he felt was its support. He could swim to Saint Amour, or much farther if he had to; as though all those years in the pool had been just for this. Eddie swam, kicking, pushing great handfuls of water aside, riding high, barely breathing; swimming his best. After a while, he stopped to make sure Jack was keeping up. He couldn't see him.

"Jack?" he shouted over the wind.

No reply.

He swam back, out to sea, pausing once or twice to call, "Jack? Jack?" and heard no answer. He found him among the litter left behind by the speedboat, not swimming.

"Jack. For Christ's sake."

"It's too far."

"It's not."

"The sharks will get me anyway."

"Swim, Jack. Like in the pool. You were the best."

"That was a long time ago. I blew it."

"You didn't blow it."

"Then how come we're here?"

A wave broke over Jack's head, left him coughing.

"Swim, Jack."

Jack started swimming, in the right direction, but so clumsy. His arms barely came out of the water, his legs hardly kicked. Eddie stroked along beside him. Twice he looked back. The first time he saw *El Liberador* moving south. The second time it was out of sight. He raised his head, looked the other way, toward the lights of Saint Amour. They had receded. Either it was his imagination or they were caught in a current. Eddie swam faster, found his rhythm again. The next time he checked, Saint Amour seemed a little closer. He looked around for Jack; and didn't see him.

"Jack," he called.

All he heard in reply were the countless sounds of sea and wind. He turned back.

He found Jack again, treading water, rising and falling with the swells, his eyes on the moon.

"Jack. You're not trying."

Jack looked at him. "How much did you get away with?"

"It's on the bottom."

"You had it all in that pack?"

"Yes."

Jack shook his head. "Bro. Even an ordinary bank account would have been better."

"Swim," Eddie said.

Jack treaded water. "Your plan was good, though," he said. "I was the one who fucked it up. You're smart, Eddie. Smarter than me, in some ways."

"That's not true. Swim."

"I'm tapped out, bro."

"If you've got the energy to argue, you've got the energy to swim."

Jack's lips chattered. As soon as he saw that, Eddie's lips started chattering too. "I don't mean tapped out that way," Jack said. "I mean financially. If the money's on the bottom, what's the point?"

"Please."

But Jack wouldn't swim. The wind blew harder, driving the sea wild. The moon disappeared. Without moonlight, he wouldn't be able to find Jack again. "Swim," he shouted at the top of his lungs, right in Jack's face.

Jack's eyes widened. He tried a few strokes, swallowed a mouthful of water, came up coughing, swallowed more, went under. Eddie dove down and got him.

"Swim."

Jack shook his head.

Eddie rolled onto his back. "Hold onto me," he said.

Jack put his arms around Eddie's neck, lay on top of him. The sea absorbed some of his weight, but Jack was heavy all the same.

"Just hold on," Eddie said. He began paddling toward Saint Amour, Jack's arms around his neck, Jack's head on his chest, Jack's body pushing him under. He had to kick hard just to keep Jack on the surface.

Eddie paddled. He looked up at the sky, moonless, starless, dark. Arms up, dig down, pull; arms up, dig down, pull. How far did they go on each cycle? A yard? Eddie counted five hundred strokes, then said: "How're we doing, Jack?"

Jack raised his head. The movement drove Eddie under. He swallowed water, came up sputtering, Jack's arms still tight around his neck. "Gettin' there," Jack said.

"You can see the lights?"

"Billions of them."

Eddie turned toward Saint Amour. He could barely make out the lights at all. They were farther away than ever. He lowered his head, kicked hard, paddled. Arms up, dig down, pull. Arms up, dig down, pull. Jack held on.

Eddie counted two thousand strokes, forced himself not to look, began two thousand more. Jack said something. Eddie could feel Jack's lips moving against his chest, couldn't hear him.

"I can't hear you."

Jack raised his head, looked into Eddie's eyes. "I said forget it."

Eddie stopped paddling. The sea tossed them up and down, the wind sang all around. "Fifteen years, Jack," Eddie said.

"I was jealous."

"Of me and Mandy?"

"No, no. I didn't give a shit about Mandy. It was you."

"Me?"

"Sure. Always so fucking happy. Even now, you're not really bitter."

"I'm bitter," Eddie said.

Jack didn't hear him. He went still, his arms around Eddie's neck; Eddie treaded water for both of them. A faraway look appeared in Jack's eyes. "Remember how I used to hog the puck from you? And you'd be skating around yelling, 'Pass, pass,' and not even knowing I was ragging you. Just pleased as punch to be out there. I wasn't like that, bro. Sorry for calling you bro. I had resentments, like everybody else I've ever met."

"That's all bullshit," Eddie said.

"See? You haven't changed a bit." Jack laughed, a strange sound out there in the wild night. Then he brought his head up a little and kissed Eddie's face.

Eddie could have cried, but he didn't. He leaned back and started paddling. Arms up, dig down, pull. He was on stroke two thousand six hundred and fifty-three when Jack went stiff and said: "Did you feel that?"

"Feel what?" Eddie said; his lips were numb, and the words came out ill-formed.

"That bump."

"I didn't feel any bump." Eddie lost his stroke count but kept paddling.

"A fish," Jack said. "A big fish. Down there in Davy Jones's locker. They can smell blood."

"There's no blood," Eddie said.

"Dream on." Jack tightened his grip on Eddie's neck.

Eddie paddled. That was all he had to do. Keep them safe from Davy Jones. Paddle and count. His job. Jack's job was to hold onto his neck. Arms up, dig down, pull.

"Are you doing your job, Jack?"

No answer.

Arms up, dig down, pull.

"I asked you a fucking question."

No answer.

Arms up, dig down, pull.

"Answer me, bro."

No answer. But Jack's arms held him tight. He was doing his job. He just didn't want to talk about it, that was all.

Eddie paddled. He counted twenty thousand strokes. He refused to stop and look, didn't want to see Saint Amour slipping farther and farther away. He did his job. He didn't notice the sky paling, the sea growing gentler, the wind dying down. He paddled and counted. Sometimes he yelled at Jack and called him bad names for not answering. But he had no right to be angry at Jack. Jack was doing his job perfectly, holding on tight. He just didn't want to talk about it.

Eddie started on a fresh twenty thousand. Arms up, pull, dig down. Was that right? He got mixed up, began again. Pull down, dig up, arms. Arms, arms, arms.

"Jack. I've forgotten the stroke."

No answer.

"What's the stroke, Jack? I've forgotten the goddamn stroke."

No answer. Eddie started to cry.

He lay motionless in the water, Jack on top of him. He felt something bump the back of his head. Something big and powerful; it wasn't his imagination.

"Davy Jones is here," he told Jack, and held his brother close. They were each other's albatross. Maybe everybody had one.

He heard a voice. "What's that over there?"

Davy Jones had a strange voice. A woman's voice. He sounded like a woman, and not just any woman, but a woman Eddie knew.

Maybe he was already dead, or having one of those dying experiences people talked about on TV.

Davy Jones came nearer. "There. Just past those rocks."

Eddie whispered: "Jack. Do you hear him?" He looked down at his brother. Jack was sleeping.

Davy Jones spoke, very close. "Oh, my God."

Eddie turned his head. It touched something. Sand. He looked around, saw tiny waves sliding on a beach an arm's length away. Karen was there, and behind her many black men in snappy uniforms. He was lying in six inches of water.

Karen ran splashing to him. One of her eyes was blackened and closed; the other was damp. He focused on that one and said, "You don't look like Davy Jones."

"Oh, my God."

"My brother here and I, we did our jobs. I know you don't like him, but he's brave as a lion. Admit it, Jack."

Jack wouldn't admit it.

"He's sleeping."

Karen leaned down, extending her hand. Eddie saw that all the buttons on her shirt were missing.

"Where are your buttons?" he asked.

Karen put her hand on Jack's shoulder, tried to pull him off.

"It's okay, One-Eye," Eddie said. "You can let go. It's not Davy Jones."

But Jack wouldn't let go. It took two of the snappily uniformed men to pry him off.

"God Almighty," said one of them when he'd had a look at Jack.

Without his brother's arms around him, Eddie felt free and light, so light he knew he could just bounce right up to his feet. But when he tried, he found he couldn't move at all. He could only lie where he was, letting the water lap at him.

Overhead helicopters whirred south across a blue sky.

Inside

Chapter Thirty-Four

They tried to make a go of it, but Karen wasn't the same.

When Eddie got out of the hospital in Nassau, they went to another island, three or four stops down the chain from Saint Amour. They ate, drank, swam. At first, they made love often, in a nice room with air-conditioning, balcony, maid service, and private pool. Then there was less lovemaking. A nice room, but lacking love poetry on the walls and ceiling.

Soon Karen wanted to return to her job. Eddie went with her, stayed in her co-op. She worked long hours. He found a job at the NYU library. It didn't work out. The system was computerized. He'd known that; his supervisor had assured him he'd pick it up in no time. But he didn't. He couldn't concentrate. He even lost his interest in reading; didn't want to be near books. He wanted to be out. He wandered around the city, went to bars, handed in his resignation. Maybe if he hadn't lost the backpack, things would have been different.

Karen said she wanted some space.

Maybe they had needed Jack to keep it hot.

Eddie bought a cheap ticket to L.A. and had a look at USC. He went to the pool and watched the team work out. They were very young and very fast. He tried to put himself in their place and couldn't. He went to a lecture on nineteenth-century English poetry and left after twenty minutes.

Eddie took a bus across the country and got off in the Dunkin' Donuts parking lot: the Dunkin' Donuts on the strip with Motel 6, Mufflers 4U, Lanny's Used Tires, Bud Lite, Pink Lady Lounge, All the Shrimp You Cn Eat $6.95, XXX Video, Happy Hour. He had a glazed honey donut and black coffee. He met some people. They found him a job in a garage, working as a mechanic's helper.

The garage serviced all the prison vehicles. The C.O.s checked them thoroughly going out, not as thoroughly going in. Millions of men have dreamed of breaking out of jail, and some have succeeded, but who wants to break in?

One day they brought in the big forklift from the prison workshop. Something about the starter, Eddie didn't get the details. The mechanic put in a new one. That night Eddie remained behind to lock up. He locked up from the inside, went into the bathroom, removed his overalls. Underneath he wore denims. He found an old razor blade and shaved the gray hair off his head. Then he raised the seat on the forklift and wedged himself into the tool space underneath.

The mechanic sent the forklift back next morning. Trusties hauled it off the truck at the gate and drove it to the workshop. After ten or fifteen minutes, Eddie took a peek. There were lots of denim-clad men around, but no one was looking. Eddie climbed out.

He joined a line of prisoners moving toward the mess hall. Eddie didn't stay with them all the way. He turned into the east wing and went through a scanner to the door of the library. A C.O. was on duty, someone new. He patted Eddie down.

"Got a pass?" he said.

"I forgot a book in there last night."

"Step on it."

Eddie entered the library. There was no one inside but El Rojo, bent over a law book. He had new lines on his face and gray roots in his hair. He didn't look up as Eddie approached, so Eddie said, "This isn't a bullshit macho Latin thing."

El Rojo looked up then; and Eddie was on the move.

"It's a bullshit crazy inmate thing."

El Rojo was quick: quick to pull a homemade knife, quick to shout for help. The C.O. was quick too. But none of it was quick enough. El Rojo died on the library table.

Eddie saw Prof in the yard a few months later.

"Hey, Nails. Want your watch back?"

"Don't need it," Eddie said.